STAR WARS®

THE ESSENTIAL GUIDE TO PLANETS AND MOONS

STAR WARS GUIDES AND RESOURCE MATERIALS
PUBLISHED BY THE BALLANTINE PUBLISHING GROUP

STAR WARS TECHNICAL JOURNAL
STAR WARS ENCYCLOPEDIA
A GUIDE TO THE STAR WARS UNIVERSE

STAR WARS: THE ESSENTIAL GUIDE TO CHARACTERS
STAR WARS: THE ESSENTIAL GUIDE TO VEHICLES AND VESSELS
STAR WARS: THE ESSENTIAL GUIDE TO WEAPONS AND TECHNOLOGY
STAR WARS: THE ESSENTIAL GUIDE TO PLANETS AND MOONS
STAR WARS: THE ESSENTIAL GUIDE TO DROIDS*

* FORTHCOMING

STAR WARS®

THE ESSENTIAL GUIDE TO PLANETS AND MOONS

DANIEL WALLACE

ORIGINAL ILLUSTRATIONS BY
BRANDON McKINNEY AND
SCOTT KOLINS

THE BALLANTINE PUBLISHING GROUP ● NEW YORK

A Del Rey® Book
Published by The Ballantine Publishing Group

®, ™, and copyright © 1998 by Lucasfilm Ltd. Title and
character and place names protected by all applicable
trademark laws.
All Rights Reserved. Used Under Authorization.

All rights reserved under International and Pan-American
Copyright Conventions. Published in the United States by The
Ballantine Publishing Group, a division of Random House, Inc.,
New York, and simultaneously in Canada by Random House of
Canada Limited, Toronto.

http://www.randomhouse.com/delrey/
http://www.starwars.com

Library of Congress Catalog Card Number: 97-97133

Interior and cover design by Michaelis/Carpelis Design
Associates, Inc.

Edited by Sue Rostoni (Lucasfilm) and Steve Saffel (Del Rey)

Manufactured in the United States of America

First Edition: August 1998

10 9 8 7 6 5 4 3 2 1

To Kelly
Wife, friend, supporter, sweetheart, inspiration

ACKNOWLEDGMENTS

The author Anne Morrow Lindbergh wrote, "One can never pay in gratitude; one can only pay 'in kind' somewhere else in life." If this is true, I've got a lot of work ahead of me. Big thanks are due to the following people for making this project possible. I owe you one.

To Lucy Autrey Wilson for giving me the chance.

To Sue Rostoni for outstanding help above and beyond the call of duty.

To Brandon McKinney and Scott Kolins for building cities and bringing aliens to life.

To Steve Saffel at Del Rey for editorial flair.

To Kevin J. Anderson for opening doors.

To Alec Usticke, Mike Beidler, Ryan Silva, Charlene Newcomb, and Jim Fisher for keeping this thing alive during its embryonic stage.

To Jack Camden, Brendon Wahlberg, and Rich Handley for hunting down rare, out-of-print reference material.

To the many *Star Wars* authors for expanding on such a fun universe and to the following saints for putting up with my questions: Tom Veitch, Mike Stackpole, Kristine Kathryn Rusch, Michael P. Kube-McDowell, Barbara Hambly, Steve Perry, A.C. Crispin, Rebecca Moesta, Timothy Zahn and especially Steve Sansweet.

To the editorial staff of West End Games, including Eric Trautmann, Peter Schweighofer, George Strayton, and Paul Sudlow, for their aid and their indispensable role-playing guidebooks.

To Craig Robert Carey for the Kashyyyk tour, Alex Newborn for the sympathetic ear, Bill Smith for the war stories, and Mary Jo and James at *Blue Harvest* for keeping things in perspective.

To the fans in the many *Star Wars* on-line communities, including AOL and rec.arts.sf.star-wars.misc, for their observations, encouragement, and ideas.

To the inspiring music of John Williams, Joel McNeely, and They Might Be Giants.

To my family and friends for absolutely everything I have in this world.

And finally, to George Lucas for brainstorming this wonderful phenomenon in the first place.

INTRODUCTION

"*An epic of heroes, villains, and aliens from a thousand worlds.*"

That's what the stentorian announcer promised to deliver in the first theatrical previews for a new sci-fi extravaganza called *Star Wars*. The flickering trailer offered tasty flashes of zooming spaceships, strange beasties, and double sunsets, hinting at a fantastic galaxy that was utterly unlike our own.

When the movie finally broke in May 1977, the "gee whiz" factor didn't diminish one bit. Our heroes' planet-hopping adventures took them from the hot sands of Tatooine to the cool mists of Yavin 4. And the phantasmagoric menagerie of bizarre barflies knocking 'em back in the Mos Eisley cantina hinted at a thousand other points of origin.

The Empire Strikes Back and *Return of the Jedi* added several strange new locales to the canon, leading one to speculate that the *Star Wars* galaxy has a peculiar number of single-climate worlds: Tatooine is a desert planet, Hoth an ice ball, Dagobah a slimy mudhole, Endor the "forest moon." (But hey, this is space opera—why not?)

Though the films have been loved by generations of moviegoers and VCR buffs, they spotlight only a small fraction of the countless planets in that galaxy far, far away. The books, comics, computer games, and television specials have done their best to rectify that. Even places that were mentioned only in passing on the big screen, such as Dantooine, Kessel, and Taanab, have been given climates, geographies, and elaborate histories by dozens of new authors and artists. If you're interested in tracking down the original source material on any given planet, the back of this volume contains a coded bibliography to help you in your search.

From Abregado-rae to Zhar, planets and moons are the backdrops for the world's most popular space fantasy. This book covers a hundred of the most notable. But galaxies are big places, and there is still much to explore.

Enjoy the bus tour, and don't feed the Wookiees.

Daniel Wallace
Detroit, Michigan

STAR WARS

THE ESSENTIAL GUIDE TO PLANETS AND MOONS

TABLE OF CONTENTS

A TIMELINE OF IMPORTANT EVENTS

-25,000 YEARS

The Old Republic, the first galaxywide government, is formed in the Core Worlds. The Jedi Knights act as the Republic's loyal guardians and peacemakers.

-4,000 YEARS

The Jedi Knights Ulic Qel-Droma and Nomi Sunrider train on Arkania and Ambria and help stop a war on the planet Onderon.
Tales of the Jedi (comics)

-3996 YEARS

Ulic Qel-Droma and Exar Kun join forces in the Great Sith War and devastate Ossus.
The Sith War (comics)

-10 YEARS

A young Han Solo learns the smuggling trade on Ylesia and later joins the Imperial Academy.
The Paradise Snare (novel)

-10-5 YEARS

R2-D2 and C-3PO have a series of memorable adventures on Kalarba and Roon as they move from master to master.
Droids (comics and animated television series)

-3 YEARS

Lando Calrissian, in a recently acquired starship called the *Millennium Falcon*, gambles his way across the Centrality, including Rafa V.
Lando Calrissian and the Mindharp of Sharu, Lando Calrissian and the Flamewind of Oseon, Lando Calrissian and the Starcave of ThonBoka (novels)

-2-1 YEARS

Han Solo and Chewbacca, now full-time smugglers, leave Nar Shaddaa to seek adventure on Mytus VII, Ammuud, Dellalt, and elsewhere.
Han Solo at Stars' End, Han Solo's Revenge, Han Solo and the Lost Legacy (novels)

0 YEARS

Luke Skywalker and Han Solo rescue Princess Leia from the Death Star, which is destroyed in the triumphant Battle of Yavin.
Star Wars: A New Hope (film)

0-3 YEARS

The Alliance evacuates Yavin 4 and searches for a new base, while Leia visits the worlds of M'haeli and Mimban.
Classic Star Wars (comics), *Splinter of the Mind's Eye* (novel), *River of Chaos* (comics), and X-Wing (computer game)

3 YEARS

The Alliance is routed at the Battle of Hoth, but Yoda teaches Luke to become a Jedi Knight on Dagobah. Han Solo is encased in carbonite on Bespin by Darth Vader.
Star Wars: The Empire Strikes Back (film)

3.5 YEARS

Prince Xizor, criminal overlord of Black Sun, plots to kill Luke Skywalker at Zhar and Coruscant, while Boba Fett delivers a frozen Han Solo to Jabba the Hutt.
Shadows of the Empire (novel, comics, and video game)

4 YEARS

Han Solo is rescued from Jabba's palace on Tatooine, and the second Death Star is destroyed at the Battle of Endor. Mon Mothma, leader of the Rebel Alliance, proclaims the birth of a New Republic.
Star Wars: Return of the Jedi (film)

4+ YEARS

The Alliance answers a distress call from the planet Bakura, where the Rebels join forces with the Imperials to fight off the Ssi-ruuk invasion.
The Truce at Bakura (novel)

IN THE *STAR WARS* UNIVERSE

6.5–7.5 YEARS

The courageous pilots of Rogue Squadron capture the Imperial capital world of Coruscant and liberate Thyferra.

The X-Wing series: Rogue Squadron, Wedge's Gamble, The Krytos Trap, The Bacta War (novels)

8 YEARS

Leia is courted by the handsome Prince Isolder of Hapes, but a jealous Han kidnaps her and takes her to the wilderness of Dathomir. Leia and Han are married upon their return.

The Courtship of Princess Leia (novel)

9 YEARS

Grand Admiral Thrawn takes command of the Empire and leads a devastating campaign against the New Republic with help from the mad Jedi Joruus C'baoth of Wayland. Leia and Han's twins, Jacen and Jaina, are born.

Heir to the Empire, Dark Force Rising, The Last Command (novels)

10–11 YEARS

Emperor Palpatine returns in the body of a clone on Byss as rejuvenated Imperial forces drive the New Republic from Coruscant. Palpatine is eventually defeated, and Leia and Han's third child, Anakin, is born.

Dark Empire, Dark Empire II, Empire's End (comics)

11 YEARS

Luke Skywalker founds the Jedi academy on Yavin 4 while Admiral Daala strikes at the upstart Rebels on Dantooine and Mon Calamari. Leia becomes Chief of State of the New Republic.

Jedi Search, Dark Apprentice, Champions of the Force (novels)

12–13 YEARS

Luke falls in love with Callista, a fellow Jedi Knight. The burgeoning New Republic is menaced by the *Eye of Palpatine* near Belsavis, the Hutts' Darksaber project, and the Death Seed plague in the Meridian sector.

Children of the Jedi, Darksaber, Planet of Twilight (novels)

14 YEARS

Jacen, Jaina, and Anakin are kidnapped by Hethrir, cruel leader of the Empire Reborn, on Munto Codru.

The Crystal Star (novel)

16–17 YEARS

Leia's leadership is put to the test when the Yevetha, a fanatically xenophobic alien species, emerge from N'zoth with an armada of Imperial warships.

Before the Storm, Shield of Lies, Tyrant's Test (novels)

17 YEARS

One of Luke's former Jedi students masterminds a plan to overthrow the New Republic from the planet Almania.

The New Rebellion (novel)

18 YEARS

Han returns to the Corellian system with his family and gets caught up in a violent revolution.

Ambush at Corellia, Assault at Selonia, Showdown at Centerpoint (novels)

22 YEARS

Eleven-year-old Anakin Solo enrolls at Luke Skywalker's Jedi academy and finds adventure with his friend Tahiri on Yavin 8.

The Junior Jedi Knights series (young reader novels)

23 YEARS

Jacen and Jaina Solo, now fourteen, train at the Jedi academy and foil the Second Imperium's attack on Kashyyyk.

The Young Jedi Knights series (young adult novels)

THE GALAXY

The galaxy contains billions of stars, forming a brilliant pinwheel disk more than 100,000 light-years in diameter. From the beginning its inhabitants looked up at these twinkling points of light and dreamed. The earliest spaceships could hardly escape their own star systems, but the miraculous discovery of the faster-than-light dimension known as hyperspace ushered in a new age of discovery and exploration.

The first galactic scouts struck out from the Core Worlds along two stable hyperspace paths—the Perlemian Trade Route and the Corellian Run. These twin hyperlanes outlined a vast wedge-shaped region of space that was soon dubbed "the Slice." Though it contains many of the oldest and best-known planets, the Slice encompasses only a fraction of the known galaxy.

For ease of classification, Old Republic cartographers divided the galaxy into regions, sectors, and systems.

- *Regions* are the largest divisional groupings. Regions vary greatly in size and location, from small pockets of space such as the Centrality to vast expanses such as the Outer Rim Territories.
- *Sectors* are subdivisions of regions. The original definition of a sector was any area of space with fifty inhabited planets, but increased exploration has caused many sec-tors to grow far beyond their original boundaries.
- *Systems* consist of individual stars and their orbiting planets. Some systems have many life-bearing planets, some have none, while others contain only drifting asteroids or comets. Only a fraction of stars are encircled by planets, and only a fraction of those planets can sustain life. Despite this, any galactic atlas will readily list over a million inhabited worlds and thousands of intelligent alien species.

A list of some of the major areas of the galaxy follows, though this list is far from exhaustive.

DEEP CORE

The Deep Core is the densely packed mass of stars lying at the very heart of the galaxy. Since the gravitational pull of its myriad suns snarls the fabric of hyperspace, the region was long thought to be impenetrable. Emperor Palpatine, however, discovered several safe hyperlanes into the protected region, and it remained a stubborn Imperial stronghold for nearly two decades after the Battle of Endor. The star systems within the Deep Core are sometimes called the Core Systems.

- Byss
- Khomm

KOORNACHT CLUSTER

The Koornacht Cluster, a luminous disk of blazing stars and interstellar gas, sits in the Farlax sector near the fringes of the Deep Core. It was Imperial territory from the end of the Clone Wars until soon after the Battle of Endor, when the alien Yevetha successfully hijacked the Empire's retreating Black Fleet armada. Twelve years later the Yevethans rabidly annihilated all "foreign" colonies inside the Cluster's borders, forcing the New Republic to retaliate.

- Galantos
- J't'p'tan
- N'zoth

CORE WORLDS

This ancient region bordering the Deep Core contains the most prestigious and densely-populated planets in the galaxy. There are, of course, exceptions, like the seedy Abregado-rae, but most of the Core Worlds are universally revered. The Old Republic was born in the Core Worlds and spread out from there to settle other distant star systems. A bastion of Imperial support, the Core Worlds were finally liberated by the New Republic approximately three years after Endor. But an Imperial resurgence led by Palpatine's clone forced the Alliance to withdraw temporarily, and the Rebels had to capture the Core Worlds a second time.

- Abregado-rae
- Alderaan
- Chandrila
- Coruscant
- Kuat
- Ralltiir

CORELLIAN SECTOR

Situated within the Core Worlds, this legendary area contains the five worlds of the Corellian system and dozens of other neighboring systems known as the Outliers. Formerly ruled by the Corellian Diktat, the sector became increasingly hermetic during the Empire's rule. Fourteen years after the Battle of Endor, the Sacorrian Triad attempted to use the Starbuster weapon to bully the New Republic into recognizing the Corellian sector as an independent state. Duro sits at the edge of the sector, though it is not considered an Outlier system.

- Corellia
- Drall
- Duro
- Sacorria
- Selonia
- Talus and Tralus

THE COLONIES

The first Old Republic explorers and settlers to leave the Core Worlds colonized this adjacent region, which they named the Colonies. Over the millennia many of these planets became just as industrialized and wealthy as their old-world counterparts, though the antiquated term "Colonies" has stuck. The New Republic picked undeveloped planets in the Colonies region to use as stepping-stones for its first Core Worlds invasion.

- Arkania
- Balmorra
- Borleias (Blackmoon)
- Carida
- Talasea
- Teyr

TAPANI SECTOR

The Tapani sector is located in the Colonies, but by tradition it is considered a respected part of the Core Worlds community. Elite and ancient noble houses rule much of the sector, though border planets called the Freeworlds are slowly encroaching on house-held territory.

- Fondor
- Mrlsst

INNER RIM PLANETS

This diverse region features many agricultural and industrial powerhouses. The Inner Rim was finally freed by the New Republic five years after the Battle of Endor—just in time for Grand Admiral Thrawn to sweep in and recapture the territory. Though Thrawn was defeated, many Inner Rim planets resent the New Republic for its failure to protect them.

- Ambria
- Antar Four
- Atzerri
- Bestine
- Bilbringi
- Carratos
- Myrkr
- Onderon
- Taanab
- Telti
- Thyferra

HAPES CONSORTIUM

A fabulously wealthy cluster of sixty-three inhabited planets, the Hapes Consortium has become synonymous with fierce protectionism and zealously guarded borders. Though very few had ever seen the cluster's worlds, rumors abounded of astounding treasures such as rainbow gems, wisdom trees, and mind-controlling weaponry. Left largely to its own devices during Emperor Palpatine's reign, the Consortium broke its millennia-long isolation when the Hapan Queen Mother unexpectedly contacted Princess Leia Organa of the New Republic.

- Hapes

EXPANSION REGION

The Expansion Region began as an experiment in corporate-controlled space—wealthy conglomerates were allowed to profit from the area's planets as they saw fit. Eventually the ruling companies moved on to exploit the Corporate Sector. The Expansion Region is still a producer of raw materials, metals, and ores, though many of its resources have been exhausted.

- Aquaris
- Aridus
- M'haeli
- Mimban
- Nkllon
- Tynna

CENTRALITY

The Centrality is an old-fashioned, regressive corner of space best known for the Oseon casinos and the life-crystals of the Rafa system. The Centrality swore allegiance to Palpatine soon after the Empire's formation. Its puppet government was allowed a certain degree of autonomy, though this was mostly because Imperial forces had little interest in directly controlling the trivial region.

- Rafa V

MID RIM

With a smaller population and fewer natural resources than many other regions, the Mid Rim is a territory where residents work hard for what they have. Several planets have built up impressive economies, while pirate raiding fleets often hide in the unexplored spaces far from the trade lanes.

- Ando
- Belsavis
- Bimmisaari
- Bothawui
- Garos IV
- Ithor
- Kalarba
- Kashyyyk
- Kothlis
- Ord Mantell
- Rodia
- Umgul
- Vortex

HUTT SPACE

A lawless expanse near the Outer Rim Territories, Hutt Space is controlled by the most corrupt and powerful Hutt clans. The region is infamous throughout the galaxy for its widespread smuggling, piracy, and open criminal activity. Imperial authorities largely left the Hutts to their own devices, in part because many influential citizens (including Black Sun's Prince Xizor) had a covert stake in their illegal commerce.

- Da Soocha V
- Nal Hutta and Nar Shaddaa
- Ylesia

TION HEGEMONY

Once the seat of power for the pre-Republic conqueror Xim the Despot, the Tion Hegemony is now a crumbling backwater whose glory days are long past. It sits in an undistinguished area bordered by the Cronese Mandate and the Allied Tion.

- Dellalt

MERIDIAN SECTOR

The Meridian sector is a lightly populated region near the Outer Rim Territories. The New Republic has several bases in the sector, but most of the planets remain neutral despite the close proximity of the Imperially held Antemeridian sector. Nine years after the Battle of Endor a devastating outbreak of the Death Seed plague raced across three-quarters of the sector and killed millions.

- Nam Chorios
- Nim Drovis

OUTER RIM TERRITORIES

The Outer Rim is the last widely settled expanse before one reaches Wild Space and the Unknown Regions. An incredibly vast region of space, it is strewn with obscure alien homeworlds and rugged, primitive frontier planets. As a result of its distance from the Core, the area was a hotbed of support for the Rebel Alliance. Grand Moff Tarkin was given the formidable task of bringing the Outer Rim into line.

- Agamar
- Alzoc III
- Anoth
- Bakura
- Barab I
- Bespin
- Dagobah
- Dantooine
- Dathomir
- Endor
- Eriadu
- Firrerre
- Gamorr
- Honoghr
- Hoth
- Kessel
- Korriban
- Mon Calamari
- Munto Codru
- Ossus
- Pzob
- Roon
- Ryloth
- Sullust
- Tatooine
- Vergesso Asteroids
- Wayland
- Yavin 4
- Yavin 8
- Zhar

CORPORATE SECTOR

Located at the wispy edge of one galactic arm, the Corporate Sector is a free-enterprise fief that contains no native intelligent species. Despite its considerable distance from the Core Worlds, the sector is easy to get to, thanks to several well-established hyperspace routes. The ruthless Corporate Sector Authority (CSA) was given a free hand in governing its territory by the Empire as long as Emperor Palpatine received regular kickbacks. The CSA was interested in profit, not ideology, and commonly sold weapons to both sides during the frequent Imperial–New Republic skirmishes.

- Ammuud
- Bonadan
- Etti IV
- Mytus VII

WILD SPACE

The frontier of the galaxy, Wild Space is the ragged fringe separating civilization from the Unknown Regions. Planets such as Almania lie so far from the galactic centers of power that they are virtually ignored.

- Almania
- Pydyr

UNKNOWN REGIONS

Even after twenty-five millennia of interstellar travel, much of the galaxy remains unexplored. Scouting missions were drastically curtailed during the height of the Empire, though Grand Admiral Thrawn spent several years mapping portions of the Unknown Regions. Recent attacks by unfamiliar foes such as the Ssi-ruuvi Imperium have helped convince the New Republic that further exploration of this area is a military necessity.

- Lwhekk

THE ESSENTIAL GUIDE TO PLANETS AND MOONS

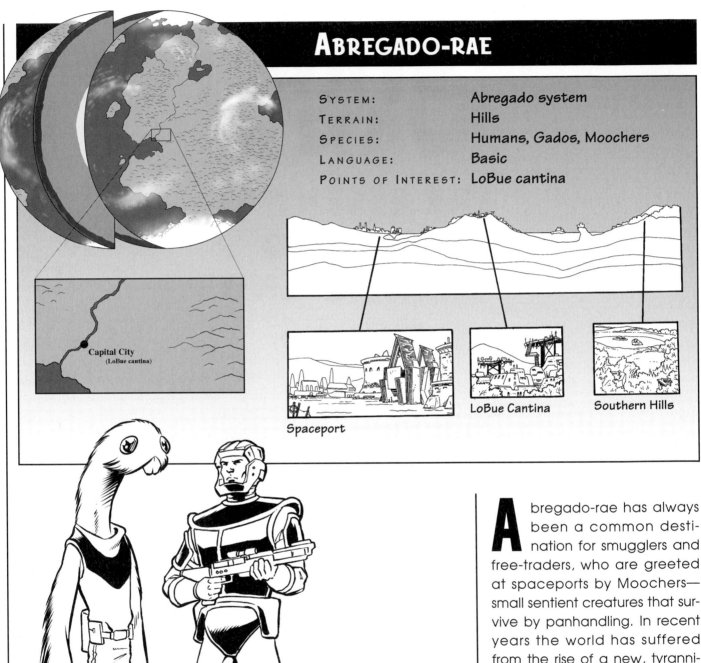

ABREGADO-RAE

SYSTEM: Abregado system
TERRAIN: Hills
SPECIES: Humans, Gados, Moochers
LANGUAGE: Basic
POINTS OF INTEREST: LoBue cantina

Capital City
(LoBue cantina)

Spaceport

LoBue Cantina

Southern Hills

Native Gados maintain the spaceports. Local security officer.

Abregado-rae has always been a common destination for smugglers and free-traders, who are greeted at spaceports by Moochers—small sentient creatures that survive by panhandling. In recent years the world has suffered from the rise of a new, tyrannical government that has modernized Abregado-rae but demanded total obedience from its citizens. A peaceful separatist group in the southern hills made the mistake of publicly protesting; as an example, the regime cut off its supply lines, forcing the group to submit or starve.

During the New Republic's

war against Grand Admiral Thrawn, Han Solo and Lando Calrissian went to Abregado-rae to make contact with Talon Karrde's smuggling organization. The planet's notoriously seedy starport was now gleaming and polished, but the sight of grim police thugs made it clear that the native Gados had lost a measure of freedom.

Ducking into the LoBue cantina, Lando spotted their contact, Fynn Torve, in an intense game of sabacc with several other players. All too aware of the security officers casing the place, Han purchased a pile of betting chips and took a seat at the table. As he was easing into the game, a burly religious minister shoved forward, seemingly plucking a "skifter"—an illegal face-changing sabacc card—from Han's hand. Law enforcement toughs converged to harass the suspected cheater, and Torve quietly slipped away.

Lando and Han finally met Torve back onboard the *Falcon*. Since Abregado-rae's constabulary had impounded Torve's ship, the *Etherway*, for running contraband food to the hill dissidents, the smuggler had wisely been lying low. The "reverend" back In the cantina had actually been one of Torve's local contacts, happy to create the needed diversion. After Han and Lando expressed their

Spaceport Moochers panhandle visitors.

desire to meet his boss, Torve reluctantly agreed to take them to Talon Karrde's hidden base on Myrkr.

Later, Mara Jade arrived at Abregado-rae to pick up the confiscated *Etherway* on behalf of Karrde and discovered that the smuggling ship had been released from the impound yard thanks to a generous bribe given by Wedge Antilles. After briefly chatting with Rogue Squadron's leader, Mara board-ed the *Etherway* and piloted through the outer fringes of the planet's atmosphere.

Accelerating to full speed, Mara rapidly prepared the jump to hyperspace, but the *Victory*-class Star Destroyer *Adamant* roared from the planet's far side and expertly cut off her escape route. The Imperial warship's smug commander called for the outlaw vessel's immediate and unconditional surrender.

Mara was out of options. Though she had enjoyed her years of anonymity, she had no choice but to transmit the unmistakable recognition signal that identified her as the long-lost Emperor's Hand.

His valuable prize safely aboard, the *Adamant*'s commander left Abregado-rae with all possible haste, bound for Endor and a very interested Grand Admiral Thrawn.

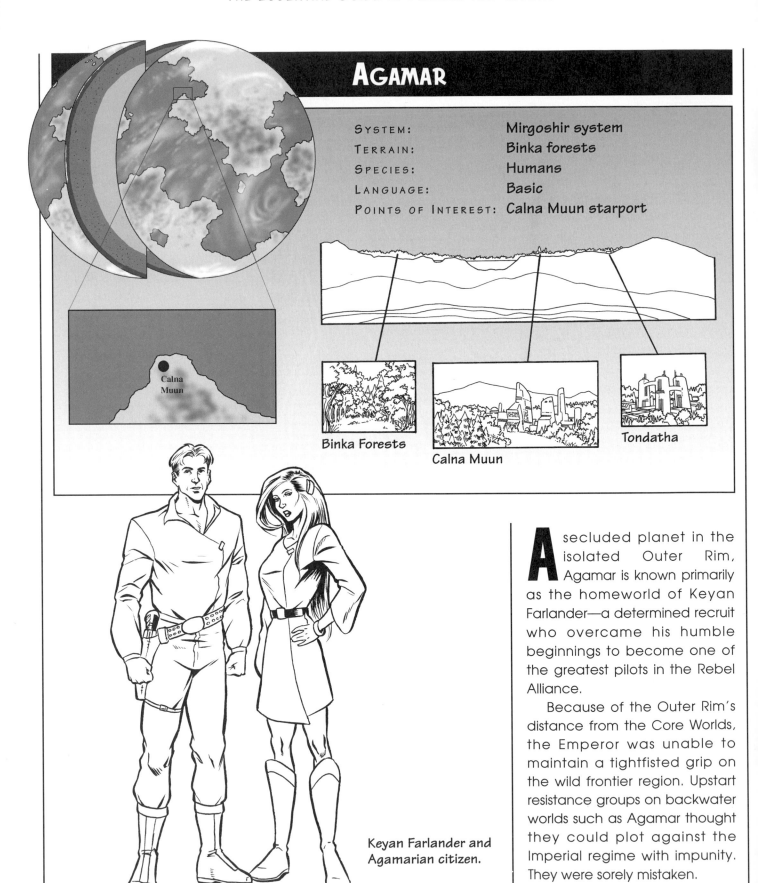

AGAMAR

SYSTEM: **Mirgoshir system**
TERRAIN: **Binka forests**
SPECIES: **Humans**
LANGUAGE: **Basic**
POINTS OF INTEREST: **Calna Muun starport**

Calna Muun

Binka Forests

Calna Muun

Tondatha

Keyan Farlander and
Agamarian citizen.

A secluded planet in the isolated Outer Rim, Agamar is known primarily as the homeworld of Keyan Farlander—a determined recruit who overcame his humble beginnings to become one of the greatest pilots in the Rebel Alliance.

Because of the Outer Rim's distance from the Core Worlds, the Emperor was unable to maintain a tightfisted grip on the wild frontier region. Upstart resistance groups on backwater worlds such as Agamar thought they could plot against the Imperial regime with impunity. They were sorely mistaken.

An Imperial assault craft was

dispatched to Agamar to quell its fledgling insurrectionist movement. Over deafening loudspeakers, the warship's commander announced the inescapable penalty for Imperial citizens who dared harbor traitors. Proton torpedoes were then dropped from the sky.

A young Keyan Farlander, racing home through the binka forest, heard the screams of the wounded and dying. When the bombardment finally ceased, his hometown of Tondatha was a smoking ruin. At the blast crater that had once been his family's struggling mugruebe ranch Keyan found the lifeless bodies of his mother and father.

With no reason to remain, Keyan drifted to the main city, Calna Muun, where he joined the Agamar Resistance. The dissident group had been shaken by the Empire's brutal attack but was now more driven than ever to continue the fight.

Mon Mothma, the distinguished leader and founder of the Rebel Alliance, arrived on Agamar for a secret meeting with the planetary resistance, hoping to persuade them to join her larger cause. Keyan listened intently as the dignified woman recited a litany of the Emperor's atrocities and called upon all free beings of the galaxy to make a stand against tyranny. Inspired by her eloquence, Farlander asked how he could become a starfighter pilot to strike back against the butchers who had devastated his life.

Flight Cadet Farlander was sent to the Alliance star cruiser *Independence* for orientation and intensive training. It was far from easy, but the young Agamarian displayed a natural skill in the cockpit—and manifested an uncanny ability to wield the Force.

Over the next few years Farlander distinguished himself in extraordinary service to the Alliance. Between countless dogfights, Farlander helped annihilate the Star Destroyer *Intrepid*, participated in the Battle of Yavin, spearheaded the successful Operation Ram's Head, oversaw the deployment of the new B-wing fighter, and helped cover the Rebel fleet's evacuation to the ice world of Hoth. Agamar has every reason to be proud of its most famous son.

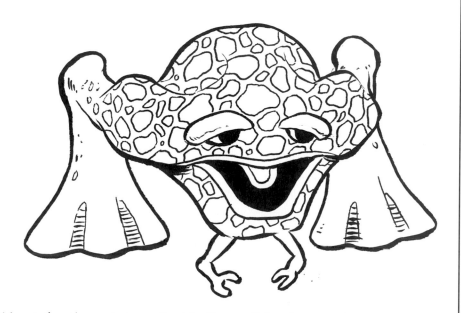

Mugruebe, the main ingredient in the traditional mugruebe stew.

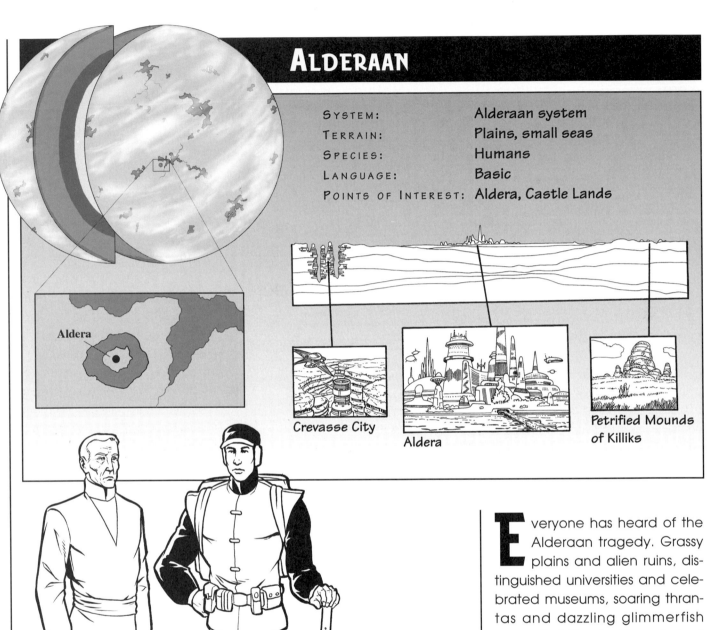

ALDERAAN

SYSTEM: Alderaan system
TERRAIN: Plains, small seas
SPECIES: Humans
LANGUAGE: Basic
POINTS OF INTEREST: Aldera, Castle Lands

Aldera

Crevasse City

Aldera

Petrified Mounds of Killiks

Citizens of Alderaan were peaceful and prosperous.

Everyone has heard of the Alderaan tragedy. Grassy plains and alien ruins, distinguished universities and celebrated museums, soaring thrantas and dazzling glimmerfish were all obliterated in an instant by the Death Star's superlaser, leaving only a ragged debris field fittingly called the Graveyard.

For thousands of years Alderaan was famous as a world of unspoiled beauty and a center of art, culture, and education. The earliest colonists refused to pave their new home with ferrocrete—*one* Coruscant was enough for them. Instead, cities were built into canyon

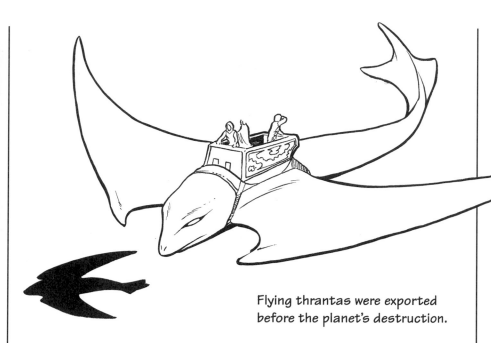

Flying thrantas were exported before the planet's destruction.

crevasses, beneath the polar ice, and on stilts in the shallow saline seas.

The rolling plains and gentle breezes attracted some of the greatest artists and philosophers who ever lived. Some sought inspiration in the Castle Lands (empty dirt mounds left by long-vanished aliens), while others used the endless fields as their canvas in vast "grass paintings."

Though Alderaan had long been a democracy, it still retained a royal family: House Organa. The Organas, ruling from the capital, Aldera, took an active role in the Old Republic government and helped oversee the voluntary demilitarization of their world after the bloody Clone Wars. After Palpatine's rise, Bail Organa became a founding member of the Rebel Alliance, and his adopted daughter, Leia,

followed in his footsteps.

But Princess Leia was captured above Tatooine by Darth Vader and brought aboard the newly completed Death Star. Grand Moff Tarkin had planned to use his new weapon on Alderaan—as an example to other free-thinking worlds—but now he could also finally crush the Rebellion.

The princess was brought to the control center and led to believe that she could save her homeworld by divulging the site of the secret Rebel base. Leia named a location, but it made no difference—the defenseless planet was obliterated.

Tarkin, however, had made a disastrous error. The callous murder of billions struck anger—not fear—into the galaxy. New allies, seeing the Empire's true face, flocked to the Rebel banner.

Imperial spokespeople put

their best spin on the story, initially claiming that Alderaan had destroyed itself with titanic internal detonations. When a pirated holoclip exposed the lie, the Empire claimed that its action had been necessary to prevent the release of "Bail Organa's biowar virus." Few, save the staunchest Imperial loyalists, believed that.

Today those Alderaanians who were safely offworld during the incident make regular pilgrimages to the Graveyard. Among the drifting rocks they leave flowers, poems, and mementos of their lost loved ones. The survivors leave with a new determination: the galaxy must never forget.

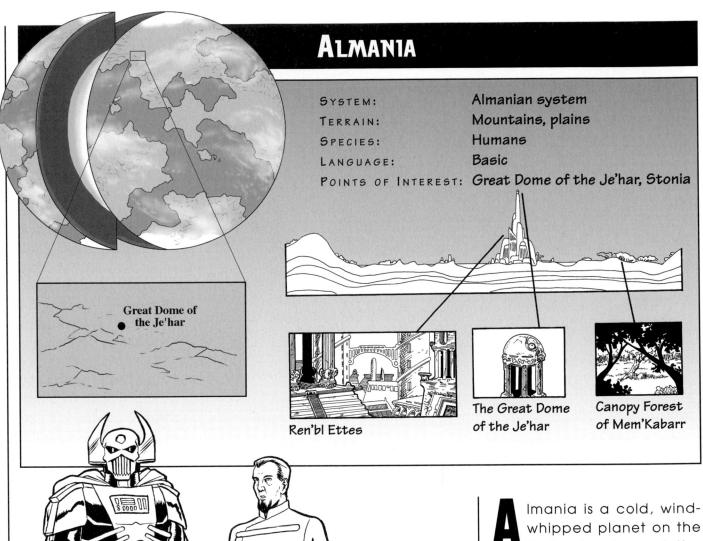

ALMANIA

SYSTEM:	Almanian system
TERRAIN:	Mountains, plains
SPECIES:	Humans
LANGUAGE:	Basic
POINTS OF INTEREST:	Great Dome of the Je'har, Stonia

Great Dome of
the Je'har

Ren'bl Ettes

The Great Dome
of the Je'har

Canopy Forest
of Mem'Kabarr

Kueller (left)
massacred many
Je'har officials,
hoping to vindicate
his parents'
murders.

Almania is a cold, wind-whipped planet on the farthest edges of the galaxy. Its three moons, Pydyr, Auyemesh, and Drewwa, are also habitable and have been settled for generations. Almania is so far from the galaxy's hub that even the Empire ignored the remote outworld.

For years the planet was ruled by the Je'har, a group that lent financial support to the Rebel Alliance. During the New Republic's battle against Grand Admiral Thrawn, however, the Je'har changed to a new, merciless regime. Thousands of Almanian dissenters were brutally executed. Some of them sent a distress signal to the New Republic, but the government was preoccupied with other problems. The slaughter continued for years.

During that time Dolph, a Force-sensitive Almanian studying at Luke Skywalker's Jedi academy on Yavin 4, received terrible news about his family. Rashly, Dolph abandoned his Jedi training and rushed back to his homeworld, only to find his parents' bodies hanging outside the Je'har ruling palace. Not yet able to control the Jedi powers he had learned, Dolph allowed his anger to consume him, tapping deep into the powers of the dark side.

Dolph assumed the name Kueller, after an ancient Almanian general, and began a crusade against his parents' murderers. Through the eyeholes of a chilling death's-head mask, he watched as his armies killed their former oppressors and then massacred all who stood in their way. Only a thousand handpicked Almanian citizens survived Kueller's holocaust.

Thirteen years after the Alliance's victory at Endor, Kueller set his sights on the galaxy. He murdered the populations of Pydyr and Auyemesh with explosive-rigged droids,

The Thernbee is psychic and quite playful.

using the acquired wealth to finance his campaign of conquest. Luke Skywalker felt the deaths in the Force and tracked the disturbance to Almania. When his X-wing unexpectedly exploded, a severely wounded Luke was captured and imprisoned. With the Jedi Master in his possession, Kueller contacted President Leia Organa Solo and demanded that she transfer all governmental power to him—or her brother's life would be forfeit.

Unintimidated, Leia arrived at Almania with a New Republic fleet. While Wedge Antilles battled Kueller's warships and their TIE squadrons, Leia rescued Luke from the dungeon, but the pair ran straight into Kueller.

An inexperienced Leia and an injured Luke were no match for Kueller's dark side power. Han and Chewbacca arrived with Force-canceling ysalamiri, but the lizards were promptly swallowed by a huge, hairy Thernbee. The ysalamiri still projected their nullifying bubble even as they were digested. Without the Force, Kueller's advantage vanished. In a last desperate move he tried to detonate the bombs in every rigged droid he had spread across the galaxy. Leia killed him with a blaster shot, finally putting a stop to his reign of terror.

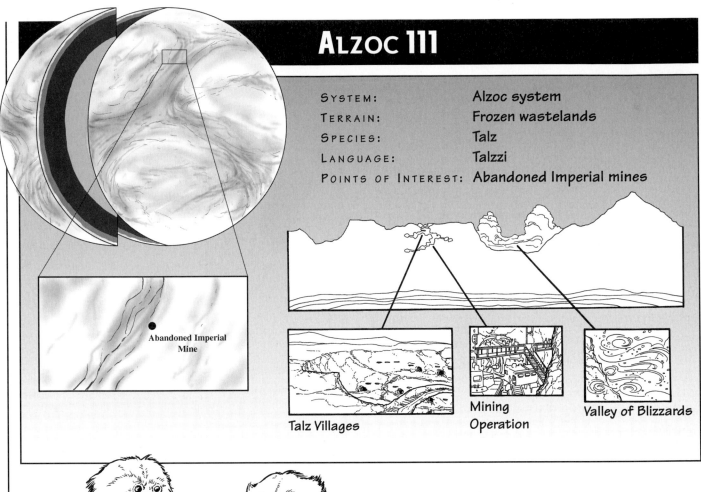

ALZOC 111

SYSTEM:	Alzoc system
TERRAIN:	Frozen wastelands
SPECIES:	Talz
LANGUAGE:	Talzzi
POINTS OF INTEREST:	Abandoned Imperial mines

Abandoned Imperial Mine

Talz Villages

Mining Operation

Valley of Blizzards

Talz are nearly as tall as Wookiees.

Alzoc III is the frozen home-world of the Talz. Standing nearly as tall as Wookiees, Talz are covered with shaggy white pelts and speak their buzzing language through a flexible proboscis. Their four specialized eyes allow for perfect vision even during the blinding daylight hours.

When the Empire discovered the out-of-the-way ice world, it realized that the Talz—massive but meek—would make excellent slave laborers. The gentle giants were set to work digging raw ore from deep pits bored into Alzoc III's crust. The Empire failed to record this find in the planetary registry, and the Talz's oppression continued, unnoticed by the freedom fighters of the Rebel Alliance.

When an unconventional Imperial officer named Pter Thanas was assigned to the Alzoc III garrison, he was impressed by the work ethic of its natives. Reasoning that the slaves would work more efficiently if they were well fed, he increased their daily rations. Soon afterward, Thanas accidentally stumbled near the edge of an open mine shaft, but a furry paw yanked him back to solid ground, saving his life.

Months later, when the food allotments were reduced again, Thanas was ordered to demolish the village of a Talz headman who had protested. He refused to comply. Furious at his insubordination, the garrison commander had Thanas reassigned to the even more remote Rim world of Bakura. The lessons Thanas learned from the Talz served him well at his new post, especially when a group of Rebels arrived at Bakura, offering a truce.

Perhaps the best known Talz is Muftak of Mos Eisley. Muftak lived in the sweltering heat of Tatooine almost all his life, with no idea how he had gotten there and no memories of his homeworld. The shaggy alien imagined Alzoc III to be a verdant paradise blooming with sweet nectar flowers, and no one had the knowledge to correct him. Muftak and Kabe, his Chadra-Fan companion, were

in the Mos Eisley cantina when Luke Skywalker and Ben Kenobi first met Han Solo. Soon afterward the two friends had an adventure that allowed them to leave the desert planet, and Muftak plotted a course for Alzoc III.

Four years later the Empire suffered a crushing defeat at the Battle of Endor. Retreating Imperial soldiers were forced to abandon many of their posts in the Outer Rim, including Alzoc III. Eight years after Endor the long-dormant Imperial battle-moon *Eye of Palpatine* was reactivated and, with Luke Skywalker aboard, began making preprogrammed troop pickups. When the ship arrived at the ice planet, it found no trace of the once-thriving Imperial base. Determined to fulfill its programming in spite of this fact, the *Eye* brought aboard a bewildered group of Talz instead. Fortunately, Luke was able to defeat the automated Dreadnaught and return the peaceful aliens to their homeworld.

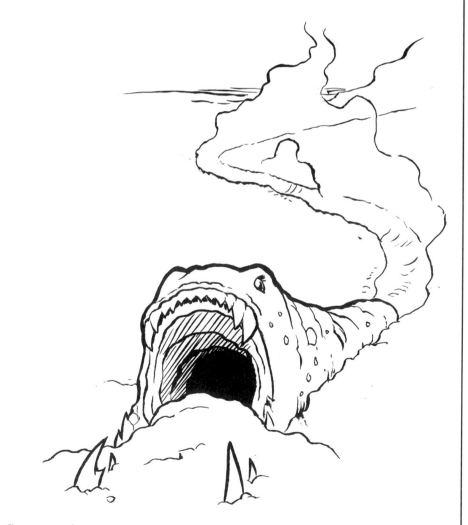

The snow slug captures unwary prey in its cavelike mouth.

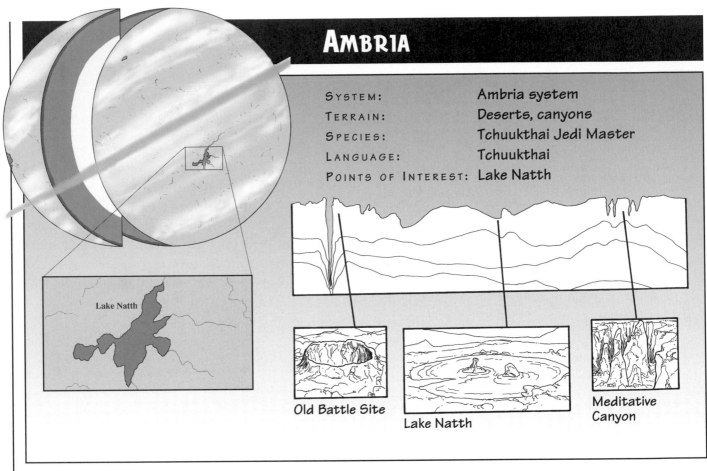

AMBRIA

SYSTEM:	Ambria system
TERRAIN:	Deserts, canyons
SPECIES:	Tchuukthai Jedi Master
LANGUAGE:	Tchuukthai
POINTS OF INTEREST:	Lake Natth

Lake Natth

Old Battle Site

Lake Natth

Meditative Canyon

Jedi Master Thon.

Four thousand years before the conflict between the Alliance and the Empire, the desert planet Ambria was a world of bottled tension—a place where a great evil was kept at bay through the tireless efforts of a Jedi Master.

Ambria sits at the heart of the Stenness Node, a dense cluster of profitable mining systems whose inhabitants ply the shipping lanes in wasp-shaped ore haulers. This dry world of plateaus and canyons is girded by a spectacular set of rings that encircle the dusty brown orb in pulsing hues of brilliant violet.

Despite its striking appearance, Ambria was too harsh for colonization. It was, however, a battleground for an epic clash between the forces of good and evil. Though the exact details have been lost to history, the great Master Thon, a rare Tchuukthai (or "Wharl") Jedi, defeated potent Sith spirits that threatened to consume the entire sector. The Jedi Master contained the sinister energy beneath the waters of Lake Natth. Unable to escape its confinement, the dark side malevolence mutated the local lifeforms, manifesting itself in vicious flesh-eating monstrosities called hssiss. Thon chose to remain on Ambria as a guardian and continued to initiate others into the Jedi Order.

One of Thon's most celebrated students was Nomi Sunrider. Her arrival on Ambria was not as she had planned. Nomi's husband, Andur, a Jedi Knight, had just been murdered, and the grief-stricken woman had no desire to train in the Force—only to deliver Andur's gift of lightsaber crystals to the Jedi Master. Thon persuaded Nomi to stay and train with him, but she was still reluctant to commit herself fully.

When her master's life was threatened by Great Bogga the Hutt, nefarious underlord of the Stenness Node, Nomi finally released herself to the Force. Using elementary battle meditation, she put the Hutt's thugs and enforcers at each other's throats. Thon looked on with

pride—Nomi Sunrider had become a Jedi.

Years later, during the devastating Sith War, Ambria was the site of an attempted assassination. Oss Wilum, once an eager disciple of Thon's wisdom, had been seduced and corrupted by the vile Sith teachings of Exar Kun. Joining forces with the former Jedi Knight Crado, Oss returned to Ambria to slay his own master.

Drawing on the powers of the Sith, Oss summoned two hssiss from the stagnant waters of Lake Natth and commanded them to tear the meat from Thon's bones. The old Tchuukthai, however, had vanquished this evil before. Flocks of terrified neeks scurried out of the way as the Jedi Master joined the fray. Faced with failure, Crado cravenly abandoned the battlefield, leaving a beaten Oss Wilum alone with his shame. Though Thon eventually brought his fallen pupil back to the light, the pain of betrayal never fully healed.

Flesh-eating hssiss inhabit Lake Natth.

Terrestrial neeks are playful creatures.

AMMUUD

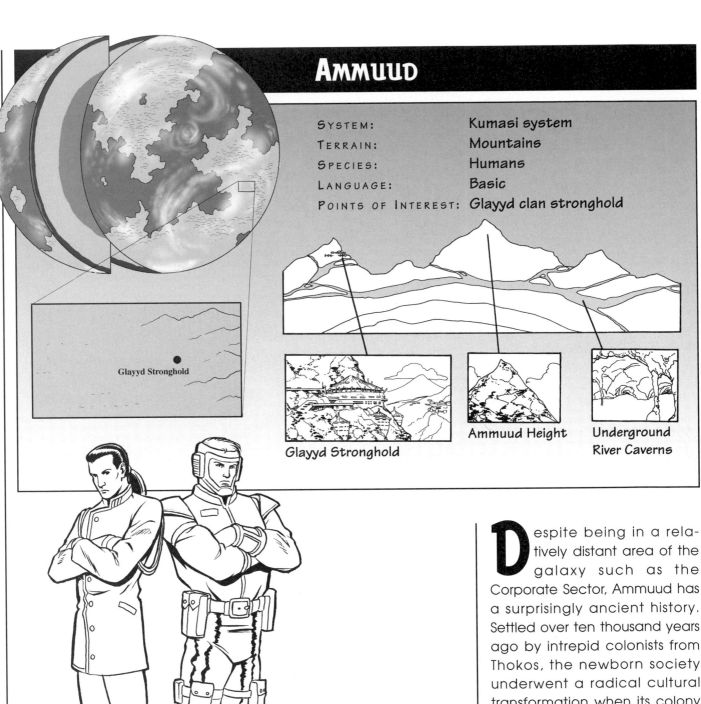

SYSTEM:	Kumasi system
TERRAIN:	Mountains
SPECIES:	Humans
LANGUAGE:	Basic
POINTS OF INTEREST:	Glayyd clan stronghold

Glayyd Stronghold

Glayyd Stronghold

Ammuud Height

Underground River Caverns

Mor Glayyd (left) and Mor Reesbon (right) are descendants of the founding colonist clans.

Despite being in a relatively distant area of the galaxy such as the Corporate Sector, Ammuud has a surprisingly ancient history. Settled over ten thousand years ago by intrepid colonists from Thokos, the newborn society underwent a radical cultural transformation when its colony lost contact with the outside galaxy.

The seven original colony ships—the *Reesbon*, *Tikeris*, *Owphrin*, *Melchett*, *Almowri*, *Odoon*, and *Glayyd*—evolved into seven ruling clans, with each clan headed by a hereditary patriarch, or "Mor." The opportunity to move Ammuud

Pterosaurs glide through the Ammuud sky.

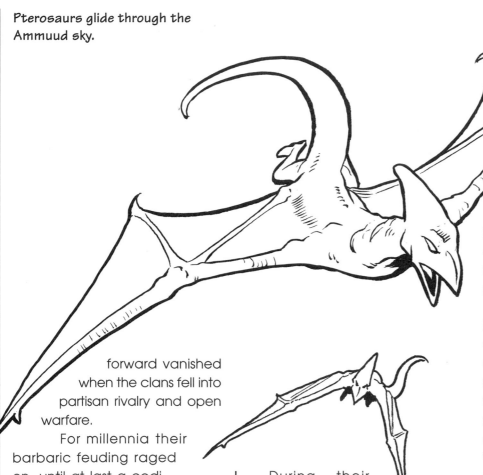

forward vanished when the clans fell into partisan rivalry and open warfare.

For millennia their barbaric feuding raged on, until at last a codified system of laws was adopted by each of the seven nation-states. The Code of Ammuud, established approximately a hundred years before the Rebel Alliance's victory at Yavin, specified that disputes were to be settled by a formal challenge and death duel between the two aggrieved parties. Only one fatality resulted instead of the scores from a typical clan war.

In Ammuud's terms this was true progress. When the Corporate Sector sprang up around the planet, the CSA allowed its backward neighbors to continue practicing their quaint laws, albeit under Authority subcontract.

During their early smuggling years Han Solo and Chewbacca adventured with Fiolla, a high-ranking Corporate Sector officer. Fiolla was trying to crack a secret slavery ring; Han and Chewie just wanted the ten thousand credits the slavers owed them. Their group followed the trail to Ammuud, where the Mor Glayyd had been allowing the slaver ships to be cleared through his agency, no questions asked.

Upon their arrival, Han discovered that the infamous gunman Gallandro had challenged the Mor Glayyd to a death duel on behalf of the rival Reesbon

clan. To protect their only lead, Han agreed to take the Mor's place under the arcane code's bylaws. When Gallandro saw the Mor was no longer a target, he withdrew—but not before demonstrating his lethally accurate speed draw on a spread of nearby holotargets.

At the same time, Chewbacca, in Ammuud's mountains with the *Millennium Falcon*, was caught in a frenzied grazer stampede. In inventive Wookiee fashion, he swiftly downed a gliding pterosaur with a bowcaster quarrel. Lashing its lightweight carcass to the frame of a metal tripod, he soared to safety on the makeshift hang glider as the snorting herd trampled his position.

Back in the Glayyd stronghold, Han revealed that the slavers had poisoned the Mor's father. Outraged, the Mor Glayyd turned over all evidence on the slaving ring, enough to shut it down for good. After a harrowing shoot-out with the slavers' ship—and a tense negotiation with Authority execs aboard a *Victory*-class Star Destroyer—Han and Chewie departed from Ammuud ten thousand credits richer.

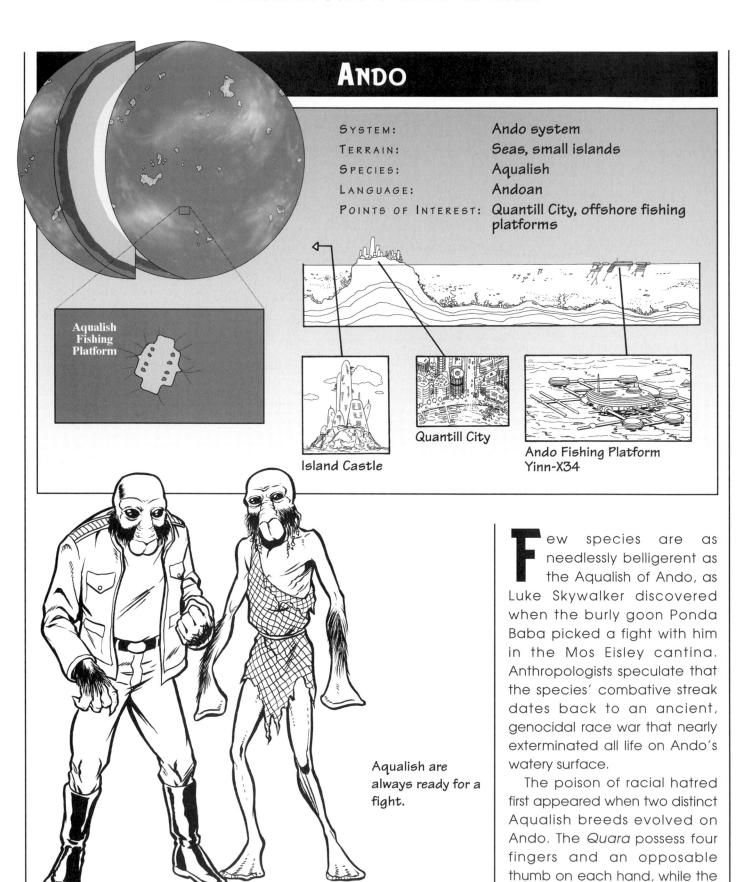

ANDO

SYSTEM:	Ando system
TERRAIN:	Seas, small islands
SPECIES:	Aqualish
LANGUAGE:	Andoan
POINTS OF INTEREST:	Quantill City, offshore fishing platforms

Aqualish Fishing Platform

Island Castle

Quantill City

Ando Fishing Platform Yinn-X34

Aqualish are always ready for a fight.

Few species are as needlessly belligerent as the Aqualish of Ando, as Luke Skywalker discovered when the burly goon Ponda Baba picked a fight with him in the Mos Eisley cantina. Anthropologists speculate that the species' combative streak dates back to an ancient, genocidal race war that nearly exterminated all life on Ando's watery surface.

The poison of racial hatred first appeared when two distinct Aqualish breeds evolved on Ando. The *Quara* possess four fingers and an opposable thumb on each hand, while the *Aquala* have less dexterous, cup-shaped fins. The fingered Aqualish, representing only a tenth of Ando's population, retreated to the planet's marshy islands, while the Aquala sailed the ocean currents on interlocking rafts, casting drift nets for the elusive Andoan mineral-fish.

On a world covered with oceans and soggy atolls, metals are a rare and valuable commodity. The mineral-fish, which digested ores and secreted them to form rock-hard carapaces, were the most important natural resource on the planet. When their numbers began declining as a result of overfishing, the Aquala looked for someone to blame and settled on their terrestrial cousins.

Ando erupted in a savage fratricidal bloodbath that raged for generations. The Aqualish species might have vanished altogether if not for the arrival of a visitor from the stars. A small scout ship, possibly piloted by Duros explorers, set down in the middle of the war zone and promptly became the new target of hate for both Aquala and Quara. Reverse-engineering the ill-fated scout ship, the Aqualish soon slapped together a ragtag space fleet. Their armada left the star system on a bold crusade to conquer the peaceful civilizations of the Old Republic.

The galactic government, however, had the best-trained soldiers and most advanced armaments in existence. Warships of the Republic's navy

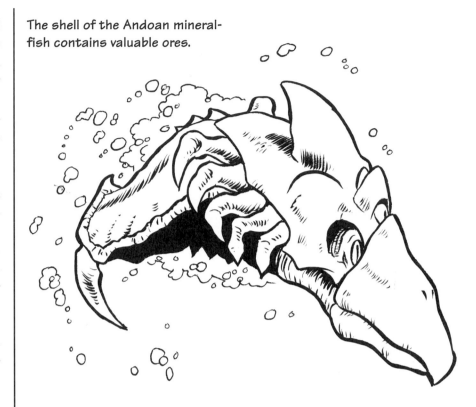

The shell of the Andoan mineral-fish contains valuable ores.

smashed the inferior fleet and swiftly took the war to Ando. Smart enough to realize that they were hopelessly outmatched, the cowed Aqualish sued for peace.

Ando was forcibly demilitarized under the watchful eye of the Republic. Though they could no longer be part of a conquering Aqualish space fleet, many of the tusked aliens found offworld employment as strikebreakers, bill collectors, and other vocations where their bellicose temperaments were an asset.

Ponda Baba was lucky to survive his brief scuffle with Skywalker, which ended when Ben Kenobi's lightsaber severed his hairy arm at the elbow. With his companion, the murderous madman Dr. Evazan, Ponda

soon returned to his aquatic homeworld.

There, in a remote island castle, Evazan developed a brain-switching apparatus with funding from a corrupt Aquala senator. Evazan planned to transfer Ponda's consciousness into the senator's healthy, two-armed body, but a vengeful bounty hunter chose that moment to attack. When the smoke cleared, the Andoan senator was trapped in Ponda's form, Ponda had disappeared, and Evazan left Ando to practice his vile trade on another world.

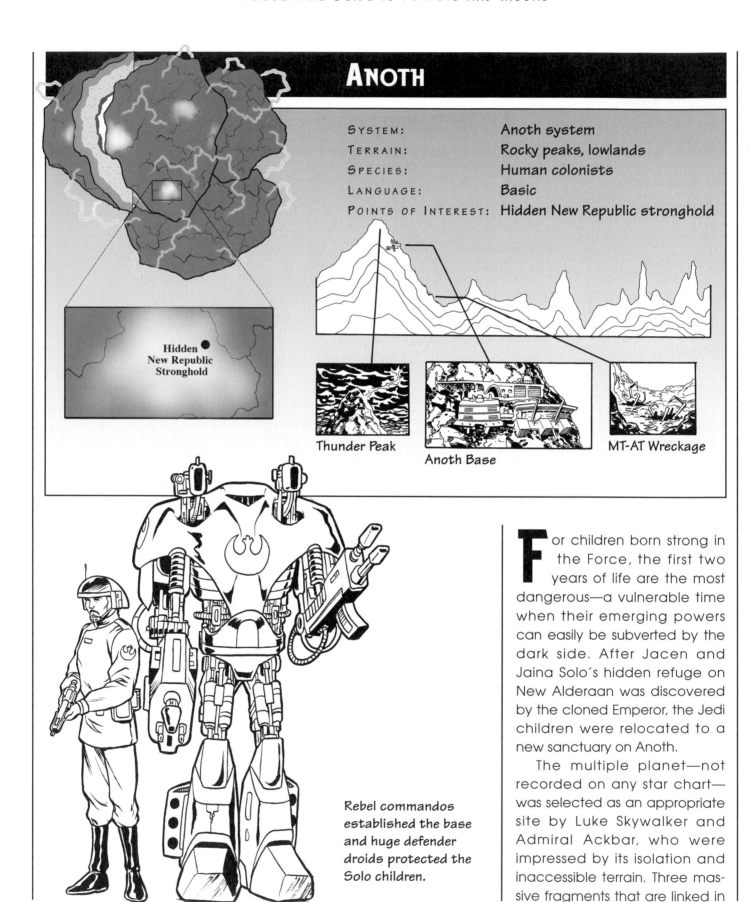

ANOTH

SYSTEM:	Anoth system
TERRAIN:	Rocky peaks, lowlands
SPECIES:	Human colonists
LANGUAGE:	Basic
POINTS OF INTEREST:	Hidden New Republic stronghold

Hidden New Republic Stronghold

Thunder Peak

Anoth Base

MT-AT Wreckage

Rebel commandos established the base and huge defender droids protected the Solo children.

For children born strong in the Force, the first two years of life are the most dangerous—a vulnerable time when their emerging powers can easily be subverted by the dark side. After Jacen and Jaina Solo's hidden refuge on New Alderaan was discovered by the cloned Emperor, the Jedi children were relocated to a new sanctuary on Anoth.

The multiple planet—not recorded on any star chart—was selected as an appropriate site by Luke Skywalker and Admiral Ackbar, who were impressed by its isolation and inaccessible terrain. Three massive fragments that are linked in formation by weak gravity drift through space amid crackling bolts of static electricity. The two largest chunks are seething wastelands, but a breathable atmosphere clings to the lowlands of the smallest piece. No one, Luke reasoned, would look for a settlement *here*.

Precautions were taken nonetheless. A secure operations base was built deep in a grotto network within one of the tallest stone spires. A squad of camouflaged assassin droids stood ready to annihilate any invader who made it past the FIDO anti-intruder system installed at the cave's mouth. Even the gentle, nurturing nanny droid was programmed to unleash a deadly flurry of blaster bolts if her charges were ever threatened. Leia's old friend Winter remained at the Anoth base full-time as guardian of and teacher to Jacen, Jaina, and Anakin Solo.

After the twins reached the age of two, they were sent to live with their mother; Anakin, still an infant, remained on Anoth. All was well until Ambassador Furgan, a zealous Imperial loyalist, learned the location of the concealed stronghold from his personal spy.

Furgan, fleeing Carida's destruction aboard the Dreadnaught *Vendetta*, angled toward Anoth with a hold full of MT-AT "spider walkers." The pompous bureaucrat was seized with the conceit that if he could kidnap the Solo

Anothian living crystals barely survive in Anoth's harsh terrain.

baby, he could raise him as a new Emperor Palpatine—with himself as a "trusted adviser," of course.

Furgan's arachnid destroyers began scaling the sheer rock of the cliff face. The cool-headed Winter immediately activated the security systems, eliminating half the attackers before they could even reach the hangar doors, but the surviving troopers were persistent. Furgan soon had the Jedi infant.

Leia and Ackbar arrived aboard the *Galactic Voyager*, just in time to rescue the baby Anakin. The *Vendetta* tried to flee between Anoth's two largest chunks, where it was skewered by a static bolt and vaporized. A panicked Furgan abandoned his prize in order to reach the safety of his beloved MT-AT. In a tussle at the cliff's edge the pudgy ambassador fell to his death with a wordless scream of terror.

ANTAR FOUR

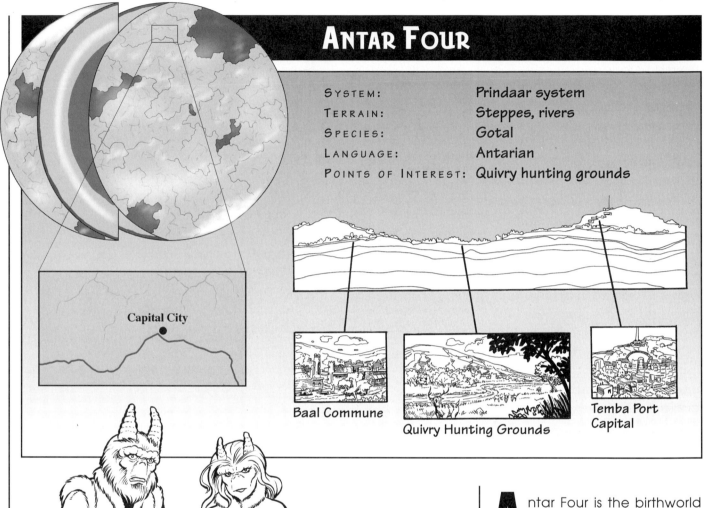

SYSTEM:	Prindaar system
TERRAIN:	Steppes, rivers
SPECIES:	Gotal
LANGUAGE:	Antarian
POINTS OF INTEREST:	Quivry hunting grounds

Capital City

Baal Commune

Quivry Hunting Grounds

Temba Port Capital

Gotals detect energy through their head cones.

Antar Four is the birthworld of the Gotal, whose flat faces and twin head cones are a common sight in every starport throughout the galaxy. Some ignorant spacers distrust the Gotal, claiming they can "read minds"—this is untrue. Gotals can, however, pick up on the emotional states of other beings, an evolutionary by-product of their world's bizarre environment.

Antar Four is a moon, the fourth of six large bodies orbiting the gas giant Antar. The satellite's severe axial tilt causes unusual day/night cycles and exceptionally harsh seasonal changes. Sometimes Antar Four is lit on *both* sides by the sun and the reflective surface of Antar; at other times it is plunged into total darkness within its primary's massive shadow. The tenacious creatures that evolved under such conditions are quite different from the norm.

Since the availability of light was never guaranteed, animals developed senses other than sight—hearing, olfaction, and echolocation are some of the more common. The Gotal, however, evolved knobby protuberances atop their skulls, called "head cones," that specialized in the detection of radiation, electromagnetism, neutrino waves, and many other types of energy. A Gotal hunter can track a herd of migrating quivry for weeks, identifying their passive energy emissions from kilometers away. The Gotal pride themselves on the trials and dangers of a difficult hunt. They often say, "What is easily achieved is easily lost."

With practice, Gotal energy sensing can be used to detect the empathic state of another being, even when the subject is outwardly attempting to mask her or his feelings. No sabacc player tries to bluff when a Gotal is at the table. The head

Hunting quivry sharpens a Gotal's senses.

cones' sensitivity, however, can also be a curse—droids and other automatons create an unpleasant "buzzing" sensation, and the Force has an even more painful effect. Luke Skywalker tended to hurry past Gotal members of the Rebel Alliance for fear that his Jedi abilities would leave them with splitting headaches.

Some Gotal are so skilled at reading emotions that they can actually anticipate an enemy's actions a split second before he or she makes them. Glott, the most notorious of these Gotal "precogs," went into business as a bounty hunter, tracking fugitives for the thrill and the credits. Glott met his match on the planet M'haeli when he ran up against a young Imperial named Ranulf Trommer.

Feltipern Trevagg embarked on a different sort of hunt. The Gotal tax official tried to win the heart of a delicate H'nemthe female in the Mos Eisley cantina on Tatooine. The two lovers were snuggling in a darkened booth when Luke Skywalker and Ben Kenobi entered to hire a star pilot. But a day later Trevagg learned the hard way that mating customs differ greatly from planet to planet.

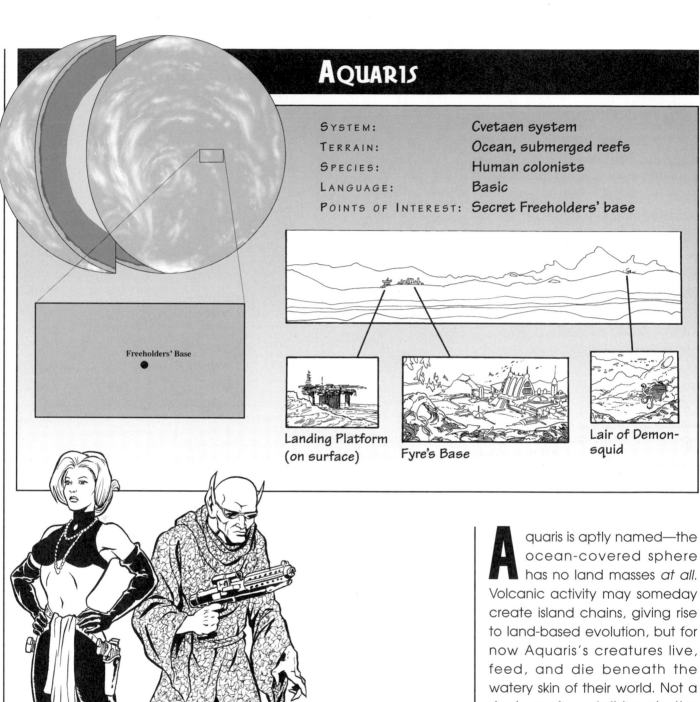

AQUARIS

SYSTEM:	Cvetaen system
TERRAIN:	Ocean, submerged reefs
SPECIES:	Human colonists
LANGUAGE:	Basic
POINTS OF INTEREST:	Secret Freeholders' base

Freeholders' Base

Landing Platform (on surface)

Fyre's Base

Lair of Demon-squid

Silver Fyre, leader of the Freeholders, and her deputy commander, Kraaken.

Aquaris is aptly named—the ocean-covered sphere has no land masses *at all.* Volcanic activity may someday create island chains, giving rise to land-based evolution, but for now Aquaris's creatures live, feed, and die beneath the watery skin of their world. Not a single reef or atoll breaks the surface, and humans long ago dismissed Aquaris as unfit for colonization.

An uninhabited, overlooked world was just what Silver Fyre and her Freeholders were looking for. Fyre, leader of one of the galaxy's largest smuggling and piracy groups, bypassed obvious choices such as Myrkr and the Vergesso Asteroids to build a new base of operations on Aquaris.

Fyre sank thousands of hard-won credits into the construction of her extensive base, which was then sunk beneath Aquaris's briny surf—safe from prying eyes and casual sensor scans. A landing platform could be extended above the waves to accommodate arriving ships, then sealed and brought beneath the surface to the main facility on the ocean floor. The base's transparisteel viewports offered a stunning vista of Aquaris's diverse fish, mollusks, and cetaceans. At first some of the larger creatures tried to drive this strange metal behemoth from their territory; Fyre's Freeholders learned to keep the monsters at bay with the weapons on their maneuverable aqua-skimmers.

Just after the Battle of Yavin, Silver Fyre attended a conference with Princess Leia on the planet Kabal. After years of evading Imperial escort frigates and customs vessels, Fyre had decided to throw in her lot with the Rebel Alliance. Leia arrived at the Aquaris base on the *Millennium Falcon* soon afterward.

Han was very familiar with Fyre's shady past and was suspicious of her sudden Rebel sympathies. Since R2-D2 was carrying sensitive Alliance data, Han dangled the droids as bait, hoping that Fyre—or one of her Freeholders—would snap them up.

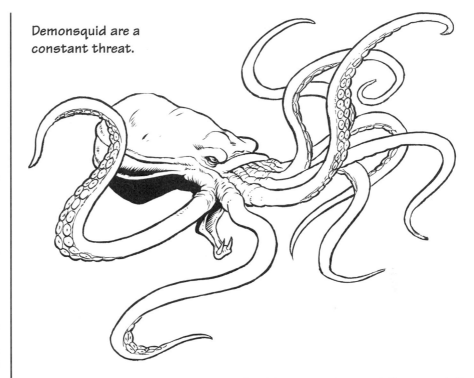

Demonsquid are a constant threat.

In the morning the group boarded aqua-skimmers for an underwater hunting expedition. As they neared their quarry, a monstrous demonsquid, Luke's skimmer plunged straight toward its waiting tentacles.

They'd been tricked. Kraaken, Fyre's deputy commander, had stunned Luke and placed his skimmer on autopilot. Kraaken hoped to steal the droids for himself while the others were preoccupied with the rescue. Han, donning an oxygen mask, popped the canopy of his skimmer and swam to save his friend.

Han freed Luke, only to be grabbed by the beast's suckered tentacle. Chewbacca doesn't take kindly to seeing his "honor family" menaced—a vicious jab with a metal shard allowed their escape, while a clean shot from Fyre's aqua-skimmer pierced the squid's brain sac.

Back at the Freeholders' base, Leia succeeded in uncovering Kraaken's treachery and preventing his theft of the droids. Grateful, Silver Fyre pledged all her resources—including her formidable space fleet—to the service of the Rebel Alliance.

Gnooroop travel in dense schools that can reach more than ten kilometers in length.

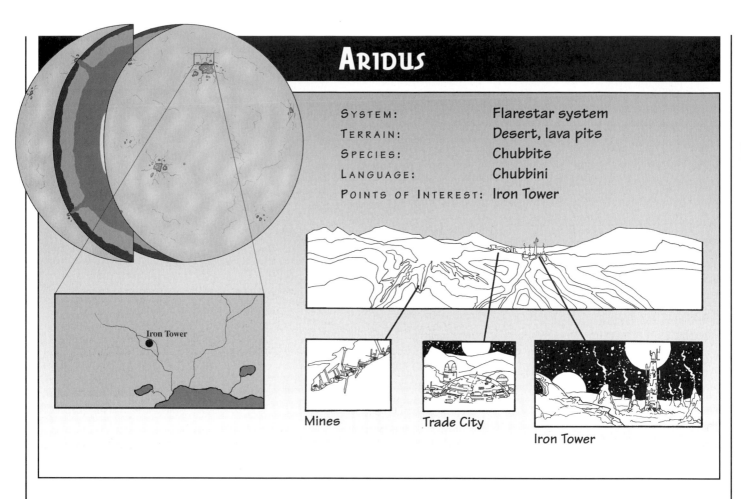

ARIDUS

SYSTEM:	Flarestar system
TERRAIN:	Desert, lava pits
SPECIES:	Chubbits
LANGUAGE:	Chubbini
POINTS OF INTEREST:	Iron Tower

Iron Tower

Mines

Trade City

Iron Tower

Chubbits.

The galaxy is filled with tragic examples of the Empire's lack of respect for native peoples, cultures, environments, and ecosystems. Aridus is one of them.

When Imperial scouts located valuable natural resources on the desert planet, Imperial mining teams rushed to exploit them. However, Aridus's ionized atmosphere wreaked havoc with the tunneling equipment. Mole miners would suddenly switch off while drilling a shaft; comlink communications would be lost in a burst of static. The mining foreman pleaded with his superiors to authorize the construction of a massive power transformer and signal amplifier; otherwise, operations on Aridus would have to be scrapped.

Anxious to protect his investment, the sector Moff approved the Iron Tower, a monumental structure that could punch its signal through any interference. The mining picked up again, and Imperial hovertrains began ferrying workers to the dig sites.

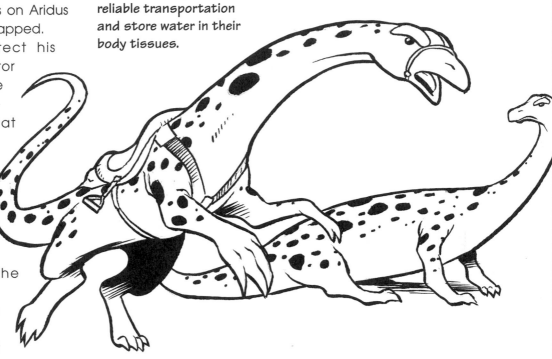

Droffi steeds provide reliable transportation and store water in their body tissues.

The Imperials never stopped to consider what effect this might have on the native Chubbits. The diminutive lizards had quietly watched the Empire ravage their world, but the new Iron Tower was a lethal threat. Its powerful emanations had crippling effects on the Chubbit nervous system, and they were forced to take up arms for their continued survival.

The Rebel Alliance gladly supplied weapons to their cause. Soon after the Battle of Yavin, Luke Skywalker heard that one of the Rebel gunrunners had spotted Ben Kenobi on Aridus. Unwilling to dismiss the possibility that his slain master had come back from the dead, Luke rushed to investigate the rumor. When he finally met the brown-robed figure, Luke allowed himself to believe that Obi-Wan Kenobi had returned.

However, this "Ben Kenobi" was merely a trained actor altered by Imperial surgeons to resemble the fallen Jedi. Luke joined the imposter on a purported mission to destroy the Iron Tower. Darth Vader was secretly lying in wait to snare the Rebel.

As the two set off across the desert astride droffi steeds, the actor began to have doubts about his mission. The respect the Chubbits had shown him and the awe in the young man's eyes indicated what a great man Obi-Wan had been—and what a small, cowardly man the actor must be to willingly serve as an Imperial puppet.

When the two split up inside the Iron Tower, Vader ordered "Ben" to lure Luke into his trap. But the actor refused to obey Vader's command and pulled a control lever to start a catastrophic overload spiral in the structure's upper levels. When the blast smoke cleared, the Iron Tower was disabled and Vader had vanished.

Luke rushed to the old man's side, but his wounds were too severe. As he died, the actor revealed the truth—he was not Luke's mentor, "just an imposter, who came to love the part. I only hope I played it well."

ARKANIA

SYSTEM:	Perave system
TERRAIN:	Tundra, canyons
SPECIES:	Arkanians, Yaka
LANGUAGES:	Basic, Yakan
POINTS OF INTEREST:	Diamond mines

Master Arca's Training Center

Trade City

Depleted Diamond Mine

Master Arca's Training Center

Master Arca (left) is a typical Arkanian. Luwingo (right) is a Yaka cyborg with brain implants.

"I wouldn't miss this for all the diamonds in Arkania!" A common spacers' saying, this old cliché reveals the popular image of a planet where miners extract gems of all sizes—from brilliant, glittering crystal fragments to massive faceted stones the size of bowvine melons. Arkania is a jeweler's dream.

The robust aliens who inhabit this resource-rich world possess impressive stamina and sharp minds and have a particular gift for manipulating science and technology. Arkanians can be distinguished from baseline humans by their milky-white eyes and four-fingered, clawed hands.

It was from this hardy stock that a great Jedi Master arose over four millennia before the rise of the Empire. Master Arca Jeth was one of the wisest of all Jedi Knights, with an astounding ability to influence the coordination and morale of an attacking army—a skill known as Jedi Battle Meditation. Arca served the Old Republic during the Great Droid Revolution on Coruscant and, many years later, returned to his homeworld to train others in the ways of the Force.

The old Arkanian established a wilderness training center in the outback, far from the most remote diamond mines. Arca's apprentices—the brothers Ulic and Cay Qel-Droma and the Twi'lek Tott Doneeta—meditated in austere yurts, practiced lightsaber moves against an ancient dueling droid, learned the lightning strike of the Arkanian dragon, and listened to their master's teachings in the glowing campfire light.

Though all three pupils showed remarkable potential, Ulic stood out, mastering every challenge his master set before him. In a graduation ceremony of sorts Master Arca dispatched

The Arkanian dragon is intelligent enough to be classified as semi-sentient.

his three Jedi-in-training to quell a civil war on the planet Onderon. After only three days, however, he was forced to leave Arkania in his starship *Sungem* and intervene personally on his students' behalf.

Later, in a surprise attack on a Jedi assembly, Arca was struck down by a Krath war droid. "The enemy has found me, Ulic," he told his finest disciple, "but the enemy knows only darkness. I know the light." With those words, the greatest Arkanian Jedi became one with the Force.

Many generations later the descendants of Arca's people reached new heights in their understanding of cyborging and microcircuitry. After conquering the neighboring Yaka system, they embarked on an ethically questionable medical experiment: enhancing the intelligence of the stocky, slow-witted Yaka with implanted cybernetic brain links.

Though some Arkanians protested, the experiment was a success—the muscle-bound Yaka became one of the most intelligent species in the galaxy. Yakans are so intelligent, in fact, that most beings find them thoroughly inscrutable, with a bizarre sense of humor to match. Large numbers of Yakans now live on Arkania, using their superior minds to further the cause of science. One Yaka, the smuggler Luwingo, helped Lando Calrissian's invasion team escape from Byss after a disastrous assault on the Emperor's Citadel.

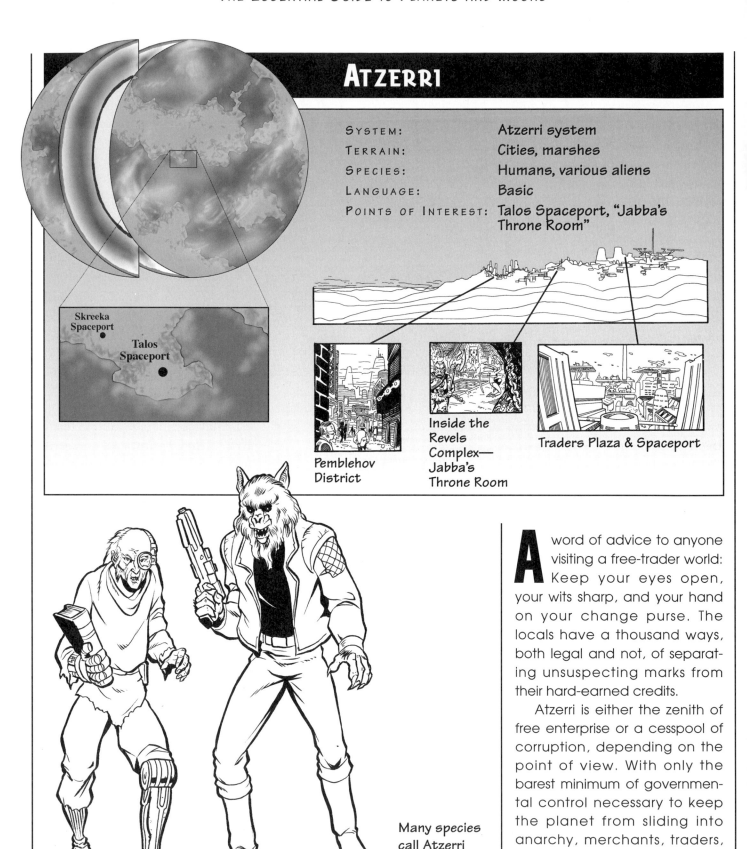

ATZERRI

SYSTEM: Atzerri system
TERRAIN: Cities, marshes
SPECIES: Humans, various aliens
LANGUAGE: Basic
POINTS OF INTEREST: Talos Spaceport, "Jabba's Throne Room"

Skreeka Spaceport

Talos Spaceport

Pemblehov District

Inside the Revels Complex— Jabba's Throne Room

Traders Plaza & Spaceport

Many species call Atzerri home.

A word of advice to anyone visiting a free-trader world: Keep your eyes open, your wits sharp, and your hand on your change purse. The locals have a thousand ways, both legal and not, of separating unsuspecting marks from their hard-earned credits.

Atzerri is either the zenith of free enterprise or a cesspool of corruption, depending on the point of view. With only the barest minimum of governmental control necessary to keep the planet from sliding into anarchy, merchants, traders, and outright swindlers (it's often difficult to tell the difference) compete in an environment of unbridled competition. Almost everything can be found on Atzerri, and *absolutely* everything is for sale.

Some thirteen years after the Battle of Endor, Luke Skywalker arrived on Atzerri with the mysterious Fallanassi woman called Akanah. She had told Luke that the sisters of the Fallanassi Order—including his long-lost mother—could be found there, but Akanah was spinning a snarled web of lies. She had no real information on Luke's mother and had led them to Atzerri to search for her own *father*.

Inventing a false pretense, Akanah vanished into the streets of Talos, leaving Luke behind with their ship, *Mud Sloth*. After several hours the Jedi Master grew tired of waiting. With his famous face masked behind a Force-made illusion, Luke headed out exploring.

Traders Plaza, just outside the landing pads, was a jumble of noisy, gaudy stalls designed to "hook" new arrivals while their pockets were still stuffed with hard currency. Amused but intrigued in spite of himself, Luke stopped into the "Galactic Archives" and purchased a copy of the lurid *Secrets of Jedi Power*—after haggling with the owner and getting it for less than half the outrageous cover price.

Pushing his way past the milling crowds and trash-foraging Meeks, Luke eventually reached the Revels, a raucous entertainment complex easily recognized by its strobing spotlights and drunken screams. Wanting to read his tabloid tome in peace, Luke started to leave, but his eye caught a familiar name lit in holographic lights: Jabba's Throne Room.

"Jabba's" turned out to be a themed restaurant and bar, painstakingly re-created to resemble the Hutt lord's former palace. Greeted by a Twi'lek actor playing Bib Fortuna, led to a table by a scantily clad dancing girl, and seated underneath an ersatz Han Solo frozen in carbonite, Luke had to admit that his exploits and those of his friends had spawned a bizarre cottage industry. He left just as an unconvincing Chewbacca was dragged down the stairs in chains.

Meanwhile, Akanah trudged through the flesh-market Pemblehov District and the Demon's Lair to reach Atrium 41—the decrepit home of her estranged father. But a joyous reunion was not to be. Joreb Goss, his brain rotted by the drug Rokna blue, had no recollection of even *having* a daughter.

A tearful Akanah returned to the ship, and Luke piloted them out of the system. Both had failed to find what they were looking for on Atzerri.

The Atzerrian Meek is a relative of the Abregado Moocher.

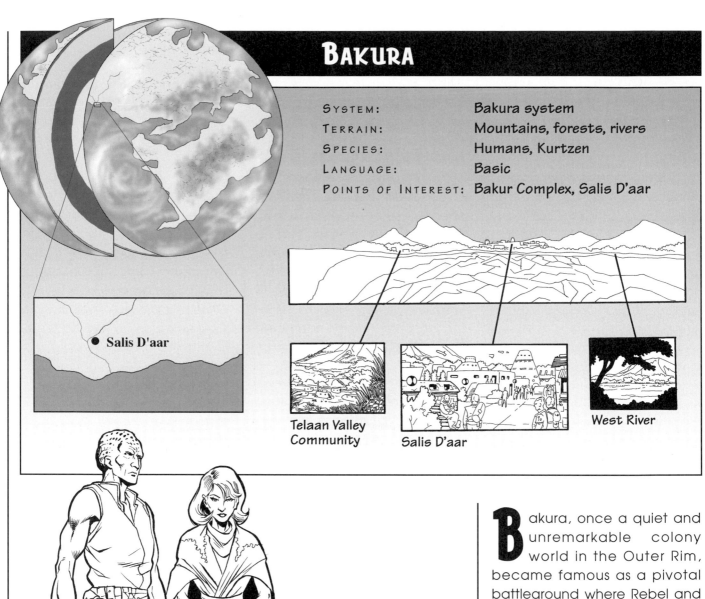

BAKURA

SYSTEM: **Bakura system**
TERRAIN: **Mountains, forests, rivers**
SPECIES: **Humans, Kurtzen**
LANGUAGE: **Basic**
POINTS OF INTEREST: **Bakur Complex, Salis D'aar**

Salis D'aar

Telaan Valley Community

Salis D'aar

West River

The indigenous species Kurtzen (left) make up 5% of Bakura's population, led by Prime Minister Gaeriel Captison (right).

Bakura, once a quiet and unremarkable colony world in the Outer Rim, became famous as a pivotal battleground where Rebel and Imperial forces fought side by side for the very survival of the galaxy.

The lush world is a green and blue sphere whose capital city, Salis D'aar, sits on a sparkling river delta of white quartz. Bakura's modest economy is centered on the production of repulsorlifts and the export of namana fruit. Droids are banned on the planet, since malfunctioning machines killed many of the earliest settlers.

Bakura, a new member of

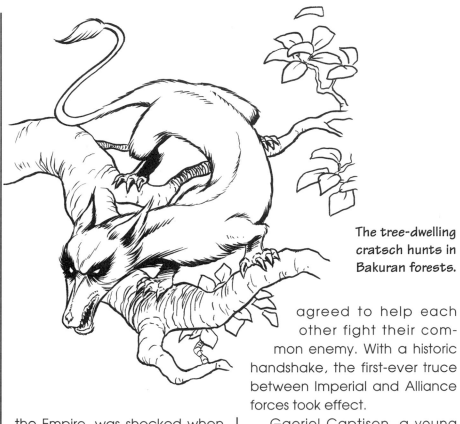

The tree-dwelling cratsch hunts in Bakuran forests.

the Empire, was shocked when an invasion fleet roared into the system immediately after the Battle of Endor. The strange egg-shaped warships were an advance force from the reptilian Ssi-ruuvi Imperium, striking from their homeworld of Lwhekk. The Ssi-ruuk's unnatural "entechment" technology harnessed human life energies to battle-droid control systems. An outpost world such as Bakura would provide the alien invaders with thousands of lives to fuel their war machines, spelling doom for every inhabited world in the galaxy.

At Endor the victorious Rebel Alliance intercepted the planet's urgent plea and sent its greatest heroes to assist. When the Rebels arrived, Princess Leia and Imperial Governor Nereus agreed to help each other fight their common enemy. With a historic handshake, the first-ever truce between Imperial and Alliance forces took effect.

Gaeriel Captison, a young and attractive Bakuran senator, caught the eye of Luke Skywalker. Gaeriel believed that great power in the Force was counterbalanced by tragic weakness in the lives of others and was reluctant to be close to the young Jedi Knight.

Meanwhile, aboard the mighty Ssi-ruuvi flagship *Shriwirr*, the brainwashed human Dev Sibwarra used his own Force sensitivity to detect Luke's presence below. Reasoning that this powerful Jedi might be able to entech subjects from a distance, Dev's Ssi-ruuk masters captured Skywalker.

Dev changed after witnessing Skywalker's heroism. When Luke made his move to escape from the *Shriwirr*'s entechment chamber, Dev fought by his side. Hundreds of Ssi-ruuk fled the ship in escape pods.

A full-fledged space battle raged around the *Shriwirr* as Imperial and Alliance ships forced most of the alien cruisers to flee into hyperspace. At the moment of their triumph, however, Nereus turned on the Rebels. The short-lived truce was at an end.

The Alliance was able to defeat the traitorous Imperials in an exhausting battle, while the citizens of Salis D'aar rose up in arms on the planet below. Both enemies—the Ssi-ruuk and the Empire—had been vanquished.

Bakura was now a member of the New Republic, but its people feared a return visit by the Ssi-ruuk. Four powerful vessels—the *Intruder*, *Watchkeeper*, *Sentinel*, and *Defender*—were built to safeguard the system. Gaeriel Captison was elected Prime Minister of Bakura and married Pter Thanas, the former commander of the Imperial garrison, who had defected to the Alliance.

Fourteen years after the truce Luke Skywalker returned to Bakura to ask for Gaeriel's help—he needed the planet's warships for a mission to the Corellian system. Gaeriel agreed, and Bakura was grateful for the opportunity to finally repay its longstanding debt to the New Republic.

BALMORRA

SYSTEM:	Nevoota system
TERRAIN:	Plains, urban centers
SPECIES:	Humans
LANGUAGE:	Basic
POINTS OF INTEREST:	State-of-the-art weapons plants

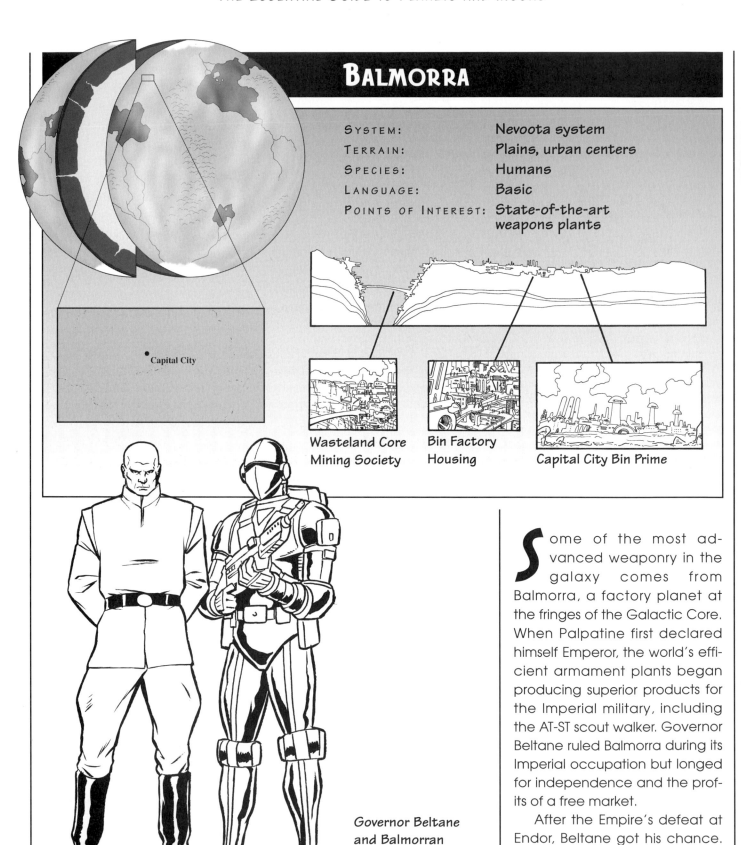

Capital City

Wasteland Core
Mining Society

Bin Factory
Housing

Capital City Bin Prime

Governor Beltane
and Balmorran
soldier.

Some of the most advanced weaponry in the galaxy comes from Balmorra, a factory planet at the fringes of the Galactic Core. When Palpatine first declared himself Emperor, the world's efficient armament plants began producing superior products for the Imperial military, including the AT-ST scout walker. Governor Beltane ruled Balmorra during its Imperial occupation but longed for independence and the profits of a free market.

After the Empire's defeat at Endor, Beltane got his chance. Balmorra threw off Imperial rule and became a neutral world for five years, until it was forced

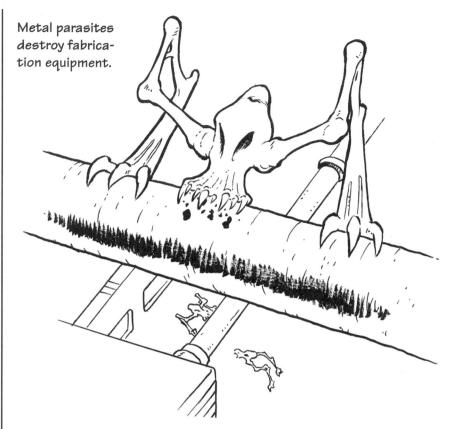

Metal parasites destroy fabrication equipment.

back into service during the reappearance of Emperor Palpatine. When the cloned Emperor supposedly died at Da Soocha V, a defiant Beltane began arming the New Republic.

Imperial Military Executor Sedriss traveled to the treasonous world aboard the Star Destroyer *Avenger* to dispense the appropriate punishment. Not wanting to risk damaging the valuable armament factories with an orbital bombardment, Sedriss landed his troops for open combat.

Thirty-six thousand stormtroopers and seven hundred scout walkers were ordered to guard the flanks of Sedriss's deadly battle droids, the SD-9s. Unfortunately, the metal com-

batants ran straight into a phalanx of Balmorran SD-10s. Beltane's droids were the latest models, incorporating the newest advancements in self-healing metal, and had been programmed to exploit all the weaknesses of their out-of-date forebears. The SD-9s were swiftly decimated.

Eager to regain the advantage, Sedriss unleashed his Shadow Droids—sleek ebony fighters containing the circuit-wired brains of former Imperial pilots. Sweeping down from the *Avenger*'s hangar bay, the Shadow Droids quickly wiped out the defending SD-10s and opened a clear path into Beltane's fortified city.

But Beltane had one more surprise in store—the X-1 Viper

Automadons. These metal behemoths were armored with molecular plating, allowing them to absorb blaster fire and use the energy to power their own cannons. Nothing the Empire had on the battlefield was able to resist the mechanical destroyers.

Sedriss was furious that Beltane had developed such a devastating weapon without informing the Empire. However, he shrewdly realized the power he could wield with a legion of Automadons. Publicly he agreed to a truce—the Empire would give Balmorra its freedom in return for a shipment of the new battle droids. Privately he resolved to reduce Balmorra to ashes at the earliest possible opportunity.

Governor Beltane was no fool. He knew that his planet's survival depended on the victory of the New Republic. He arranged for Sedriss's Automadons to be shipped to the Imperial headquarters on Byss but informed the Alliance leaders of the time and place his freighter could be captured. Rebel commandos intercepted the shipment, and Lando Calrissian led an attack on Byss with the war droids. Though Lando's assault was unsuccessful, the forces of the resurrected Emperor were soon defeated, allowing Balmorra to continue arming the New Republic.

BARAB 1

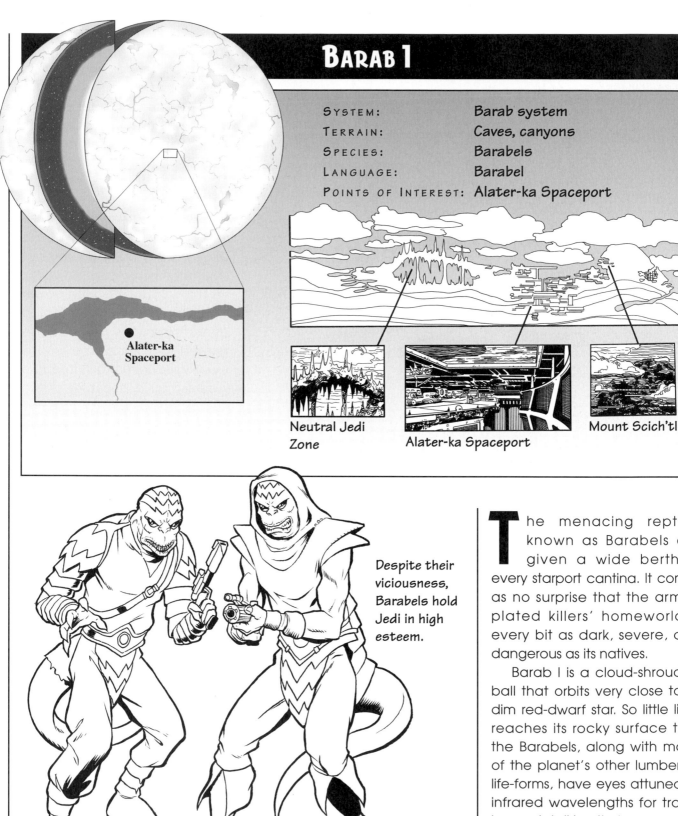

SYSTEM: Barab system
TERRAIN: Caves, canyons
SPECIES: Barabels
LANGUAGE: Barabel
POINTS OF INTEREST: Alater-ka Spaceport

Alater-ka Spaceport

Neutral Jedi Zone

Alater-ka Spaceport

Mount Scich'tl

Despite their viciousness, Barabels hold Jedi in high esteem.

The menacing reptiles known as Barabels are given a wide berth in every starport cantina. It comes as no surprise that the armor-plated killers' homeworld is every bit as dark, severe, and dangerous as its natives.

Barab I is a cloud-shrouded ball that orbits very close to its dim red-dwarf star. So little light reaches its rocky surface that the Barabels, along with many of the planet's other lumbering life-forms, have eyes attuned to infrared wavelengths for tracking and stalking their prey.

All activity on Barab I is strictly dictated by the cycles of its sixty-hour-long rotation. Though the world is always murky, the intense heat and radiation thrown off by Barab's star drive every ambulatory creature underground during the day. Sessile, bulb-shaped plants wrap themselves in silvery reflective cocoons as pools of standing water evaporate into clouds of low-hanging steam. Late in the day, as the planet slowly spins toward shadow, the surface temperature drops and creatures of every imaginable size and shape slink from their sheltered caverns.

Barabel hunters live for these few hours, catching and slaughtering shenbit bonecrushers and other prey many times their size. When the steam clouds condense into torrential rain, the hunters drag the oozing carcasses back to their subterranean dwellings.

Though they are a crude and often merciless species, the Barabel have a deep respect for the ancient order of Jedi Knights. Centuries ago a band of passing Jedi helped settle a conflict over choice hunting grounds that was threatening to erupt into full-scale butchery. Even today a Barabel will accept the judgment of a Jedi in any dispute, great or small.

But those early Jedi peacemakers did not record Barab I in the galactic registry. The planet remained cloaked in obscurity until the rise of the Empire.

An Imperially chartered corporation, Planetary Safaris, scouted Barab I and was

Barabels enjoy stalking shenbit bonecrushers for sport and meat.

impressed by its rapacious monsters. Legions of big-game hunters descended on the world to bag prize trophies, including the stuffed and mounted heads of Barabel warriors. When the great Barabel chieftain Shaka-ka retaliated, the Empire realized the value of these rugged and tenacious fighters.

The modest spaceport of Alater-ka was soon constructed to accommodate Imperial landing craft, and it remains the only city ever built on Barab I. Many Barabels were exported to the galaxy as mercenaries, shockboxers, and commandos, though some found work as bounty hunters. One of the best, Skahtul, captured Luke

Skywalker on Kothlis but made the foolish mistake of negotiating with both Prince Xizor and Darth Vader.

Barab I was liberated from its Imperial overseers after the Battle of Endor, but the Barabels' hostility caused continual headaches for the New Republic. Four years after Endor, furious over a broken shipbuilding contract, the reptiles nearly went to war with the insectoid Verpine. The Barabel even arranged to sell freeze-dried Verpine body parts to the insect-eating Kubaz. The crisis was averted without undue bloodshed, but no diplomat can predict what the ferocious Barabel will do next.

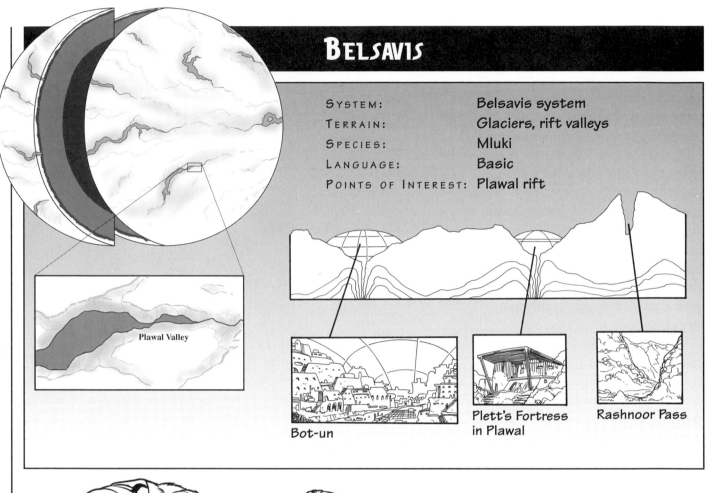

BELSAVIS

SYSTEM:	Belsavis system
TERRAIN:	Glaciers, rift valleys
SPECIES:	Mluki
LANGUAGE:	Basic
POINTS OF INTEREST:	Plawal rift

Plawal Valley

Bot-un

Plett's Fortress in Plawal

Rashnoor Pass

The native Mluki.

Belsavis is a world of fire and ice, of steaming tropical rifts separated by vast stretches of wind-scoured glaciers. Geothermal heat, bubbling up in sheltered valleys, allows vegetation to thrive in the warmth immediately surrounding the vents. This unique flora attracted the great Jedi Master Plett, whose Belsavis fortress became a sanctuary for the children of the Jedi.

Plett watched the actions of Emperor Palpatine with dismay. Though the old Jedi wished to remain at peace, tending to exotic plants in the Plawal rift, his conscience compelled him to harbor fugitives from

Palpatine's purges—many of them children. Unfortunately, Plett underestimated the depth of the Empire's hatred. The galactic tyrant commissioned a battlemoon, the *Eye of Palpatine*, and commanded it to obliterate Plawal.

Thanks to Jedi sabotage, the deadly destroyer never arrived. A backup wing of TIE fighters caused minor damage, but Plett and his charges successfully escaped to parts unknown.

With the Jedi gone, Belsavis survived as a profitable agricultural exporter. Several agronomic corporations capped the humid rift valleys with transparent domes, keeping out the glacial winds and providing a perfect growing environment for hanging beds of vine-coffee. About a year after the Empire's defeat at Endor, Roganda

Ismaren—one of the Emperor's Hands—set up shop in Plawal.

Roganda's teenage son Irek was rumored to be the offspring of Emperor Palpatine himself. With his Force talents and a cybernetic brain implant, the arrogant youth could control machines with his mind. Seven long years passed while Roganda made overtures to the aristocratic and powerful Senex Lords and Irek located the long-dormant *Eye of Palpatine*. Responding to the boy's call, the automated battlemoon awoke from its thirty-year sleep.

Han Solo and Leia Organa Solo were on Belsavis investigating a cryptic warning. When Leia learned too much for her own good, Roganda had her captured and imprisoned. The haughty woman's carefully laid plans crumbled, however, when

the *Eye* suddenly appeared in the system and Irek could no longer control it. The unstoppable Dreadnaught prepared to carry out its original program: *Shell the Plawal rift into oblivion.*

Leia escaped from her prison as Roganda and her son fled the planet in their personal starship. Luke Skywalker and his companions stopped the *Eye* by overloading the reactor before it could exterminate hundreds of innocent lives.

Afterward, Leia, Luke, and Luke's new love, Callista, explored old Master Plett's forgotten Jedi storerooms hidden deep in the kretch-infested tunnels. Plett's training tools, dusty from years of neglect, would be used once again by the new children of the Jedi: Jacen, Jaina, and Anakin Solo.

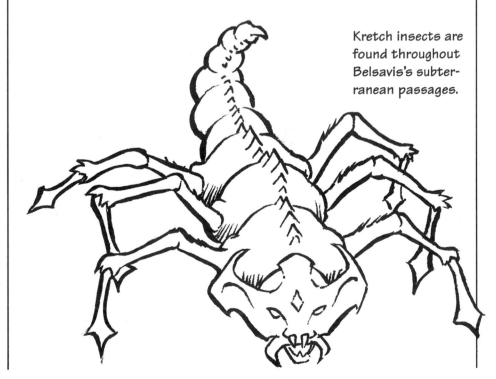

Kretch insects are found throughout Belsavis's subterranean passages.

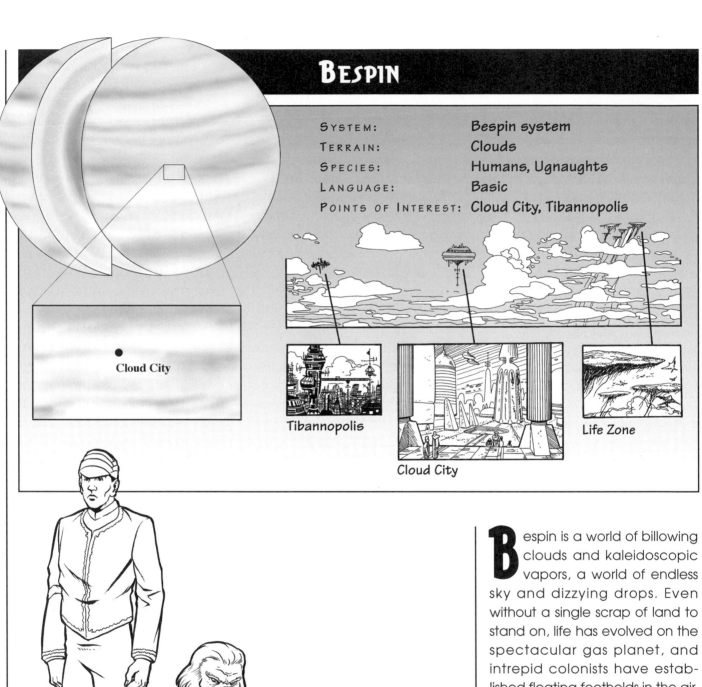

BESPIN

SYSTEM:	Bespin system
TERRAIN:	Clouds
SPECIES:	Humans, Ugnaughts
LANGUAGE:	Basic
POINTS OF INTEREST:	Cloud City, Tibannopolis

Cloud City

Tibannopolis

Cloud City

Life Zone

Humans and Ugnaughts keep Bespin operational.

Bespin is a world of billowing clouds and kaleidoscopic vapors, a world of endless sky and dizzying drops. Even without a single scrap of land to stand on, life has evolved on the spectacular gas planet, and intrepid colonists have established floating footholds in the air.

Gas giant planets are common sights, but few are inhabited. Like most, Bespin has a roiling atmosphere hundreds of kilometers deep and a liquid core under tremendous pressure. Unlike most, a narrow band of temperate, breathable air exists in the upper altitudes.

Within this "Life Zone" drift clouds of phosphorescent

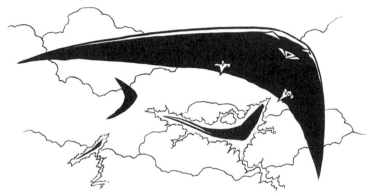

Giant gas bags, beldons metabolize natural chemicals, perhaps producing the valuable Tibanna gas itself. Packs of velkers, emitting energy fields, shred and devour beldons.

algae and colossal jellyfish beasts called beldons. Most animals steer clear of these sluggish leviathans, but flocks of sharp-toothed velkers can carve one up in minutes, gulping down chunks of flesh before the carcass plunges into the misty depths.

Floating cities are possible but are fiendishly difficult and expensive. No one would have bothered to build them on

Bespin if the world hadn't been a prime source of valuable Tibanna gas. Although the fact is not widely known, Bespin's Tibanna is naturally "spin-sealed," making it useful in boosting blaster firepower and causing it to be worth a fortune on the black market.

Cloud City is the largest of the airborne Tibanna refineries. It is also unique, doubling as a top-notch vacation resort and entertainment complex. In the bowels of the station, Tibanna is frozen into carbonite blocks for transport; in the uppermost towers, idle tourists win and lose fortunes in the Royal, Trest, and Pair O'Dice casinos.

Years ago Cloud City was won by the charming gambler Lando Calrissian in a sabacc game. Lando proved surprisingly capable in his role as Baron Administrator, keeping the factories running smoothly and enjoying his new status as a "respectable businessman." Together with his cyborg aide Lobot, he once battled the psychotic robot EV-9D9 after she dismantled a quarter of the city's droid population.

Later Calrissian was forced into an uncomfortable situation when the Empire arrived at his station. Darth Vader was setting a trap for someone named Skywalker, and his old friend Han Solo was the bait. Lando initially played along—he had a city to protect, after all, and he hadn't seen Han in years—but his conscience got the better of him. Activating Cloud City's Wing Guard, Lando freed Han's friends and fled from Bespin in the *Millennium Falcon*.

Cloud City changed hands many times over the ensuing years, but Lobot remained there as the computer liaison. Seven years after Endor Luke Skywalker returned to Bespin to recruit a gas prospector named Streen into his new Jedi academy. Five years after that Lando made his way back to Cloud City and convinced Lobot to help him solve the mystery of the Teljkon vagabond. Despite its turbulent history, Bespin is still a profitable exporter and one of the most beautiful sights in the galaxy.

BESTINE

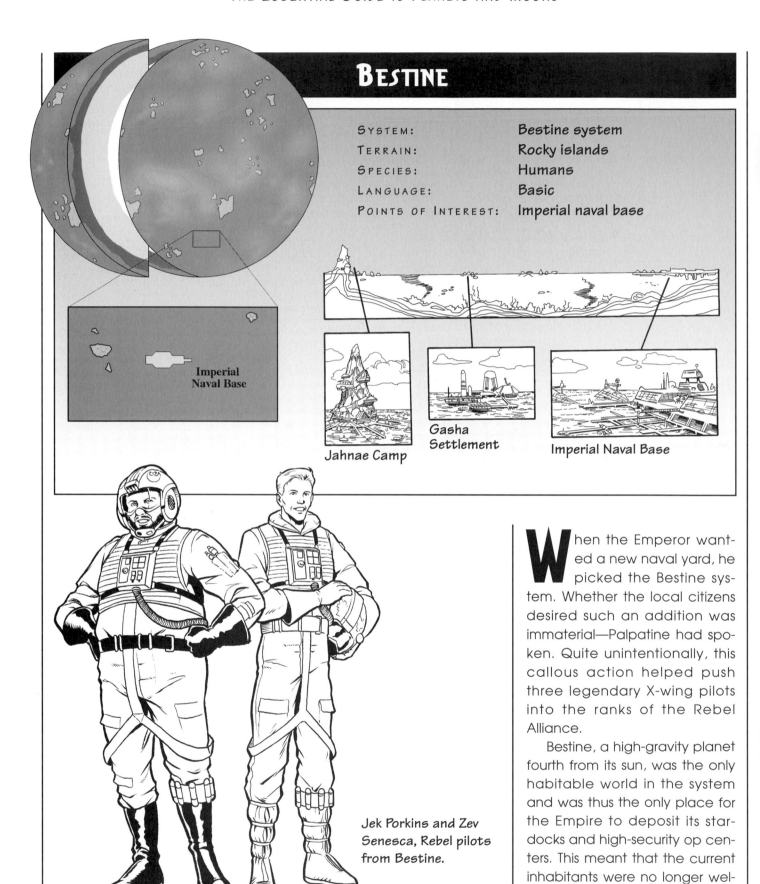

SYSTEM:	Bestine system
TERRAIN:	Rocky islands
SPECIES:	Humans
LANGUAGE:	Basic
POINTS OF INTEREST:	Imperial naval base

Imperial Naval Base

Jahnae Camp

Gasha Settlement

Imperial Naval Base

Jek Porkins and Zev Senesca, Rebel pilots from Bestine.

When the Emperor wanted a new naval yard, he picked the Bestine system. Whether the local citizens desired such an addition was immaterial—Palpatine had spoken. Quite unintentionally, this callous action helped push three legendary X-wing pilots into the ranks of the Rebel Alliance.

Bestine, a high-gravity planet fourth from its sun, was the only habitable world in the system and was thus the only place for the Empire to deposit its stardocks and high-security op centers. This meant that the current inhabitants were no longer welcome.

Bestine's colonists were a stubborn, independent lot. They had struggled for years to establish their modest settlements atop island spires, next to surging tidal pools, and on the waves to be carried along by the ocean currents. Reluctantly, they agreed to leave, trusting in the Empire's promises of a better life elsewhere.

Those promises proved empty. Outraged, the Bestine expatriates swore revenge, but on their *own* timetable. The Rebel Alliance was too hot-headed and impulsive, they said, and none joined—save one.

Jek Porkins was a first-rate pilot. He'd learned the craft as a boy, racing his T-16 skyhopper through Bestine's atolls and spearing sink-crabs with precise bursts of laser fire. Vowing that the Empire would pay, he became a courageous Rebel fighter.

As the naval base neared completion, an Imperial informant tipped the commanding officer off to some shady dealings on Kestic Station. Kestic, a free-trader outpost orbiting on the fringes of the Bestine system, had been supplying weapons to the Rebellion for some time. In retaliation, the Star Destroyer *Merciless* blasted it to glowing scrap. The young smuggler Zev Senesca lost his parents in the catastrophe, but the Alliance gained one more talented pilot.

Later an active Rebel cell sprang up on Bestine's watery

Oceanic sink-crabs use bladders to propel themselves.

surface for the purposes of sabotage and infiltration. In one of its most notorious exploits, the small band helped coordinate the theft of the Imperial freighter *Rand Ecliptic* just before the Battle of Yavin.

The *Ecliptic*'s first mate, Biggs Darklighter, was a fresh Academy graduate and the childhood friend of Luke Skywalker. He was determined to defect to the Alliance, and the Bestine cell made it easy. The freighter's captain, a secret Rebel spy, *allowed* his vessel to be hijacked and put up only token resistance. Biggs flew through a cloud of patrolling TIEs and leapt to the safety of hyperspace.

Tragically, both Biggs and Porkins were killed while challenging the first Death Star, and Zev was downed by walker fire in the Battle of Hoth. Though none of them lived to see it, their determined comrades in arms eventually freed Bestine from its Imperial oppressors.

BILBRINGI

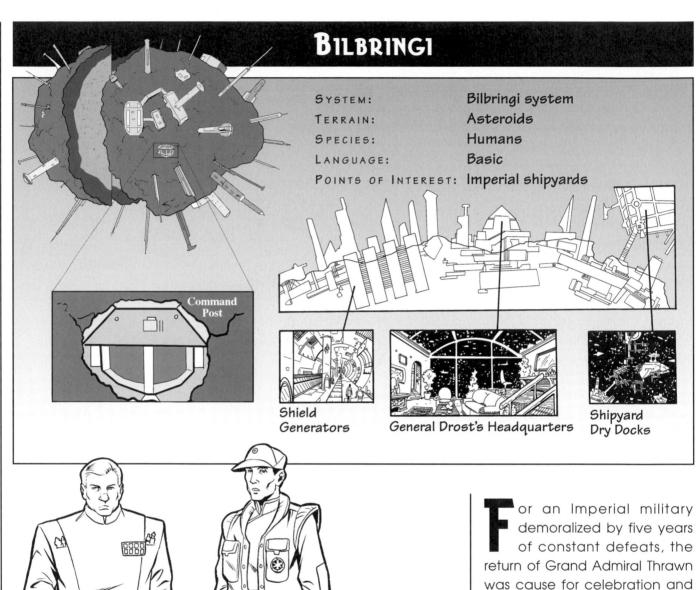

SYSTEM: **Bilbringi system**
TERRAIN: **Asteroids**
SPECIES: **Humans**
LANGUAGE: **Basic**
POINTS OF INTEREST: **Imperial shipyards**

Command Post

Shield Generators

General Drost's Headquarters

Shipyard Dry Docks

General Drost (left) protected the Bilbringi shipyards and oversaw the dry-dock workers (right).

For an Imperial military demoralized by five years of constant defeats, the return of Grand Admiral Thrawn was cause for celebration and represented a real hope that they might win back their former glory. Thrawn's death at the celebrated Battle of Bilbringi pounded one more nail into the Empire's coffin.

The Bilbringi system is choked with asteroids, planetoids, and drifting debris. Since it lies close to several military transshipment lanes and since its orbiting rocks are rich in strategic metals, the Imperial navy developed the system as a starship construction facility and a testing ground for experimental weaponry.

One of the largest chunks of ore, designated Bilbringi VII, became the headquarters for the commanding officer, General Drost. Sprouting signal relays and observation towers like a bloated insect, the airless planetoid hovered amid thousands of dry docks and half-completed warships. This unnatural tableau of slate-gray plasteel was illuminated by blue ion flashes and scarlet plasma bursts from the adjacent weapons-firing range. The Imperial shipyards of Bilbringi could not compare to the facilities at Corellia, Fondor, and Kuat, but they were the best the Empire could command during Thrawn's campaigns.

General Drost knew the importance of his commission. He defended Bilbringi with four Golan II battle platforms, each one bristling with turbolasers, tractor beams, and torpedo launchers. Arriving freighters were thoroughly scrutinized by flight control, and any deviation from the preapproved approach vectors was prevented by a bobbing string of shield barriers.

Late in his war Grand Admiral Thrawn ordered technicians to fit twenty-two of the local asteroids with cloaking devices. He then ingeniously used them to blockade the Rebels' capital world of Coruscant. Since the invisible obstacles could be detected only by a Crystal Gravfield Trap, Talon Karrde and several of his smuggling associates decided that the New Republic would pay a bundle for a working CGT, so they decided to steal one from Bilbringi.

Meanwhile, Admiral Ackbar and Wedge Antilles were also planning to attack the Bilbringi yards. For secrecy they made it appear as if Tangrene were their true target, but Thrawn saw the diversion for what it was. The brilliant Grand Admiral anticipated the New Republic but not the smugglers' coalition.

Karrde's people arrived first and assumed that the Imperial ambush was for them—after all, they'd hit Bilbringi once before. But Thrawn's Star Destroyers pounced on Ackbar instead. Overlooked, the smugglers were free to make attack runs on the Golan stations, forcing Thrawn to split his forces.

On the Imperial command ship *Chimaera*, Thrawn's personal Noghri bodyguard stabbed his master through the heart to avenge his people's betrayal on Honoghr. As the red glow dimmed from the eyes of the last Grand Admiral, Captain Pellaeon ordered a full and immediate retreat.

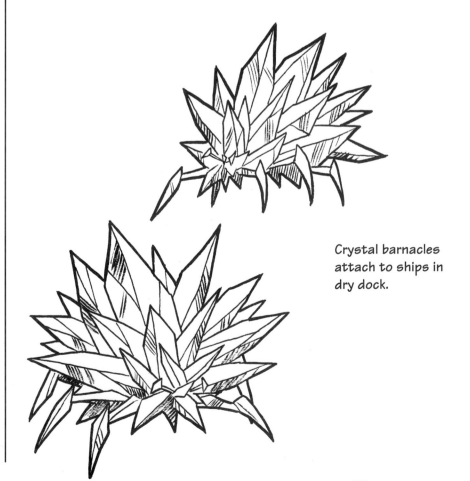

Crystal barnacles attach to ships in dry dock.

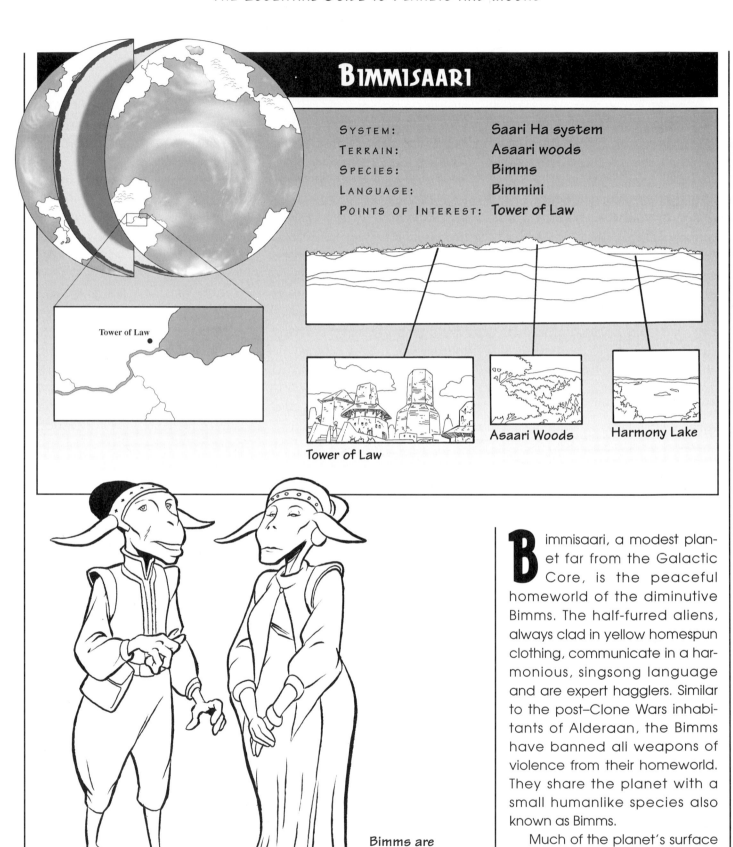

BIMMISAARI

SYSTEM: **Saari Ha system**
TERRAIN: **Asaari woods**
SPECIES: **Bimms**
LANGUAGE: **Bimmini**
POINTS OF INTEREST: **Tower of Law**

Tower of Law

Tower of Law

Asaari Woods

Harmony Lake

Bimms are excellent hagglers.

Bimmisaari, a modest planet far from the Galactic Core, is the peaceful homeworld of the diminutive Bimms. The half-furred aliens, always clad in yellow homespun clothing, communicate in a harmonious, singsong language and are expert hagglers. Similar to the post–Clone Wars inhabitants of Alderaan, the Bimms have banned all weapons of violence from their homeworld. They share the planet with a small humanlike species also known as Bimms.

Much of the planet's surface is covered with thick forests of asaari trees, which move their leafy fronds in response to stimuli. Flocks of brightly colored tiga loreng nest in the mobile branches like dartfish among sea anemones. The sight of gently waving asaari groves on the calmest days has delighted many star travelers.

Five years after the Battle of Endor, during the earliest days of the war against Grand Admiral Thrawn, Leia Organa Solo arranged a diplomatic mission to Bimmisaari in hopes of bringing the planet into the New Republic. The hero-oriented Bimms requested that Luke Skywalker come along as well, and the group landed at Bimmisaari's capital city in Han Solo's *Millennium Falcon*.

When she was greeted at the landing pad, Leia was informed that the Bimm negotiator had fallen ill and there would be a slight delay. To pass the time, Luke investigated the Tower of Law while Leia, Han, and C-3PO were taken on a tour of the adjacent marketplace.

Leia realized their danger when their hosts abruptly vanished and were replaced by a squad of eleven steely-eyed Noghri assassins. Their Stokhli spray sticks indicated that they wanted to capture their targets alive but immobilized. As the menacing aliens moved forward, Leia called to her brother through the Force.

Luke, in the tower's top level, heard the call and sprinted for the stairs but was intercepted by seven more Noghri. Unwilling to spill blood needlessly, Luke tried to pin his attackers beneath a heavy, Force-flung tapestry, but the Noghri were astonishingly quick. Realizing he had no choice, Luke threw his lightsaber, mentally guiding it through a long arc, and cut down all seven attackers.

Meanwhile, Han created a welcome distraction by having Leia scoop up a handful of jewelry from a nearby storefront. The enraged Bimm merchants piled on the shoplifter, allowing Han to signal Chewbacca back on the *Falcon*. The Wookiee roared to the rescue, clearing the area with the *Falcon*'s quad cannons. Luke joined the action, swinging down from the tower on a rope of hardened Stokhli spray, and the group escaped to safety aboard the hovering ship.

An obstinate Leia demanded to be set back on the surface immediately to continue their diplomatic mission. But Han's stubborn streak ran just as deep, and he refused to risk the lives of his wife and their unborn twin children. "We made the jump to lightspeed about two minutes ago," he announced to an incensed Leia. "Next stop, Coruscant."

The Bimmisaari tiga loreng thrives on this world where hunting is banned.

BONADAN

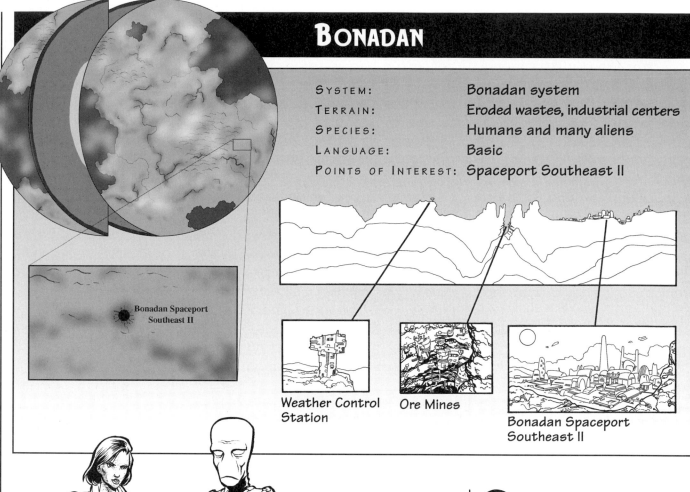

SYSTEM:	Bonadan system
TERRAIN:	Eroded wastes, industrial centers
SPECIES:	Humans and many aliens
LANGUAGE:	Basic
POINTS OF INTEREST:	Spaceport Southeast II

Bonadan Spaceport Southeast II

Weather Control Station

Ore Mines

Bonadan Spaceport Southeast II

Fiolla (left), an agent in the CSA, with a Duros pilot (right).

Bonadan is one of the busiest ports in the thriving free-enterprise fief known as the Corporate Sector. At all hours of the local day or night, thousands of ore barges, freight haulers, passenger liners, military cruisers, and commercial starships are either landing at or taking off from one of Bonadan's ten colossal spaceports.

The Corporate Sector Authority has a well-deserved reputation for ruthlessness in its pursuit of the almighty credit, and Bonadan is a prime example of the excesses of unchecked greed. Where it is not covered by factories or scrap yards, the planet's surface is a bleak, cracked wasteland. Rare species such as the Bonadanian tortapo are on the verge of extinction because of massive strip mining and industrial dumping, but no checks have been implemented. When Bonadan's resources are completely played out, the Authority will pack up and move operations to the next exploitable world.

With a booming population of miners, laborers, freighter bums, and visiting execs, the local Security Police have taken a major preventive step to curb violence: with the exception of law enforcement "specials," no weapons are permitted on Bonadan. Specialized detectors are visible on every street corner to enforce the decree. Assassins must be particularly inventive to circumvent the devices. The lethally modified protocol droid C-3PX eliminated a target on Bonadan by using hidden internal blasters. R2-D2 and C-3PO later witnessed the noble end of C-3PX on Hosk Station.

Years before they helped destroy the Empire's mighty Death Star at Yavin, Han Solo and Chewbacca were tricked into making a slaving run to the planet Lur. Though they were able to defeat the slavers and free the captives, Han stubbornly insisted that he was still owed his ten-thousand-credit fee. The pair flew to Bonadan to meet the slavers' contact.

Instead of meeting that per-

The Bonadanian tortapo is one of the last surviving species on this industrial planet.

son, they ran into Fiolla, a high-ranking agent of the Corporate Sector Authority. When Fiolla headed off into the Bonadan countryside to intercept members of the slaving ring, Han followed on a rented repulsor scooter. The meeting suddenly turned deadly when one of the slavers jumped Han with a vibroknife. After dispatching the attacker, Han and Fiolla fled aboard his abandoned swoop as four more swoops screamed in pursuit.

The swoop riders neared and death seemed imminent, but Han seized on the opportunity to prove his frequent boast: "Inspiration's my *specialty*." Veering into the structural girders of a massive weather-control station, he jinked and weaved until the vehicle emerged in the station's vast aiming cylinder. Their pursuers slowly followed, a bit confused by the Corellian's erratic flight, and Han and Fiolla roared past them at full throttle. Their protesting swoop

shot out of the tube's end. As it cleared the durasteel gridwork by millimeters, the swoop's fairing was torn loose in the suicidal squeeze. A luckless pursuer, hoping to copy Solo's reckless move, ended his unsavory career in a bright fireball.

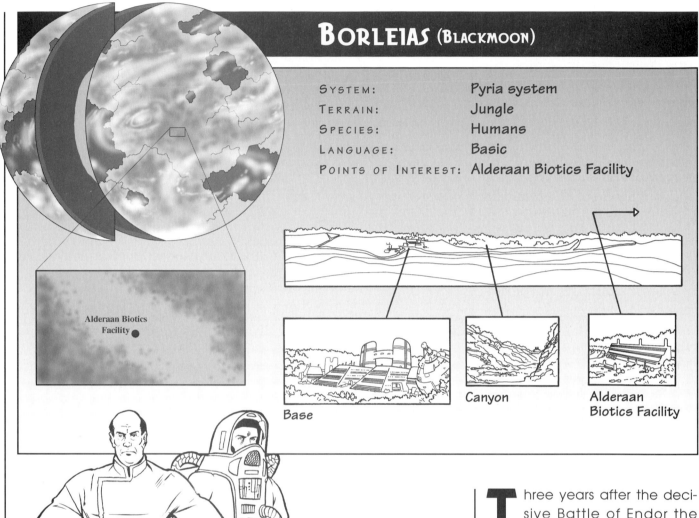

BORLEIAS (BLACKMOON)

SYSTEM: Pyria system
TERRAIN: Jungle
SPECIES: Humans
LANGUAGE: Basic
POINTS OF INTEREST: Alderaan Biotics Facility

Alderaan Biotics Facility

Base

Canyon

Alderaan Biotics Facility

General Evir Derricote and a Borleian scientist.

Three years after the decisive Battle of Endor the Rebel Alliance seemed poised to become the galaxy's rightful government. Buoyed by a string of victories, the daring pilots of Rogue Squadron—the Alliance's elite fighter team—prepared to conquer the Imperial capital world of Coruscant.

To do that, they first needed to capture a fortified planet close to the Galactic Core. Borleias, code-named Blackmoon, would serve as a stepping-stone to Imperial Center and to ultimate victory over Palpatine's self-appointed heirs.

Borleias is a lush tropical

world covered with steamy jungles where venomous imoodas drop from the treetops on unwary prey. Only two facilities were ever built on its overgrown surface: an Imperial military base and a biotics facility specializing in exotic flora from the destroyed planet of Alderaan. Both were under the command of General Evir Derricote, a cruel genius who was too canny to leave his world vulnerable to Rebel predation.

Derricote secretly siphoned funds from the Imperial treasury, adding additional TIE interceptors, ion cannons, and shield generators to bolster Borleias's meager defenses. Unaware of Derricote's private armory, Rogue Squadron attacked Borleias with misguided tactics and inadequate firepower. Rogue pilots were slaughtered.

Limping back to headquarters with nearly half his squadron mates incapacitated or killed, Wedge Antilles formulated a new attack plan. No base could fall while its shields were intact, and Derricote was reinforcing his with power from the biotics facility. If an X-wing fighter could sever the pipeline with a volley of well-aimed torpedoes, the shields would collapse and Blackmoon would be theirs.

When Wedge asked for volunteers, every member of Rogue Squadron wanted to fly this "suicide mission." The chosen pilots tried to sneak into Borleias's atmosphere by mimicking falling meteors, but a patrol

The Borleian imooda inhabits the jungle regions.

of TIE interceptors cut them off. Smashing through the defense line, the Rogues angled straight for the power conduit.

In a harrowing flight reminiscent of the Death Star trench run, Wedge sliced through a narrow rift valley and then lit up a juggernaught assault vehicle with his quad lasers and perforated the ferrocrete conduit with a pair of torps. The shields fell and Derricote's base soon followed.

The Rebels took immediate advantage of the strategic foothold Blackmoon's capture had given them. Within months, thanks once again to the efforts of Rogue Squadron, Coruscant was in the hands of the Rebel Alliance. Their victory, however, was tainted by the Krytos virus the retreating Imperials had left behind.

At the Alderaan Biotics Facility on Borleias, Alliance scientists worked around the clock to synthesize a cure. Mixing Rylothean ryll spice with Thyferran bacta, researchers created a Krytos vaccine called rylca. Massive quantities of the remedy were shipped out from Borleias to end the Empire's plague.

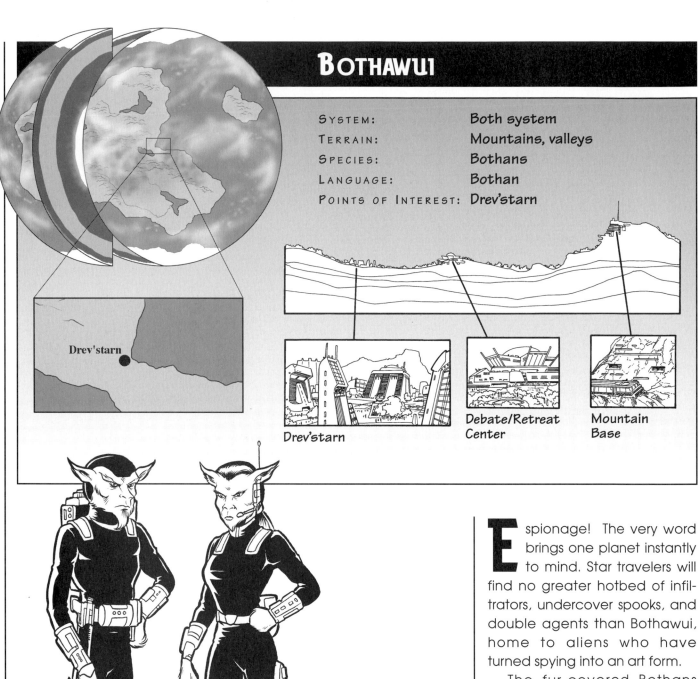

BOTHAWUI

SYSTEM:	Both system
TERRAIN:	Mountains, valleys
SPECIES:	Bothans
LANGUAGE:	Bothan
POINTS OF INTEREST:	Drev'starn

Drev'starn

Drev'starn

Debate/Retreat Center

Mountain Base

The galaxywide reputation of Bothan spies is undisputed.

Espionage! The very word brings one planet instantly to mind. Star travelers will find no greater hotbed of infiltrators, undercover spooks, and double agents than Bothawui, home to aliens who have turned spying into an art form.

The fur-covered Bothans developed their natural talents through a peculiar form of cultural evolution. Predators such as the krak'jya are numerous on Bothawui, but draft animals never emerged. Advancing armies, forced to haul their own equipment, provisions, and heavy armaments, quickly grew disgusted at this inefficient method of combat. Eventually, the Bothans learned to defeat an enemy from *within*.

Over the centuries the aliens became masters at gathering intelligence and exploiting it for political gain. Bothan statesmen rarely fall to assassins' blades, but they often step down when their allies suddenly desert them or when an ugly scandal is deliberately brought to light. This ruthless pursuit of power and influence, known as the "Bothan Way," causes many non-Bothans to view the species as untrustworthy opportunists waiting to pounce on the slightest misstep.

It is precisely this environment of mutual suspicion that has made the Bothan Spynet the finest in the galaxy. In the mountain-ringed valley city of Drev'starn intelligence agents from the Empire, the Rebel

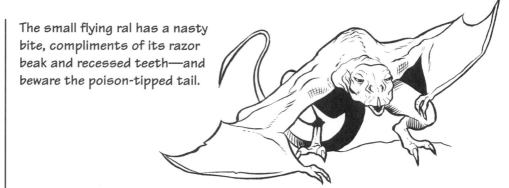

The small flying ral has a nasty bite, compliments of its razor beak and recessed teeth—and beware the poison-tipped tail.

Alliance, Black Sun, Hutt Space, and countless other confederacies mingle freely among the sparkling glitterstone buildings. Bothawui is a clean, cosmopolitan trading hub and is the closest thing to "neutral space" allowed within the Empire's borders.

Just before the Battle of Endor the Bothan Spynet uncovered evidence that the freighter *Suprosa*, carrying a top-secret Imperial information core, was scheduled to arrive at the Both system within days. Luke

Skywalker and his new acquaintance, Dash Rendar, journeyed to Bothawui to help capture the vessel and its vital cargo of intelligence data.

At a secluded mountain base Luke prepared twelve Bothan Y-wing pilots for their upcoming mission. When the squadron intercepted the *Suprosa* and demanded its surrender, the "helpless" freighter revealed a bristling array of turbolasers and missile launchers. Half the Bothans were killed by a diamond-boron torpedo before Luke could disable the ship with his X-wing's cannons.

Further deaths followed as the computer core made its way to the nearby planet Kothlis and into the hands of the Rebel Alliance's leadership. The payoff, however, seemed worth it—the decoded data revealed the location of the unfinished second Death Star. "The time for our attack has come," Mon Mothma proudly announced to a spirited Alliance war room, but she took care to remember the tragic cost. "Many Bothans," she explained in a hushed voice, "*died* to bring us this information."

Krak'jya are named after their loud bellowing growl.

BYSS

SYSTEM:	Beshqek system
TERRAIN:	Plateaus, lakes
SPECIES:	Humans
LANGUAGE:	Basic
POINTS OF INTEREST:	Imperial Citadel, Imperial Freight Complex

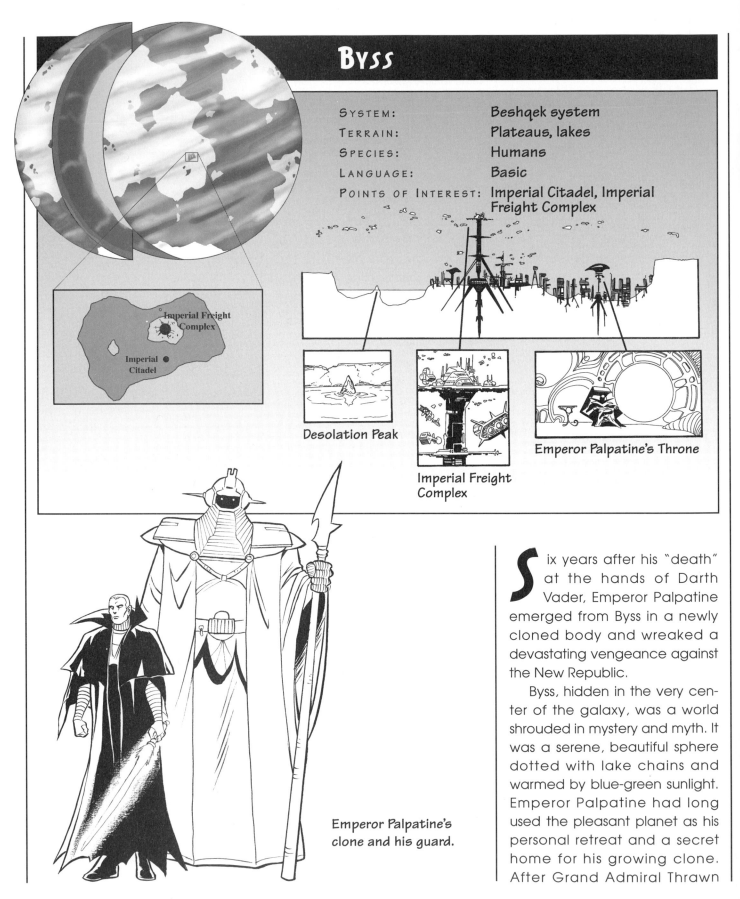

Imperial Freight Complex

Imperial Citadel

Desolation Peak

Imperial Freight Complex

Emperor Palpatine's Throne

Emperor Palpatine's clone and his guard.

Six years after his "death" at the hands of Darth Vader, Emperor Palpatine emerged from Byss in a newly cloned body and wreaked a devastating vengeance against the New Republic.

Byss, hidden in the very center of the galaxy, was a world shrouded in mystery and myth. It was a serene, beautiful sphere dotted with lake chains and warmed by blue-green sunlight. Emperor Palpatine had long used the pleasant planet as his personal retreat and a secret home for his growing clone. After Grand Admiral Thrawn succeeded in weakening the New Republic, the reborn Emperor made his move—his loyal armies forced the upstart government to evacuate Coruscant. Flush with victory, Palpatine sent his World Devastators to ravage Mon Calamari and captured his old nemesis, Luke Skywalker.

Brought before the Emperor on Byss, Luke decided on a risky strategy—he would become Palpatine's servant and conquer the dark side from within. Leia sensed her brother's danger and convinced Han Solo to mount a rescue operation.

After hitching passage with Han's smuggling friends, the *Falcon* landed in the Emperor's Citadel. As Leia had intended, they were brought before Luke—but he had changed. Distant and cold, he watched as his friends were imprisoned.

But Luke had not gone as far into the dark side as it appeared. He loaded a control code that would stop the World Devastators into the memory banks of R2-D2 and urged Leia to escape back to the New Republic with the information. The group fled aboard the *Falcon*.

Left behind on Byss, Luke lost to the Emperor in a lightsaber duel. Palpatine took his beaten foe and boarded his flagship for a showdown with the New Republic at Da Soocha V.

The Emperor was defeated at the Pinnacle Moon, but the war was far from over. Taking a new clone body, Palpatine struck with a new planet-destroying weapon in orbit around Byss—the deadly Galaxy Gun.

The New Republic came up with a bold plan. Rebel commandos hijacked a shipment of new X-1 Viper battle droids on its way to Byss and rode the freighter to its destination. Once they arrived, Lando Calrissian and the other soldiers wheeled out the armored droids in a do-or-die attempt to capture the Imperial Citadel.

The Citadel's turbolasers couldn't scratch the sturdy Vipers' molecular shielding, but the high-tech hulls were no match for the teeth of Palpatine's monstrous "chrysalis beasts." Lando and the rest were saved from certain death by a group of courageous smugglers.

Soon afterward, in a battle near Onderon, the Rebels boarded the Emperor's new flagship, *Eclipse II*. R2-D2 sent the ship through hyperspace on a ramming course with the Galaxy Gun at Byss. As the two weapons collided, the Galaxy Gun mistakenly fired one of its missiles straight at Byss's core.

The projectile set off an unstoppable nucleonic chain reaction. Within moments the Emperor's throne world was nothing but a cloud of rubble, and the New Republic had won another hard-fought victory.

The Emperor keeps pet chrysalides which attack on his command.

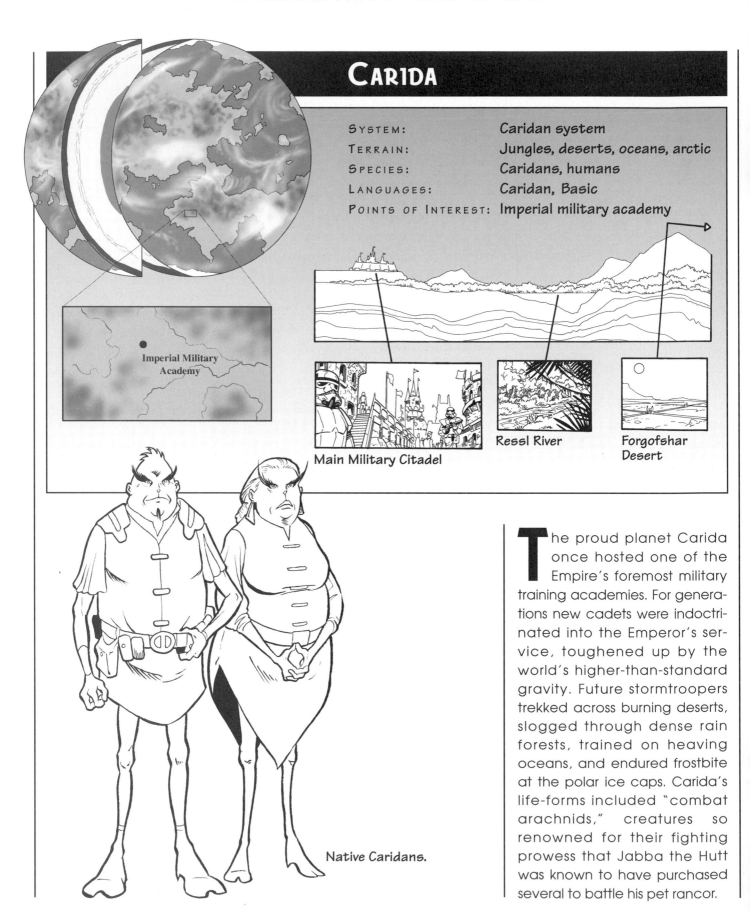

CARIDA

SYSTEM:	Caridan system
TERRAIN:	Jungles, deserts, oceans, arctic
SPECIES:	Caridans, humans
LANGUAGES:	Caridan, Basic
POINTS OF INTEREST:	Imperial military academy

Imperial Military Academy

Main Military Citadel

Ressl River

Forgofshar Desert

Native Caridans.

The proud planet Carida once hosted one of the Empire's foremost military training academies. For generations new cadets were indoctrinated into the Emperor's service, toughened up by the world's higher-than-standard gravity. Future stormtroopers trekked across burning deserts, slogged through dense rain forests, trained on heaving oceans, and endured frostbite at the polar ice caps. Carida's life-forms included "combat arachnids," creatures so renowned for their fighting prowess that Jabba the Hutt was known to have purchased several to battle his pet rancor.

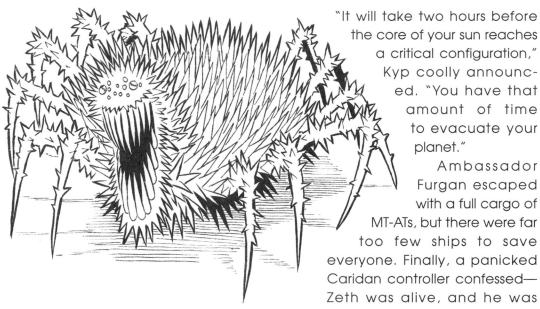

The combat arachnid enjoys a good battle.

Admiral Daala was trained at the academy on Carida, despite the Emperor's well-known prejudices against women. Daala excelled in the hostile environment, developing ingenious battle strategies under a false computer persona. When Grand Moff Tarkin arrived to meet this brilliant tactician he promoted Daala to the rank of admiral, placing her in charge of the top-secret Maw Installation near Kessel.

As the Empire continued to fragment after the disastrous Battle of Endor, Carida remained one of the stubborn strongholds of Imperial might. Development continued on the MT-AT "spider walker," but the planet's lack of capital ships left it somewhat isolated.

Seven years after Endor, Carida's Ambassador Furgan made a diplomatic mission to Coruscant. Furgan reaffirmed his planet's Imperial loyalties and even tried to poison Mon Mothma, the New Republic's chief of state.

Soon afterward the renegade Jedi trainee Kyp Durron stole the Sun Crusher superweapon and flew to the Caridan system. Years before, Kyp's brother Zeth had been forcibly inducted into the stormtrooper program. The young man delivered an ultimatum: If the Caridans did not provide immediate information on Zeth's fate, he would fire a resonance torpedo into their sun.

Stalling for time, Caridan officials uploaded a falsified file stating that Zeth had frozen to death on routine maneuvers. Meanwhile, sixty TIE fighters launched and, lasers blazing, swarmed around Kyp's quantum-armored vessel.

Furious at their effrontery, Kyp fired a torpedo. The pulsating weapon buried itself deep into the heart of the yellow star.

"It will take two hours before the core of your sun reaches a critical configuration," Kyp coolly announced. "You have that amount of time to evacuate your planet."

Ambassador Furgan escaped with a full cargo of MT-ATs, but there were far too few ships to save everyone. Finally, a panicked Caridan controller confessed—Zeth was alive, and he was stranded on the doomed planet. Knowing he could not reverse the chain reaction he'd started, Kyp raced to the main military citadel to rescue his long-lost brother.

He was too late. Carida's sun exploded in a furious rush of blinding energy. The first shock wave annihilated every living thing on the surface; the second cracked the planet open like an avril's egg. Kyp, safe in the invulnerable Sun Crusher, fled the system in anguish with the blood of millions on his hands.

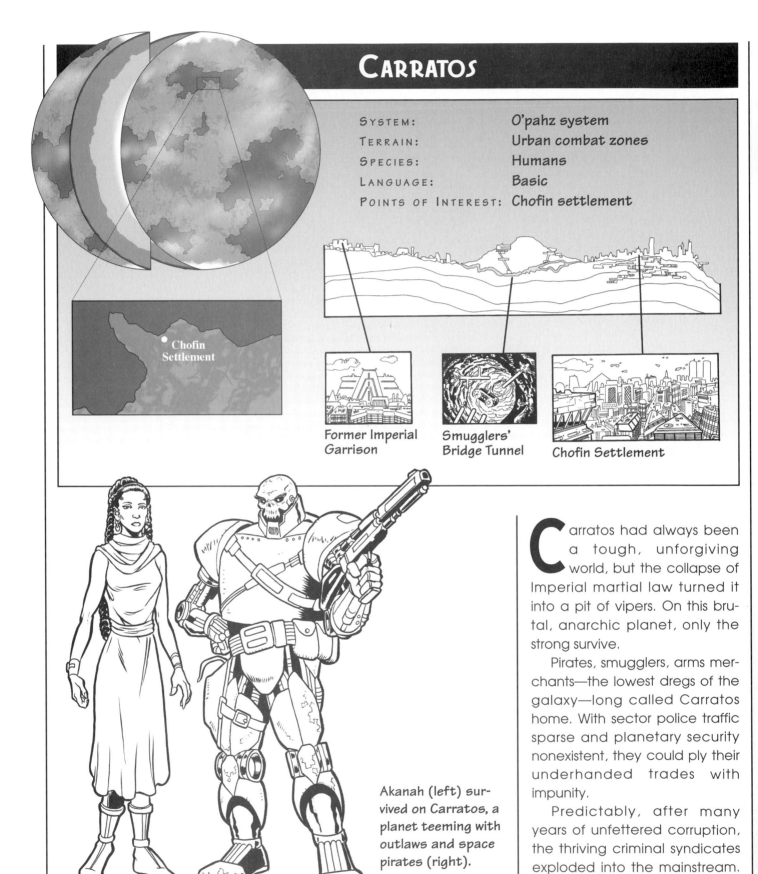

CARRATOS

SYSTEM:	O'pahz system
TERRAIN:	Urban combat zones
SPECIES:	Humans
LANGUAGE:	Basic
POINTS OF INTEREST:	Chofin settlement

Chofin Settlement

Former Imperial Garrison

Smugglers' Bridge Tunnel

Chofin Settlement

Akanah (left) survived on Carratos, a planet teeming with outlaws and space pirates (right).

Carratos had always been a tough, unforgiving world, but the collapse of Imperial martial law turned it into a pit of vipers. On this brutal, anarchic planet, only the strong survive.

Pirates, smugglers, arms merchants—the lowest dregs of the galaxy—long called Carratos home. With sector police traffic sparse and planetary security nonexistent, they could ply their underhanded trades with impunity.

Predictably, after many years of unfettered corruption, the thriving criminal syndicates exploded into the mainstream. Wealthy citizens fled the ensuing mayhem by escaping offworld or chose to seal themselves behind locked and barricaded manor gates. The less fortunate struggled to survive among an army of thugs, cutpurses, killers, and feral shooks.

The Empire briefly clamped down on Carratos, and its "shoot on sight" edict helped quell some of the more noisome troublemakers. But then came Endor, and the Imperial troops suddenly had more important battles to fight. The Liberty Movement, a ragged military junta, overran the abandoned stormtrooper garrison and burned nearly all the governmental records. Everyone with a criminal past was given a clean slate, and the planet once again descended into chaos.

An innocent girl, Akanah Norand, was dumped into this hostile environment at the age of twelve. Her mother, Talsava, had been a member of the Fallanassi religious order on Lucazec but had been forced into exile after betraying her fellow adepts to the Empire. Lazy and irresponsible, Talsava mistreated her daughter and spurned a Fallanassi woman named Nashira who once visited Carratos to welcome Akanah back into the circle.

Just three years after their ill-fated arrival in the Chofin settlement, Talsava vanished, taking her daughter's savings with her. Left alone in a sea of predators, Akanah quickly learned how to survive.

Voracious shooks hover over unwary prey.

Using her street smarts and her Fallanassi skill at manipulating reality through the White Current, the young girl persevered despite overwhelming odds. After several years she married Andras Pell, a kindhearted man thirty-six years her senior, and inherited his ancient Verpine Adventurer starship upon his death.

Finally free to leave Carratos, Akanah was eager to rejoin her Fallanassi sisters. But she was also intrigued by the Jedi Master Luke Skywalker. To test his motivations—and secure his help—she told Luke that Nashira, the mysterious woman who had visited her on Carratos years earlier, was his long-lost mother.

Akanah had no real evidence to support her dubious claim, but Luke was so starved for information that he was willing to grab at the smallest crumb. Despite some misgivings, the Jedi joined this beautiful new arrival in her quest. The two companions set off in the newly christened *Mud Sloth*, and Akanah left Carratos behind for good.

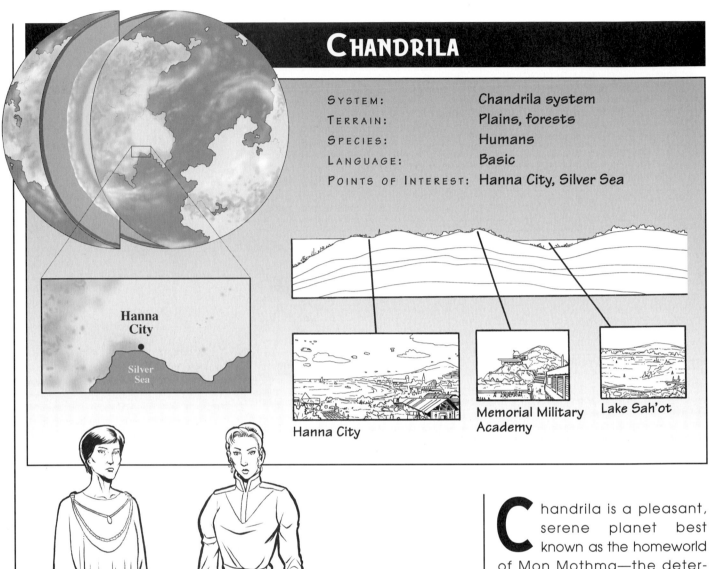

CHANDRILA

SYSTEM:	Chandrila system
TERRAIN:	Plains, forests
SPECIES:	Humans
LANGUAGE:	Basic
POINTS OF INTEREST:	Hanna City, Silver Sea

Hanna City

Silver Sea

Hanna City

Memorial Military Academy

Lake Sah'ot

After Mon Mothma (left) went underground, Canna Omonda (right) filled her Senate position.

Chandrila is a pleasant, serene planet best known as the homeworld of Mon Mothma—the determined Senator who forged the Rebel Alliance, tempered it with idealism and iron will, and used it to pierce the black heart of Palpatine's corrupt Empire.

For a Core World, Chandrila is sparsely populated and surprisingly rural. Cities, small and scattered, are separated by terraced gardens and kilometers of gentle rolling plains. Livestock herds and hopping squalls are allowed to roam freely, sometimes tying up traffic on the sparse thoroughfares. Residents and tourists are

Docile, free-roaming squalls often cause traffic jams.

entranced by the Hanna Wild Game Reserve, the Gladean State Parks, and the crystal waters of Lake Sah'ot. The planet's unspoiled beauty in fact has often been compared to that of Alderaan. Fresh air must be a catalyst for independent thought, for the Emperor experienced nearly as much opposition from Chandrila as from Princess Leia's rebellious homeworld.

The native inhabitants have always felt they could discuss—and more often *debate*—their political opinions without fear of official reprisal. It was in this tolerant environment that Mon Mothma grew up in a sparkling port city on the shores of the Silver Sea.

Both of her parents were respected politicians in their own right, and Mon Mothma soon became one of the youngest persons ever elected to the Republic Senate. When Palpatine declared himself Emperor, she worked with her old friend Bail Organa to curb the tyrant's excesses. Branded a traitor to the New Order, Mon Mothma went underground, never flagging in her belief that justice eventually would prevail.

Chandrila suddenly found itself without representation in the senate. The people elected Canna Omonda to fill Mon Mothma's vacancy, and Omonda's firebrand rhetoric quickly attracted the ire of Imperial loyalists. Already enraged by Mon Mothma's growing insurgent movement, Palpatine would tolerate no further humiliation from Chandrila.

Three Imperial Star Destroyers dropped into orbit and seized the troublesome senator. Omonda was tortured into a false confession of "crimes" against the Empire and was scheduled for public execution on Coruscant during the Emperor's festive new year celebrations. In another move clearly designed to hurt Chandrila, stiff agricultural tariffs were slapped on the Bormea sector. The planet's inhabitants were indignant, but many considered themselves lucky to have escaped the fate of Ralltiir—or Alderaan.

Six months after the Battle of Endor, with Grand Vizier Sate Pestage at the Empire's helm, seven Star Destroyers mysteriously appeared in Chandrilan space and enforced a strict blockade—*nothing* was permitted in or out. Pestage, alarmed at the recent string of Imperial defeats, had apparently decided to hold Chandrila hostage in case the Rebels threatened Coruscant. Fortunately, the Vizier's plot crumbled when Ysanne Isard forced him from office.

A mere handful of years later the New Republic's navy liberated nearly all the Core Worlds. Mon Mothma, proud beyond words, returned to her homeworld to see her people finally freed from beneath the Empire's boot heel.

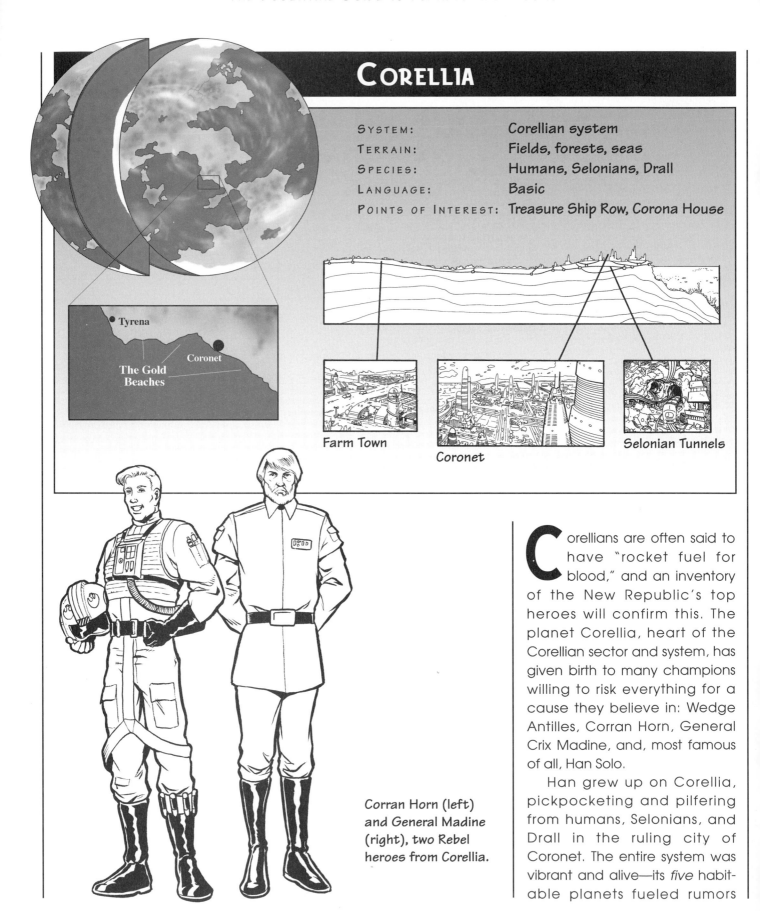

CORELLIA

SYSTEM: Corellian system
TERRAIN: Fields, forests, seas
SPECIES: Humans, Selonians, Drall
LANGUAGE: Basic
POINTS OF INTEREST: Treasure Ship Row, Corona House

Tyrena

Coronet

The Gold Beaches

Farm Town

Coronet

Selonian Tunnels

Corran Horn (left) and General Madine (right), two Rebel heroes from Corellia.

Corellians are often said to have "rocket fuel for blood," and an inventory of the New Republic's top heroes will confirm this. The planet Corellia, heart of the Corellian sector and system, has given birth to many champions willing to risk everything for a cause they believe in: Wedge Antilles, Corran Horn, General Crix Madine, and, most famous of all, Han Solo.

Han grew up on Corellia, pickpocketing and pilfering from humans, Selonians, and Drall in the ruling city of Coronet. The entire system was vibrant and alive—its *five* habitable planets fueled rumors that it was an artificial alien construct, but this was a topic reserved for scholars. Burgeoning commercial trade, smuggling, and the colossal stardocks operated by the Corellian Engineering Corporation brought a great deal of space traffic to Corellia, and most visitors would stop in at Treasure Ship Row, the lively, garish open-air bazaar of Coronet.

Like many Corellians, young Han yearned for the stars and eventually enrolled in the Imperial Academy. A promising career in the Corellian Sector Fleet was cut short when the outspoken young officer helped free a Wookiee slave named Chewbacca. Court-martialed and disgraced, Han left the sector with Chewie to begin a new life as a smuggler.

As the war against the Rebel Alliance intensified, the Corellian system became increasingly isolated. Trade dried up, and corporations began relocating to more lucrative markets. The ruling Corellian Diktat lost more and more power to the Triad on Sacorria and eventually disappeared altogether. He was replaced by a New Republic governor-general, but it was too late. The Corellian economy had suffered irreparable damage from its closed borders.

Fourteen years after the Battle of Endor, Han Solo finally returned to his birthworld—this

time with his wife and three young children in tow. Chief of State Leia Organa Solo was there for a standard trade conference, but her entire family was trapped when the Sacorrian Triad activated a systemwide interdiction field, preventing hyperspace travel. The Triad then threatened the galaxy with a weapon capable of destroying stars. Just when things looked their bleakest, Han's cousin, Thrackan Sal-Solo, emerged as the leader of an antialien faction called the Human League and kidnapped Han's children.

Thrackan, who'd proclaimed himself the new Diktat, hoped

While the Corellian sand panther hunts during daylight hours, few have actually seen this poison-clawed beast.

to double-cross his Triad bosses and emerge as the leader of an independent Corellian sector. The key to his scheme lay in the control of an ancient technological device. Eons earlier the system's planets had been moved into their orbits by planetary repulsors and the hyperspace tractor called Centerpoint Station.

Unfortunately for the would-be dictator, Han's children had inherited their father's ingenuity. They escaped, and a Bakuran warship apprehended Thrackan. When seven-year-old Anakin used the Drall repulsor to fire an interference shot, the starbuster was rendered harmless. The Corellian crisis was over.

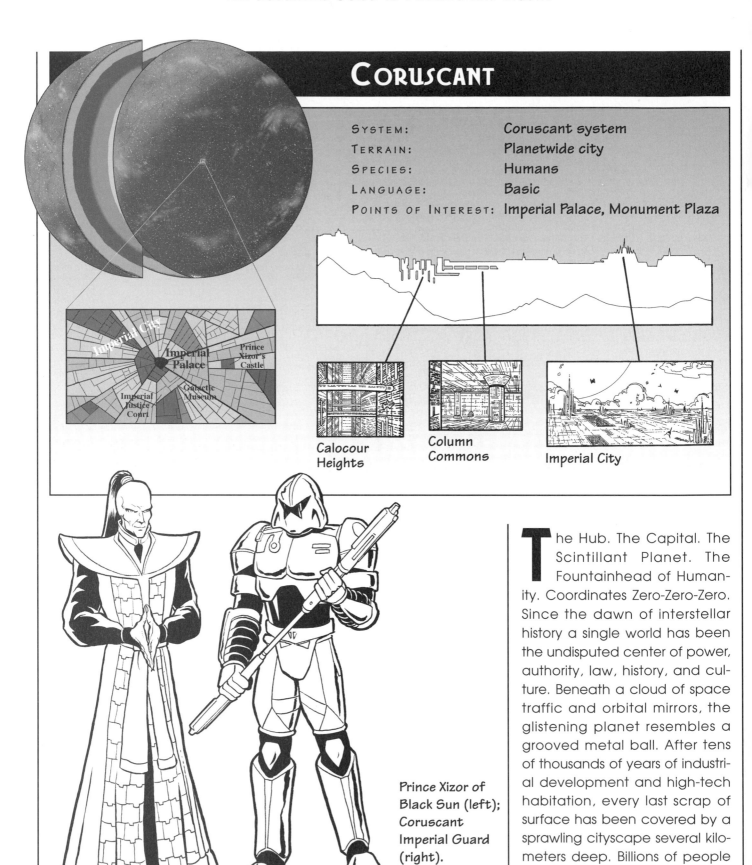

CORUSCANT

SYSTEM:	Coruscant system
TERRAIN:	Planetwide city
SPECIES:	Humans
LANGUAGE:	Basic
POINTS OF INTEREST:	Imperial Palace, Monument Plaza

Imperial City

Imperial Palace

Prince Xizor's Castle

Imperial Justice Court

Galactic Museum

Calocour Heights

Column Commons

Imperial City

Prince Xizor of Black Sun (left); Coruscant Imperial Guard (right).

The Hub. The Capital. The Scintillant Planet. The Fountainhead of Humanity. Coordinates Zero-Zero-Zero. Since the dawn of interstellar history a single world has been the undisputed center of power, authority, law, history, and culture. Beneath a cloud of space traffic and orbital mirrors, the glistening planet resembles a grooved metal ball. After tens of thousands of years of industrial development and high-tech habitation, every last scrap of surface has been covered by a sprawling cityscape several kilometers deep. Billions of people live layer upon layer in the ferrocrete labyrinth; the well-to-do

Corridor ghouls terrorize unwary citizens in the lower levels of Imperial City.

escape to top-level luxury penthouses or tethered satellites called skyhooks.

As power and wealth climbed higher into the sparkling towers and causeways, the lowest levels were abandoned to darkness and disrepair. This gloomy undercity is strewn with seedy taverns and wrecked equipment; its dismal shadows conceal granite slugs, corridor ghouls, and shambling mutated subhumans.

The essence of Coruscant is Imperial City. Built on an eons-old battlefield between the ancient Taungs and the Battalions of Zhell, the metropolis is the shining glory on a planet filled with wonders. The Galactic Museum and Monument Plaza are marvelous attractions in their own right, but the city is dominated by a single spectacular structure—the Imperial Palace.

A glittering gray-green pyra-

mid just north of the Manarai Mountains, the immense Imperial Palace houses governmental offices, Palpatine's throne room, and the breathtaking Grand Corridor with its double lines of greenish-purple ch'hala trees. Some distance away lies the artificial Western Sea and the walled-off alien district called Invisec.

Coruscant, temporarily renamed Imperial Center, was the dark heart of Palpatine's foul Empire. For years the Rebel Alliance avoided the heavily fortified capital world out of necessity. But soon after the Battle of Hoth, Princess Leia and her companions infiltrated Prince Xizor's opulent castle in Imperial City and destroyed it.

Several years after Endor the Rebel fleet captured the planet from the forces of Ysanne Isard, only to find the long-awaited victory spoiled by an outbreak of the virulent Krytos plague. The Alliance successfully held Coruscant for three years, until

Hawk-bat eggs are a delicacy to be treasured.

the cloned Emperor Palpatine (taking advantage of Grand Admiral Thrawn's recent gains) forced them to evacuate to Da Soocha V. The Emperor was driven out within a year, but the battle damage to Imperial City was extensive.

Since then, the rebuilt Coruscant has been a living symbol of the New Republic's perseverance and determination. Whatever damage it has seen and whatever changes it has gone through, Coruscant and its new government will undoubtedly endure for years to come.

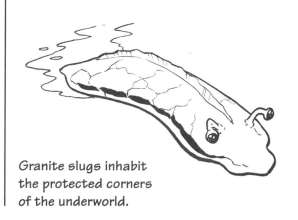

Granite slugs inhabit the protected corners of the underworld.

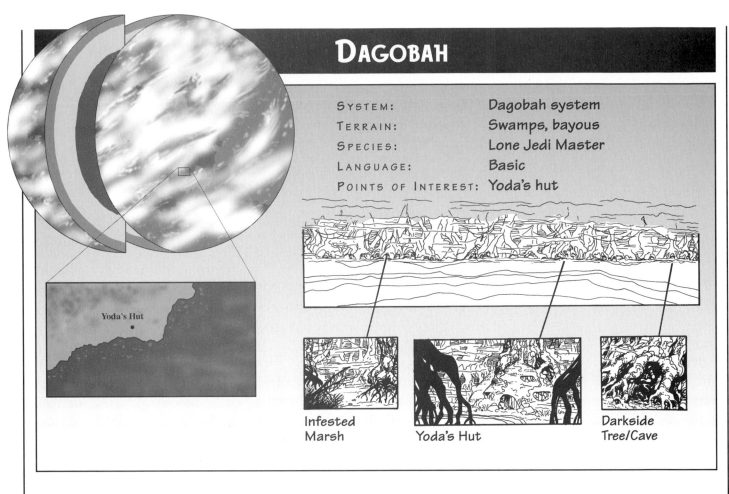

DAGOBAH

SYSTEM:	Dagobah system
TERRAIN:	Swamps, bayous
SPECIES:	Lone Jedi Master
LANGUAGE:	Basic
POINTS OF INTEREST:	Yoda's hut

Yoda's Hut

Infested Marsh

Yoda's Hut

Darkside Tree/Cave

The knobby white spider eventually grows into a gnarltree.

Caught in the driving snow of a Hoth blizzard, Luke Skywalker saw a vision of Obi-Wan Kenobi. "Luke," the apparition intoned, "you must go to the Dagobah system. There you will learn from Yoda, the Jedi Master who instructed me."

Dagobah, in the Sluis sector, is a world of murky swamps, steaming bayous, and petrified gnarltree forests. Gnarltrees have a fascinating life cycle—the ubiquitous white spiders that roam the swamp are actually newly sprouted seedlings that will take root and grow into new, adult gnarltrees.

Their dense branches and

roots house butcherbug colonies, nightbat nests, and roaming packs of lazy spotlight sloths. Some of the more lethal creatures living beneath the canopy include swamp slugs, dragonsnakes, and carnivorous fungi.

This obscure, sodden bog planet eventually became the home of Yoda. The diminutive Jedi Master inhabited a primitive mud-walled hut, demanding little from his surroundings. Yoda spent his days taking long walks through the tangled marsh undergrowth, gathering edible plants to make rootleaf stew, and meditating on the Force created by the millions of growing, breathing life-forms all around him.

After the Rebel Alliance's crushing defeat at the Battle of Hoth, Luke Skywalker, following Obi-Wan's mysterious

instructions, told R2-D2 to plot a course for Dagobah.

As Luke prepared to land on the cloud-covered globe, something inexplicable fouled his X-wing's sensors. With a sickening jolt the blinded starfighter nose-dived into a watery peat bog. Frustrated and angry at his absurd situation, Luke was ill prepared to deal with a meddlesome, exasperating green gnome who began poking through his supplies. Yoda was testing his tolerance and discernment, and Luke utterly flunked.

Luke's stubborn impatience would be his greatest challenge throughout Yoda's intense training. During one trial Luke faced a nightmare vision of himself—beneath Darth Vader's black mask—in the bowels of a dark-side cave. During another trial, Yoda taught him not to overestimate appearances by raising his X-wing from the muck with seemingly little effort.

Dragonsnakes are known to battle giant swamp slugs.

Though he still had much to learn, Luke abandoned his training to rescue his friends on Bespin's Cloud City. After a nearly fatal confrontation with Vader, Luke returned to Dagobah, only to watch his master die. After nine hundred years Yoda became one with the Force.

Luke would return to the swamp planet several more times: once during the bitter war against Grand Admiral Thrawn and again three years later in the hope he could restore his love Callista's lost connection to the Force. Though Yoda's mud hut has been obliterated by years of rainstorms and spreading swampland, Dagobah remains a world of flourishing life and a potent center of the Force.

The giant swamp slug hides in Dagobah's numerous bogs.

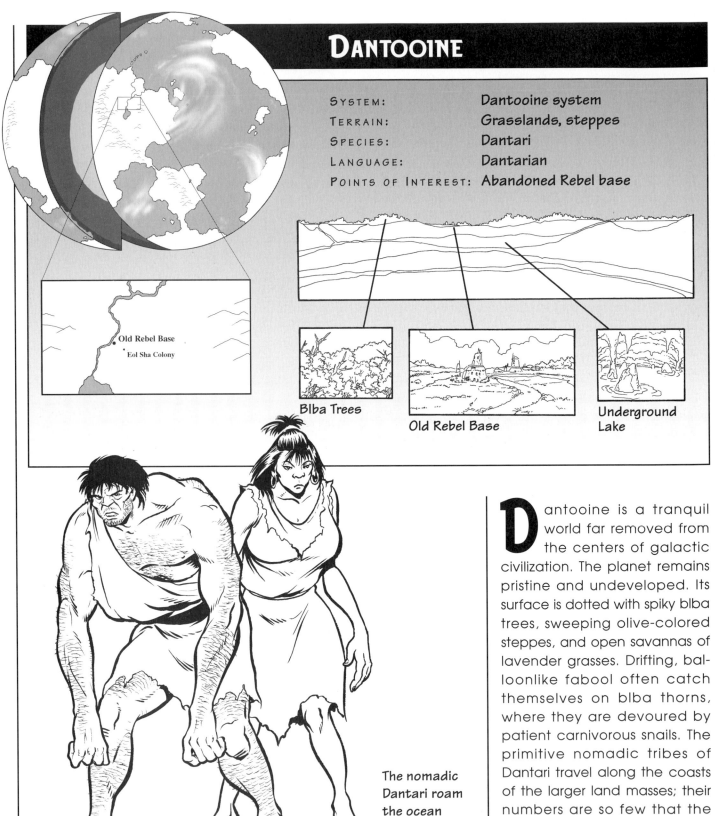

DANTOOINE

SYSTEM:	Dantooine system
TERRAIN:	Grasslands, steppes
SPECIES:	Dantari
LANGUAGE:	Dantarian
POINTS OF INTEREST:	Abandoned Rebel base

Old Rebel Base
Eol Sha Colony

Blba Trees

Old Rebel Base

Underground Lake

The nomadic Dantari roam the ocean coasts.

Dantooine is a tranquil world far removed from the centers of galactic civilization. The planet remains pristine and undeveloped. Its surface is dotted with spiky blba trees, sweeping olive-colored steppes, and open savannas of lavender grasses. Drifting, balloonlike fabool often catch themselves on blba thorns, where they are devoured by patient carnivorous snails. The primitive nomadic tribes of Dantari travel along the coasts of the larger land masses; their numbers are so few that the planet is essentially uninhabited.

Nearly four millennia ago the great Jedi Master Vodo-Siosk

Balloonlike fabool are often punctured by the thorny blba tree...

...and eaten by carnivorous snails.

Baas established a training center among the peaceful ruins of Dantooine. His students included the Cathar warriors Crado and Sylvar, but his most adept pupil was the arrogant human Exar Kun. In a spirited lightsaber training duel with the young Jedi, Vodo was cruelly defeated when Kun split his wooden staff in two. After that confrontation, Exar Kun abandoned his master and left Dantooine forever to fulfill his dark destiny.

Thousands of years passed. The Empire arose, and so did the Rebel Alliance. The remote world of Dantooine seemed to be the perfect place for a hidden Rebel base. Alliance engineers constructed a command facility from temporary self-erecting modules that could be moved at a moment's notice.

When a Rebel soldier discovered an Imperial tracking device hidden in the latest cargo shipment, all personnel scrambled to evacuate the base in a single day. Only a few permanent structures were left behind.

Later, Princess Leia Organa was captured by Darth Vader and brought aboard the Death Star. When torture droids and mind probes could not force Leia to reveal the location of the Rebels' new base on Yavin 4, Grand Moff Tarkin threatened to destroy the Princess's home planet of Alderaan.

Hoping to spare Alderaan and still protect the Yavin 4 base, Leia resorted to a deception. "Dantooine," she lied, knowing it had long been safely evacuated. "They're on Dantooine."

The confession made no difference to Tarkin. Reasoning that Dantooine was too remote for an effective demonstration of the Death Star's power, he destroyed Alderaan before Princess Leia's unbelieving eyes.

Imperial scout ships were immediately dispatched to Dantooine. When they found only the abandoned remains of a Rebel base, Tarkin was furious. He ordered the Princess's immediate execution but didn't foresee the trouble that could be caused by a farm boy, a smuggler, two droids, and a two-and-a-half-meter-tall Wookiee.

Seven years after the Alliance's great victory at Endor, fifty colonists from the volcanic planet Eol Sha were relocated on Dantooine at Luke Skywalker's suggestion. After generations spent on their hellish homeworld, Dantooine's open grasslands seemed like a paradise to the colonists.

Their newfound peace was shattered when Admiral Daala discovered the Dantooine colony. The renegade warrior woman decimated the settlement, landing AT-AT walkers that set the grasses ablaze with blaster fire and crushed prefabricated buildings beneath their lumbering feet. It remains to be seen whether Dantooine will ever again be colonized.

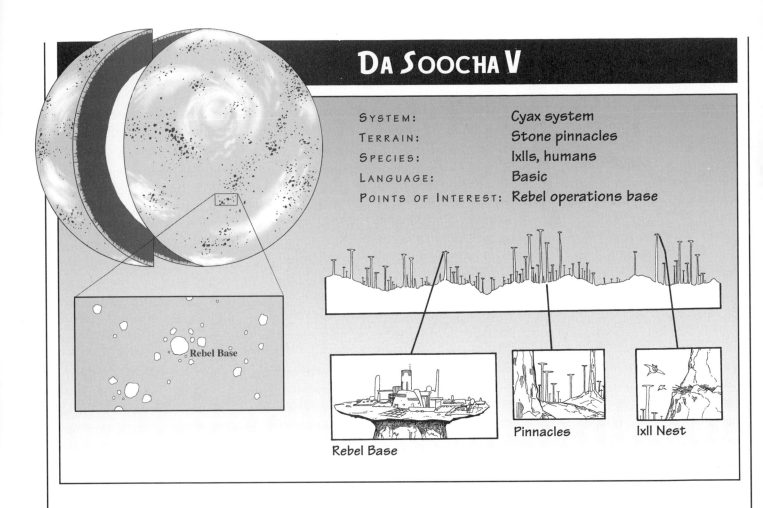

DA SOOCHA V

SYSTEM:	Cyax system
TERRAIN:	Stone pinnacles
SPECIES:	Ixlls, humans
LANGUAGE:	Basic
POINTS OF INTEREST:	Rebel operations base

Rebel Base

Rebel Base

Pinnacles

Ixll Nest

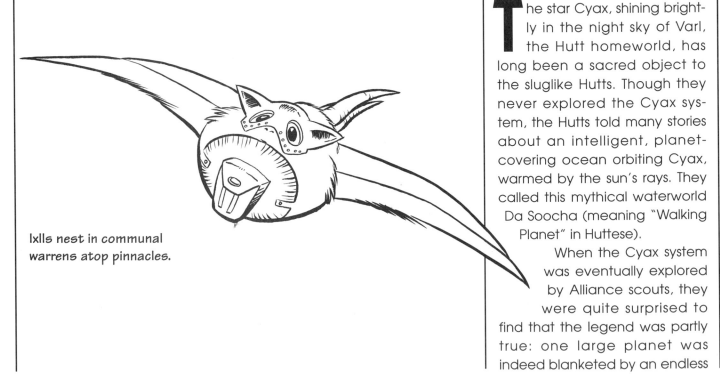

Ixlls nest in communal warrens atop pinnacles.

The star Cyax, shining brightly in the night sky of Varl, the Hutt homeworld, has long been a sacred object to the sluglike Hutts. Though they never explored the Cyax system, the Hutts told many stories about an intelligent, planet-covering ocean orbiting Cyax, warmed by the sun's rays. They called this mythical waterworld Da Soocha (meaning "Walking Planet" in Huttese).

When the Cyax system was eventually explored by Alliance scouts, they were quite surprised to find that the legend was partly true: one large planet was indeed blanketed by an endless briny sea. They named their discovery Da Soocha in honor of the Hutt fable.

Six years after the Battle of Endor and the Rebel Alliance's declaration of a New Republic, the Empire struck back with a vengeance. Forced from Coruscant by forces loyal to the cloned Emperor Palpatine, Mon Mothma, Admiral Ackbar, and the other Republic leaders established a new command base on Da Soocha's uncharted fifth moon.

They found Da Soocha V to be covered with an array of kilometers-high rocky spires and nicknamed it the Pinnacle Moon. Caverns within the huge stone columns were cleared and expanded by Alliance engineers to hold hangars and operations decks for the New Republic fleet. The native Ixlls were delighted by the strange two-legged visitors, particularly since their loud flying machines frightened away the predatory tumnors.

After Luke Skywalker fell under the Emperor's thrall on Byss, the evil galactic despot arrived at Da Soocha in his flagship, the *Eclipse*. With Luke as his prisoner and reluctant servant, Palpatine demanded that Leia Organa Solo surrender to him.

Leia did so, knowing that this was the only way she could save her brother. Aboard the *Eclipse* she broke the dark side grip that was holding Luke in bondage. Enraged at her success and defiance, Palpatine

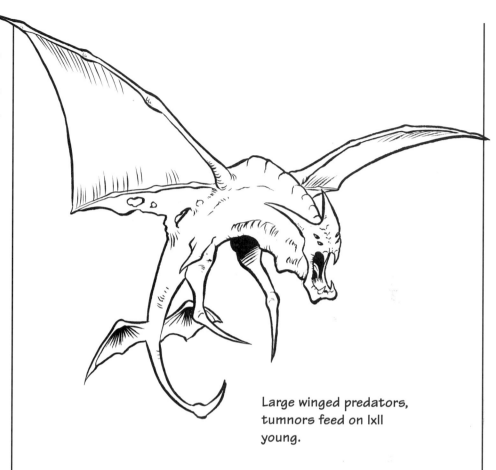

Large winged predators, tumnors feed on Ixll young.

conjured up a hideous Force storm that threatened to consume the orbiting New Republic fleet.

Joining their powers, brother and sister Jedi created a wave of life energy that repelled the unnatural Force storm and turned it back on its maker. Luke and Leia escaped on a shuttle-craft as the implacable tempest devoured the *Eclipse*.

Palpatine survived by inhabiting another clone body. He then fired a projectile from his powerful new Galaxy Gun at the Rebel base. Luke, returning from Ossus with his student Kam Solusar, saw the deadly missile

emerge from hyperspace, but his weapons were unable to penetrate its heavy shielding. Fortunately, the New Republic leaders had been evacuated safely.

As the shell buried itself deep into the crust of Da Soocha V, it triggered a nucleonic chain reaction, devastating the world with the speed and fury of burning starfire. In a flash the Pinnacle Moon was no more.

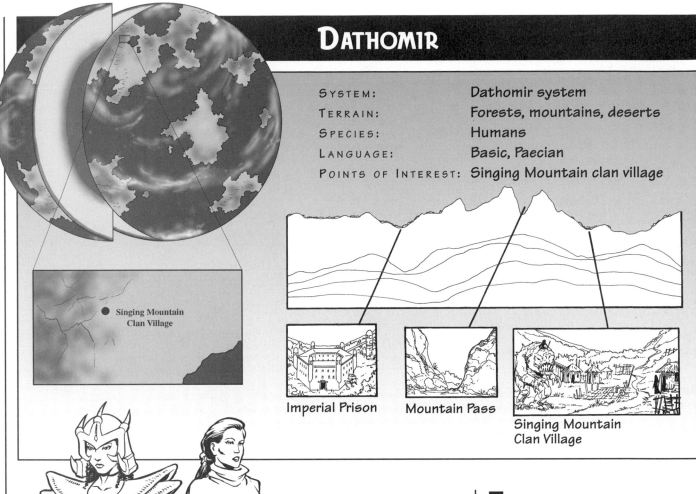

DATHOMIR

SYSTEM:	Dathomir system
TERRAIN:	Forests, mountains, deserts
SPECIES:	Humans
LANGUAGE:	Basic, Paecian
POINTS OF INTEREST:	Singing Mountain clan village

Singing Mountain Clan Village

Imperial Prison

Mountain Pass

Singing Mountain Clan Village

The witches of Dathomir are Force-sensitive warriors.

In the biggest sabacc game of Han Solo's gambling career he won a habitable planet valued at well over two billion credits. That savage world, Dathomir, would be the appropriate backdrop for his nearly disastrous courtship of Princess Leia.

Centuries ago the Old Republic banished a rogue Jedi Knight named Allya to Dathomir's primitive wilderness, where she encountered a colony of former exiles. The thriving world was strong with life energy, and Allya taught the colony's women to master the Force—even how to tame the terrifying rancors that ran wild through the thick evergreen forests.

These spellcasters, the witches of Dathomir, formed female-dominant clans where males were treated as property and forbidden to make major decisions. Those women who were seduced by the Force's dark side formed their own corrupt clan: the Nightsisters.

Nearly four hundred years before the rise of the Empire, the Jedi spaceborne academy *Chu'unthor* crashed in a Dathomir tar pit. The Jedi sent to recover the wrecked ship, including the great Master Yoda, were driven off by the sorceresses.

Much later, not knowing about the native witches, Imperial forces built a penitentiary for political dissidents on the planet's surface. When the Nightsisters made contact, the Emperor was stunned by the depth of their leader Gethzerion's power. Wanting to keep her abilities safely bottled up, Palpatine ordered the prison's ships destroyed from orbit; the stranded guards were enslaved by Gethzerion and her twisted followers.

After Han won the deed to Dathomir in a cutthroat round of high-stakes sabacc, he decided to take Leia there for seven

Tamed rancors carry the witches from clan to clan.

relaxing days. However, Leia was busy with Prince Isolder of Hapes—*too* busy, Han thought. When she refused to come, Han kidnapped her.

Dathomir, unfortunately, was not a romantic vacation spot. Han and his companions smashed through Warlord Zsinj's Imperial fleet, crashed the *Falcon* in an impenetrable thicket, fled from rancors, and were captured by the witches of the Singing Mountain clan. On top of that, the Nightsisters

threatened to wipe them out with an army of captive Imperials.

Gethzerion, meanwhile, shrewdly plotted to turn Han over to Warlord Zsinj in exchange for transport off-planet. In a vicious game of double cross, Zsinj tried to freeze Dathomir with an orbital nightcloak while Gethzerion hijacked an armed shuttle and blasted into the sky. Her ship was blown to bits by one of Zsinj's Star Destroyers, but the warlord met his own end during a furious space battle with the Hapan navy. With the Nightsisters' malignant taint removed, Han turned the ownership to Dathomir over to the sisters of the Singing Mountain clan.

Some fifteen years later the dark side threat was reborn. A new breed of Nightsisters emerged in the wilds and helped supply the Second Imperium's Shadow Academy with a ready supply of Force-sensitive warriors. Dathomir, it seems, will remain a trouble spot for years to come.

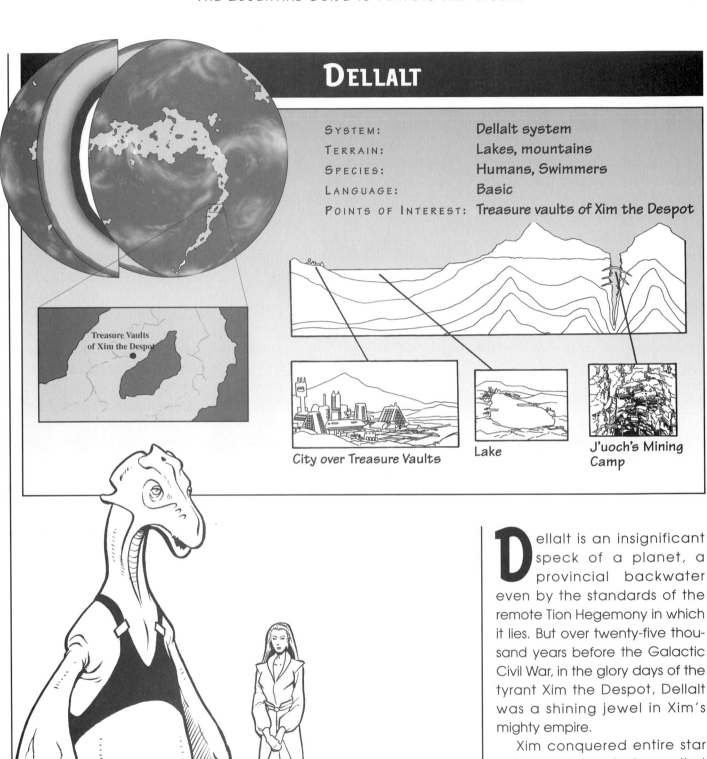

DELLALT

SYSTEM:	Dellalt system
TERRAIN:	Lakes, mountains
SPECIES:	Humans, Swimmers
LANGUAGE:	Basic
POINTS OF INTEREST:	Treasure vaults of Xim the Despot

Treasure Vaults of Xim the Despot

City over Treasure Vaults

Lake

J'uoch's Mining Camp

Gigantic Swimming People (left) dwarf humans on Dellalt.

Dellalt is an insignificant speck of a planet, a provincial backwater even by the standards of the remote Tion Hegemony in which it lies. But over twenty-five thousand years before the Galactic Civil War, in the glory days of the tyrant Xim the Despot, Dellalt was a shining jewel in Xim's mighty empire.

Xim conquered entire star systems in the ancient years that preceded the formation of the Old Republic. His defeated subjects, cowed by his military might, offered extravagant gifts and tributes from their worlds. To house his plunder Xim commissioned a vast network of vaults

The Dellalt canoid has needlelike teeth and a prehensile tail.

and chambers to be built on Dellalt.

The warlord's engineers set to work, incorporating the most advanced technologies available in their day. The true vaults were concealed beneath an entire level of empty corridors and were guarded with lethal antiweapon defenses. Outside, the surrounding city gleamed with opulent towers and monorails. Xim's treasure arrived aboard the *Queen of Ranroon*, guarded by his war droids and a brotherhood called the Survivors, but the dictator was killed soon afterward by Kossak the Hutt at the Third Battle of Vontor.

Dellalt's heyday was over. The planet drifted into obscurity as the nascent Old Republic shifted the geographic centers of power. Hopeful treasure hunters arrived to investigate the vaults but, finding only the vacant dummy chambers, left empty-handed. Xim's war droids were kept safe in their mountain stronghold by the Survivors.

Thousands of years passed. Xim's city decayed into a soggy ruin, haunted only by roving canoids and a few thousand die-hard locals. Dellalt saw only a handful of starship visits each year; its inhabitants regressed to tried-and-true technologies such as pullcart-hauling dray beasts.

Not long before their adventures with the Rebel Alliance, Han Solo and Chewbacca, with associates both old and new, went to Dellalt to search for Xim's lost treasure. Unfortunately, there was one other interested party—J'uoch, the operator of a brutal mining operation in the Dellaltian mountains.

The stakes were raised when J'uoch brazenly stole the *Millennium Falcon*. Hitching a

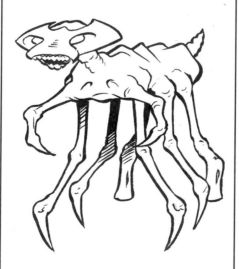

Skeletal, eight-legged dray beasts are a common sight.

ride across the nearest lake on a native sauropteroid (and starting a Swimmer dominance battle in the process), they set off on foot over the mountains to reach the mining camp and their cherished ship. They were captured by the Survivors, managed to escape, and lived through the carnage as the Survivors unleashed Xim's war droids on J'uoch's encampment.

Near the end of their quest Han had one final showdown with the gunman Gallandro, who had traveled a great distance to settle an old score. All that remained was the looting of the vaults. But when the anxious fortune hunters finally breached the inner walls, the "treasure" of Xim the Despot was revealed to be roomfuls of kiirium and heaps of mytag crystals—priceless in their day but as common as Socorran sand now. Xim's vaults had only *historical* value. Disappointed but eager for new challenges, the two adventurers departed to take up work for Jabba the Hutt.

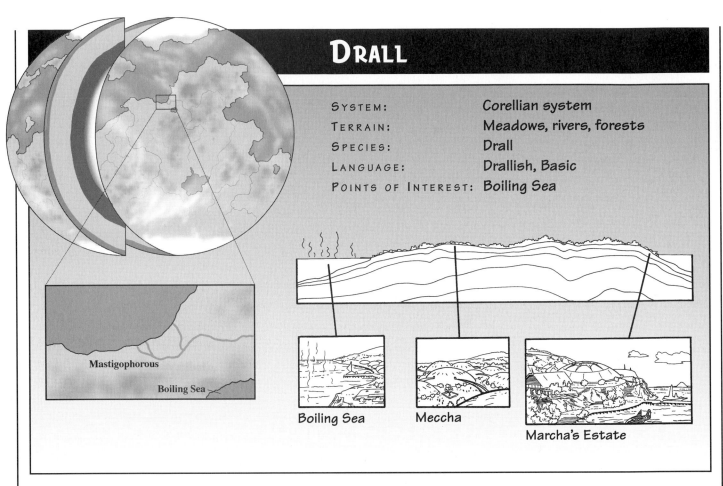

DRALL

SYSTEM: Corellian system
TERRAIN: Meadows, rivers, forests
SPECIES: Drall
LANGUAGE: Drallish, Basic
POINTS OF INTEREST: Boiling Sea

Mastigophorous

Boiling Sea

Boiling Sea

Meccha

Marcha's Estate

The peaceful Drall generally stay at home.

Drall, one of the "Five Brothers" of the Corellian system, bears the name of the sensible alien species that calls it home. Drall are short, furred creatures descended from burrowing mammals. Despite their diminutive stature, they carry themselves with dignity and poise.

The Drall are very practical and orderly. It is said that there is *no* prehistory on Drall, since its inhabitants have meticulously noted and recorded every trivial event since the dawn of intelligence. Though the cautious creatures seldom venture from their home system, some Drall have been seen in

Drallish ibbots
feed off algae
on the banks of
the Boiling Sea.

J'uoch's mining camp on Dellalt and other locations throughout the galaxy.

Drall is a quiet world, neither a hub of commerce nor a significant industrial producer. Most visitors come to the planet to visit the famous Boiling Sea, a landlocked body of water that actually bubbles and steams during the hottest summer months. Other attractions include abundant varieties of avians, including sixty-eight different subspecies of the colorful ibbot.

When Chief of State Leia Organa Solo went to the Corellian system for a trade summit, she hired a Drall named Ebrihim to tutor her three young children during their stay. Just days after their arrival Corellia exploded in violence. As the thugs of the antialien Human League attacked, Chewbacca took the children and their tutor to safety in the *Millennium Falcon*. Ebrihim, with help from his temperamental droid Q9-X2, led the ragged group to his aunt's secure estate on Drall.

Ebrihim's aunt, the Duchess Marcha, discussed the crisis with her nephew, and their sharp Drallish minds settled on a course of action. Their group found Drall's subterranean planetary repulsor, which had been used in ancient times to move the world into its current orbit, and seven-year-old Anakin, using his uncanny skill with machines, got the device working again. Unfortunately, Anakin's experiments attracted the attention of Thrackan Sal-Solo, the leader of the Human League.

Thrackan planned to double-cross the Sacorrian Triad—the masterminds behind the starbuster plot—and a working planetary repulsor was the key. His troops couldn't find the Corellian repulsor, so he ordered an assault boat to seize the one on Drall. Chewbacca, the children, and the two Drall were captured and imprisoned behind a force field.

Q9, however, had gone unnoticed. With the droid's help, the children escaped and blasted off in the *Millennium Falcon*. Thrackan pursued in the assault craft, but the Solo children had inherited their father's knack for piloting. With an expert inside loop, Jacen and Jaina disabled Thrackan's vessel just before both ships were picked up by the Bakuran cruiser *Intruder*.

Anakin Solo was returned to the planet's surface in the long-shot hope that the boy could use the Drall repulsor to disable Centerpoint Station before it fired a supernova-inducing energy burst. At the last instant, with millions of lives at stake, Anakin reached out with the Force and fired a precise interference shot. Centerpoint's deadly volley dispersed in a harmless cloud of white light.

DURO

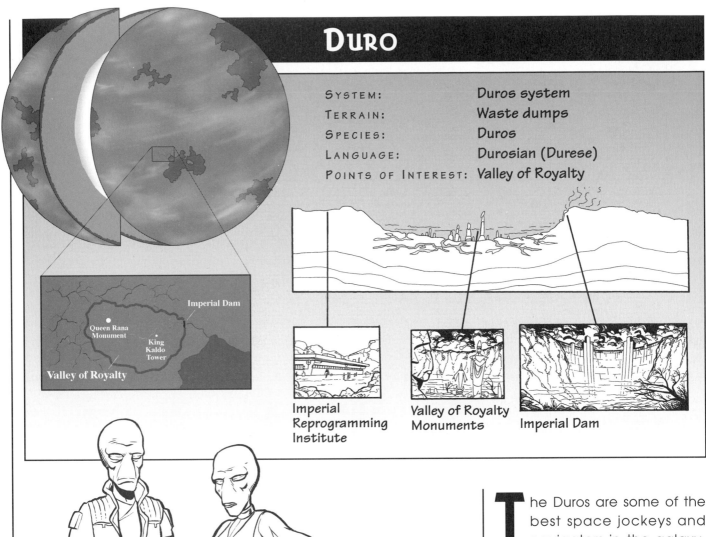

SYSTEM: Duros system
TERRAIN: Waste dumps
SPECIES: Duros
LANGUAGE: Durosian (Durese)
POINTS OF INTEREST: Valley of Royalty

Imperial Dam

Queen Rana Monument

King Kaldo Tower

Valley of Royalty

Imperial Reprogramming Institute

Valley of Royalty Monuments

Imperial Dam

Duros live to ride the hyperlanes.

The Duros are some of the best space jockeys and navigators in the galaxy. They have traveled the hyperlanes since the dawn of the Old Republic. But when a species constantly searches for adventure among the stars, its birthworld can be forgotten and neglected. Such is the case with Duro.

Tens of thousands of years before the Galactic Civil War, Duros culture entered a golden age. The temperate, terrestrial planet provided a bountiful food supply and abundant natural resources. Under the wise rule of the benevolent Queen Rana, scientists made profound

Mutant fefze beetles can convert any organic material into an edible protein paste.

breakthroughs in the science of interstellar flight. Within decades the Duros had established orbital waystations and began striking out into the inky blackness of unexplored space.

Queen Rana died at the advanced age of two hundred. Her heir, King Dassid, continued his mother's policies of galactic expansion and watched as more and more Duros relocated to space stations and far-flung colony worlds.

Duros explorers, meanwhile, were blazing new hyperspace routes and encountering other early star travelers, such as the human Corellians. As they became less dependent on their homeworld, many questioned the need to take orders from an isolated and out-of-touch monarchy.

The Duros shipping conglomerates agreed. In a swift coup they wrested power from the sitting ruler, Duchess Geneer. From that day forward all governmental authority lay in a coalition of megacorporations and their countless stockholders.

That was bad news for Duro. Nearly every citizen abandoned the planet, heading out as galactic traders and pathfinders to enrich their home companies. Mammoth

automated food factories sprang up on the surface, transporting their harvests to the six space cities orbiting overhead. As the ecosystem gradually collapsed, millions of animal species—including Duro's legendary cannibal arachnid—vanished forever.

Most Duros didn't care. They possessed an indelible sense of wanderlust, and the stars had become their new home. But with the rise of Palpatine's Empire, things got much worse.

The Imperial military seized

the Duros system and its resources, setting up ore mines near the ancient Valley of Royalty. Bubbling toxic waste pumped into vast reservoirs was kept in check by towering dams of duracrete. Clouds of acrid smoke hung close to the splintered ground, and mutant fefze beetles were the only creatures rugged enough to survive in the irradiated hellhole.

The Rebel Alliance tried to free Duro in the premature Battle of Vnas, but the attack was a failure despite the impressive performance of the new Y-wing starfighters. It wasn't until several years after the Battle of Endor that the shrinking Empire left Duro in peace.

The planet in all likelihood will never recover, but only Duros historians and archaeologists mourn its loss. The rest of their red-eyed race, spread across the face of the galaxy, have other worlds to visit, new routes to discover, and fresh stories to tell.

The cannibal arachnid died out as Duro's ecosystem collapsed.

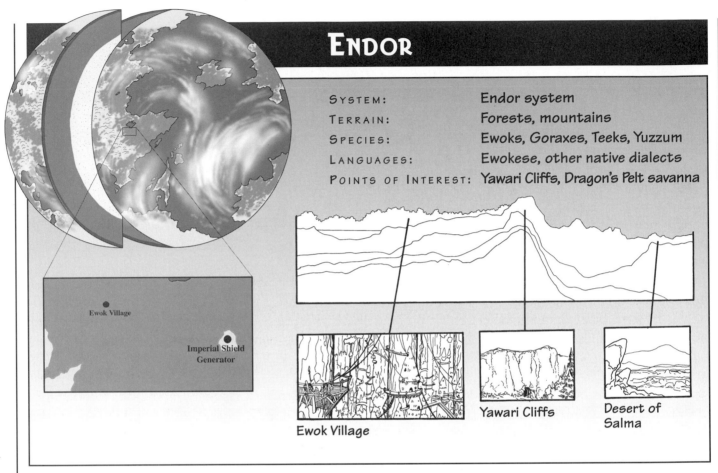

ENDOR

SYSTEM: Endor system
TERRAIN: Forests, mountains
SPECIES: Ewoks, Goraxes, Teeks, Yuzzum
LANGUAGES: Ewokese, other native dialects
POINTS OF INTEREST: Yawari Cliffs, Dragon's Pelt savanna

Ewok Village

Imperial Shield Generator

Ewok Village

Yawari Cliffs

Desert of Salma

The Ewoks were instrumental in the Battle of Endor.

Above a humble forest moon, Emperor Palpatine was killed and the Imperial fleet was permanently crippled. The justice and light of the New Republic spread from Endor to encompass the galaxy.

Located in the remote Moddell sector, the gas giant Endor is orbited by nine moons. The largest of the moons is a lush green sphere known as the Forest Moon, but often simply called Endor.

The Forest Moon of Endor is covered with woodlands, savannas, and mountains. The thriving satellite has given birth to numerous intelligent species, including gigantic Goraxes,

The Moon of Endor is home to the superfast and trinket-loving Teeks.

superfast Teeks, stilt-legged Yuzzums, and Ewoks.

Though the short, furry Ewoks appear cuddly to many observers, they are actually master hunters and fierce warriors. Ewoks live in lakeside dwellings and in villages built high in the trees, which can reach heights of a thousand meters.

A young Ewok named Wicket W. Warrick played an active role in many events on Endor. When a starship belonging to a human family crashed on the moon, Wicket befriended young Cindel Towani after her parents were captured and later killed. After the Ewoks defeated a giant Gorax and a tribe of alien Marauders, Cindel was able to leave the Forest Moon with a kindhearted old man named Noa.

Emperor Palpatine later used the moon as a construction site for his second Death Star, protecting the battle station with an impenetrable energy shield projected from a generator on Endor's surface. The Rebels couldn't resist striking at such a rich target.

Han Solo, Princess Leia, and the Alliance's other heroes landed on the moon with the intention of disabling the shield generator. They were taken captive by members of Wicket's tribe, but surprisingly, the furry warriors held a religious reverence for the golden droid C-3PO. Their adoration, combined with a demonstration of Force levitation, won the prisoners their freedom. After Threepio included the Ewoks in his rousing tale of the Empire's downfall, the excited tribe agreed to help.

As the group invaded the Imperial bunker the following morning, an entire legion of crack stormtroopers appeared. Things looked bleak until the Ewoks sprang up in a surprise attack, unleashing a deadly salvo of spears and arrows. Imperial scout walkers were tripped, snared, and crushed between logs as the Ewoks activated their traps.

Once again the Empire had made the fatal mistake of underestimating its opponent. With a roar, the shield projector went up in flames. In space overhead, Lando Calrissian and Wedge Antilles flew into the now-vulnerable Death Star and overloaded its reactor.

Meanwhile, Luke Skywalker endured an epic showdown with Darth Vader and the Emperor aboard the battle station. Overcoming decades of evil, Vader threw his master down a reactor shaft to his doom. Luke escaped in a shuttle just in time, and the Death Star exploded spectacularly behind him.

Realizing that the battle was lost, Captain Pellaeon of the Star Destroyer *Chimaera* ordered the Imperial fleet's immediate retreat. The weakened Empire would live to fight another day, but the Battle of Endor marked the end of the Galactic Civil War.

The giant Gorax keeps its prey in hanging cages.

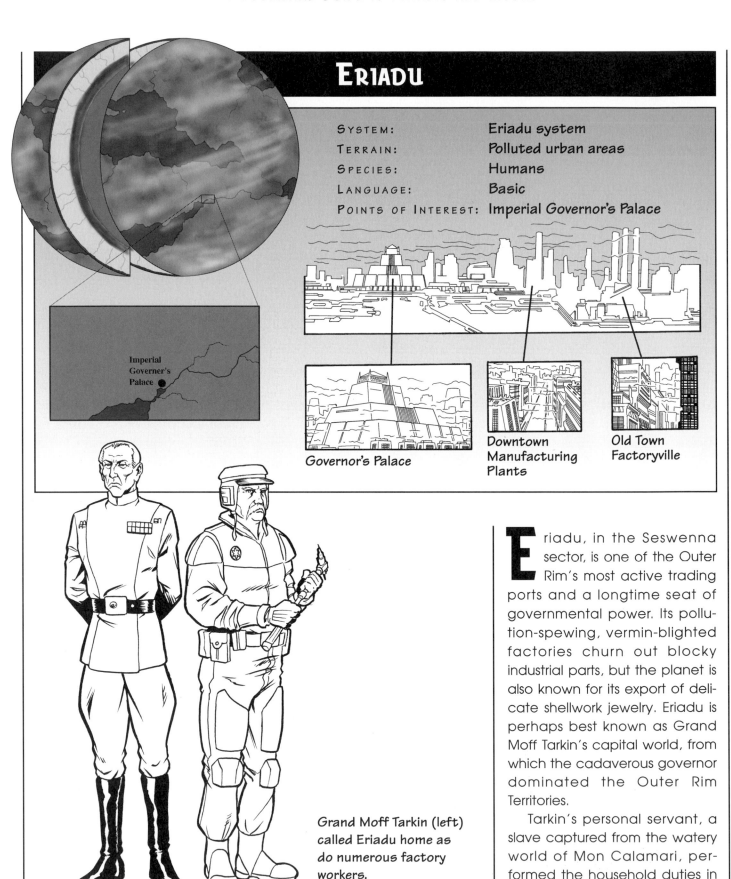

ERIADU

SYSTEM:	Eriadu system
TERRAIN:	Polluted urban areas
SPECIES:	Humans
LANGUAGE:	Basic
POINTS OF INTEREST:	Imperial Governor's Palace

Imperial
Governer's
Palace

Governor's Palace

Downtown Manufacturing Plants

Old Town Factoryville

Grand Moff Tarkin (left) called Eriadu home as do numerous factory workers.

Eriadu, in the Seswenna sector, is one of the Outer Rim's most active trading ports and a longtime seat of governmental power. Its pollution-spewing, vermin-blighted factories churn out blocky industrial parts, but the planet is also known for its export of delicate shellwork jewelry. Eriadu is perhaps best known as Grand Moff Tarkin's capital world, from which the cadaverous governor dominated the Outer Rim Territories.

Tarkin's personal servant, a slave captured from the watery world of Mon Calamari, performed the household duties in Eriadu's luxurious Governor's

The Eriaduian rat flourishes in
the polluted urban environment.

Palace. The Grand Moff spent many hours explaining to his alien the secrets of Imperial might. He saw no harm in this idle pursuit, for the Mon Calamari were clearly subhuman—even his seemingly intelligent slave, Ackbar. Tarkin also developed a new policy (modestly called the "Tarkin Doctrine") that would become the guiding principle behind the Emperor's regime: *rule by fear.*

Ambitious enough to covet the Emperor's throne, Tarkin convinced Palpatine to fund a new military undertaking that would be the living embodiment of the Tarkin Doctrine—the Death Star. As the battle station neared completion, the Grand Moff was increasingly absent from Eriadu as he made more and more visits to the remote Horuz system to oversee the project.

At last his superweapon was finished. Ready to assume command, Tarkin and the Death Star's primary designer, Bevel Lemelisk, boarded a *Lambda*-class shuttle piloted by Ackbar. As the Mon Calamari slave plotted a course away from Eriadu, three Rebel Y-wing fighters appeared out of nowhere, spitting lasers from their twin cannons. Tarkin, fearing for his life, ordered his servant to make the jump to hyperspace at once.

Ackbar switched off the shuttlecraft's shields and calmly awaited their destruction as the Y-wings swung around for another pass at the now-helpless vessel. "*I* have brought this upon you," he told Tarkin, "in exchange for all the pain you have inflicted upon me and others like me."

Tarkin fled, cramming into the single-occupant escape pod with the portly Lemelisk. Looking back, he was surprised to see that the Rebel starfighters had not delivered the killing blow. Instead, they were pulling alongside and attaching air links to the unprotected ship. If Ackbar had not been a worthless alien, Tarkin would have thought they were actually *rescuing* the creature.

Admiral Motti's personal Star Destroyer arrived before the Rebel raiders could menace Tarkin's escape pod. Regretful at losing a valuable slave but relieved to have survived a Rebel assassination attempt, Tarkin took command of his impregnable Death Star. Surely he was safe from Rebel attack there.

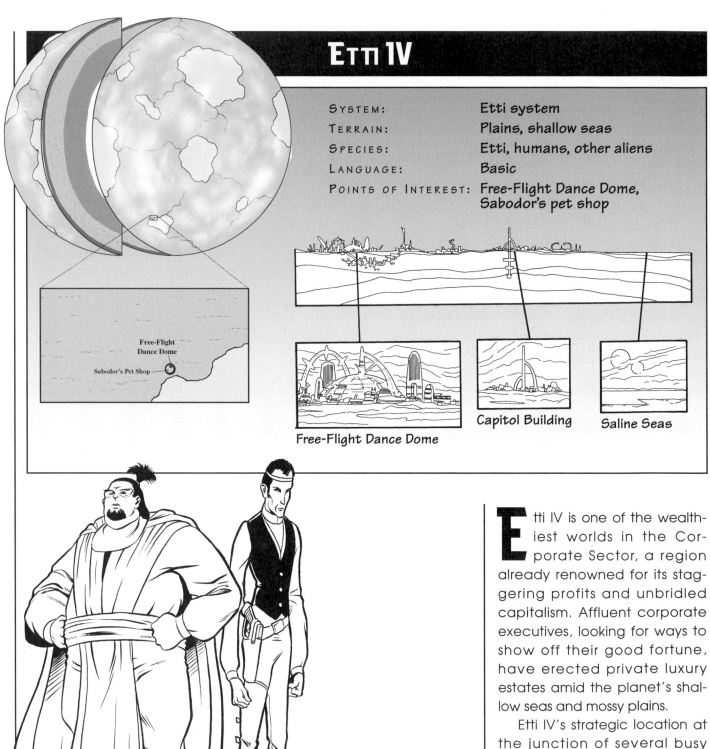

ETTI IV

SYSTEM: **Etti system**
TERRAIN: **Plains, shallow seas**
SPECIES: **Etti, humans, other aliens**
LANGUAGE: **Basic**
POINTS OF INTEREST: **Free-Flight Dance Dome, Sabodor's pet shop**

Free-Flight
Dance Dome

Sabodor's Pet Shop

Free-Flight Dance Dome

Capitol Building

Saline Seas

The crime lord Ploovo Two-For-One's size contrasts with the thin native Etti.

Etti IV is one of the wealthiest worlds in the Corporate Sector, a region already renowned for its staggering profits and unbridled capitalism. Affluent corporate executives, looking for ways to show off their good fortune, have erected private luxury estates amid the planet's shallow seas and mossy plains.

Etti IV's strategic location at the junction of several busy hyperspace routes has also made it a bustling epicenter of mercantile trade. The sheer volume of credits on the planet, both those arriving through commerce and those hoarded by the corporate lords, has led to the inevitable appearance of thieves, pickpockets, swindlers, and kingpins of organized crime.

The very rich have both the freedom and the means to indulge in exotic and idle pursuits, and Etti IV doesn't disappoint them. Near the spaceport are numerous shops and boutiques, some of which sell exotic and rare animals from every corner of the galaxy. The Free-Flight Dance Dome is the most opulent dining establishment on the planet and possesses a variable gravity field that can be extended selectively anywhere on the premises. The dance floor is typically kept at zero gee; revelers spin and twist freely, their boots never touching the ground.

Unlike the xenophobic Empire, the free-enterprise Corporate Sector welcomes aliens of all kinds—after all, a Rodian's credits are just as good as a human's. Though no known native intelligent species are found on its many worlds, the human offshoot race known as the Etti was given control of Etti IV by the Corporate Sector Authority. An ambitious Etti named Wumdi, after making a fortune in the Corporate Sector, became one of Prince Xizor's most trusted lieutenants in Black Sun.

Before their famous adventures with the Rebel Alliance, Han Solo and Chewbacca smuggled for Ploovo Two-For-One, a heavyset crime lord

Dinkos are biting, clawing, stink-squirting creatures originally from Proxima Dibal.

whom they thoroughly despised. After surviving a nearly fatal gunrunning operation to Duroon, the pair came to Etti IV to give Ploovo his cut of the profits. Before heading for their rendezvous at the Free-Flight, Han stopped off in Sabodor's pet shop to make a unique purchase.

Entering the dome, they sat down with the crime lord and prepared to settle their account. But a knot of Espo security police barged in and demanded Han's surrender—tipped off by Ploovo, they had impounded the *Millennium Falcon* because of its failure to comply with starfreighter safety regulations. As he prepared to leave with the armed escort, Han opened the box containing Ploovo's "payment"—a biting, clawing, stink-squirting dinko.

The bistro erupted in chaos as the enraged dinko hissed and launched itself at the other patrons. Han and Chewbacca exchanged fire with the startled Espos as they sprinted to the bar and its gravity controls, which they promptly punched up to 3.5 gees. Yanked down by their own weight, the customers, police, and Ploovo lay pinned to the floor while the inventive Corellian and his Wookiee first mate made their escape.

FIRRERRE

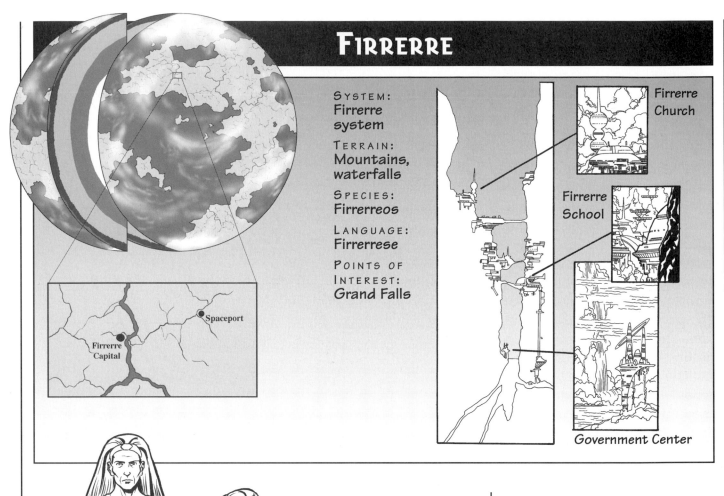

SYSTEM:
Firrerre system

TERRAIN:
Mountains, waterfalls

SPECIES:
Firrerreos

LANGUAGE:
Firrerrese

POINTS OF INTEREST:
Grand Falls

Spaceport

Firrerre Capital

Firrerre Church

Firrerre School

Government Center

Firrerreos are a rare species closely resembling baseline humans on the outside.

Although not as infamous as the destruction of Alderaan, the utter devastation suffered by the planet Firrerre is another tragic monument to the unmatched cruelty of Emperor Palpatine and those who served him.

Firrerreos are one of the rarest species in the galaxy, with perhaps only a few thousand survivors still in existence. A near-human species with varicolored striped hair, Firrerreos possess nictitating membranes to protect their eyes and have remarkable healing powers. Their society was separated into a rigid clan system, and uttering another Firrerreo's name was believed to give the speaker special power over the one named.

Two Force-sensitive Firrerreos, Hethrir and his mate, Rillao, were early students of Darth Vader's. Vader, pleased with Hethrir's aptitude, appointed the alien to the position of Imperial Procurator of Justice. Hethrir condemned dozens of "treasonous" planets by imprisoning their inhabitants in suspended animation and sending them off in sublight passenger ships, ostensibly to colonize distant worlds. Desperate to prove his loyalty to his master, Hethrir fulfilled Vader's most chilling order of all and condemned his own homeworld to death.

Thousands of adult Firrerreos were ordered onto passenger freighters, but millions of others—and *all* the planet's children—were left behind. Aboard the departing ships Firrerre's sons and daughters watched as the Emperor's elite Starcrash Brigade released an incurable strain of hive virus. Every last one of their friends, neighbors, and children died in agony as the gruesome pathogen ate its way through their bodies. Within days Firrerre was a dead world. It was swiftly quarantined to prevent the plague from spreading to other, more pro-Imperial planets.

Horrified at what her mate had become, Rillao fled to a backwater planet, carrying their unborn child. After the Empire lost the Battle of Endor and

Mishalopes once thrived in the mountains near Grand Falls.

Hethrir's power base deteriorated, the former Procurator tracked down all the passenger ships he had dispatched into deep space. After towing them to a secret location, Hethrir was free to visit and select captive children to sell into slavery. When he finally tracked down Rillao and his young son, Tigris, Hethrir imprisoned his mate in a torture web on one of the freighters and took Tigris away to be the heir of his "Empire Reborn."

Ten years after the Battle of Endor, while searching the galaxy for her three kidnapped children, Princess Leia Organa

Solo discovered Hethrir's freighters and their suspended-animation cargoes of living beings. Boarding the nearest ship, Leia noticed that it was filled with natives of Firrerre.

The princess freed Rillao from her torment, but when she woke another Firrerreo from stasis, the alien refused to escape with her. Though it would take decades for the sublight freighter to reach another world, the proud Firrerreo would not abandon his surviving people. "If all memory of the Empire has vanished when we wake," he declared, "so much the better."

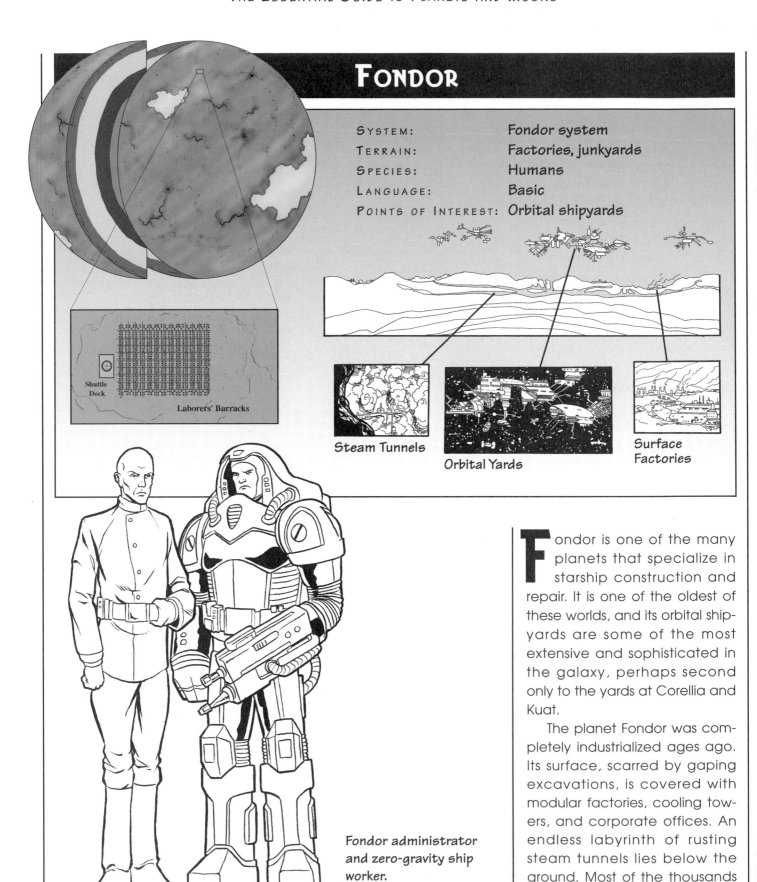

FONDOR

SYSTEM: **Fondor system**
TERRAIN: **Factories, junkyards**
SPECIES: **Humans**
LANGUAGE: **Basic**
POINTS OF INTEREST: **Orbital shipyards**

Shuttle Dock

Laborers' Barracks

Steam Tunnels

Orbital Yards

Surface Factories

Fondor administrator and zero-gravity ship worker.

Fondor is one of the many planets that specialize in starship construction and repair. It is one of the oldest of these worlds, and its orbital shipyards are some of the most extensive and sophisticated in the galaxy, perhaps second only to the yards at Corellia and Kuat.

The planet Fondor was completely industrialized ages ago. Its surface, scarred by gaping excavations, is covered with modular factories, cooling towers, and corporate offices. An endless labyrinth of rusting steam tunnels lies below the ground. Most of the thousands of orbital dockworkers, at the end of their zero-gee shifts, board shuttles that take them to the endless square kilometers of identical laborers' barracks on the planet below. The droid Bollux was first activated at the Fondor yards nearly a century before the Battle of Yavin; he later had several remarkable adventures with a young smuggler named Han Solo.

Though the stardocks at Kuat were the primary builders of the Empire's prestigious Star Destroyers, Fondor was unexpectedly handed the contract to manufacture the Super Star Destroyer *Executor*. The first in a new line of staggeringly large naval warships, the *Executor* would serve as Lord Darth Vader's personal flagship. The Empire demanded total secrecy and closed off the system to all nonmilitary traffic. The Fondor executives were outraged that they could no longer serve their best clients, but the mammoth project took up nearly all their resources, and they knew better than to risk Vader's anger. If they did their job well, they might also be able to steal more lucrative military contracts from their competitors on Kuat.

Some leading Imperial admirals did not view the *Executor* as the newest pride of the Emperor's navy. To them the horribly expensive undertaking was merely Vader's latest pet project and one more example of the Dark Lord's favored status with Emperor Palpatine. They

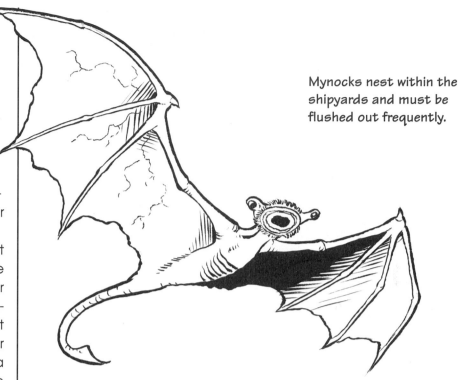

Mynocks nest within the shipyards and must be flushed out frequently.

would be quite pleased to see Vader fail.

One of their members, Admiral Griff, secretly contacted the Rebel Alliance. If a Rebel agent sabotaged the *Executor*, they would conveniently look the other way. Luke Skywalker agreed to infiltrate the Fondor yards.

Though the traitorous officers didn't know it, Griff was actually Vader's spy, working to expose his co-conspirators' treachery. When the admirals arranged to meet with Skywalker in Fondor's underground steam tunnels, Griff informed his master, and Vader prepared to strike.

In the cavernous steam shafts the disloyal Imperials discussed their next moves with the Rebel saboteur. But the young

man suddenly sensed a dark presence in the Force and warned them that the malignancy was coming their way. The plotters broke and ran as Vader charged in with a full complement of stormtroopers.

Luke was trapped, but the resourceful R2-D2 activated the tunnel's steam flow. White mist rushed through the passage, blinding the troopers and obscuring their breakout. Stowing away on a drone barge, Luke and Artoo escaped from the Fondor system.

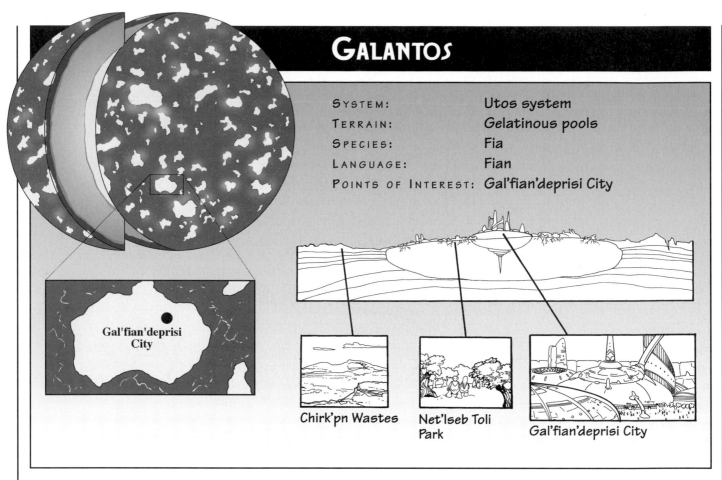

GALANTOS

SYSTEM:	Utos system
TERRAIN:	Gelatinous pools
SPECIES:	Fia
LANGUAGE:	Fian
POINTS OF INTEREST:	Gal'fian'deprisi City

Gal'fian'deprisi City

Chirk'pn Wastes

Net'lseb Toli Park

Gal'fian'deprisi City

Fia live on an ever-moving world.

The myriad stars of the Koornacht Cluster fill the night sky of Galantos as a blazing oval of light. The awestruck Fia revered the dazzling sight and referred to it as the Multitude. But twelve years after the Battle of Endor the Fia of Galantos became convinced that their beloved Koornacht would be the source of their imminent destruction.

Lying deep in the Farlax sector, Galantos keeps a low profile but is well known among planetary geologists for its bizarre alien terrain. Its rocky surface is dotted with thousands of pools ranging in size from tiny puddles to vast seas hundreds of kilometers square. These depressions hold pale-green organic gelatin, a springy substance that provides life-giving nutrients for every creature on the planet.

Bulbous *toli* trees sink their needle-roots beneath the pools' rubbery skin, while skree-skaters glide along the smooth surface on the hunt for smaller prey. The Fia, with wide, splayed bodies for navigating their undulating environment, were the first of Galantos's creatures to evolve sentience.

The surrounding wastelands provided metal and stone for the Fia to construct impressive cities. Since the largest gelatinous pools tended to roll and heave during strong storms, Fian dwellings were flexible, built with plenty of "give."

Because of a scarcity of usable space, the Fian population never expanded beyond a half million individuals. But Galantos traded goods with its neighbors and continued on a stable, peaceful, and predictable course until the chilling message of Plat Mallar.

The bigoted Yevethan aliens, denizens of the neighboring Koornacht Cluster, had just exterminated all "foreign" settlements in their territory. Plat Mallar, an innocent young pilot, had barely escaped one such attack and was trying to reach Galantos in a short-range starfighter when he was rescued by a passing freighter. *If the Yevethans have done this,* the Fia thought, gazing fearfully

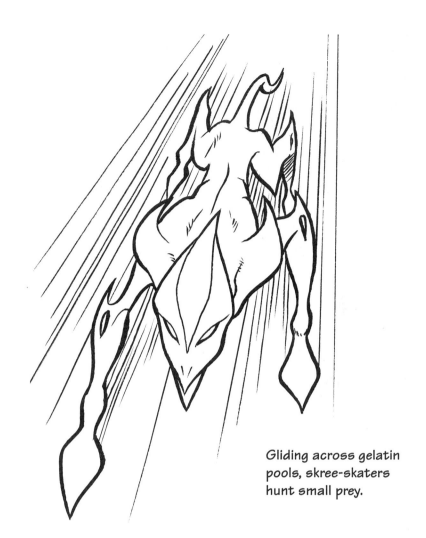

Gliding across gelatin pools, skree-skaters hunt small prey.

up at the Multitude, *we could be next.*

Jobath, councillor of the Fia, desperately sought an audience with Leia Organa Solo on Coruscant. He camped out at her personal residence—breaking all protocols for properly addressing the chief of state—but Jobath's dire warnings were heeded. Galantos's emergency petition for New Republic membership was swiftly approved, and the warships *Gol Storn* and *Thackery* arrived to protect the planet from Yevethan aggression.

The devastating attack that so terrified the Fia never materialized, thanks to the Republic's navy. The fleet, carrying Luke Skywalker and a group of Fallanassi from J't'p'tan, leapt into the heart of the Koornacht Cluster and decimated the Yevethan military at the epic Battle of N'zoth. Galantos and its relieved citizens returned to business as the latest members of the New Republic.

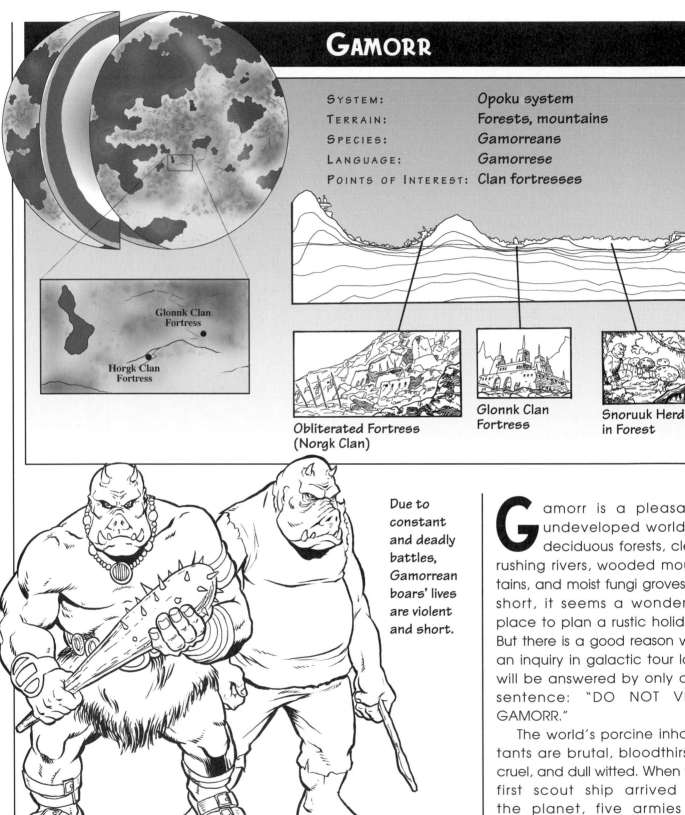

GAMORR

SYSTEM: **Opoku system**
TERRAIN: **Forests, mountains**
SPECIES: **Gamorreans**
LANGUAGE: **Gamorrese**
POINTS OF INTEREST: **Clan fortresses**

Glonnk Clan Fortress

Horgk Clan Fortress

Obliterated Fortress (Norgk Clan)

Glonnk Clan Fortress

Snoruuk Herd in Forest

Due to constant and deadly battles, Gamorrean boars' lives are violent and short.

Gamorr is a pleasant, undeveloped world of deciduous forests, clear rushing rivers, wooded mountains, and moist fungi groves. In short, it seems a wonderful place to plan a rustic holiday. But there is a good reason why an inquiry in galactic tour logs will be answered by only one sentence: "DO NOT VISIT GAMORR."

The world's porcine inhabitants are brutal, bloodthirsty, cruel, and dull witted. When the first scout ship arrived on the planet, five armies of Gamorreans battled for days to win the right to approach the strange visitor. Finally, one victo-

Gamorreans herd the shuffling snoruuks.

rious troop strode forth to claim its prize—and promptly battered the vessel to tiny pieces.

Simply put, Gamorrean boars love warfare and killing. They prefer face-to-face combat whenever possible, using swords, clubs, and vibro-axes. Their entire year is organized around warfare, which occurs between rival clans with little or no provocation.

Spring is taken up with training for the coming season, and eager prospects show off their gladiatorial prowess at open-air tourneys and festivals. Summer is a veritable orgy of bloodlust as vast clan armies clash in

Fascinated by shiny objects, quizzers will steal whatever they fancy.

grand conflict. Fall and winter are spent resting and recuperating from the gashes, skewerings, and lost body parts of a typical campaign. Nearly ten times as many boars are born each year as sows, a ratio that evens out when one considers their substantial seasonal attrition rate.

Since boars are so single-minded, Gamorrean sows must do the basic work of running a feudal society. Sows own all the property and oversee trade, manufacturing, and agriculture. Clans make their homes in fortresses encircled by wooden stockades and guarded by Gamorrean watch-beasts. These sinewy creatures are so vigilant and so fierce when provoked that the Imperial army has taken to stationing them at facilities such as the Sirpar training center.

Gamorr's cool forests harbor no animal life larger than a meter long. It is believed that the piglike aliens hunted all major beasts to extinction long ago. In the dense green canopy, mischievous, chattering quizzers leap from branch to branch; below them, mobile colonies of snoruuk mushrooms shuffle through the fallen leaves on the overgrown forest floor. Snoruuks are a staple in the Gamorrean diet, and shep-

herds patiently herd the fungi along at a glacially slow pace. Status in Gamorrean society is exhibited through the display of morrts, slimy bloodsucking parasites that are lovingly treated as pets. A great Gamorrean warlord can have as many as twenty morrts decorating his body, gorging themselves on his bodily fluids.

The Empire has tried to "civilize" Gamorr, with disastrous

Watch-beasts protect and defend the clan fortresses.

results. After the well-known Native Management and Industrialization debacle, it was decided that Gamorreans should be left to do what they do best. Gamorreans in the galaxy often find work as bodyguards, mercenaries, bouncers, or any other job requiring raw muscle and a tough hide. Jabba the Hutt employed several Gamorreans in his criminal palace on Tatooine, including the stupid but good-natured Gartogg.

GAROS IV

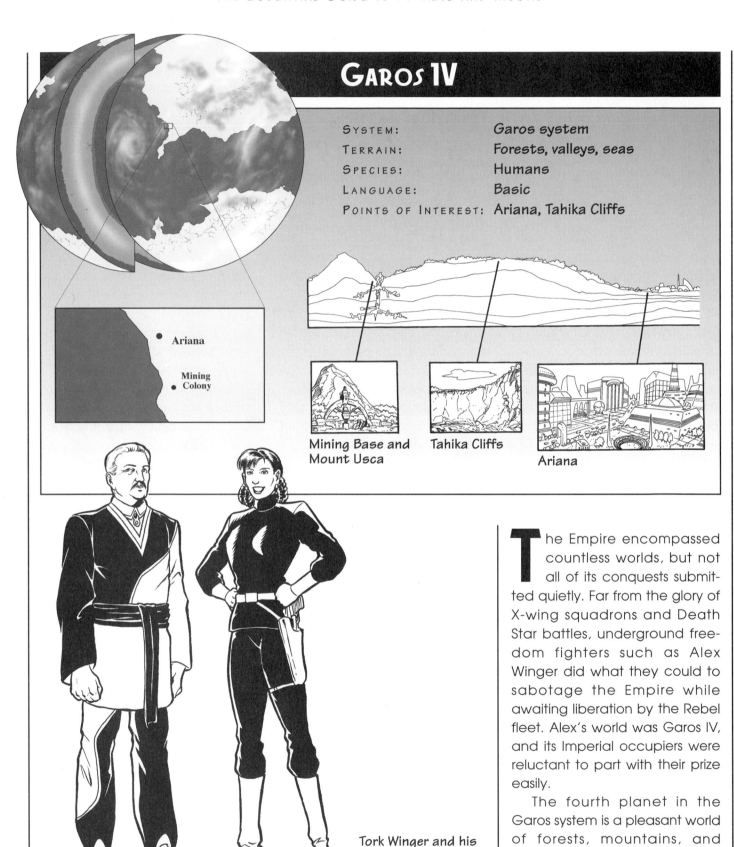

SYSTEM:	Garos system
TERRAIN:	Forests, valleys, seas
SPECIES:	Humans
LANGUAGE:	Basic
POINTS OF INTEREST:	Ariana, Tahika Cliffs

Ariana

Mining Colony

Mining Base and Mount Usca

Tahika Cliffs

Ariana

Tork Winger and his daughter, Alex.

The Empire encompassed countless worlds, but not all of its conquests submitted quietly. Far from the glory of X-wing squadrons and Death Star battles, underground freedom fighters such as Alex Winger did what they could to sabotage the Empire while awaiting liberation by the Rebel fleet. Alex's world was Garos IV, and its Imperial occupiers were reluctant to part with their prize easily.

The fourth planet in the Garos system is a pleasant world of forests, mountains, and oceans. Its population is concentrated on a single continent in three major centers: the waterfront resort town of Zila, the manufacturing seat (and agricultural breadbasket) of Garan, and Ariana, the shining capital city. Ariana boasts the prestigious University of Garos, and students can always relax at the never-empty Chado's Pub. Just a short distance away lie the breathtaking Tahika Cliffs, from which visitors can watch the pounding surf of the Locura Ocean and listen to wild boetays howling mournfully at the twin moons.

Garos IV has a long history; it was first settled four thousand years ago by human colonists. The hazardous Nyarikan Nebula cut the arrivals off from most outside contact, and they developed into a tough, self-reliant people.

When colonists from the neighboring planet Sundari began migrating en masse to Garos, tensions rose and tempers flared. Accusations of unfair competition escalated into a full-blown civil war that raged for generations. It ended when the Empire arrived and violently "forced a peace."

The respected local politician Tork Winger was installed as the Imperial governor. He struggled to find a middle ground, but his adopted daughter, Alex, could not compromise her principles. Behind her father's back she began meeting with the secret Garos resistance movement in the tunnels beneath Ariana.

After the Battle of Endor the Garos resistance thought that it might soon triumph, but then the Empire stepped up its research into the local hibridium ore deposits. This rare mineral produces a natural cloaking effect, and that made it invaluable to the Imperial war effort. A well-defended quarry was built in the mountains south of Ariana to mine hibridium and transport it off-planet.

Over the next few years Alex and her comrades scored many victories against the Imperial occupation force. They successfully ambushed hibridium convoys, destroyed a landing platform at the hibridium mines, and wiped out a disassembled ion cannon that was being stored in Zila. Soon after the defeat of Grand Admiral Thrawn, Alex teamed up with Luke Skywalker on a covert mission to the frozen planet Sarahwiee.

Her actions brought Garos's plight to the attention of the New Republic. Soon X-wing fighters and Mon Calamari star cruisers leapt from hyperspace and forced the outnumbered Imperials to abandon their only source of hibridium. With her homeworld emancipated, Alex Winger went on to face new challenges.

Wild boetays stake out the Tahika Cliffs.

HAPES

SYSTEM: **Hapan system**
TERRAIN: **Tropical mountains**
SPECIES: **Humans**
LANGUAGE: **Hapan**
POINTS OF INTEREST: **Fountain Palace, Reef fortress**

Fountain Palace

Reef Fortress

Famous Lorell Raider Wreck

Fountain Palace

The Queen Mother Ta'a Chume and her son Prince Isolder reign over the Hapes Consortium.

For the secretive and fabulously wealthy nobility of Hapes one proverb sums up the philosophy behind their matriarchal society: "Never let a man believe he is the intellectual equal of a woman. It only leads him to evil."

Hapes is the ruling planet of the Hapes Consortium, a cluster of sixty-three worlds settled over four thousand years ago by a pirate band called the Lorell Raiders. While pillaging nearby systems, the bandits would seize beautiful women and drag them back to the Hapes Cluster. The barbaric practice continued for generations, until the Jedi Knights eliminated the

Raiders permanently.

Once they were free, the women took control of their cluster and invested all power in a hereditary monarch to be known as the Queen Mother. Men assumed a subservient role, with little voice in politics or business. After several prosperous centuries the Queen Mother sealed the Hapan borders, and they remained closed for over three millennia.

Four years after the Battle of Endor the Hapans broke their long isolation with an unexpected offer to the New Republic. They would form a political and military alliance if Princess Leia would agree to marry their Prince Isolder. As the *Chume'da*, or heir, of the Hapan worlds, the handsome Isolder had the power to make Leia the next Queen Mother, giving her unprecedented resources with which to fight Imperial warlords such as Zsinj. Before she could give her answer, Leia was kidnapped by a jealous Han Solo and taken to the untamed planet of Dathomir.

Isolder and Luke Skywalker formed a tentative partnership to track down the princess but found more than they bargained for in Dathomir's wilderness. While battling the vicious Nightsisters, the Prince fell in love with Teneniel Djo, a beautiful Force-strong spellcaster. Isolder was captivated. Though she was of low birth and dressed in reptile hides, Isolder

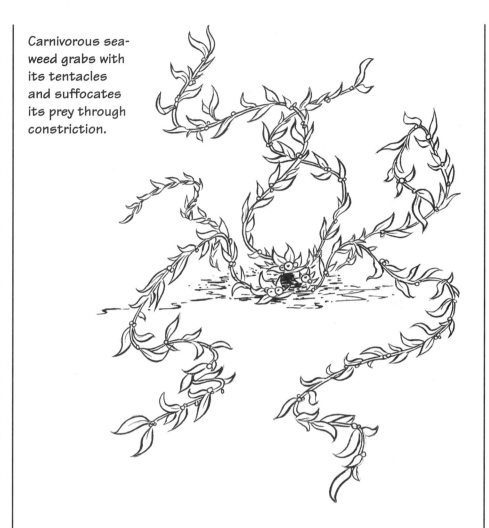

Carnivorous seaweed grabs with its tentacles and suffocates its prey through constriction.

decided that only this fierce warrior woman could be his bride.

Ta'a Chume, the current ruler, did not react well to her son's choice of a bride—political backstabbing and infighting had been a court tradition for centuries. The two were married, however, and bore a daughter who shared her mother's gift for the Force. Young Tenel Ka trained at Luke Skywalker's Jedi academy, where she befriended Han and Leia's twin children, Jaina and Jacen. After a horrifying lightsaber accident in which her

left arm was severed, Tenel Ka returned to Hapes.

Even her grievous injury could not halt the internecine maneuvering of her grandmother and those in power. While Tenel Ka stayed at the royal family's secure Reef Fortress, the treacherous Ambassador Yfra plotted to kill the young heir. A rigged wavespeeder, a patch of carnivorous seaweed, and a squad of Bartokk assassins were not enough. Tenel Ka handily foiled the plot, proving beyond a doubt that she had the skills necessary to rule Hapes as a capable Queen Mother.

HONOGHR

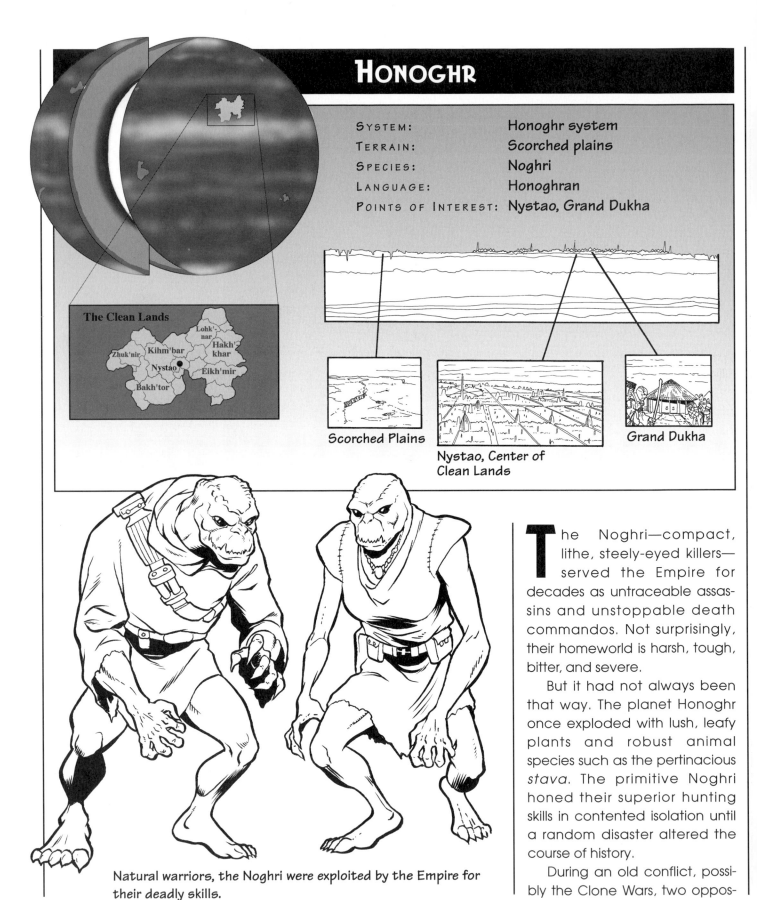

SYSTEM:	Honoghr system
TERRAIN:	Scorched plains
SPECIES:	Noghri
LANGUAGE:	Honoghran
POINTS OF INTEREST:	Nystao, Grand Dukha

The Clean Lands

Lohk'-nar
Zhuk'nir
Kihm'bar
Hakh'khar
Nystao
Éikh'mir
Bakh'tor

Scorched Plains

Nystao, Center of Clean Lands

Grand Dukha

Natural warriors, the Noghri were exploited by the Empire for their deadly skills.

The Noghri—compact, lithe, steely-eyed killers—served the Empire for decades as untraceable assassins and unstoppable death commandos. Not surprisingly, their homeworld is harsh, tough, bitter, and severe.

But it had not always been that way. The planet Honoghr once exploded with lush, leafy plants and robust animal species such as the pertinacious *stava*. The primitive Noghri honed their superior hunting skills in contented isolation until a random disaster altered the course of history.

During an old conflict, possibly the Clone Wars, two opposing starships slugged it out in Honoghran orbit. The loser, irreparably damaged, tumbled through the sky and slammed into the ground, releasing toxic chemicals that ruined the soil and poisoned the rain.

The devastated Noghri were on the verge of catastrophic famine when a visitor from the stars arrived—a black-garbed nightmare who called himself Darth Vader. He offered the Empire's help in healing Honoghr's wounds if trained Noghri warriors would join his cause. The awed aliens respectfully agreed.

However, the Empire had no intention of restoring Honoghr. Instead, it seeded the planet with a hybrid *kholm*-grass that prevented all other plants from taking root. Legions of Imperial decon droids purified tiny parcels of land, but at such a slow rate that the Noghri were always kept just below the verge of self-sufficiency. As long as the land stayed contaminated, the Noghri would remain in the Empire's pocket.

After Vader's death Grand Admiral Thrawn took over as lord of the Noghri people. Thrawn ordered death squads to kidnap Leia Organa Solo and her unborn twins, but one commando got close enough to recognize his target's scent. The soldier, Khabarakh, identified Leia as the *Mal'ary'ush*—the daughter and heir of his late master Darth Vader—and begged her forgiveness. At her

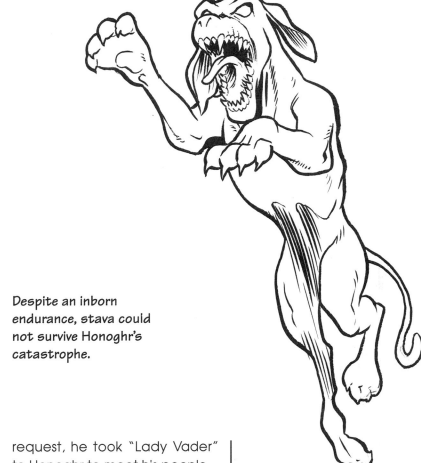

Despite an inborn endurance, stava could not survive Honoghr's catastrophe.

request, he took "Lady Vader" to Honoghr to meet his people.

From orbit the dying planet was an ugly hue of singed brown, but a small patch of green stood out like an emerald landing beacon. "The Clean Lands," noted Khabarakh, explaining that all Noghri settlements had been relocated to that tiny disinfected area.

Leia was taken in by the clan Kihm'bar and narrowly escaped capture by Grand Admiral Thrawn. Leia knew a little about decon droids and could see that the Empire's droids were working ridiculously slowly. When she learned the Noghri had been kept in bondage for *decades*, she was horrified.

Full of righteous anger, Leia

met with the Noghri clan dynasts in the ruling city of Nystao. The dynasts did not take their honor-bond lightly, but it was impossible to ignore the evidence the *Mal'ary'ush* was presenting—the Empire had played them for fools.

Their debt was over. The Noghri now controlled their *own* destiny and took their revenge on Thrawn at the Battle of Bilbringi. Since then new crops have been harvested from an irrigated river valley, but the ecological damage is so far-reaching that Honoghr may never fully recover.

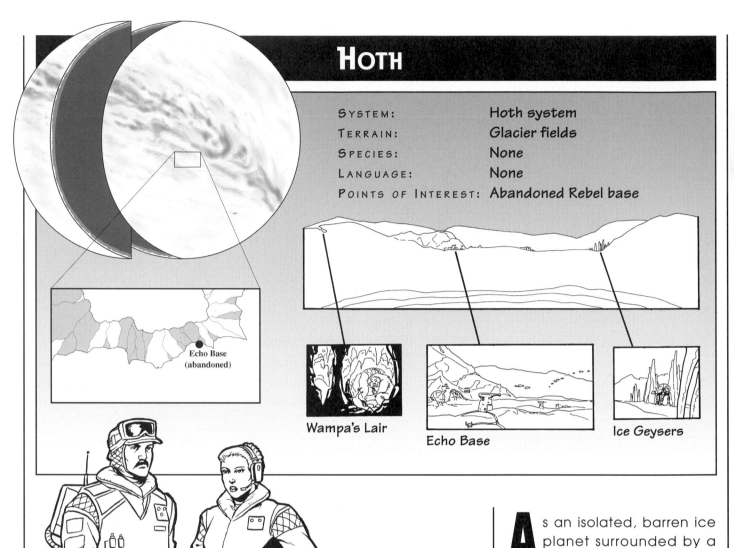

HOTH

SYSTEM:	Hoth system
TERRAIN:	Glacier fields
SPECIES:	None
LANGUAGE:	None
POINTS OF INTEREST:	Abandoned Rebel base

Echo Base
(abandoned)

Wampa's Lair

Echo Base

Ice Geysers

Echo Base Rebels.

As an isolated, barren ice planet surrounded by a hazardous asteroid belt, Hoth seemed to be the perfect spot for a secret Rebel base. Unfortunately, that unforgiving world became famous as the site of one of the Rebellion's greatest defeats.

The unpopulated world of Hoth is blanketed with snow and battered by meteors. Despite claims that the frozen wastes don't hold enough life to fill a space cruiser, the planet's tenacious animals include ornery tauntauns and ferocious wampa ice creatures.

Hoth first came to the attention of the Rebellion by blind

Indigenous tauntauns smell worse on the inside.

chance, when Luke Skywalker crash-landed on its glacier fields and encountered a pair of human replica droids. After his rescue, Luke reported that Hoth's isolation made it a perfect candidate for a new headquarters base, and the Rebel leadership agreed.

The Alliance Corps of Engineers carved a vast command center from the ice. Echo Base became home to several thousand soldiers, technicians, and pilots, though the numbing temperatures caused breakdowns in the T-47 snowspeeders. To compensate, the inventive Rebels corralled several wild tauntauns and trained them as riding mounts.

Just one month after the base's official opening Luke was attacked by a wampa ice creature while on tauntaun patrol. Fortunately, Han Solo was able to rescue his friend, keeping Luke alive through the subzero night and beating survival odds of 725 to 1.

Not long afterward a strange metal object was detected in Zone Twelve. The invader self-destructed when Han and Chewbacca investigated, but the smoking remains were clearly those of an Imperial probe droid. With a heavy heart, General Rieekan ordered the evacuation of Echo Base.

Light-years away, Darth Vader studied the probot's vital data and ordered his personal fleet to jump immediately to the Hoth system. The Star Destroyers, however, emerged from hyperspace too close to the ice planet, allowing the Rebels to engage their protective energy shield. Lord Vader ordered General Veers to prepare his AT-AT walkers—the Battle of Hoth would now be a surface engagement.

As Veers's juggernaught marched south toward the shield generator, Rogue Group's snowspeeders decided on the unorthodox strategy of tripping the four-legged behemoths with harpoons and tow cables. They met with some success but were hopelessly outnumbered and outgunned. The Rebels retreated, abandoning their positions in the face of devastating losses.

Han Solo and Princess Leia escaped aboard the hastily repaired *Millennium Falcon* as the base fell apart around their ears. After bringing down a walker, Luke departed from the battle in his X-wing and set a course for the swamp planet Dagobah to meet a mysterious Jedi Master named Yoda.

Luke finally returned to Hoth a decade later with his new love, Callista. There they encountered a desperate band of wampa-pelt hunters whose luck had turned and who were now holed up in the deserted Echo Base while their quarry waited hungrily outside. Though the two Jedi tried to rescue the wretched group, the wampas demonstrated their uncanny ability to work together as a killing team. Luke and Callista barely escaped from Hoth with their lives.

The fierce wampa ice creature.

ITHOR

SYSTEM: *Ottega system*
TERRAIN: Rain forests
SPECIES: Ithorians
LANGUAGE: Ithorian
POINTS OF INTEREST: *Tafanda Bay*, Falls of Dessiar

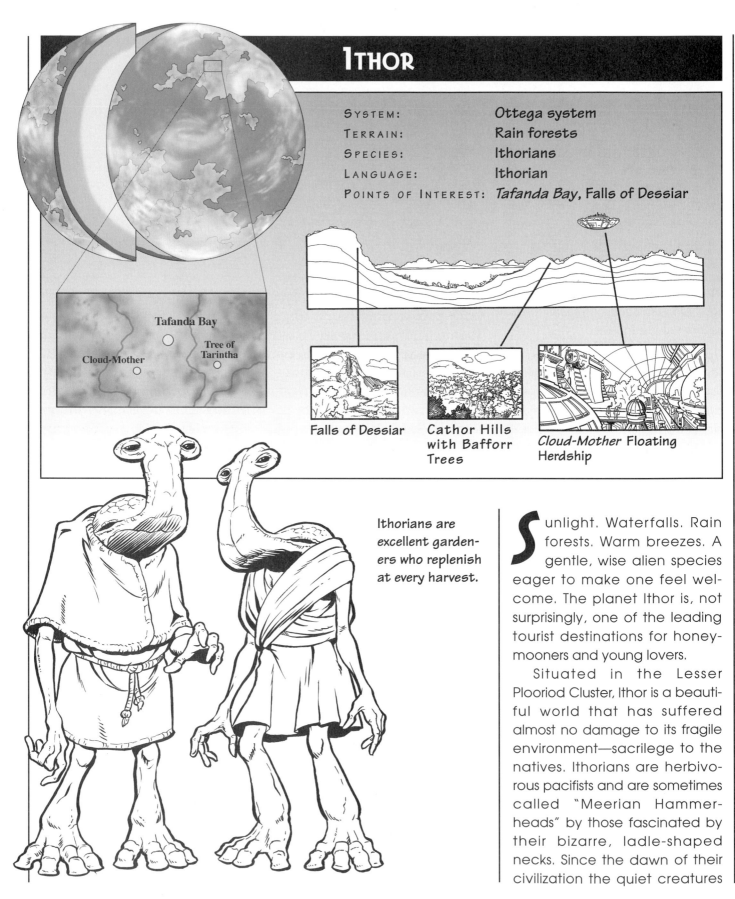

Tafanda Bay
Cloud-Mother
Tree of Tarintha

Falls of Dessiar

Cathor Hills with Bafforr Trees

Cloud-Mother Floating Herdship

Ithorians are excellent garden-ers who replenish at every harvest.

Sunlight. Waterfalls. Rain forests. Warm breezes. A gentle, wise alien species eager to make one feel welcome. The planet Ithor is, not surprisingly, one of the leading tourist destinations for honey-mooners and young lovers.

Situated in the Lesser Plooriod Cluster, Ithor is a beautiful world that has suffered almost no damage to its fragile environment—sacrilege to the natives. Ithorians are herbivorous pacifists and are sometimes called "Meerian Hammerheads" by those fascinated by their bizarre, ladle-shaped necks. Since the dawn of their civilization the quiet creatures

The lush rain forests support varied life-forms incuding manollium birds...

...and shamarok flitters.

Meet, for those off-worlders lucky enough to be part of it, is always an awe-inspiring sight.

Ithorian horticultural and cloning expertise is second to none, so Emperor Palpatine sent the Star Destroyer *Conquest* to persuade the kindhearted aliens to "donate" their secrets to the cause of Imperial science. Captain Alima knew that the Hammerheads were docile, but his ship also bristled with sixty turbolaser batteries. A blazing grove of bafforr trees would be a wonderful incentive if they proved recalcitrant.

Momaw Nadon was high priest of the *Tafanda Bay* and could not bear to see the Mother Jungle threatened. Over the vehement protests of his fellows, Nadon tearfully surrendered the accumulated knowledge of generations of Ithorian botanists. The shocked herd banished the traitor to the sand-scoured oven of Tatooine, where he was to remain until he had served his sentence.

have worshiped the Mother Jungle.

The rain forests held everything they could possibly need. The indyup trees, the donar flowers, and the bull-ferns were all part of a delicately balanced ecosystem supporting the manollium bird, the shamarok flitter, and the arrak snake. Semi-intelligent bafforr trees ruled benevolently over all the forest's organisms. Living in complete harmony with their surroundings—for every vegetable plucked, they planted two—the Ithorians were overjoyed when they discovered repulsorlift technology. Now the Mother Jungle could remain pristine forever.

The Ithorians moved to the sky, gliding casually above the bafforr treetops in "herd cities" such as *Tafanda Bay*, *Cloud-Mother*, and *Tree of Tarintha*. Every few years the floating terraria gathered at a central location for the sacred Time of Meeting, linking with each other in a delicate web of bridges and antigrav platforms. The

...arrak snakes...

The anguished exile endured the desert's harshness for years, until Captain Alima again entered his life as part of an Imperial task force looking for two escaped droids. An old score was finally settled, and Nadon returned to his beloved homeworld with a clear conscience.

Years later, during the New Republic's war with Admiral Daala, Wedge Antilles and the beautiful scientist Qwi Xux arrived on Ithor. The two assumed that Momaw Nadon's personal protection would prevent anyone from using Qwi's weapons knowledge for evil. Sadly, the loyalty of Ithorian friends proved to be no match when Kyp Durron, under influence of the dark side, erased Qwi's mind.

J'T'P'TAN

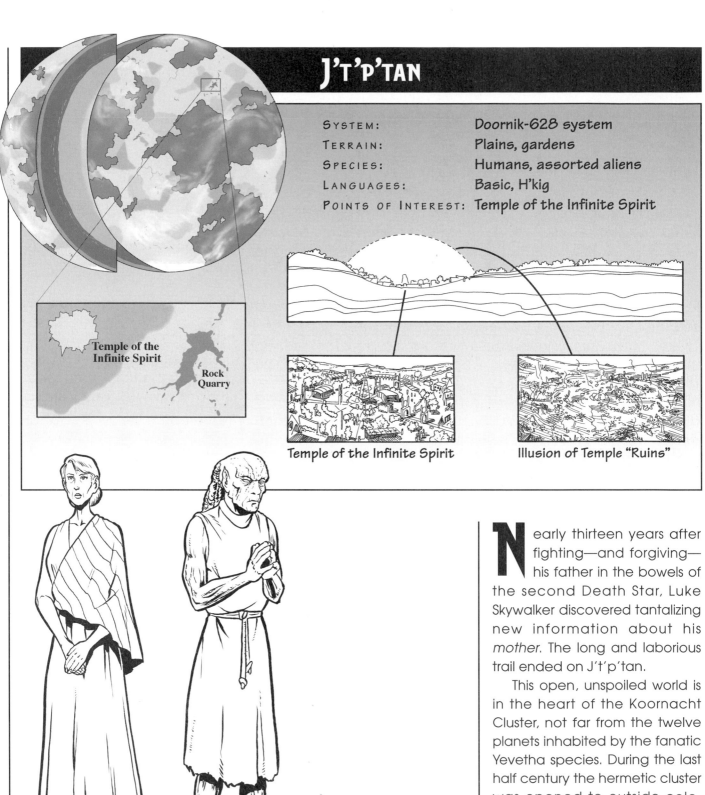

SYSTEM:	Doornik-628 system
TERRAIN:	Plains, gardens
SPECIES:	Humans, assorted aliens
LANGUAGES:	Basic, H'kig
POINTS OF INTEREST:	Temple of the Infinite Spirit

Temple of the Infinite Spirit

Rock Quarry

Temple of the Infinite Spirit

Illusion of Temple "Ruins"

Wialu of the Fallanassi (left) protected the H'kig monks (right).

Nearly thirteen years after fighting—and forgiving—his father in the bowels of the second Death Star, Luke Skywalker discovered tantalizing new information about his *mother*. The long and laborious trail ended on J't'p'tan.

This open, unspoiled world is in the heart of the Koornacht Cluster, not far from the twelve planets inhabited by the fanatic Yevetha species. During the last half century the hermetic cluster was opened to outside colonization. Among the interested settlers was a group of persecuted H'kig pilgrims.

The religious acolytes had fled their homeworld of Rishi

during a doctrinal conflict and viewed "Doornik-628E" as their promised land. They named their new home after four sacred glyphs in H'kig: "jeh," the immanent; "teh," the transcendent; "peh," the eternal; and "tan," the conscious essence. Only the last syllable was secular enough to be written out fully.

H'kig believers are hardworking, often humorless ascetics. After settling in a sheltered valley, the apostles excavated several rock quarries, using simple hand tools. They then began work on the Temple of the Infinite Spirit, a monumental stone edifice of courtyards and meditation gardens sprawling across two thousand hectares.

Quiet monks hewed stones from the soil with iron picks, hauled them away on pull-carts drawn by native tybis and lovingly fitted them into place with aching, callused fingers. The backbreaking work continued for decades—a physical tribute to the mystical essence could *never* be considered "complete."

Halfway across the galaxy another religious order was also being persecuted for its beliefs and abilities. The Fallanassi, who were able to manipulate reality by tapping into the White Current, fled their homes on Lucazec ahead of Imperial stormtroopers. Eventually they were welcomed by the peaceful H'kig commune on J't'p'tan.

Then the genocidal Yevetha began exterminating all non-

Yevethan settlements within the Koornacht Cluster. Although their lives and the lives of the H'kig were at stake, the Fallanassi would not use their power as a weapon. The Circle sisters protected the Temple from Yevethan orbital bombardment by *merging* it with the Current. Yevethan gunners saw a blackened, smoking ruin, but behind the illusion thirteen thousand H'kig continued their holy tasks in perfect safety.

Soon afterward Luke arrived on J't'p'tan with the Fallanassi woman Akanah. Akanah hoped to rejoin her sisters, and Luke—led on by her false promises—thought he would at last meet his mother. But while his companion's dreams were fulfilled, Luke's were cruelly shat-

tered. Wialu, the leader of the Fallanassi, refused to answer any questions about "Nashira" or her possible relationship to Luke Skywalker.

Undaunted, Luke continued to press the Fallanassi for help. Awed by the manner in which they had hidden the H'kig temple from outside eyes, he persuaded Wialu to trick the Yevetha by creating an illusory New Republic "phantom fleet." The tactic proved instrumental in the Republic's victory at the Battle of N'zoth.

Immediately afterward, with the Yevethan threat crushed, the Fallanassi felt they were no longer needed on J't'p'tan. Aboard the liner *Star Morning*, they departed the planet, never to return.

The native tybis is a gentle beast of burden.

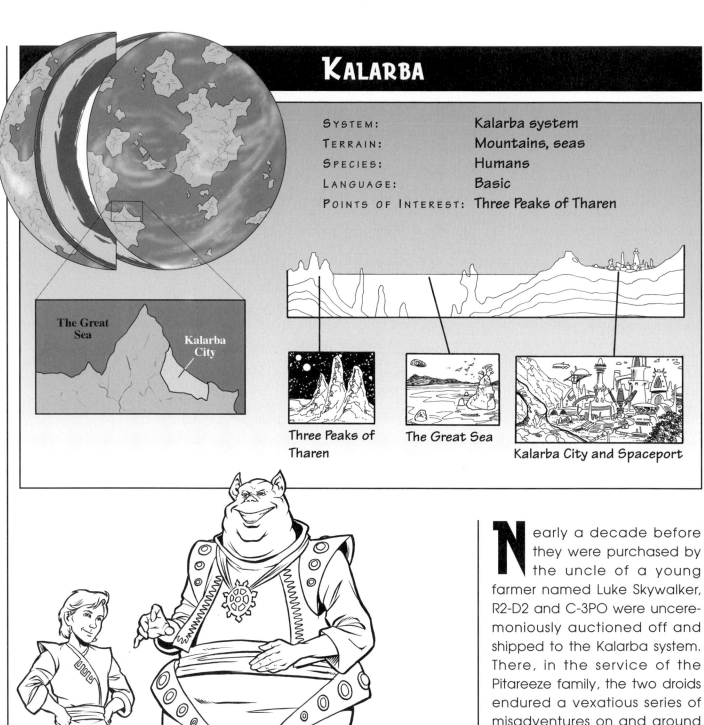

KALARBA

SYSTEM: Kalarba system
TERRAIN: Mountains, seas
SPECIES: Humans
LANGUAGE: Basic
POINTS OF INTEREST: Three Peaks of Tharen

The Great Sea

Kalarba City

Three Peaks of Tharen

The Great Sea

Kalarba City and Spaceport

Nak Pitareeze (left) had his favorite droid duo stolen by the pirate Captain Huba (right).

Nearly a decade before they were purchased by the uncle of a young farmer named Luke Skywalker, R2-D2 and C-3PO were uncere-moniously auctioned off and shipped to the Kalarba system. There, in the service of the Pitareeze family, the two droids endured a vexatious series of misadventures on and around the temperate planet.

The pleasant, largely unde-veloped world of Kalarba is near several influential systems in the Mid Rim. Human colonists settled the planet centuries ago and have since developed a high (some would say *inflated*) opinion of their self-worth. The

Kalarbans' great strength of spirit is said to be embodied in the Three Peaks of Tharen, a unique and often visited mountain range near the vast equatorial zone. Kalarba's twin moons are worth noting: Ash-covered Indobok is home to the alien B'rknaa, while high-tech Hosk is enveloped by a sprawling *Esseles*-class space station.

Artoo and Threepio were taken in by the Pitareeze family and put to work as household servants and full-time guardians for the young Pitareeze boy Nak. The prosperous family was quite kind as masters went, but Nak's relentless string of mischievous pranks threatened to unbalance poor Threepio's AA-1 VerboBrain permanently.

During their tenure the droids also worked as cooks aboard the Pitareeze family cruise ship, which took visitors on guided tours of the ancient Kalarban ancestral lands. On one occasion, as the prodigious vessel glided above the peaceful expanse of the Great Sea, it was set upon by a ragged band of swoop-riding sky pirates.

After relieving the terrified passengers of their valuables, the bandits departed, taking Artoo and Threepio with them. Captain Huba, the leader of the mangy group, had apparently developed an appreciation for the droid chefs' skill at baking a hot Stenness pie.

Threepio didn't like this at all. First he and Artoo were brought to the pirates' wretched lair in a

The vynock flourishes in atmosphere whereas its cousin, the mynock, does not.

dank cave along the rocky coastline. Then they were forced to race Ripter, one of Huba's muscle-bound enforcers, in a swoop contest, all because the thug had supposedly maligned Threepio's "honor."

With Artoo at the repulsor bike's controls—and Threepio wailing in terror—the two droids shot through the Kalarban sky, trying to reach a rocky promontory before the other racer and return with the golden medallion hanging there. Though the spirited astromech proved an able pilot, the droids won the contest when a swarm of native vynocks—planetbound cousins

of the spacegoing mynock— flew straight into Ripter's face.

The two friends soon returned to the Pitareeze family but eventually departed from Kalarba. While visiting Hosk, they foiled the plans of the villainous Olag Greck by preventing the station's destruction, and Unit Zed (the robotic head of Hosk security) deputized the two heroes on the spot. Zed convinced his new lieutenants to help him pursue Greck to the lawless smugglers' moon of Nar Shaddaa. The droids left Kalarba behind, but their adventures were just beginning.

KASHYYYK

SYSTEM:
Kashyyyk system

TERRAIN:
Wroshyr forests

SPECIES:
Wookiees

LANGUAGE:
Shyriiwook

POINTS OF INTEREST:
Wookiee tree villages

Rwookrrorro

Nursery Ring

Rwookrrorro

Shadow Forest

It is unwise to upset a Wookiee.

Kashyyyk, the home planet of the Wookiees, boasts one of the most unusual—and lethal—ecosystems in the galaxy. Awe-inspiring wroshyr trees cover its surface, stretching several kilometers from the planet's sheltered surface to its wispy cloud layer.

The cutthroat struggle for survival began eons ago on the planet's surface; species that could climb higher, such as the ancestors of Wookiees, did so. The creatures that remained either evolved deadly defenses or became extinct. The survivors now thrive in the towering wroshyr forests, and peculiar plants and animals fill every pos-

The forest depths are home to the flesh-shredding katarn...

levels, inhabiting extensive, technically sophisticated cities. These engineering marvels hang kilometers above the ground with nothing but wroshyr branches to support them. Liftcars held by unbreakable kshyy vines carry Wookiees from one level to the next, while imported banthas and multilegged sureggies serve as beasts of burden.

Wookiees have long feuded with the reptilian Trandoshans, who inhabit another planet in the same star system. In fact, it was a Trandoshan official who convinced the Empire to exploit the powerful species as slave labor. One Wookiee, Chewbacca, was saved from slavers by a young soldier named Han Solo, and Chewie swore his people's traditional "life debt" to his rescuer. The two became constant companions and fast friends.

Five years after the Battle of Endor, Leia Organa Solo went to Kashyyyk with Chewbacca to hide from the Noghri strike teams that had been trying to kidnap her for Grand Admiral Thrawn. The steel-gray aliens soon found her in the city of Rwookrrorro. Leia tried to escape beneath Rwookrrorro, clinging tightly to Chewbacca, but the Noghri followed in a hovercar. Desperate, Leia tied her lightsaber to a kshyy vine and swung the weapon into the

...the smothering protoplasmic slug...

hovercar's underside. Her attackers plunged into the misty depths.

Over fourteen years later Leia and Han's twin children, Jacen and Jaina, visited Kashyyyk with Lowbacca, Chewbacca's nephew and fellow Jedi student. The friends were caught in the middle of a full-scale battle when the Second Imperium raided Thikkiiana City's computer factory. Imperial pursuit forced them into the dangerous lower levels of the wroshyrs, but they survived the frightening ordeal.

sible niche in the vertical environment.

The millions of years of competitive evolution created what many have called a "layered death trap" amid Kashyyyk's wroshyrs. Visitors are generally safe as long as they remain among the highest of the interlaced branches, but the threat steadily increases as one descends toward the surface. Carnivorous syren plants, flesh-shredding katarns, poisonous webweavers, and smothering protoplasmic slugs are just a few of the known dangers. Below a certain level, sunlight can no longer penetrate the leafy canopy; toothy bioluminescent predators are the only visible things in the utter darkness. Very few have touched the soil of Kashyyyk and lived to tell about it.

Wookiees have established a civilized society in the highest

...and the carnivorous syren plant.

KESSEL

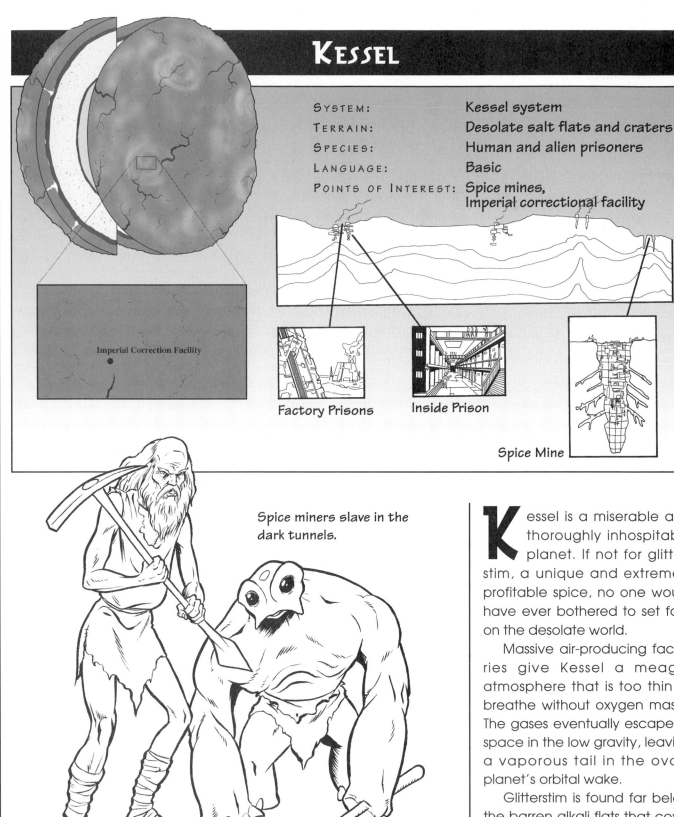

SYSTEM:	Kessel system
TERRAIN:	Desolate salt flats and craters
SPECIES:	Human and alien prisoners
LANGUAGE:	Basic
POINTS OF INTEREST:	Spice mines, Imperial correctional facility

Imperial Correction Facility

Factory Prisons

Inside Prison

Spice Mine

Spice miners slave in the dark tunnels.

Kessel is a miserable and thoroughly inhospitable planet. If not for glitter-stim, a unique and extremely profitable spice, no one would have ever bothered to set foot on the desolate world.

Massive air-producing factories give Kessel a meager atmosphere that is too thin to breathe without oxygen masks. The gases eventually escape to space in the low gravity, leaving a vaporous tail in the ovoid planet's orbital wake.

Glitterstim is found far below the barren alkali flats that cover the surface. The fibrous, photoactive spice, primarily used for therapeutic purposes, induces

The bogey, a glittering creature in the spice mines.

a telepathic boost when ingested, and it can quickly turn a casual user into a hollow addict. Few "glit-biters" realize that their daily fix was once a strand in a spice spider's cobweb spun by the nightmarish arachnids to snare passing bogeys.

For years the Empire had a stranglehold on Kessel and the spice industry. Criminals and political prisoners were forced to toil in the infamous spice mines, and the planet's moon boasted a fully stocked Imperial garrison. Crime lords such as Jabba the Hutt obtained glitterstim from corrupt officials, and the smugglers who made this "Kessel Run" often argued over who could fly the route in the fastest time and shortest distance.

After the Empire lost the Battle of Endor, a Rybet prison official named Moruth Doole seized total control of the planet. Three years later the pilots of Rogue Squadron helped free members of the Black Sun crime syndicate from Kessel to assist in the capture of Coruscant.

Seven years after Endor, Han Solo and Chewbacca were sent on a diplomatic mission to reestablish contact with Kessel. They were captured by a nervous Doole and forced to work in the spice mines, where they met a young prisoner named Kyp Durron.

The three of them escaped from Kessel on a stolen shuttle and flew into the Maw, a nearby black hole cluster, where they stumbled across a secret Imperial weapons-research facility. Captured by the ruthless Admiral Daala, the group managed to escape aboard the experimental Sun Crusher. When Daala pursued them out of the Maw, her ships ran straight into Doole's ragtag Kessel fleet, which she promptly decimated.

Later a New Republic strike force attempted to capture Daala's Maw Installation. Their soldiers met with little resistance, but the Installation's weapons scientists chose to flee aboard a fully operational Death Star prototype. The befuddled researchers mistakenly destroyed Kessel's garrison moon with the weapon when they attempted to demolish Kessel itself.

Kyp Durron, aboard the Sun Crusher, knew that the galaxy had to be rid of the deadly battle station. He suicidally accelerated his vessel toward the nearest black hole while the Death Star gave chase. As Kyp escaped to safety in a message pod, both weapons were swallowed by the Maw forever.

Lando Calrissian and Mara Jade soon became business partners and secured the planet's lucrative mines, using supercooled worker droids to dig the spice. It is unclear what the future holds for Kessel, but the galaxy's hunger for glitterstim guarantees that it will never be ignored.

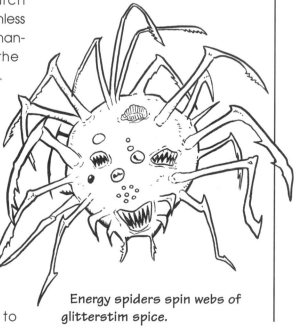

Energy spiders spin webs of glitterstim spice.

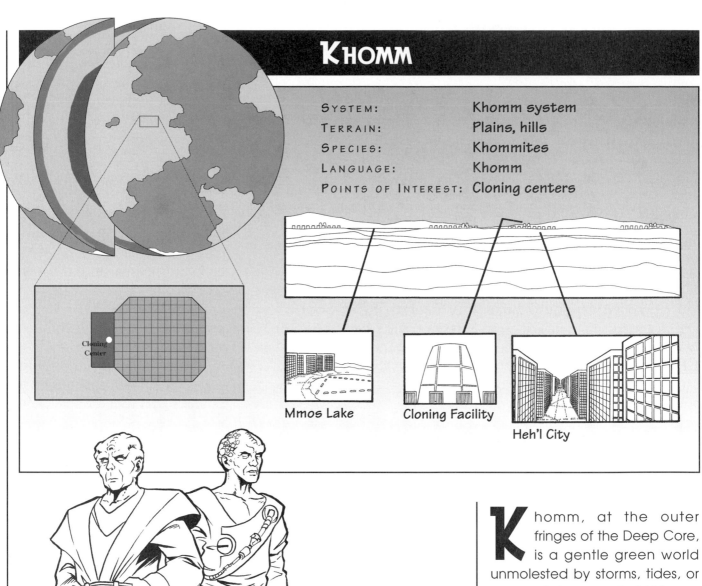

KHOMM

SYSTEM: Khomm system
TERRAIN: Plains, hills
SPECIES: Khommites
LANGUAGE: Khomm
POINTS OF INTEREST: Cloning centers

Cloning Center

Mmos Lake   Cloning Facility   Heh'l City

Kaell 116 (left) and Dorsk 82 (right) are typical Khommite clones.

Khomm, at the outer fringes of the Deep Core, is a gentle green world unmolested by storms, tides, or seasonal changes. Amid kilometers of rolling hills lie dozens of spotless, efficiently planned grid cities whose inhabitants are unfailingly polite, intelligent, and peaceful. It is little wonder, then, that those who touch down on Khomm find it insufferably *dull*.

The humanoid aliens of Khomm live in a society in which total conformity is the guiding principle. Innovation and discord are concepts so foreign to their minds that they can scarcely be *conceived*, and it has been this way for over a thousand years. A millennium ago the Khommites decided that their culture had reached perfection. Freezing development at that level, they used the science of cloning to create perfect duplicates of each citizen. Each new generation would look just like the one before it, and their society would never change.

The unique alien nature of the Khomm cloning process allowed the planet to escape the sweeping genetic restrictions imposed on the galaxy after the Clone Wars. Even animals, such as the stilt-legged strider, were genetically engineered for beauty and docility. Each new Khommite knew its place and performed the same jobs as its "parent." The Force, however, had little regard for Khomm tradition.

To his shock, the eighty-first clone of Dorsk showed an unexpected ability to control and wield the powers of the Jedi. Dorsk 81 honed his new skills during a year of intensive training at Luke Skywalker's Jedi academy and, upon graduation, returned to Khomm with his friend Kyp Durron.

Dorsk 81 was welcomed as a hero by the cheering throngs—he was the first Khommite to do anything heroic in over a thousand years. But Dorsks 80 and 82—his genetic forebear and descendant, respectively—wanted the Jedi Knight to return to his former duties at the local cloning center. Having experi-

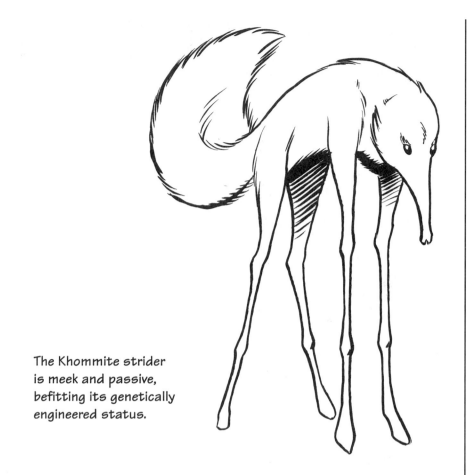

The Khommite strider is meek and passive, befitting its genetically engineered status.

enced variety, Dorsk 81 was unable to return to mediocrity. He and Kyp left the planet to investigate a suspicious Imperial buildup in the Deep Core.

The two Jedi got in over their heads. Though they escaped, Admiral Daala identified one of the meddlers as a Khommite. Reasoning that Khomm must be a supporter of the New Republic, she ordered her flotilla of Victory Star Destroyers to bombard the planet as part of an orchestrated campaign of terror.

Kyp and Dorsk 81 tried to warn Khomm of the coming attack, but nothing could wake the clones from their placid security. City-leader Kaell 116,

when exhorted to declare a state of emergency, promised only to "consider the matter." Khomm was a helpless target when the Imperial battlefleet arrived.

The perfect gridwork cities were left in ruins. Once-gleaming cloning centers were breached by concussion missiles; boxlike homes vanished in plumes of oily smoke. Though thousands tragically lost their lives, Admiral Daala's attack might just be the provocation needed to rouse Khomm from its centuries of complacency.

KORRIBAN

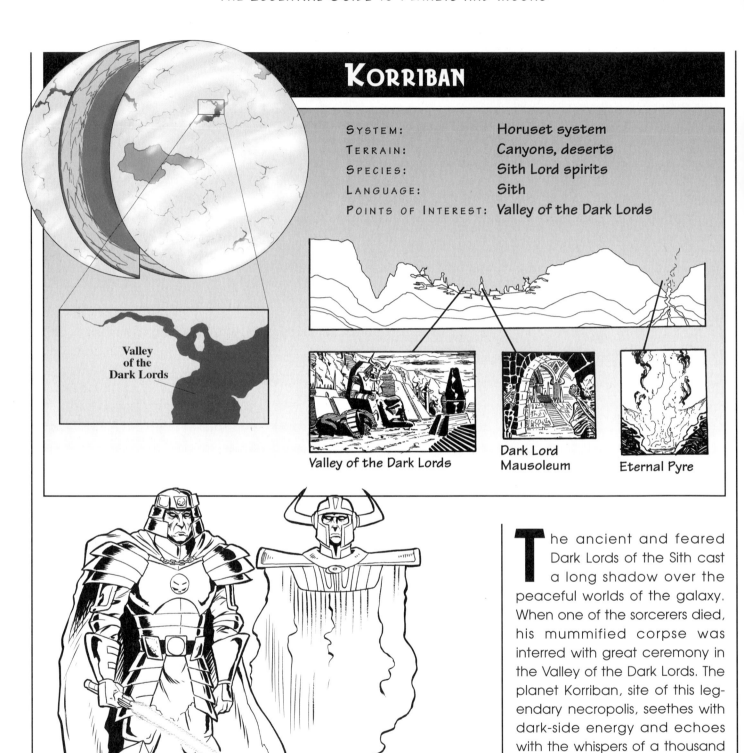

SYSTEM:	Horuset system
TERRAIN:	Canyons, deserts
SPECIES:	Sith Lord spirits
LANGUAGE:	Sith
POINTS OF INTEREST:	Valley of the Dark Lords

Valley
of the
Dark Lords

Valley of the Dark Lords

Dark Lord
Mausoleum

Eternal Pyre

Freedon Nadd (left) and the spirit of a Dark Lord of the Sith (right).

The ancient and feared Dark Lords of the Sith cast a long shadow over the peaceful worlds of the galaxy. When one of the sorcerers died, his mummified corpse was interred with great ceremony in the Valley of the Dark Lords. The planet Korriban, site of this legendary necropolis, seethes with dark-side energy and echoes with the whispers of a thousand ghosts.

For generations, during the height of their corrupt empire, the Sith Lords built intricately detailed temples, erected towering effigies of themselves, and carved statues of fanciful beasts into the sand-colored rock walls of the sloping valley. A funeral was a rare and elaborate occasion attended by hundreds of Sith slaves and dozens of ambitious rulers, each hoping to be the next Sith Lord. After the mourners departed and silence once again settled over Korriban, the restless life essence departed from the desiccated cadaver and haunted its sepulchral crypt.

The fabulous riches encased in each mausoleum lured legions of grave robbers over the years. Without exception the greedy plunderers got the messy deaths they deserved. The tomb defenses are formidable—ambulatory skeletons rise from the dust at the slightest footfall, while guardian creatures called tuk'ata prowl the ruins, waiting for an opportunity to pounce.

Nearly four thousand years in the past, after the defeat of the Sith empire by the forces of the Old Republic, a young Jedi Knight named Exar Kun arrived on Korriban. Eager to learn more about the long-departed Sith Lords, he agreed to follow the guidance of the Dark Jedi Freedon Nadd's incorporeal specter.

Exar Kun entered one tomb to inspect a swirling crystal pillar that held the wailing spirits of fallen Jedi Masters in eternal confinement. As he stepped forward, Nadd shattered the crystal into a million fragments, releasing a surge of energy that buried Kun beneath an avalanche of loose rock.

Pinned by a mountain of stone, his body broken and bleeding, Exar Kun knew he was dying. But the spirit of Freedon Nadd offered a way out; if he would embrace the dark side of the Force, his body would be healed.

Kun's hunger for life was too great—he accepted. Though he vowed never to fall to temptation again, it was too late. He had become an agent of evil. The devastating Sith War soon followed, instigated by Kun's tainted hand.

Millennia later Emperor Palpatine discovered the planet Korriban and its ghostly Sith spirits. After learning that the ancient temples focused and magnified his dark-side abilities, he made regular visits to his "place of power." Palpatine visited Korriban for the last time some seven years after the Battle of Endor in a fruitless effort to halt the genetic decay of his last remaining clone body.

The guardian tuk'ata inhabits and protects the Dark Lord tombs.

KOTHLIS

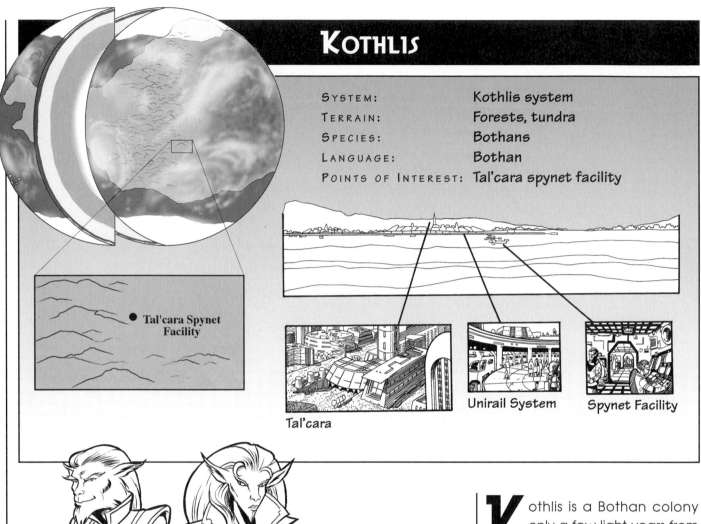

SYSTEM:	Kothlis system
TERRAIN:	Forests, tundra
SPECIES:	Bothans
LANGUAGE:	Bothan
POINTS OF INTEREST:	Tal'cara spynet facility

Tal'cara Spynet Facility

Tal'cara

Unirail System

Spynet Facility

Bothans, known for their reputed spy net, also find enjoyment engaging in politics.

Kothlis is a Bothan colony only a few light-years from the furry aliens' home-world of Bothawui. It is more rustic, remote, and run-down than its sister planet—a fertile breeding ground for under-the-table deals.

The wooded, chilly planet was purchased years ago by Raynor Mining Enterprises, which planned to build a monolithic corporate headquarters on its surface. The engineers had finished laying a colossal ferro-crete city-slab when the local ore veins unexpectedly ran dry. Bankrupt, Raynor sold the world to the Bothans at a loss, which some say was the Bothans,

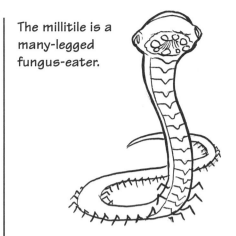

The millitile is a many-legged fungus-eater.

intent all along.

The Bothan settlers built on Raynor's existing foundation, creating the functional, unpresuming capital city of Tal'cara. A subterranean unirail tube connects most points in the dingy metropolis, from the expansive warehouse district to the opulent compound of the Imperial Consul-General. One of Kothlis's most noted citizens, Borsk Fey'lya, joined the Rebel Alliance with his sizable Bothan faction soon after the Battle of Yavin.

Away from the lights of Tal'cara, Kothlis becomes less civilized and more dangerous. Careless adventurers risk being trampled by a stampeding ganjuko or dying of exposure on the frost-pitted tundra. Menacing predators lurk in the dark gankto forests, whose fungus-covered trunks give off the ubiquitous odor (noticed by every visitor to Kothlis) of "moldy cheese."

Several months after the Rebels evacuated their Hoth base, Bothan spies stole a computer core containing the secret location of the Empire's second Death Star. Luke Skywalker escorted the prize to Kothlis, where the best data slicers on the planet began decoding the information in an isolated safe house.

Without warning, a knot of heavily armed Barabel mercenaries blasted through the room's reinforced durasteel doors. A Bothan tech grabbed the computer core and ran, but the Barabels had their eyes on a different target entirely. The grinning reptiles surrounded Luke, stunned him, and dumped him in a hidden stronghold a hundred kilometers away.

While the bounty hunters schemed to sell him to the highest bidder, Luke drew on the Force to slip from his cell. Heavy firepower—courtesy of Lando Calrissian and the *Millennium Falcon*—allowed the young Rebel to escape from Kothlis.

The Emperor, however, had learned of Skywalker's capture. Palpatine dispatched Darth Vader to the Bothan colony to collect the Jedi but also to make it appear that the Empire was concerned about the "loss" of its computer core.

Vader's *Executor* nearly

Ganjukos are hunted for their prized beaks, which are then carved into expensive daggers.

captured the *Falcon* in an asteroid trail, but the ramshackle smuggling ship safely leapt to light-speed. Thwarted, Vader destroyed the nearby space station *Kothlis II* and an illegal shadowport on the planet's second moon. Surveying the devastation, Rebel agents swallowed the Emperor's bait. *The stolen data must be very valuable indeed.*

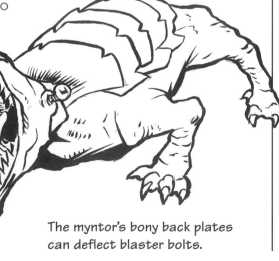

The myntor's bony back plates can deflect blaster bolts.

KUAT

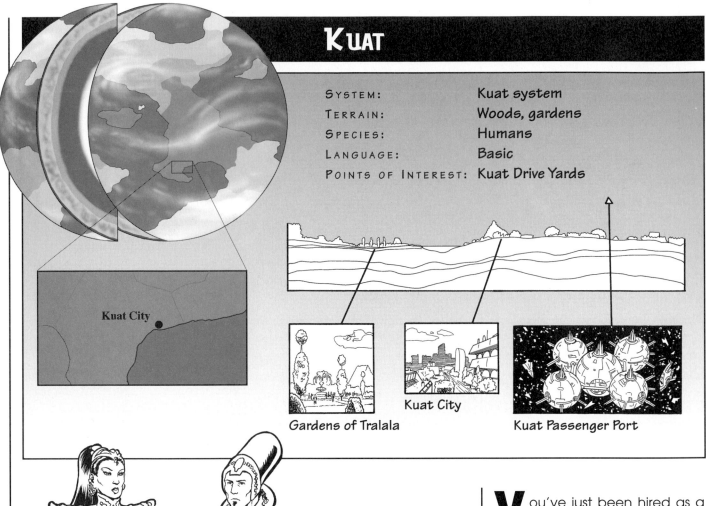

SYSTEM:	Kuat system
TERRAIN:	Woods, gardens
SPECIES:	Humans
LANGUAGE:	Basic
POINTS OF INTEREST:	Kuat Drive Yards

Kuat City

Gardens of Tralala

Kuat City

Kuat Passenger Port

A Kuat aristocrat and her *telbun*.

You've just been hired as a laser welder at the sprawling Kuat Drive Yards. Your first job? Assemble massive Imperial Star Destroyers with diligence and pride. Your second? Don't get lost.

It's no easy task. The endless stardocks encircle the system like a metallic corona, dwarfing the small green planet that lies near the peaceful center. Billions of beings are employed in the space surrounding Kuat, but almost none of them ever set foot on the terraformed world itself, with its manicured gardens and docile animals. Instead, three colossal space stations (one for passengers, one for commercial freight, and one for the Imperial military) handle all arrivals and departures and keep out any unwanted visitors.

Kuat Drive Yards, commonly known as KDY, was the primary producer of the Empire's fearsome *Imperial-* and *Super*-class Star Destroyers. Although the respectable Fondor yards won the contract to build Darth Vader's *Executor*, Kuat execs made sure that all future Super Star Destroyers had *their* logo on the hull plating. In fact, a duplicate *Executor* was built at Kuat but was soon rechristened *Lusankya* and interred on Coruscant to serve as Emperor Palpatine's secret getaway vehicle.

During his reign Palpatine oversaw the largest military buildup in galactic history, making the great Kuat merchant houses astonishingly wealthy and notoriously insular. Often composed of a single extended aristocratic family, each house long ago devised a system to prevent the unfortunate political alliances that sometimes spring from an ill-advised marriage.

When a Kuat house patriarch desires an heir, he purchases a *telbun*—a young male of the middle classes who has been raised from birth as a breeder. *Telbuns* are trained to excel in athletics, culture, mental acuity, and good looks. If they are selected, their families are handsomely compensated.

After a *telbun* sires his mis-

Drebin are herbivores providing compost for the native gardens.

tress's child, he remains with the noble family as a tutor and guardian but is *never* considered a blood relation. On the contrary, *telbuns* are ordinarily treated as chattel, swathed in heavy robes, and forced to obey their pampered mistresses's every whim.

After its shocking loss at Endor the Empire could not afford to surrender its most important manufacturing center. Palpatine's successors defended the Kuat system with fifteen Star Destroyers and rigged the stardocks with explosives in case it became necessary to scuttle them. This only

reinforced the New Republic's desire to capture Coruscant—the Imperial capital—as soon as possible.

Rogue Squadron was sent on an undercover sabotage mission to Imperial City. Pilot Erisi Dlarit posed as Ris Darsk, a bored, wealthy member of the Kuati aristocracy. Fellow Rogue Corran Horn passed as her submissive *telbun*. His very name—"Darsk Ristel"—revealed his status as mere baggage. Once they had successfully cleared starport customs, Corran was grateful to shed his ridiculous disguise and continue with the mission.

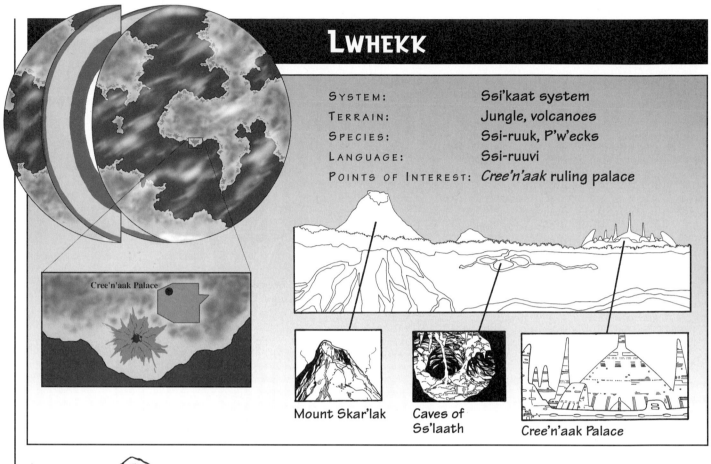

LWHEKK

SYSTEM: **Ssi'kaat system**
TERRAIN: **Jungle, volcanoes**
SPECIES: **Ssi-ruuk, P'w'ecks**
LANGUAGE: **Ssi-ruuvi**
POINTS OF INTEREST: *Cree'n'aak* **ruling palace**

Cree'n'aak Palace

Mount Skar'lak

Caves of Ss'laath

Cree'n'aak Palace

Ssi-ruuk (left) rule Lwhekk while the P'w'ecks (right) serve their masters.

In an isolated star cluster on the galaxy's fringe lies Lwhekk, the bustling heart of the Ssi-ruuvi Imperium. The Ssi-ruuk—intelligent, warm-blooded saurians—evolved on Lwhekk and eventually settled many of its closest planets.

Ssi-ruuk society is separated into rigid castes; blue-scaled members dominate politics (headed by His Potency the Shreeftut), and russet-scaled individuals make up the bulk of the military. The lowest and most despised creatures on Lwhekk are the P'w'ecks, a dull-witted servant race. Both races' chief food source consists of small multilegged fft lizards.

The Ssi-ruuks' religious beliefs dictated that if a Ssi-ruuk was killed while away from Lwhekk or another consecrated homeworld, that individual would be doomed to wander the stars forever. Unwilling to risk such a dire fate, the aliens developed a method of waging war that would not put them at personal risk.

"Entechment," when the process was perfected, transferred the life energy of a P'w'eck slave into the command circuitry of a two-meter battle droid. Sacrificing countless P'w'ecks, the Ssi-ruuk emerged from their star cluster with hordes of the compact and deadly fighters. Strikes against human outpost worlds such as G'rho resulted in the capture of the Force-sensitive boy Dev Sibwarra and led to a surprising discovery: human life energies were perfectly suited for the entechment process.

Emperor Palpatine recognized the threat and opportunity presented by these merciless conquerors. Secretly contacting the Shreeftut, the Emperor clinched a shrewd deal: he would trade thousands of Imperial citizens in exchange for his own supply of battle droids. It seems likely that once he possessed their secrets, Palpatine would have double-crossed the Ssi-ruuk and made a move against Lwhekk.

When Palpatine was killed at Endor, the Ssi-ruuk advance strike force, aboard the flagship

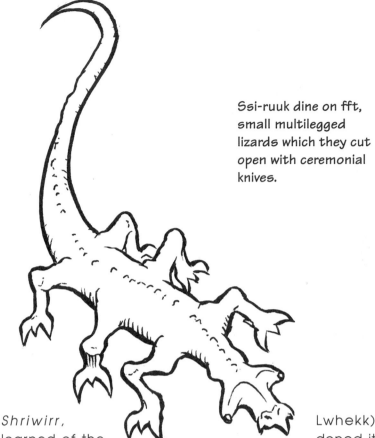

Ssi-ruuk dine on fft, small multilegged lizards which they cut open with ceremonial knives.

Shriwirr, learned of the death instantly through Dev Sibwarra's Force connection. The deal was off, and the Ssi-ruuk got ready to conquer the galaxy.

Their first target was the Outer Rim planet of Bakura, which would be a stepping-stone to the populous Core Worlds. Admiral Ivpikkis led his fleet in successful skirmishes against Bakura's Imperial defenders, but the arrival of a Rebel Alliance force—specifically, a Jedi Knight named Luke Skywalker—turned the tide against the invaders. Skywalker was nearly single-handedly responsible for capturing the *Shriwirr,* as its Ssi-ruuk crew (terrified of being killed away from

Lwhekk) abandoned its flagship before the Jedi's swinging lightsaber. The remaining ships went into full retreat.

Over the next few years the New Republic made numerous forays into Ssi-ruuk territory. Seven years after Bakura, Mon Mothma displayed their findings on a holographic galaxy map to the Caridan ambassador. "This is what remains of the Ssi-ruuk Imperium," she said, pointing to a handful of dots, "though we have not yet fully explored their worlds." Although the immediate threat from Lwhekk seems to have ended, the New Republic can never afford to let down its guard against such a formidable enemy.

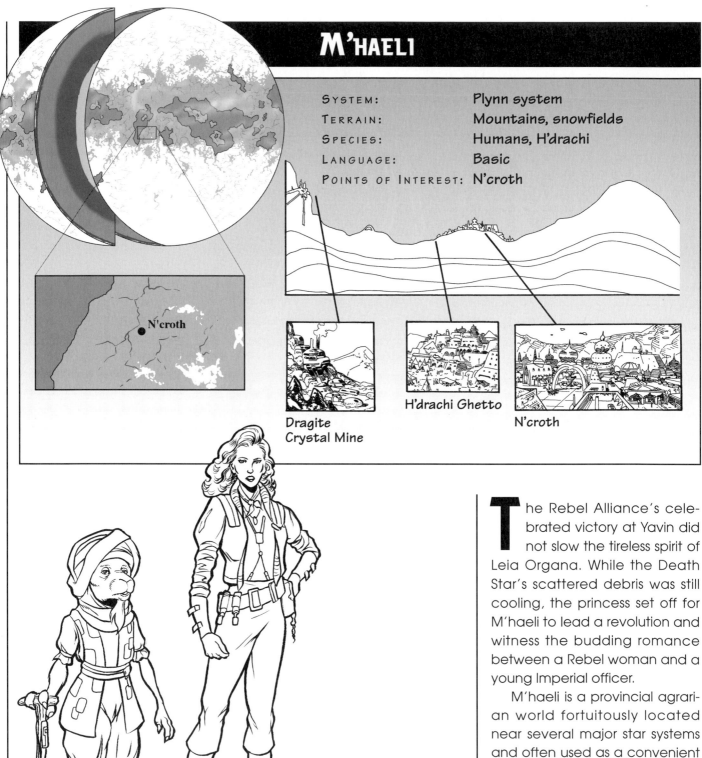

M'HAELI

SYSTEM:	Plynn system
TERRAIN:	Mountains, snowfields
SPECIES:	Humans, H'drachi
LANGUAGE:	Basic
POINTS OF INTEREST:	N'croth

N'croth

Dragite
Crystal Mine

H'drachi Ghetto

N'croth

Ch'no (left), a native
H'drachi, with Mora, the
only survivor of the
royal family.

The Rebel Alliance's cele-brated victory at Yavin did not slow the tireless spirit of Leia Organa. While the Death Star's scattered debris was still cooling, the princess set off for M'haeli to lead a revolution and witness the budding romance between a Rebel woman and a young Imperial officer.

M'haeli is a provincial agrari-an world fortuitously located near several major star systems and often used as a convenient refueling stop. Human colonists and the native H'drachi have lived for generations with only the most minimal interaction between their species. A ruling human monarchy was estab-

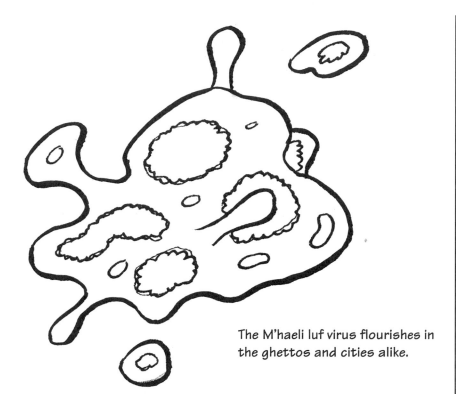

The M'haeli luf virus flourishes in the ghettos and cities alike.

lished in the capital of N'croth, but the H'drachi remained uninvolved. The withdrawn aliens had the ability to read the "timestream"—the ever-changing flux of probabilities and possible futures—and used it to justify their apathy even after the Empire took control.

An Imperial invasion force led by Governor Grigor shelled the governmental palace into ruins and erected an imposing slate-gray garrison. The royal family was ruthlessly exterminated, but the infant princess Mora went unnoticed in a loose pile of rubble. Fortunately, a kind-hearted H'drachi seer adopted the defenseless human child and raised her as his own. Governor Grigor grew crueler and more corrupt each year and secretly constructed an ille-

gal dragite mine in the snowy wastes of the D'olop range.

Grigor's superiors suspected that the governor was lining his own pockets at the Empire's expense and sent the flight officer Ranulf Trommer to spy on his dubious activities. Ranulf, operating undercover, was ordered to infiltrate a local Rebel cell led by Princess Leia. Once there, he found himself falling in love with Mora, now a beautiful, strong-willed woman of eighteen.

The young Imperial was torn. He had willingly served the Empire all his life, but the Rebels were courageously fighting Grigor's brutality to make M'haeli a better place for all. Hoping to reconcile his conflicting loyalties, Ranulf called in a force of loyal Imperials to arrest Grigor for operating an unau-

thorized mining complex. Once the immoral governor was removed, he reasoned, proper Imperial administration would eliminate the *need* for a local rebellion.

Ranulf's idealism was cruelly shattered when the Empire showed its true face. An invasion force of AT-ATs forced the Rebels from their hidden base at Red Rock; the only safe place for them now was off-world. Before leaving M'haeli with Princess Leia, Ranulf and Mora destroyed the dragite mine with a cluster of thermal charges.

Grigor was gone, but M'haeli was crawling with more Imperial troops than ever. This time, though, the situation was changed—the H'drachi elders, inspired by recent events, agreed to join the Rebellion. For once, the timestream's destinies pointed to a single, inevitable outcome: total victory over the Empire.

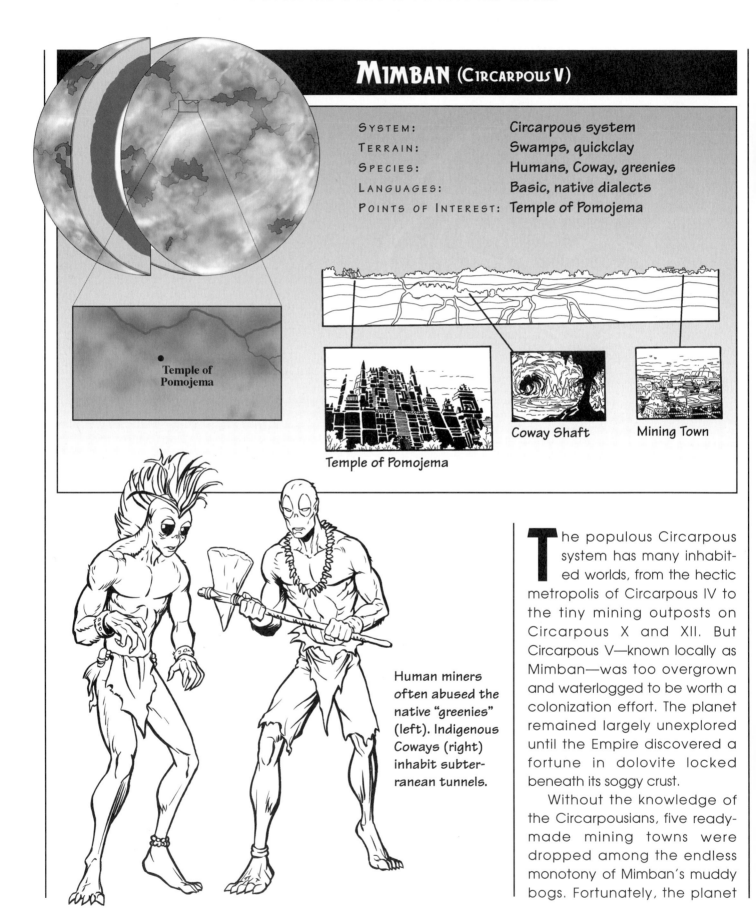

MIMBAN (CIRCARPOUS V)

SYSTEM:	Circarpous system
TERRAIN:	Swamps, quickclay
SPECIES:	Humans, Coway, greenies
LANGUAGES:	Basic, native dialects
POINTS OF INTEREST:	Temple of Pomojema

Temple of
Pomojema

Temple of Pomojema

Coway Shaft

Mining Town

Human miners often abused the native "greenies" (left). Indigenous Coways (right) inhabit subterranean tunnels.

The populous Circarpous system has many inhabited worlds, from the hectic metropolis of Circarpous IV to the tiny mining outposts on Circarpous X and XII. But Circarpous V—known locally as Mimban—was too overgrown and waterlogged to be worth a colonization effort. The planet remained largely unexplored until the Empire discovered a fortune in dolovite locked beneath its soggy crust.

Without the knowledge of the Circarpousians, five ready-made mining towns were dropped among the endless monotony of Mimban's muddy bogs. Fortunately, the planet

The wandrella sucks prey into its tooth-lined maw and can only be injured with a hit on its eyespot.

was crawling with intelligent (albeit primitive) life, and stone temples and shrines were in abundance. Captain-Supervisor Grammel, the Imperial tyrant ordered to squeeze a profit from this stinking mudpit, converted the abandoned ziggurats into offices, holding cells, and swamp-crawler garages.

Some of the native species, such as the pathetic "greenies," staggered into town to beg for gulps of alcohol; others remained aloof and mistrustful, hiding away deep behind Mimban's impenetrable foliage.

Not long after the destruction of the first Death Star, Luke Skywalker and Leia Organa were dispatched to Circarpous IV to convince its insurgent underground to throw in

with the Rebel Alliance. Unfortunately, a starship malfunction forced them to ditch on Mimban. Without a new vessel, they'd be stuck on the miserable marsh world forever. With R2-D2 and C-3PO in tow, the two disguised Rebels tried to infiltrate the Imperial mining town.

The ruse didn't last long. Captain-Supervisor Grammel captured them both and threw them behind bars. When word got out about just *who* Grammel had imprisoned, Lord Darth Vader ordered his *Executor* to head for Mimban at top speed.

With help from an old woman named Halla, Luke and Leia were soon in the thick of the jungle, tracking down a

gemstone called the Kaiburr crystal. This iridescent jewel, ensconced within the crumbling Temple of Pomojema, was rumored to have an astonishing ability to focus and magnify the Force.

Mimban, however, seemed determined to protect its treasures. A mammoth, doughy wandrella rose from the sludge and tried to suck the travelers into its greasy maw. Luke and Leia survived by going underground, but they were soon set upon by an amoebic cave creature and a horde of barbaric Coway tribesmen. To win their freedom, Luke defeated the Coway champion in single combat by drawing on his fledgling Jedi skills.

At last they were back on the trail. But Darth Vader could also sense the power of the Kaiburr crystal and confronted his progeny within the vine-covered sanctum of Pomojema. The Sith Lord was more than a match for two young, exhausted opponents. Only a trick of fate—or the Force—saved Luke and Leia's lives.

The weary Rebels left, determined to steal a ship—and this time to do it *right*. They were *very* late for a meeting on Circarpous IV.

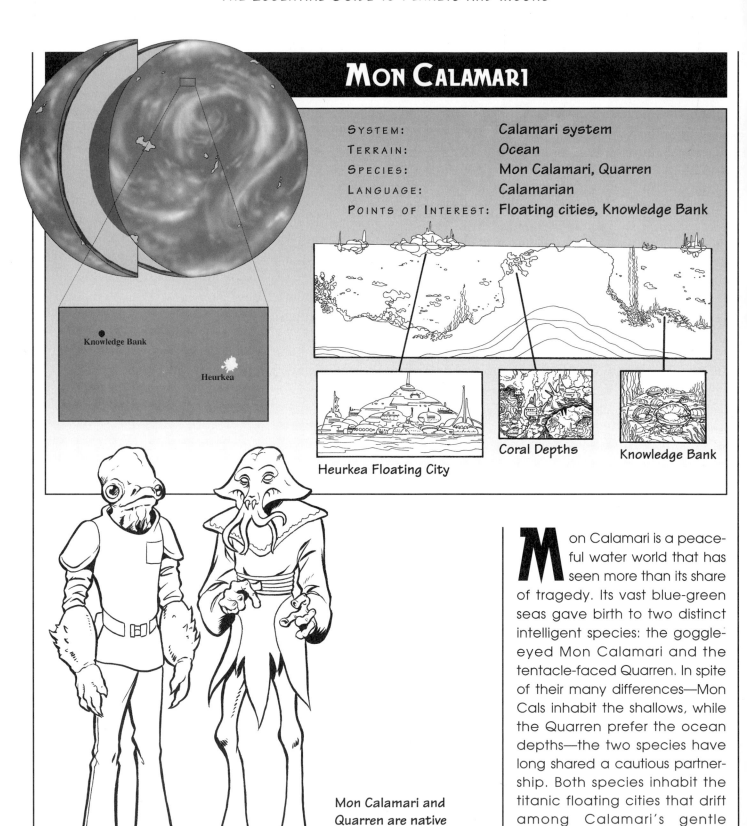

MON CALAMARI

SYSTEM:	Calamari system
TERRAIN:	Ocean
SPECIES:	Mon Calamari, Quarren
LANGUAGE:	Calamarian
POINTS OF INTEREST:	Floating cities, Knowledge Bank

Knowledge Bank

Heurkea

Heurkea Floating City

Coral Depths

Knowledge Bank

Mon Calamari and Quarren are native species, often mistrustful of one another.

Mon Calamari is a peaceful water world that has seen more than its share of tragedy. Its vast blue-green seas gave birth to two distinct intelligent species: the goggle-eyed Mon Calamari and the tentacle-faced Quarren. In spite of their many differences—Mon Cals inhabit the shallows, while the Quarren prefer the ocean depths—the two species have long shared a cautious partnership. Both species inhabit the titanic floating cities that drift among Calamari's gentle waves.

The waters teem with life, from the simple glurpfish to the swift and deadly krakana.

Within a submerged cove lies the planet's greatest treasure—the Knowledge Bank, a community of intelligent mollusks who maintain a history of every event that has ever transpired in the world's seas.

The Mon Cals' spirit of discovery inspired them to leave the oceans. Constructing immense, organic-looking starliners, they begin exploring their sector of space. Unfortunately, they were soon forced to deal with the militaristic, antialien Empire.

The Empire saw Mon Calamari as a target ripe for conquest and enslavement. When its inhabitants resisted, Imperial ships decimated three floating cities, killing millions. It is said that a Quarren lowered the planet's defenses just before the attack, a rumor that has done little to improve interspecies relations on the world.

The Mon Cals continued to yearn for freedom and managed to drive off the Imperial occupation force, using nothing more than simple hand weapons and their iron determination. Eventually they openly joined the Rebel Alliance, becoming what many observers have called "the spirit of the Rebellion." Mon Calamari starliners were converted into warships. Ackbar, a former slave rescued from Grand Moff Tarkin at Eriadu, was named Admiral of the Rebel fleet. Ackbar and other Mon Cals helped cripple the Empire in the triumphant Battle of Endor.

The krakana will *eat* anything it finds.

For six years after the battle Calamari's orbital shipyards supplied the victorious New Republic with naval vessels, but then the resurrected clone of Emperor Palpatine surfaced on Byss. Exacting revenge for his downfall, Palpatine sent his World Devastators to obliterate Mon Calamari.

As the planet eaters consumed the floating cities of Kee-Piru and Heurkea, spewing out robotic TIE fighters, Calamarian troopers and Rebel Amphibions tried vainly to stop their relentless advance. At the last possible instant R2-D2 broadcast a captured control signal that caused the World Devastators to turn on each other. The ruined machines sank beneath the waves.

With one threat ended, Mon Calamari's inhabitants were ill prepared to deal with another. Just one year later the renegade Admiral Daala pummeled the planet with an orbital strike, destroying Reef Home City. Admiral Ackbar led a brilliant counterattack that, although it sacrificed a half-built star cruiser, wiped out one of Daala's Star Destroyers. Later a female Mon Cal named Cilghal studied at Luke Skywalker's Jedi academy, becoming one of the next generation of Jedi Knights.

The Mon Cals and Quarren have suffered greatly since their world joined the galactic community, but they have also contributed much. For now the planet needs time to heal.

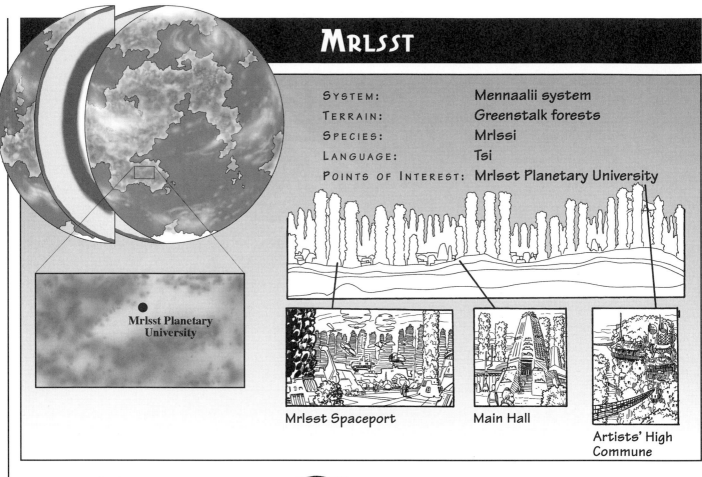

MRLSST

SYSTEM:	Mennaalii system
TERRAIN:	Greenstalk forests
SPECIES:	Mrlssi
LANGUAGE:	Tsi
POINTS OF INTEREST:	Mrlsst Planetary University

Mrlsst Planetary University

Mrlsst Spaceport

Main Hall

Artists' High Commune

Native Mrlssi descended from plumed avians.

Mrlsst, the university planet, is well known as a prestigious but harmless sanctuary for professors, scholars, and scientists. Campus peace was shattered, however, when Academy President Keela foolishly invited the Empire to a bidding war.

The native Mrlssi are a small, delicately boned race descended from plumed avians. They have always possessed a gift for physics and abstract reasoning and have a strong desire to share their knowledge with others. Mrlsst joined the galactic community ages ago. At all hours beings of every imaginable species and background can be found milling outside the labs and lecture halls, heading to and from their respective classes.

The immense main campus spreads across two hundred square kilometers, and dozens of satellite facilities are scattered over the planet's face. School buildings of white stone and crystalline glass wind between the massive trunks of "greenstalks," Mrlssi trees that stand out like the columns and pillars of a bizarre organic architecture. Greenstalks are easy to climb, and their summits often house ramshackle communes of artists, musicians, and poets. In the cracks between the greenstalks' upturned scales lie innumerable colonies of tiny (and delicious) wuorls.

During the Emperor's reign Mrlssi scientists announced that they had developed a remarkable new cloaking device code-named the Phantom

Project. What the Empire didn't know was that the project was a fake, existing only to attract Imperial research money and educational subsidies.

When the Mrlssi president Gyr Keela took office, he had no idea the cloaking device was a ruse. Several months after the Battle of Endor, Keela invited representatives from the New Republic and the Empire to meet at his offices, intending to sell the Phantom Project datacards to the highest bidder.

Wedge Antilles and the X-wing aces of Rogue Squadron arrived as the New Republic envoys. The Empire sent Loka Hask, a horribly disfigured officer who was directly responsible for the tragic deaths of Wedge's parents.

Commander Antilles didn't expect a monster such as Hask to play fair, and he wasn't disappointed. Hask's agents stole the Phantom datacards and

implicated one of Wedge's pilots in the theft.

Rorax Falken, the brilliant mathematician, then stole the datacards from Hask and destroyed them. Enraged, Hask ordered his TIE bombers to level Mrlsst with a withering salvo of concussion missiles. Hundreds of greenstalks ignited like winterfest candles as the locals struggled to douse the raging blaze.

Meanwhile, in the asteroid belt overhead, the Rogues made a shocking discovery. The Phantom Project might have been a sham, but Falken had developed something even *more* dangerous—and frighteningly real. Falken's gravitic polarization beam—more fittingly called a planet slicer—could not be allowed to fall into the Empire's clutches. Grimly, Wedge ordered that the hideous weapon be fired at Hask's cruiser.

The deadly device unexpectedly triggered a spatial wormhole, warping local space and swallowing the Imperial vessel whole, without a single scrap of flotsam to mark its extraordinary demise. Wedge and his victorious crew returned to the surface of Mrlsst to lend a hand to the university firefighters.

Delicious wuorls are easily plucked from their tree hideouts.

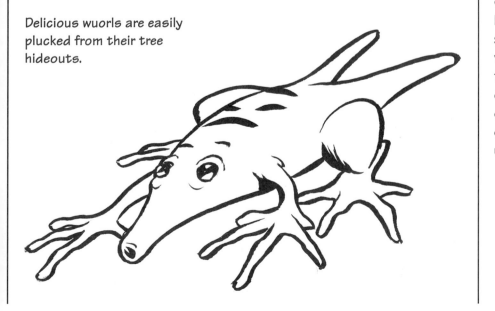

MUNTO CODRU

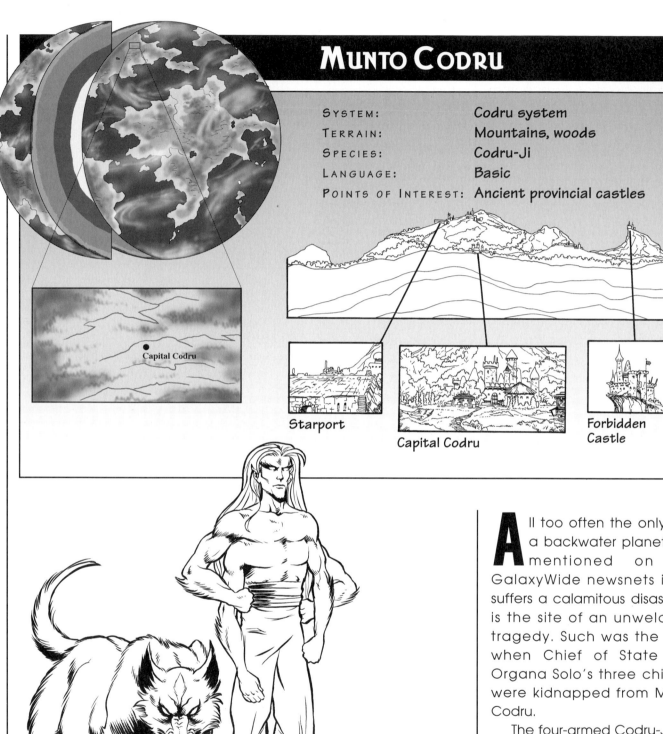

SYSTEM:	Codru system
TERRAIN:	Mountains, woods
SPECIES:	Codru-Ji
LANGUAGE:	Basic
POINTS OF INTEREST:	Ancient provincial castles

Capital Codru

Starport

Capital Codru

Forbidden Castle

The young wyrwulf (left) metamorphoses into the adult Codru-Ji (right).

All too often the only way a backwater planet gets mentioned on the GalaxyWide newsnets is if it suffers a calamitous disaster or is the site of an unwelcome tragedy. Such was the case when Chief of State Leia Organa Solo's three children were kidnapped from Munto Codru.

The four-armed Codru-Ji that inhabit the world are often considered attractive by human standards. Though they differ from humans in ways other than appearance—they sleep standing up and often communicate on a hypersonic level—their most unusual trait is their highly differentiated two-stage life cycle.

A young Codru-Ji is born as a wyrwulf—a furry six-legged animal resembling a powerful, fanged canine. At the appropriate age the wyrwulf encases itself in a rubbery blue chrysalis and undergoes a radical metamorphosis. When the cocoon splits, a fully aware Codru-Ji emerges.

The planet is perhaps best known for its delicately beautiful stone castles. Looking like fanciful illustrations from a storybook, the mazelike palaces were built ages ago by a now-vanished race. The rock walls, carved so thin that they appear translucent, are decorated with mysterious symbols and arcane petroglyphs. The Codru-Ji use the castles as provincial capitals but often avoid them entirely out of a superstitious fear that they might be haunted by their long-dead architects.

Munto Codru is the source of no valuable exports or resources, and the world never played a significant role in the Imperial or New Republic government. The Codru-Ji prefer things this way—it allows them to concentrate on their internal politics, which have evolved over hundreds of years into a highly complex and ritualized tradition. Those in power are the continual targets of "coup abductions," the formalized kidnapping of their children by members of rival political provinces. After the appropriate

Notable life-forms include the four-winged tappratine.

concessions are made and ransoms are paid, the children are always released. As long as the accepted rules are followed, the targets are not harmed.

Ten years after the New Republic's formation Leia embarked on a relaxing diplomatic tour of remote and peaceful member worlds. On Munto Codru, during the endless string of state visits and ceremonial dinners, a hysterical page burst in and delivered chilling news. A pressure bomb had just been detonated in a nearby meadow. Chewbacca was severely injured. And Leia's children—Jaina, Jacen, and Anakin—were gone.

The Codru-Ji officials tried to convince Leia that it had merely been another coup abduction—after all, Chamberlain Iyon's wyrwulf was also missing. But Leia knew differently. Someone with ties to the dark side of the Force had kidnapped her beloved children. She would find and rescue them, and the culprit would pay.

MYRKR

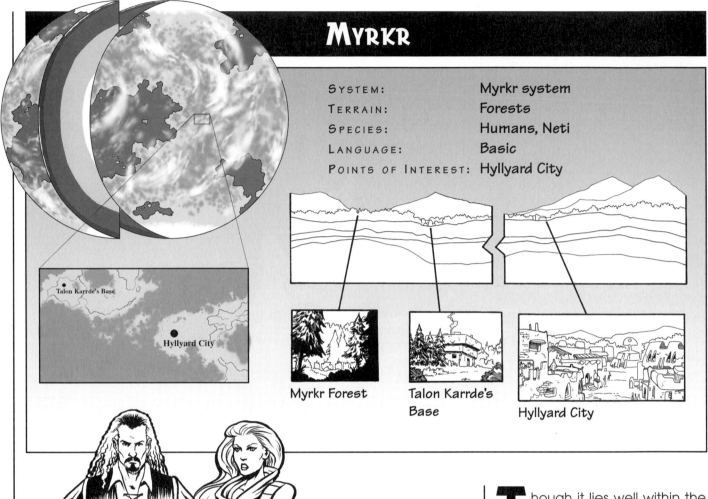

SYSTEM: Myrkr system
TERRAIN: Forests
SPECIES: Humans, Neti
LANGUAGE: Basic
POINTS OF INTEREST: Hyllyard City

Talon Karrde's Base

Hyllyard City

Myrkr Forest

Talon Karrde's Base

Hyllyard City

Talon Karrde (left) and Mara Jade (right) evacuated their base on Myrkr.

Though it lies well within the borders of civilized space, Jedi Knights have always avoided the planet Myrkr. The reason becomes clear when one visits the surface. Myrkr is home to the ysalamiri, a small creature with the bizarre ability to "push back" the Force.

It us unclear how this unique trait evolved, but a single ysalamiri can project a ten-meter bubble in which the Force does not exist. A Myrkr forest filled with ysalamiri, each one reinforcing and strengthening the others' nullifying effect, is a dangerous place for any Jedi to enter. Other indigenous animals that instinctively sense the

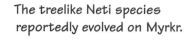

The treelike Neti species reportedly evolved on Myrkr.

The ysalamiri create Force-absent bubbles.

Force include vornskrs, deadly whip-tailed creatures that use the mystical energy field to hunt and track their prey.

Some have speculated the treelike Neti (or Ryyk) evolved on Myrkr, though this remains unconfirmed. It is known that one Neti sage, Ood Bnar, lived on Myrkr as a youth and later became one of the greatest Jedi Masters. Ood fought in the ancient Sith War, then helped Luke Skywalker defeat an enemy on Ossus over four thousand years later.

Because Myrkr attracts so little "official" attention, it is a common stop for smugglers, fugitives, and outlaws. Since the high metal content of the planet's trees fouls sensor scans, Talon Karrde placed his smuggling organization's secret headquarters deep in Myrkr's Great Northern Forest.

Five years after its defeat at Endor the Empire resurged under the brilliant leadership of Grand Admiral Thrawn. Thrawn made several trips to Myrkr to pick up ysalamiri both for use in his cloning projects and to protect himself against the mad Jedi Joruus C'baoth.

At the same time Luke Skywalker was captured by Karrde and brought to the Myrkr base. Despite losing his Force talents when the ysalamiri influence enveloped him, Luke managed to escape from his cell and steal a Skipray blastboat. Mara Jade, Karrde's second-in-command, pursued, and both ships crashed in the dense forest.

Though Mara bitterly hated Luke for ending her life as the influential Emperor's Hand, the two enemies were forced to cooperate. Several wild vornskrs tried to make a meal of them during their long trek through Myrkr's jungle. Even without his Jedi skills, Luke proved quite resourceful.

When they reached Hyllyard City, they were taken captive by an Imperial patrol. Fortunately, an ambush planned by Karrde (not to mention Luke's natural skill with a lightsaber) allowed them to escape.

Myrkr was no longer a safe place for Talon Karrde, and he evacuated his base just ahead of Thrawn's plodding AT-ATs. He had earned the wrath of the Empire. Perhaps it was time to start helping the other side.

Many subspecies of wild vornskrs detect and hunt Force-users.

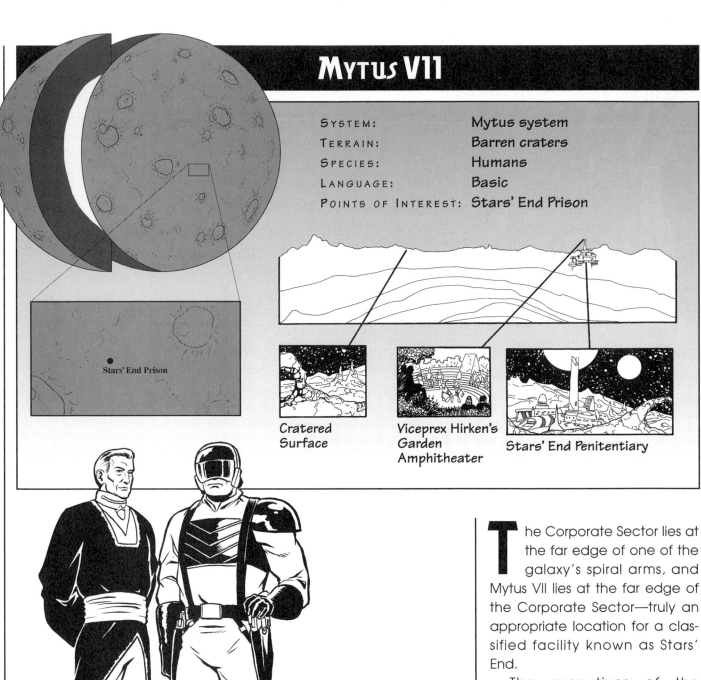

MYTUS VII

SYSTEM:	**Mytus system**
TERRAIN:	**Barren craters**
SPECIES:	**Humans**
LANGUAGE:	**Basic**
POINTS OF INTEREST:	**Stars' End Prison**

Stars' End Prison

Cratered Surface

Viceprex Hirken's Garden Amphitheater

Stars' End Penitentiary

Corporate Sector Authority Viceprex Hirken and an Espo officer.

The Corporate Sector lies at the far edge of one of the galaxy's spiral arms, and Mytus VII lies at the far edge of the Corporate Sector—truly an appropriate location for a classified facility known as Stars' End.

The executives of the Corporate Sector Authority, ruling their territory with a ruthlessness rivaling that of the Empire, determined that a top-secret prison complex was necessary to incarcerate the political dissidents who'd been inconveniencing their dogged pursuit of profit. Code-named Stars' End, the penitentiary began taking shape on Mytus VII, an airless,

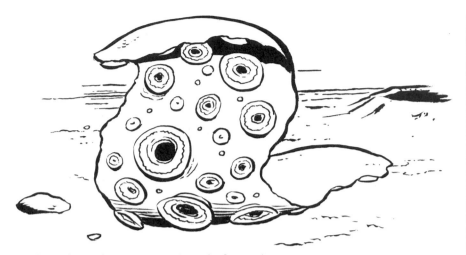

Rock suckers draw trace minerals from the stony crust.

barren rock circling the Mytus system's single star.

With billions of credits at its disposal, the Authority was able to make Stars' End utterly state-of-the-art, incorporating prodigiously expensive (and therefore vanishingly rare) technology. The main tower, thrusting up from the support buildings and defensive turbolasers, was composed of a single piece of nearly indestructible molecularly bonded armor. Behind its unassailable walls the doomed prisoners were confined in stasis booths—literally "frozen in time"—until removed for interrogation or execution.

The entire project was placed under the command of Authority Viceprex Hirken, who ordered the construction of a garden and amphitheater on the tower's top level. It was there that Hirken, indulging his private passion, watched his pet gladiator droids demolish other robotic combatants.

Before they became respected members of the Rebel Alliance, Han Solo and Chewbacca made numerous smuggling runs in bold defiance of the Corporate Sector's rulers. When Chewie was captured and imprisoned at Stars' End, Han vowed to free him. With two Trianii—Atuarre and Pakka—and the droids Bollux and Blue Max, he took the *Millennium Falcon* to the Mytus system.

Opportunity knocked when an intercepted transmission revealed that Hirken's requested troupe of entertainers had recently canceled its engagement. Posing as last-minute replacements, "Madame Atuarre and her Roving Performers" were welcomed into the impregnable fortress.

While Han scouted the lower floors with Blue Max, Atuarre realized what Hirken was expecting from his entertainers—a fully armed battle droid to pit against his Mark X Executioner. Bollux was pressed

into the role and, though he possessed not a single flamethrower or fusion cutter, outwitted and disabled the brutish destroyer. Meanwhile, Atuarre retreated to the *Falcon* and Blue Max successfully started an overload spiral in the prison's reactor. With a spectacular roar, the power plant blew.

The tower's anticoncussion field directed the blast downward, and with Mytus VII's negligible gravity, the entire penitentiary rocketed into near orbit. It was now a race against time until Stars' End reached the top of its arc and plunged to the rocky surface below. Han was reunited with Chewie, and Atuarre docked the *Falcon* with the falling tower. Their group commandeered an Authority ship and, loaded from stem to stern with refugee prisoners, blasted away just as Stars' End imploded with a flash of white light.

NAL HUTTA (AND NAR SHADDAA)

SYSTEM:
Y'Toub system

TERRAIN:
Decaying urban zones

SPECIES:
Hutts, various aliens

LANGUAGES:
Huttese, Basic

POINTS OF INTEREST:
Corellian district (on Nar Shaddaa)

Corellian Sector

Drunken Drummer

Meltdown Cafe

Shug Ninx's Garage

Nal Hutta's moon is home to smugglers and fortune-tellers.

Nal Hutta sprawls lazily in the heart of Hutt Space like one of the corpulent slugs that call it home. Its spaceport moon of Nar Shaddaa is a notorious refuge for pirates, gunrunners, and assorted riffraff. Both worlds, in all their corrupt splendor, helped shape the life of a young smuggler named Han Solo.

Millennia ago the Hutt species abandoned its blasted ancestral home of Varl. Their star caravan eventually arrived at the planet Evocar, and with typical Hutt cunning they displaced the peaceful natives. They renamed their prize Nal Hutta—"glorious jewel" in Huttese.

Tacky bathhouses and pleasure palaces sprang up like cancers as the rival Hutt merchant families vied to outdo each other. Evocar's temperate rain forests were bulldozed into stagnant swampland, creating a putrid, foul odor that pleased the Hutts immensely.

Above, on Nar Shaddaa, an even more drastic change was underway. As the moon grew in importance as a smuggling center, it was paved over with layer upon layer of docking towers, landing bays, cargo warehouses, and trading plazas. Some even said it resembled a "little Coruscant"—but a Coruscant in which the dirt, decay, and danger of the undercity had spread *everywhere*. Visitors who don't watch their backs on the Smugglers' Moon will get their throats cut, their pockets looted, and their bodies tossed down a bottomless freight shaft.

Han Solo and Chewbacca learned the tricks of the smuggling trade on Nar Shaddaa from some of the best in the business: Salla Zend, Shug Ninx, Mako Spince, and old Roa. Han, however, had no desire to get caught in a rut, and he and the Wookiee eventually left to seek adventure in the Corporate Sector.

R2-D2 and C-3PO had a wild escapade on the Smugglers' Moon during their early careers, and the Rebel agent Kyle Katarn once survived a shoot-out with dogged bounty hunters

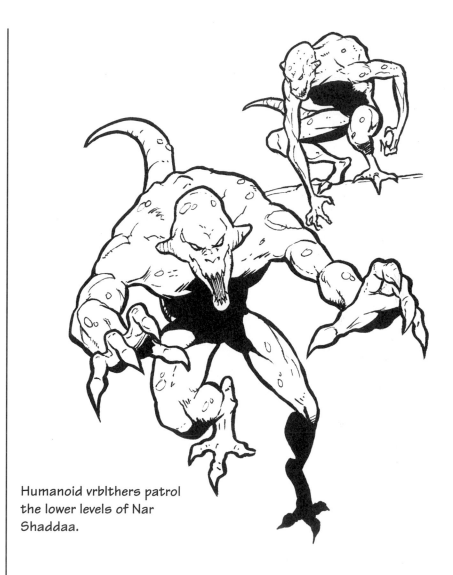

Humanoid vrblthers patrol the lower levels of Nar Shaddaa.

through the ferrocrete canyons of the vertical city. But the lawless world truly came to prominence during the cloned Emperor's reappearance.

In the middle of those turbulent times Han and Leia went to Nar Shaddaa to look up a few of Han's old friends. Hutt bosses, Gank killers, and Boba Fett himself had different plans for the Corellian and his wife. Han and Leia escaped, but a second visit nearly resulted in their messy deaths. This time they fought through a horde of half-human

vrblthers and faced Fett in a rematch. Once again the bounty hunter went away empty-handed.

Two years later Leia visited Nal Hutta in her official capacity as chief of state—rumors of a mysterious Hutt superweapon were too serious to be left uninvestigated. In the sickening showiness of Durga the Hutt's palace she and Han tried to uncover clues to the Darksaber project.

NAM CHORIOS

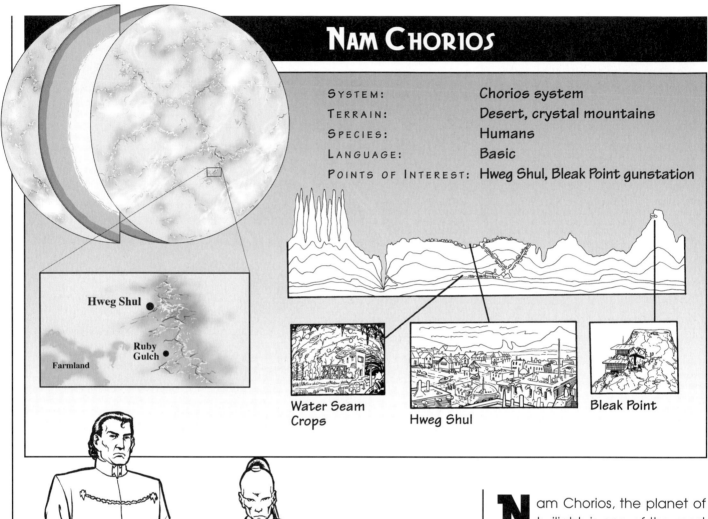

SYSTEM:	Chorios system
TERRAIN:	Desert, crystal mountains
SPECIES:	Humans
LANGUAGE:	Basic
POINTS OF INTEREST:	Hweg Shul, Bleak Point gunstation

Hweg Shul

Ruby Gulch

Farmland

Water Seam Crops

Hweg Shul

Bleak Point

Seti Ashgad (left) retained his youth through "treatments" administered by the greatly mutated droch Dzym (right).

Nam Chorios, the planet of twilight, is one of the most desolate rocks ever to support human life. Originally established as a prison colony by the Grissmath Dynasty 750 years before the Galactic Civil War, Nam Chorios later became a flashpoint between the New Republic and the Empire and the setting for two lovers' final good-bye.

When the first convicts were deposited on Nam Chorios's parched hardpan, they saw a world covered with jagged mountains of crystal and quartz. Weak sunlight filtering through the translucent facets bathed everything in perpetual dusk.

Droch insects spread the Death Seed plague.

Unable to escape the prison world because of guard-operated gunstations, they survived by farming the scarce water seams.

Generations passed. The children of the prisoners and guards joined together to keep their dismal crops from perishing. One farmer, a prophet named Theras, received a mysterious dream warning in which the rocks themselves seemed to be speaking to him: no ships large enough to carry drochs—the skittering black insects the Grissmaths had brought to the world—would ever leave the planet. Though the warning was cryptic, *something* was wrong with the drochs. Theras's followers seized control of the planet's gunstations and forbade entry and egress to anything larger than a starfighter.

Theras's dreams weren't the only oddity on Nam Chorios. For a nearly dead world it seemed to be bursting with *life*, creating a potent nexus in the Force. One Jedi, Beldorian the Hutt, went to the planet and used his newly enhanced abilities to rule the humble populace. Years later Senator Palpatine exiled his political rival, Seti Ashgad, to Nam Chorios.

Ashgad wrested control from the indolent Beldorian and spearheaded a master plan. Discovering that certain crystals—"smokies," the locals called them—could be used in synthdroids and needle fighters, Ashgad struck a deal. He would take over the Theran gunstations and give the Loronar Corporation free access to stripmine smokies. The Imperial fleet would then invade the surrounding Meridian sector, since the New Republic would be preoccupied by an unexplainable outbreak of the Death Seed plague.

At a secret diplomatic meeting Ashgad kidnapped Leia Organa Solo and unleashed the Death Seed. Tiny, squirming drochs were the vectors of the devastating epidemic—harmless on their homeworld, they become life drinkers when off it. As disease and panic spread across the sector, Ashgad took his captive princess to Nam Chorios.

Luke Skywalker had also gone to the barren world, searching for his lost love, Callista. After Leia escaped from Ashgad's fortress, the two siblings were reunited at the Bleak Point gunstation. They revealed Seti Ashgad's deceitful scheme to the locals, but it was too late. One fanatic destroyed the cannon, clearing a safe path for Ashgad's ship *Reliant* and its cargo of smokies—and drochs—to reach orbit.

Out of options, Luke made contact with the planet's dominant lifeform: the crystals. The smokies were *alive*. Convincing them of the droch threat, Luke watched as the *Reliant*'s cargo of smokies detonated in a dazzling flare.

Afterward, Luke saw Callista once again. Though they still loved each other, they realized that their lives lay along different paths. With a simple gesture of farewell Callista departed from Luke's life but not his heart.

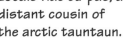

Locals ride cu-pas, a distant cousin of the arctic tauntaun.

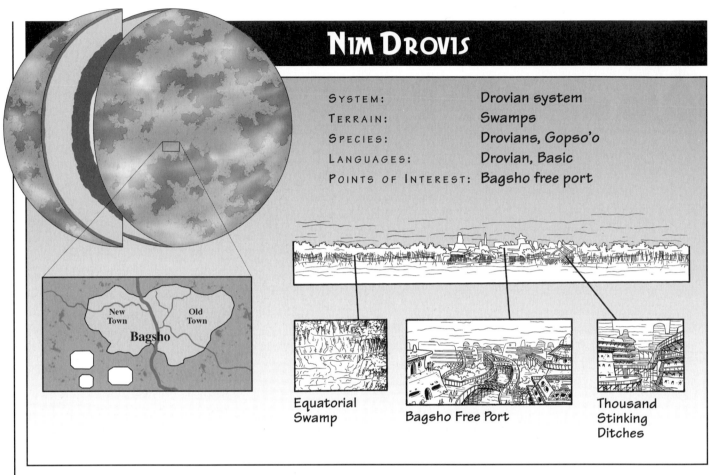

NIM DROVIS

SYSTEM:	Drovian system
TERRAIN:	Swamps
SPECIES:	Drovians, Gopso'o
LANGUAGES:	Drovian, Basic
POINTS OF INTEREST:	Bagsho free port

New Town

Old Town

Bagsho

Equatorial Swamp

Bagsho Free Port

Thousand Stinking Ditches

A Drovian military officer (left) with a primitive Gopso'o tribesman (right).

The primitive planet Nim Drovis is a dismal, rain-soaked, fungus-encrusted mudball. Tucked away in the unremarkable Meridian sector, the soggy world boasts only of an understaffed New Republic sector medical facility.

It is home to a stocky alien species divided into two fiercely insular tribes: the Drovians and the Gopso'o. Since time immemorial the two clans have feuded, resulting in countless deaths on both sides. Every inhabitant of Nim Drovis has had friends killed in the internecine struggle, a fact that only reinforces their mutual hatred.

Slimy carnivorous molds should be avoided when visiting Nim Drovis.

Contact with the greater galaxy attracted interstellar weapons traders, and their wares allowed the Drovians to quickly become the dominant tribe. It also attracted corrupt zwil pushers eager to hook a new market on their narcotic. Nearly everyone on Nim Drovis, Drovian and Gopso'o alike, is addicted to zwil, which they absorb through fist-sized plugs shoved deep into their breathing membranes.

Bagsho, the largest free port, is a rickety collection of wooden balconies and bridges built on stone foundations designed to withstand the most torrential downpours. The city's rain-swelled canals are breeding grounds for shambling, carnivorous molds whose digestive acids can strip flesh from bone in a matter of minutes. Drovians who can be spared from the Gopso'o wars are employed as mold exterminators, patrolling the city with acid- and flamethrowers.

Ten months after the fiery destruction of Admiral Daala's flagship above Yavin 4, a new threat to the New Republic emerged in the Meridian sector. On Nim Drovis and elsewhere the Loronar Corporation organized planetary rebellions, while Seti Ashgad orchestrated the release of the Death Seed plague. Armed with new Loronar blaster rifles, the Gopso'o fell on their Drovian rivals with years of pent-up bloodlust.

Han Solo had come to Nim Drovis to deliver shipwreck survivors to the sector medical facility. Though the Death Seed epidemic had been contained within the base, the bellowing Gopso'o were overrunning Bagsho, and hungry molds were oozing from their canals. Han fought his way back toward the landing pad, hoping to fly the *Falcon* off the madhouse planet as soon as possible.

Han didn't know it, but R2-D2 and C-3PO had recently been dumped on Nim Drovis by a war-zone looter. The droids vainly tried to win passage off the world by playing jizz-box tunes in a squalid tavern called the Wookiee's Codpiece. Wandering the streets after their stab at musical entertainment, they spotted Captain Solo sprinting to his ship amid slime-covered molds and a hail of Gopso'o blaster bolts.

Artoo and Threepio followed as fast as their servos would carry them, calling out for the Corellian's attention, but they were too slow, too quiet, and too late. The *Falcon* lifted off and blasted into space. Left behind, the droids could either remain in the combat zone or leave with a swinish Gamorrean captain on her rickety starship. Poor Threepio found neither option particularly appealing.

NKLLON

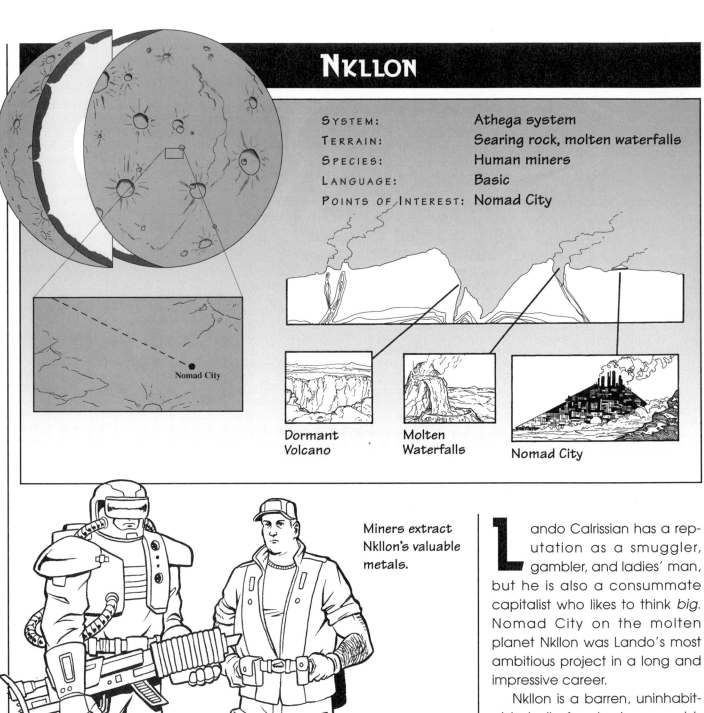

SYSTEM:	Athega system
TERRAIN:	Searing rock, molten waterfalls
SPECIES:	Human miners
LANGUAGE:	Basic
POINTS OF INTEREST:	Nomad City

Nomad City

Dormant Volcano

Molten Waterfalls

Nomad City

Miners extract Nkllon's valuable metals.

Lando Calrissian has a reputation as a smuggler, gambler, and ladies' man, but he is also a consummate capitalist who likes to think *big*. Nomad City on the molten planet Nkllon was Lando's most ambitious project in a long and impressive career.

Nkllon is a barren, uninhabitable ball of rock whose crust is rich in hfredium, kammris, and dolovite. Those metals are vital in starship construction and earn a hefty profit on the open market. Under normal circumstances Nkllon's resources would have been exploited long ago, but the tiny planetoid orbits so close to the star

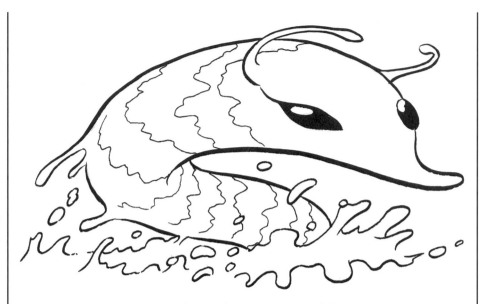

Lava worms inhabit ponds beneath molten waterfalls.

Athega that it is continuously bathed in deadly radiation and charred by broiling stellar heat. Any ship approaching Nkllon suffers sensor blindness or severe hull damage or is instantly incinerated.

Lando came up with an ingenious solution to this formidable problem. Shieldships—supercooled escort craft resembling giant umbrellas—were capable of protecting vessels until they could reach the darkness of Nkllon's night side. Once he reached the planet's shadow, Lando dropped Nomad City, a mobile mining complex that could stay on the sheltered night side throughout Nkllon's ninety-day rotation. Soon the profits were rolling in, and Lando settled down to administer his brainchild.

Unfortunately, like so many of Lando's schemes, Nomad City seemed cursed by bad luck.

Disaster struck during the New Republic's war against Grand Admiral Thrawn. Thrawn needed mole miners for his planned attack on the Sluis Van shipyards, and Nomad City had dozens of them. The Imperial Star Destroyer *Judicator*—protected by extra shielding and guided by the Jedi clone Joruus C'baoth—sailed past the sensor-blinding sun and captured fifty-one of the small excavators in a lightning raid.

A few months later, after Lando had managed to repair most of the damage to his operation, the Empire struck again. This time Thrawn's first attack was on the shieldship depot on the outer fringes of the Athega system. Commandeering one of the ungainly craft, the Grand Admiral's men flew a small Dreadnaught in behind the shieldship's protective umbra. The nearly defenseless mining complex was mercilessly hammered by the warship. Nomad City's stockpiled metals, worth millions of credits, were stolen.

The damage was more severe than Lando had feared—Nomad City could no longer move. Stranded in place, the complex's five thousand workers were doomed to a swift and painful death when Nkllon's rotation exposed them to the burning sun. Fortunately, General Garm Bel Iblis heard their distress call and evacuated all personnel. Bel Iblis did not, however, have the heavy equipment needed to recover Nomad City. The one-of-a-kind creation melted into a pool of fused metal and twisted girders.

N'ZOTH

SYSTEM:	N'zoth system
TERRAIN:	Dry plains, deserts
SPECIES:	Yevethans
LANGUAGE:	Yevethan
POINTS OF INTEREST:	Giat Nor, Hariz

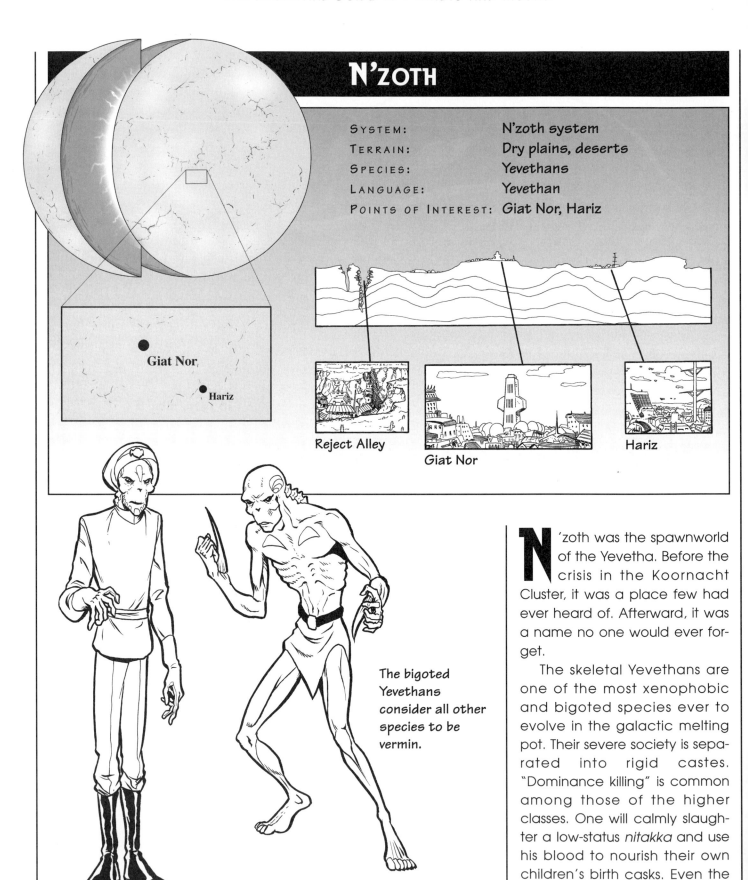

Giat Nor

Hariz

Reject Alley

Giat Nor

Hariz

The bigoted Yevethans consider all other species to be vermin.

N'zoth was the spawnworld of the Yevetha. Before the crisis in the Koornacht Cluster, it was a place few had ever heard of. Afterward, it was a name no one would ever forget.

The skeletal Yevethans are one of the most xenophobic and bigoted species ever to evolve in the galactic melting pot. Their severe society is separated into rigid castes. "Dominance killing" is common among those of the higher classes. One will calmly slaughter a low-status *nitakka* and use his blood to nourish their own children's birth casks. Even the native beasts, like the tooth-

The native siringana is as brutal as the Yevetha.

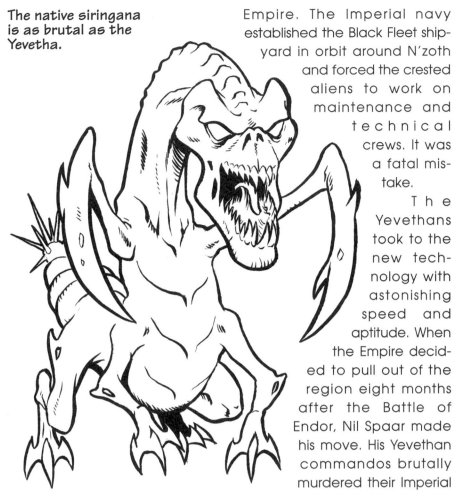

Empire. The Imperial navy established the Black Fleet shipyard in orbit around N'zoth and forced the crested aliens to work on maintenance and technical crews. It was a fatal mistake.

The Yevethans took to the new technology with astonishing speed and aptitude. When the Empire decided to pull out of the region eight months after the Battle of Endor, Nil Spaar made his move. His Yevethan commandos brutally murdered their Imperial captors and seized the entire Black Fleet, including the Super Star Destroyer *Intimidator*.

Twelve years later Nil Spaar—now viceroy of the Yevethan federation called the Duskhan League—initiated diplomatic negotiations with Leia Organa Solo on Coruscant. Though he seemed amicable, the talks were camouflage for an unholy campaign of genocide.

Spaar's Black Fleet armada, bolstered by a horde of Yevethan thrustships, executed lightning raids on all foreign settlements within Koornacht—a "purification" effort the Yevethans called the Great

faced siringana, are merciless and brutal.

If the lower classes are worthy of utter contempt, non-Yevethans are nothing but vermin. Since the blazing suns of the Koornacht Cluster blocked lesser stars from N'zoth's night sky, the Yevethans long thought they were the only intelligent species in the universe. When Imperial invasion forces proved them wrong, their opinion changed little—they were now the only *worthy* species in the universe.

Arrogance aside, Yevethan weaponry was no match for the

Purge. Extermination was swift and complete.

An outraged Leia moved to stop the violence but found her greatest opposition coming from the home front. Several influential senators accused her of "warmongering" and instituted recall proceedings. Nil Spaar was aided by spies within her own government. And Han, Leia's beloved husband, was captured and taken to N'zoth in chains.

It all came to a head in the epic Battle of N'zoth. Chewbacca and his young son rescued Han from Nil Spaar's flagship; then the two fleets clashed in a furious fray. Suddenly the New Republic was handed a welcome surprise.

The Black Fleet was crewed by numerous Imperial slaves captured years before during the shipyard seizure. Though they bore no love for the Rebellion, they liked their Yevethan captors even less. Activating a web of hidden slave circuits, the prisoners hijacked every last Star Destroyer and leapt into the Deep Core—taking Nil Spaar with them.

Since then the New Republic has kept a close eye on N'zoth. The continued peace of the galaxy is at stake.

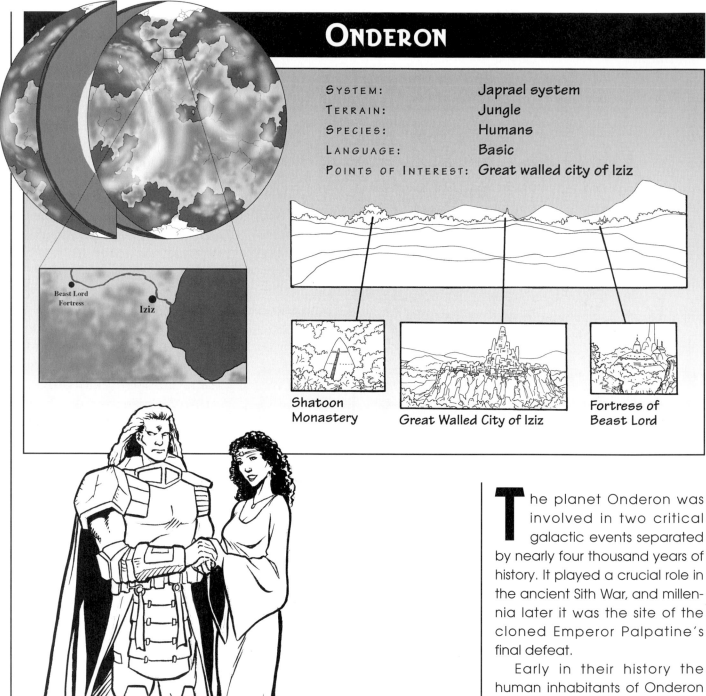

ONDERON

SYSTEM:	Japrael system
TERRAIN:	Jungle
SPECIES:	Humans
LANGUAGE:	Basic
POINTS OF INTEREST:	Great walled city of Iziz

Beast Lord Fortress

Iziz

Shatoon Monastery

Great Walled City of Iziz

Fortress of Beast Lord

In the ancient past, Oron Kira and Princess Galia united the beast-riders and city dwellers.

The planet Onderon was involved in two critical galactic events separated by nearly four thousand years of history. It played a crucial role in the ancient Sith War, and millennia later it was the site of the cloned Emperor Palpatine's final defeat.

Early in their history the human inhabitants of Onderon learned to survive. The planet's closest moon, Dxun, has an orbit so erratic that it shares atmosphere with its primary once a year. Over time the bloodthirsty winged monsters inhabiting Dxun learned that they could use this oxygen bridge to migrate to Onderon.

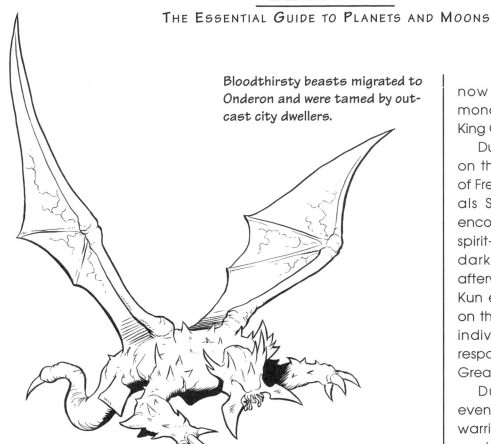

Bloodthirsty beasts migrated to Onderon and were tamed by outcast city dwellers.

To protect themselves the Onderonians built the enormous walled city of Iziz, a massive structure covering over sixteen hundred square kilometers. When a Sith magician named Freedon Nadd arrived on the planet, he instructed Onderon's royalty in the use of the dark side. Any dissidents were cast outside the city walls to be devoured by the beasts. Eventually some outcasts were able to subdue and train the creatures, and soon "beast-rider" kingdoms were flourishing in the wilds, fighting to recapture Iziz from the corrupt monarchy.

Four hundred years after Freedon Nadd's arrival on Onderon the planet was contacted by the Old Republic. Queen Amanoa, the sinister ruler of Iziz, asked the Republic for help against the "criminals" threatening to overtake her city. Master Arca of Arkania sent his three Jedi students—Ulic and Cay Qel-Droma and the Twi'lek Tott Doneeta.

The Jedi rescued Amanoa's daughter, Galia, when she was kidnapped by the beast-riders but soon learned that the abduction was a ruse. Galia intended to marry the beast-rider Oron Kira and had arranged the false capture to escape from her mother.

Ulic, hoping that this wedding could end the feud, met with Amanoa, but the furious old woman called on her dark-side powers. Oron Kira's beast-riders fought back and triumphantly captured Iziz. The people of Onderon, both beast-riders and city dwellers, were now united under the new monarchs—Queen Galia and King Oron Kira.

During a subsequent uprising on the planet by the followers of Freedon Nadd, the Tetan royals Satal Keto and Aleema encountered Nadd's intangible spirit-form, which taught them dark-side secrets. Not long afterward, the Jedi Knight Exar Kun encountered Nadd's spirit on the Dxun moon. These three individuals would be directly responsible for the devastating Great Sith War.

During that cataclysmic event Exar Kun dispatched the warrior clans of Mandalore to capture Onderon. Mandalore's men were defeated by Oron Kira's beast-riders and fled to Dxun, where Mandalore met his end.

Nearly four thousand years later Han and Leia took the *Millennium Falcon* to Onderon to hide their infant son Anakin from the resurrected Emperor. Palpatine needed a new clone body, and if his spirit did not enter the young child soon, he would die.

Palpatine found them, and as he lunged for the wailing infant, Han took him down with a single blaster shot. His body dead, Palpatine's spirit still shot toward Anakin, but the mortally wounded Jedi Knight Empatojayos Brand intercepted the evil essence. As Brand died, the Emperor's life energy expired. Emperor Palpatine would never return.

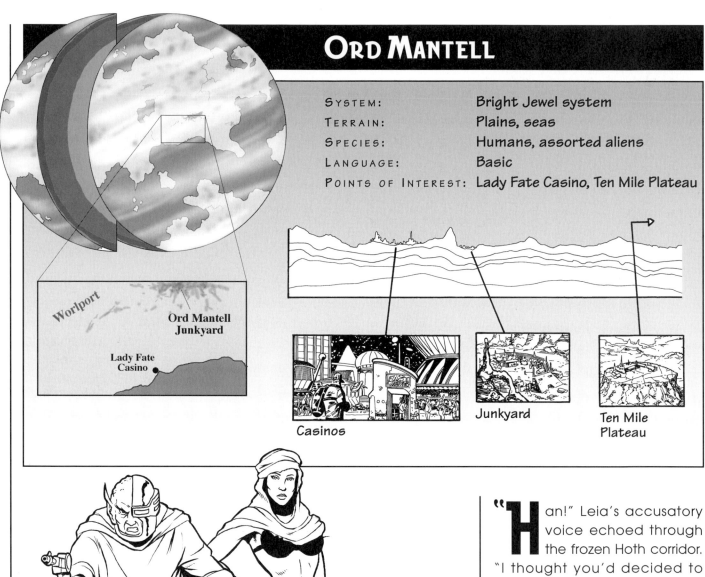

ORD MANTELL

SYSTEM:	Bright Jewel system
TERRAIN:	Plains, seas
SPECIES:	Humans, assorted aliens
LANGUAGE:	Basic
POINTS OF INTEREST:	Lady Fate Casino, Ten Mile Plateau

Worlport

Ord Mantell
Junkyard

Lady Fate
Casino

Casinos

Junkyard

Ten Mile
Plateau

Bounty hunters and molls find Ord Mantell's numerous casinos quite entertaining.

"Han!" Leia's accusatory voice echoed through the frozen Hoth corridor. "I thought you'd decided to stay!" The retreating Corellian captain spun to face her, his face flashing with annoyance. "Well, the bounty hunter we ran into on Ord Mantell changed my mind."

Exactly *which* bounty hunter Han was referring to is unclear—on Ord Mantell one can take one's pick. Situated at the heart of the Bright Jewel Cluster, the lawless world is a magnet for criminals of all stripes, from the pickpockets who frequent the shining casinos, to the pirates who hide out in the barren outback, to the assassin droids that lurk in the industrial junkyards.

Ord Mantell was first settled twelve thousand years before the Galactic Civil War as an Old Republic military outpost ("Ord" is an outdated acronym for "Ordnance/Regional Depot"). All traces of the base, however, have long since disappeared beneath coastal strips of flashing, blinking casino complexes. Farther inland lie smelters, scrap heaps, and a persistent brown haze from burning fossil fuels.

Most "legitimate" visitors to the planet never stray far from the sabacc tables, jubilee wheels, and all-night revues on the waterfront, though a few brave thrill seekers venture into the rocky backcountry on savrip-tracking expeditions. The hulking Mantellian savrip, familiar to millions as one of the standard pieces in dejarik hologames, is a formidable quarry for even the most seasoned hunter.

Other callers have less benign intentions, and Han Solo ran afoul of one of those malefactors soon after the Battle of Yavin. Forced to land on Ord Mantell to make repairs to the *Millennium Falcon*, he was noticed by an up-and-coming bounty hunter named Skorr. Drub McKumb, an old smuggling buddy, tried to warn Solo about the enormous price Jabba the Hutt had placed on his head, but Skorr got the drop on the wanted Corellian and kidnapped his valuable passen-

The Mantellian savrip is a nasty predator.

gers—Luke Skywalker and Princess Leia. In a dangerous face-off at an abandoned stellar energy plant Solo rescued his friends and humiliated Skorr, leading the manhunter straight into the hands of an angry Imperial commander.

Skorr rotted in a Kessel prison for nearly three years before going after Solo again, this time with the help of Bossk, Dengar, and Boba Fett. The capable group captured Solo and Skywalker near Hoth and took them back to Ord Mantell, locking them in an empty moisture plant. While Fett was off negotiating a suitable fee with Darth Vader, Luke used his lightsaber to slice free of his shackles. Skorr confronted the escapees and, in a scuffle with Solo, accidentally shot himself with his own blaster.

The two-time loser died of his self-inflicted wound, and the Rebel prisoners safely returned to Hoth. But Fett, Bossk, and Dengar would soon be offered a second chance to capture Han Solo, and one of them would walk away a winner.

Ossus

SYSTEM:	Adega system
TERRAIN:	Canyons, mountains
SPECIES:	Many alien Jedi, Ysanna, humans
LANGUAGES:	Classical Ossan, Ysannan
POINTS OF INTEREST:	Great Jedi Library, Knossa spaceport

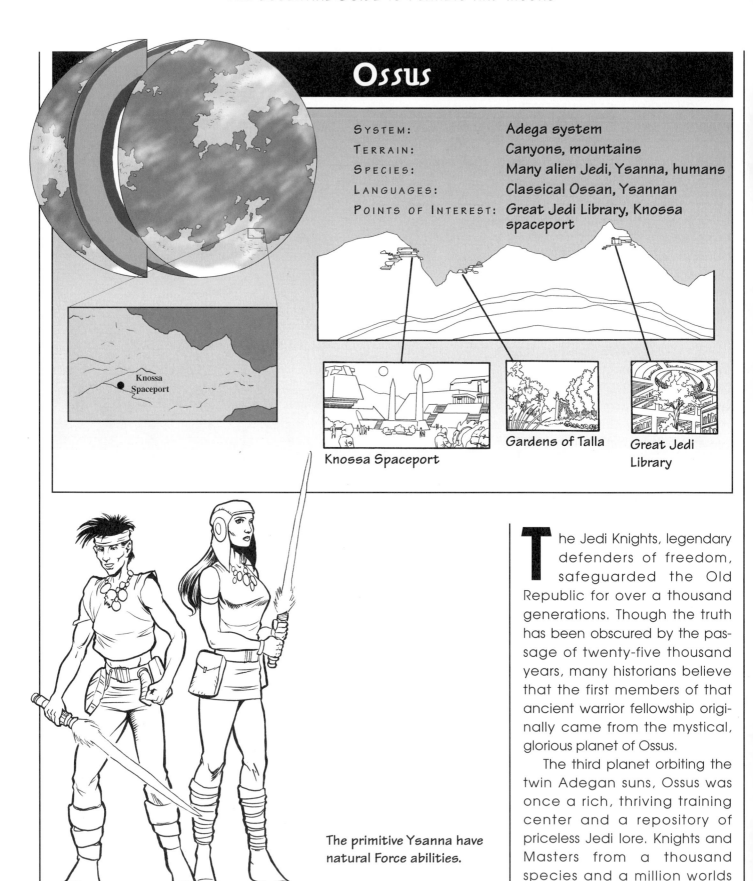

Knossa
Spaceport

Knossa Spaceport

Gardens of Talla

Great Jedi
Library

The primitive Ysanna have natural Force abilities.

The Jedi Knights, legendary defenders of freedom, safeguarded the Old Republic for over a thousand generations. Though the truth has been obscured by the passage of twenty-five thousand years, many historians believe that the first members of that ancient warrior fellowship originally came from the mystical, glorious planet of Ossus.

The third planet orbiting the twin Adegan suns, Ossus was once a rich, thriving training center and a repository of priceless Jedi lore. Knights and Masters from a thousand species and a million worlds mingled freely, sharing their knowledge and furthering the causes of peace, justice, and the Jedi Code. From the bustling Knossa spaceport to the peaceful Gardens of Talla, Ossus shone with life energy and the light side of the Force.

But tragedy of the worst kind befell Ossus during the Great Sith War. Ulic Qel-Droma, once a respected Jedi Knight, joined forces with the Sith Lord Exar Kun and ignited the ten stars of the Cron Cluster in a multiple detonation. The ensuing shock wave, tearing across space, would incinerate Ossus within days. Not even Jedi Masters could stop a supernova.

With grim acceptance, the planet was evacuated. Saving Ossus's myriad treasures would have taken a fleet of ships, and there was simply no time. For every Jedi scroll and Holocron loaded onto the transports, ten more relics were left behind to be consumed by the coming inferno.

Gloating over what his armies had unleashed, Exar Kun arrived on Ossus to loot and plunder. Master Ood, a wood-and-sap Neti, would not allow this desecration. Planting himself firmly in Ossus's soil, Ood metamorphosed into an unyielding tree, sacrificing himself to protect the lightsaber vault beneath his roots. The ravaging shockwave struck, leaving ruins and ashes in its wake, but Ood lived on.

The old Neti, however,

was not the only survivor on the scorched world. Some denizens, unable to escape in time, had taken refuge in vast subterranean caverns. Over the succeeding generations their sons and daughters forgot their Jedi origins. Their primitive tribe, the Ysanna, treated their natural Force abilities as a form of atavistic magic.

During the dark reign of Emperor Palpatine's clones Luke Skywalker went to the ancient Jedi planet with his new apprentice, Kam Solusar.

The fearful Ysanna attacked the odd strangers until they realized they were in the presence of Force Masters.

Without warning, the roar of sublight engines split the sky—Executor Sedriss, Palpatine's new right-hand man, had arrived. When his stormtrooper legion was defeated by the Ysanna shamans in pitched battle, a panicked Sedriss seized a hostage and backed up against the sturdy bole of a nearby tree.

But it was no tree. Ood Bnar, the Jedi Master, grasped Sedriss with his branches and called on energies stored deep in Ossus's core. With a dazzling flash both combatants perished. But Ood left behind a seedling to carry on his legacy.

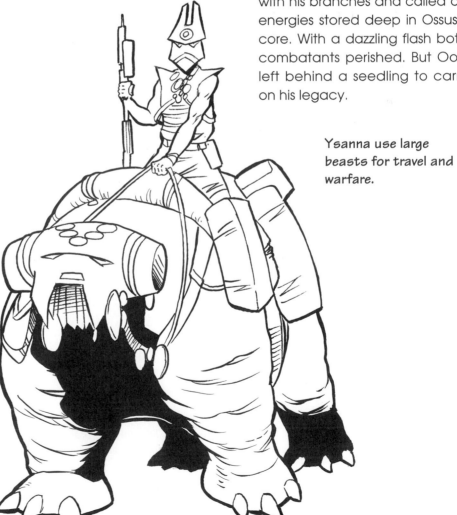

Ysanna use large beasts for travel and warfare.

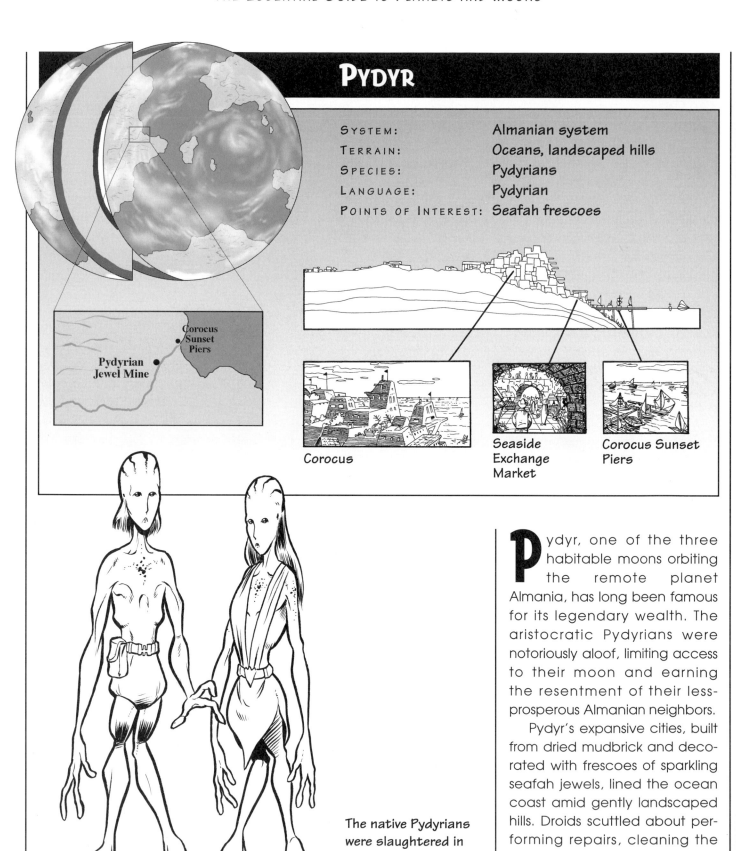

PYDYR

SYSTEM:	Almanian system
TERRAIN:	Oceans, landscaped hills
SPECIES:	Pydyrians
LANGUAGE:	Pydyrian
POINTS OF INTEREST:	Seafah frescoes

Corocus Sunset Piers

Pydyrian Jewel Mine

Corocus

Seaside Exchange Market

Corocus Sunset Piers

The native Pydyrians were slaughtered in Kueller's holocaust.

Pydyr, one of the three habitable moons orbiting the remote planet Almania, has long been famous for its legendary wealth. The aristocratic Pydyrians were notoriously aloof, limiting access to their moon and earning the resentment of their less-prosperous Almanian neighbors.

Pydyr's expansive cities, built from dried mudbrick and decorated with frescoes of sparkling seafah jewels, lined the ocean coast amid gently landscaped hills. Droids scuttled about performing repairs, cleaning the streets, and otherwise keeping their masters' immaculate society in perfect order.

Seafah shellfish are a waterfront treat, and often have brilliant jewels hidden beneath their carapaces.

Thirteen years after the decisive Battle of Endor an Almanian leader calling himself Kueller began an aggressive crusade against the New Republic. To finance his military campaign Kueller ensured that a significant portion of Pydyr's droids were equipped with explosive devices manufactured in the robotic factories of Telti.

At the appropriate moment every droid detonated. Over one and a half million Pydyrians were instantly killed, and their blasted bodies were swiftly disposed of. Kueller made arrangements to sell their jewel-encrusted homes and other possessions as "collector's sets" to the richest (and least ethical) art dealers in the galaxy. Only a thousand of the moon's citizens were spared, all of them trained seafah jewelers, so Kueller could continue harvesting Pydyr's natural wealth.

The abrupt extinguishing of so many lives created a wrenching disturbance in the Force, instantly alerting Luke Skywalker that something was amiss. Luke eventually tracked the sensation to Pydyr. As he tried to land, he inadvertently triggered a detonator concealed in his ship. Without warning, the X-wing exploded, raining flaming debris across the sandstone streets. Luke escaped from the wreckage in time but suffered a broken ankle and severe burns.

In one of the vacant residences nearby Luke treated his wounds with a Pydyrian healing stick. The archaic tool helped ease the pain, but only several days in a bacta tank could bring Luke back to full strength.

As the Jedi Master stepped back outside into the warm salty air, he was confronted by the intimidating form of Kueller.

In a flash of insight Luke realized that Kueller was actually Dolph, a former student who had abandoned his training at the Jedi academy on Yavin 4. Luke tried to reach the youthful pupil lurking behind Kueller's death's-head mask, but Dolph had fallen too deeply into the dark side.

In a fierce lightsaber duel Kueller succeeded in disarming his weakened opponent. Gloating that he could kill Skywalker with the mere flick of a wrist, the masked warrior chose instead to spare his former teacher's life. After all, Leia Organa Solo still needed to be drawn into his trap, and the Jedi Master would make excellent bait.

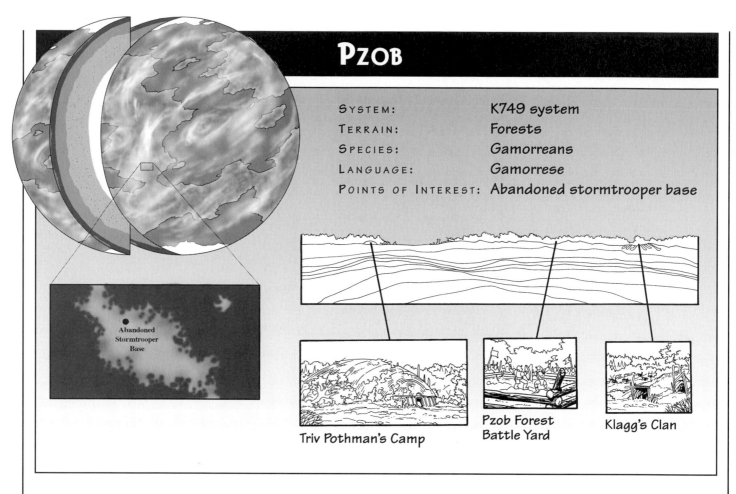

PZOB

SYSTEM:	K749 system
TERRAIN:	Forests
SPECIES:	Gamorreans
LANGUAGE:	Gamorrese
POINTS OF INTEREST:	Abandoned stormtrooper base

Abandoned
Stormtrooper
Base

Triv Pothman's Camp

Pzob Forest
Battle Yard

Klagg's Clan

Gamorreans
love armed
free-for-all
brawls.

Pzob is a heavily wooded planet in the Outer Rim that was colonized generations ago by Gamorreans. How or why the piglike settlers went to that world is anyone's guess, but for years the clans of Pzob have relished hacking and bashing each other in regular bouts of boisterous combat.

Halfway across the galaxy Senator Palpatine became Emperor and ordered a brutal purge of the Jedi Knights, who constituted the greatest threat to his power. One particularly troublesome group, led by the Jedi Master Plett, was entrenched on the planet Belsavis. To ensure the annihila-

Tiny feathered lizards come out of the forests to beg for tidbits.

tion of Plett and his followers, the Emperor constructed the unstoppable battlemoon *Eye of Palpatine*. Because of the mission's utmost secrecy, the *Eye's* elite assault troops were told to await a clandestine pickup on remote planets throughout the Outer Rim, including Alzoc III, Tatooine, and Pzob.

A company of forty-five Imperial stormtroopers arrived in Pzob's thick forests and erected a temporary headquarters not far from the territory controlled by the Klagg and Gakfedd clans. Though some troopers expressed concern about the neighboring Gamorreans, their high-tech weaponry seemed sufficient to keep the unruly aliens at bay. Besides, the rest said, the Emperor's secret warship would soon come to take them off the dirtball planet.

Years later they were still waiting. Unknown to the troop-ers, the Jedi Knight Callista had disabled the *Eye*. Decades passed, and the stormtroopers' numbers dwindled. Scores of soldiers died in border skirmishes with savage Gamorrean boars as their blasters' power cells drained. Soon only one man, Triv Pothman, remained, and he was captured by the Gakfedds.

Pothman was a sympathetic man, and he had the good sense to make himself useful to his captors. After slaving with the Gakfedds for two years and with the rival Klagg clan for one, Triv escaped back to his former encampment. There he stayed, leading a simple, peaceful life in the overgrown ruins of the stormtrooper barracks.

Thirty years after his arrival Pothman finally got a visit from the galaxy outside. Luke Skywalker and his companions had survived a perilous encounter with the reactivated *Eye of Palpatine* in a nearby nebula and needed emergency repairs to their starship. The ex-Imperial welcomed the newcomers, but the Gamorrean warriors had also noticed the arriving vessel. As the Klagg and Gakfedd clans fought over the metallic prize, a second starship hovered slowly into view. After three decades the *Eye of Palpatine* had arrived to fulfill its programming.

The *Eye's* automated lander herded every being in sight into its cavernous bay. When Luke and the rest tried to flee, the lander's artificial intelligence identified them as mutineers. Nimble tracker droids stunned the fugitives and hauled their unconscious bodies away for indoctrination on the waiting battlemoon.

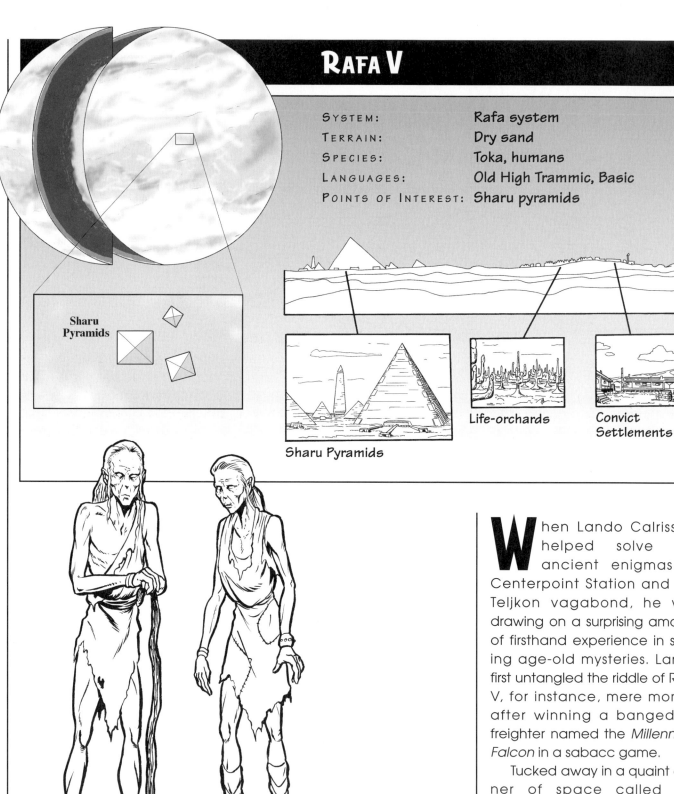

RAFA V

SYSTEM:	Rafa system
TERRAIN:	Dry sand
SPECIES:	Toka, humans
LANGUAGES:	Old High Trammic, Basic
POINTS OF INTEREST:	Sharu pyramids

Sharu Pyramids

Sharu Pyramids

Life-orchards

Convict Settlements

Toka natives.

When Lando Calrissian helped solve the ancient enigmas of Centerpoint Station and the Teljkon vagabond, he was drawing on a surprising amount of firsthand experience in solving age-old mysteries. Lando first untangled the riddle of Rafa V, for instance, mere months after winning a banged-up freighter named the *Millennium Falcon* in a sabacc game.

Tucked away in a quaint corner of space called the Centrality, the Rafa system long held interest only for archaeologists and quack physicians. The former flocked to excavate the ruins of the Sharu; the latter gathered life crystals to sell for a kilocred apiece.

"Ruins," however, is a misnomer when applied to the prehistoric edifices built by the vanished Sharu. The gaudy, variegated pyramids were made from a plastic resin that seemed completely indestructible. Even after countless millennia the edges were still sharp enough to cut a finger on. They stretched up for kilometers, blocking the sky and dwarfing the human settlements that sprang up between them.

Life crystals are the jewellike "fruit" that sprout from the indigenous silicon-based lifetrees. Though the aura generated by life-orchards saps a person's intelligence and vitality, the crystals were rumored to *extend* life spans when snapped off and worn around the neck as pendants. The sick, the elderly, and the paranoid were willing to pay outrageous prices for even the smallest Rafa crystal.

Soon after Lando's arrival in the Rafa system he was blackmailed by the local governor into searching for the Mindharp—a fabulous relic that could (the stories said) control the minds of Rafa's meek, primitive natives, the Toka. With his new pilot droid Vuffi Raa and a mysterious "key," the gambler departed for the fifth planet in the system and its colossal Sharu pyramid.

The Toka natives weren't happy to see him. Pinned down by a hail of arrows and then bound to a lifetree with only vuoles for company, Lando fully expected to die of exposure during Rafa V's frigid night.

Somehow he survived and used the key to unlock the Sharu skyscraper. *I'm losing my patience,* Lando fumed. *That Mindharp had better be inside.*

It was, and when he presented the artifact to the double-crossing governor, Lando was rewarded with a prison sentence. When his jail yard was rocked by violent groundquakes, the young captain escaped and realized that the governor had used the Mindharp.

The Toka were not primitive, after all—they *were* the ancient Sharu. Eons earlier, terrified by an overwhelming alien power, the Sharu had hidden their society beneath the ubiquitous plastic pyramids. Life-orchards sucked away their intelligence, making them appear to be docile savages. When another alien species arrived and activated the Mindharp, the Sharu would know it was safe to come out of hiding.

As the pyramids crumbled and frighteningly bizarre forms emerged from the dust, Lando and Vuffi Raa streaked away as fast as the *Falcon*'s engines could carry them. Surely there were easier ways for a droid and a con artist to make a living.

Curious vuoles live abundantly in the life-orchards.

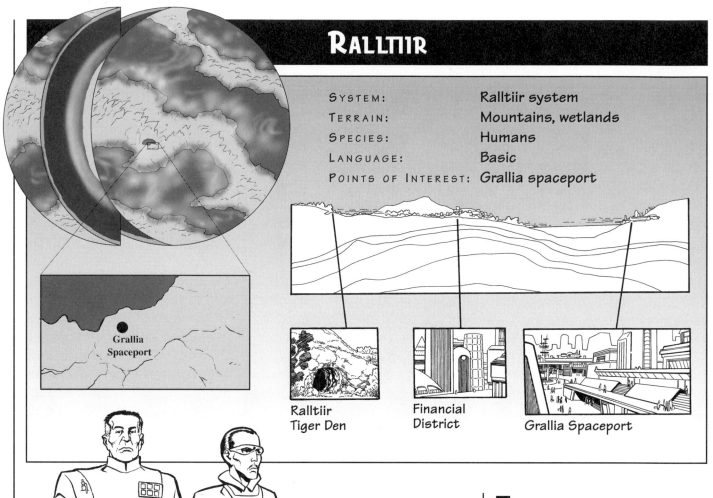

RALLTIIR

SYSTEM:	Ralltiir system
TERRAIN:	Mountains, wetlands
SPECIES:	Humans
LANGUAGE:	Basic
POINTS OF INTEREST:	Grallia spaceport

Grallia Spaceport

Ralltiir Tiger Den

Financial District

Grallia Spaceport

Lord Tion (left) commanded an Imperial task force while local bankers (right) controlled Ralltiir's economy.

Just days before the dissolution of the Imperial Senate, Palpatine ordered the brutal subjugation of Ralltiir, proving that not even a prosperous and influential Core World could stand in the way of the Emperor's New Order.

This high-tech world shares the Ringali Shell with prominent planets such as Chandrila and Esseles and lies along the busy commercial lane called the Perlemian Trade Route. For generations Ralltiir has been known as a center of banking; its financial institutions were considered some of the most stable in the galaxy.

Fanatic supporters of Pal-

The deadly Ralltiir tiger.

patine's new regime, however, infiltrated the planetwide fiscal records and tampered with them, bringing them more "in line" with existing Imperial prejudices. Nonhuman investors and known Rebel sympathizers logged in to discover that their life savings had been erased.

Knowing that the planet's reputation was at stake, the Ralltiir High Council denounced the sabotage and worked to reverse the damage. However, anything less than a public oath of loyalty to Emperor Palpatine would not be tolerated in the current political climate.

An Imperial task force under the command of Lord Tion was dispatched to quash all opposition. Tion disbanded the High Council, arrested its "treasonous" members, and set up a puppet military tribunal in its place. Roving impressment gangs dragged suspected dissidents to interrogation centers, and a naval blockade prevented anyone from leaving. Resistance from Ralltiir's citizens was dealt with swiftly and pitilessly.

Rumors of atrocities inspired Princess Leia Organa to make a mercy mission to Ralltiir. Her consular ship *Tantive IV*, loaded with relief supplies that could quickly be converted to military purposes, was permitted to land by an indulgent Lord Tion.

Tion's ruthlessness was matched only by his ego. Convinced that the princess was smitten with him, he tried to interest her in an intimate dinner. Fortunately, he was diverted by a Rebel raid at the spaceport's southern perimeter.

The attack was a trick. With Tion's forces preoccupied, a wounded Rebel stumbled across the tarmac toward the princess. He had information about a new Imperial terror weapon, code-named "Death Star," that had to be stopped at all costs. Darth Vader, on hand to observe the pacification of Ralltiir, nearly uncovered the ruse, but Leia managed to convince the Dark Lord that their intentions on Ralltiir were innocent.

With the soldier and his information safely aboard, the *Tantive IV* blasted away from Ralltiir. Though the planet had suffered horrors—its financial markets, for example, might never recover—the intelligence data passed on to the princess culminated in the destruction of the Death Star and the eventual collapse of Imperial tyranny.

RODIA

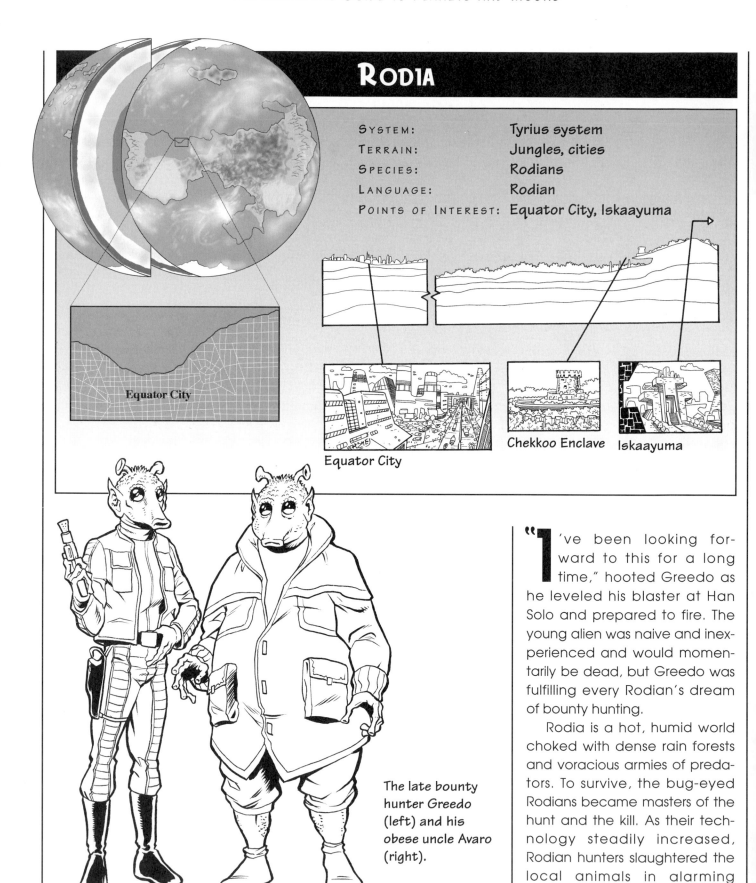

SYSTEM: **Tyrius system**
TERRAIN: **Jungles, cities**
SPECIES: **Rodians**
LANGUAGE: **Rodian**
POINTS OF INTEREST: **Equator City, Iskaayuma**

Equator City

Chekkoo Enclave   Iskaayuma

Equator City

The late bounty hunter Greedo (left) and his obese uncle Avaro (right).

"**I**'ve been looking forward to this for a long time," hooted Greedo as he leveled his blaster at Han Solo and prepared to fire. The young alien was naive and inexperienced and would momentarily be dead, but Greedo was fulfilling every Rodian's dream of bounty hunting.

Rodia is a hot, humid world choked with dense rain forests and voracious armies of predators. To survive, the bug-eyed Rodians became masters of the hunt and the kill. As their technology steadily increased, Rodian hunters slaughtered the local animals in alarming numbers. Even the bloodthirsty ghest seemed on the verge of extinction.

That was when an Old Republic scout ship landed on the Rodian homeworld. These humans were pitiful fighters, but their powerful fire weapons made them a challenging quarry. Fortunately for the Republic scouts, the Rodian Grand Protector realized the potential of joining a galactic society filled with billions of potential targets.

In exchange for high-tech imports, the Grand Protector allowed certain Rodians to leave the planet and serve the Republic by tracking down dangerous fugitives. Winning passage offworld was awarded only to hunters who had won the coveted atiang, the annual prize given for the "best catch" or the "longest trail." Rodian bounty hunters quickly earned a reputation as the best in the galaxy.

Today Rodia is dominated by sprawling cities and weapons-manufacturing plants eating into the deep green of the surrounding jungle. The capital city of Iskaayuma is the stronghold of Grand Protector Navik the Red, a barbarous warlord who won his title by exterminating the rival Tetsus clan. The surviving Tetsus— including the infant Greedo— left Rodia for their own safety. Since he never received proper instruction in the mastery of murder, poor Greedo found himself woefully outclassed by a Corellian smuggler's guile.

After Boba Fett took Han Solo away from Bespin in a solid slab of carbonite, Han's friends immediately began planning his rescue. While trying to capture Fett at a moon of Zhar, they learned that someone was trying to kill Luke Skywalker. Leia and Chewbacca journeyed to Rodia to contact Black Sun, the galaxywide criminal cabal that might hold the key to unraveling the assassination plot.

The *Millennium Falcon* touched down in Equator City, a noisy jumble of casinos and pleasure houses on the ocean coast. Lando led them past advertising holoboards and phony ornamental shrubbery to the Flip of the Credit casino owned by the late Greedo's obese uncle, Avaro Sookcool.

Sookcool was a Tetsus but had avoided Navik the Red's death sentence as a result of his close ties to Black Sun. The lisping Rodian bore no ill will toward the friends of his nephew's killer—he knew Greedo had gotten in over his head— and agreed to contact the crime syndicate on Leia's behalf.

Several days later, just as the group was beginning to tire of squandering further credits at Sookcool's sabacc tables, Black Sun arrived. Guri was a human replica droid; exotic, deadly, and utterly lifelike. Leia and Chewie departed from Rodia on Guri's *Stinger*, bound for Coruscant and a clandestine meeting with Prince Xizor.

It is not uncommon for a ghest to attack a primitive village and devour all its inhabitants.

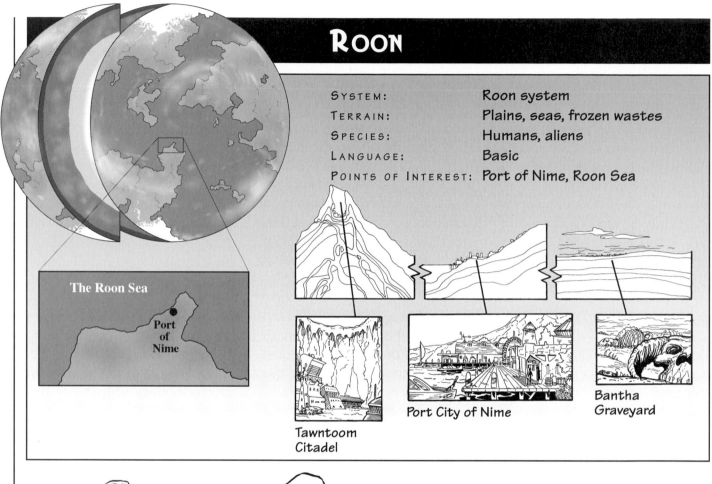

ROON

SYSTEM:	Roon system
TERRAIN:	Plains, seas, frozen wastes
SPECIES:	Humans, aliens
LANGUAGE:	Basic
POINTS OF INTEREST:	Port of Nime, Roon Sea

The Roon Sea

Port of Nime

Tawntoom Citadel

Port City of Nime

Bantha Graveyard

The depraved Governor Koong (left) and a native mudman (right).

In a remote pocket of the Outer Rim lies a navigator's nightmare ominously known as the Cloak of the Sith. This dark mass of seething gases and spinning asteroids is so hazardous that it is officially classified as impenetrable. For the brave few who attempt the crossing, the reward is worth the risk—the Cloak harbors the galaxy's only source of Roonstones.

The legendary planet Roon sits at the heart of the Cloak like a bright sapphire in a well of ink. It rotates on its axis once a year, so one side is perpetually lit while the other is cold and caliginous.

The many-legged mogo pack beast undulates as it walks.

The world's inhabitants, an eclectic mix of humans, near humans, and aliens, arrived over the centuries by following the tails of the Rainbow comets. These itinerant ice balls pass close to Roon's small sun once a year and trace out the only safe path through the Cloak of the Sith.

Because of their nearly total isolation, Roon's colonists are tough and self-reliant. They seldom ride a landspeeder when a sturdy mogo will do and still use oar-driven wooden galleys on the sparkling Roon Sea. The annual Colonial Games pit the local provinces against each other in no-holds-barred relay races, the most difficult being the climactic "drainsweeper." The victorious territory secures bragging rights and a measurable political edge for the coming season.

Primitive mudmen are native to Roon. The semisentient creatures can be broken down into many smaller versions of themselves with a concentrated spray of water. The tiniest mudmen are sometimes captured in glass containers and sold as pets.

Roonstones drive the economy of the planet. These fist-sized iridescent gems are worth a fortune on the open market, but their scarcity prevents them from becoming a major export. For generations frustrated miners have drilled empty shafts in vain, searching for the elusive Roonstone source.

A number of years before the Battle of Yavin, R2-D2 and C-3PO journeyed to Roon in the company of their master, Mungo Baobab. Mungo hoped to discover the source of the Roonstones and establish a lucrative trade route in the name of the Baobab Merchant Fleet.

But the villainous Governor Koong had other plans. Koong, the ironfisted ruler of Tawntoom province, would settle for nothing less than the total conquest of Roon and the death of Mungo Baobab. With Emperor Palpatine's observer, Admiral Screed, watching over his shoulder, Koong's agents woke a ravenous shamunaar from hibernation, then tried to fix the

Colonial Games. When both schemes failed to eliminate his rivals, Koong blanketed the Umboo province with germ-warfare gas.

To stop the power-mad governor, Mungo and the droids infiltrated his frozen citadel. There they discovered that the stronghold was built on a mountain of Roonstones but lost the gems when the fortress self-detonated.

Mungo, however, had salvaged a few. To his surprise, the rocks contained an embedded poem describing an eons-old battle on Coruscant. This amazing revelation hints at an ancient, alien origin for the Roonstones.

Artoo and Threepio eventually departed from Roon and soon found themselves on a barge bound for the Kalarba system. They thought their lives were about to slow down but they were in for a rude surprise.

The monster shamunaar is a constant threat to wild banthas.

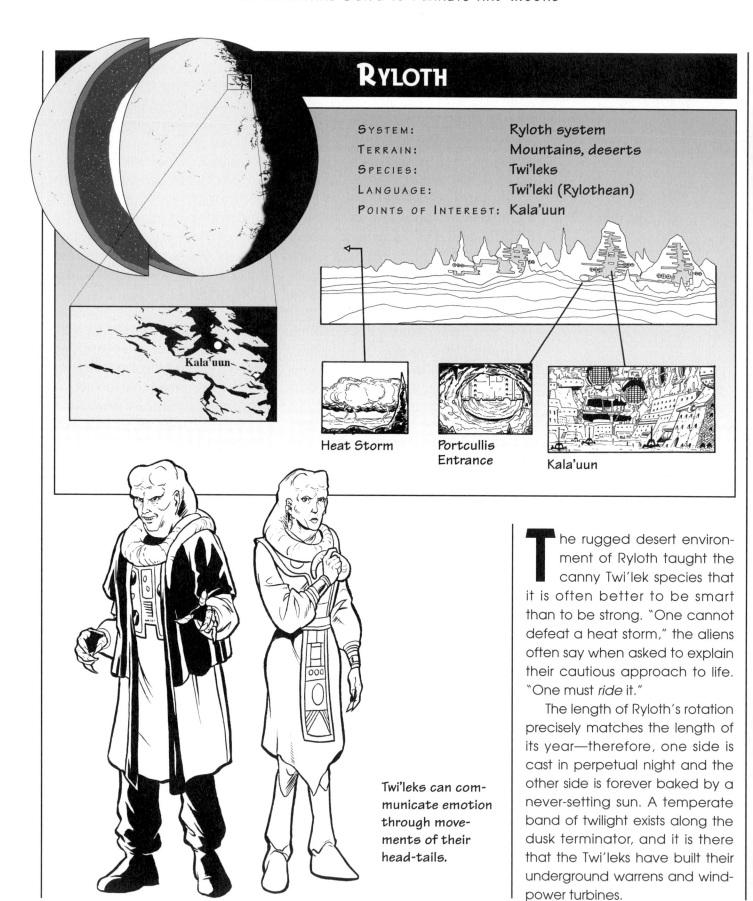

RYLOTH

SYSTEM:	Ryloth system
TERRAIN:	Mountains, deserts
SPECIES:	Twi'leks
LANGUAGE:	Twi'leki (Rylothean)
POINTS OF INTEREST:	Kala'uun

Kala'uun

Heat Storm

Portcullis Entrance

Kala'uun

Twi'leks can communicate emotion through movements of their head-tails.

The rugged desert environment of Ryloth taught the canny Twi'lek species that it is often better to be smart than to be strong. "One cannot defeat a heat storm," the aliens often say when asked to explain their cautious approach to life. "One must *ride* it."

The length of Ryloth's rotation precisely matches the length of its year—therefore, one side is cast in perpetual night and the other side is forever baked by a never-setting sun. A temperate band of twilight exists along the dusk terminator, and it is there that the Twi'leks have built their underground warrens and wind-power turbines.

Twi'leks are easily recognized by their *lekku*, or "head-tails," two fleshy appendages that hang from the base of the skull. These prehensile growths are a source of great personal pride and can be used to sign in a secret and subtle gestural language that only other Twi'leks can read.

Their society is divided into families and tribes ruled by a five-member council called the head clan. When one of the five rulers dies, the remaining four are exiled to certain death in the sun-scorched "Bright Lands." A new head clan is then appointed swiftly and pragmatically.

Kala'uun is a typical Twi'lek city. Buried within a black basaltic mountain peak in the Lonely Five range, it is accessible only through a winding subterranean tunnel. A heavy portcullis protects the city from the frequent heat storms, which will incinerate any traveler unlucky enough to be caught outside. The stone barrier also deters some of Ryloth's more persistent predators, such as the spear-footed lylek. Within Kala'uun's main cavern a hundred thousand industrious Twi'leks live, raising livestock, growing edible fungi, and mining ryll spice.

Bib Fortuna, Jabba the Hutt's majordomo, was one of the first Twi'leks to bring slavers to his world. Branded as an outcast for turning against his own kind, Fortuna soon had his revenge. He gathered an army of Jabba's most vicious thugs and laid waste to seven cities. Fortuna's plans to rule Ryloth, however, were temporarily sidetracked when Tatooine's B'omarr monks surgically removed his brain from his body.

Years later, after New Republic forces captured Coruscant, they found that their victory had been spoiled by a deadly outbreak of the Krytos virus. Wedge Antilles and Rogue Squadron were dispatched to Ryloth to secure a large amount of ryll *kor*, which would be used to synthesize a cure. The pilots got their ryll, but Wedge nearly had to fight Tal'dira, leader of a homegrown fighter squadron called the Chir'daki ("death-seeds").

The Krytos vaccine was a success thanks to the Twi'leks, and soon the watchful aliens got another chance to help defeat the Empire. Several Chir'daki pilots teamed up with Rogue Squadron and fought with distinction in the Bacta War.

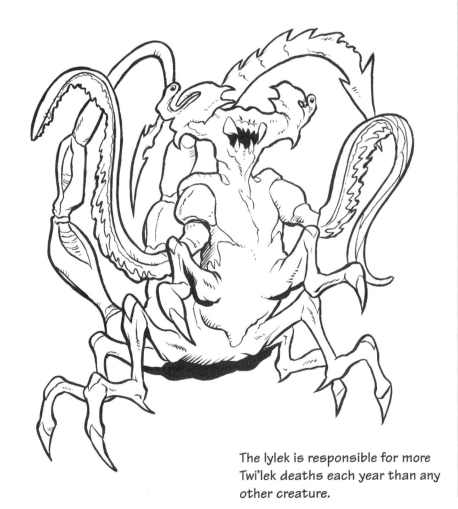

The lylek is responsible for more Twi'lek deaths each year than any other creature.

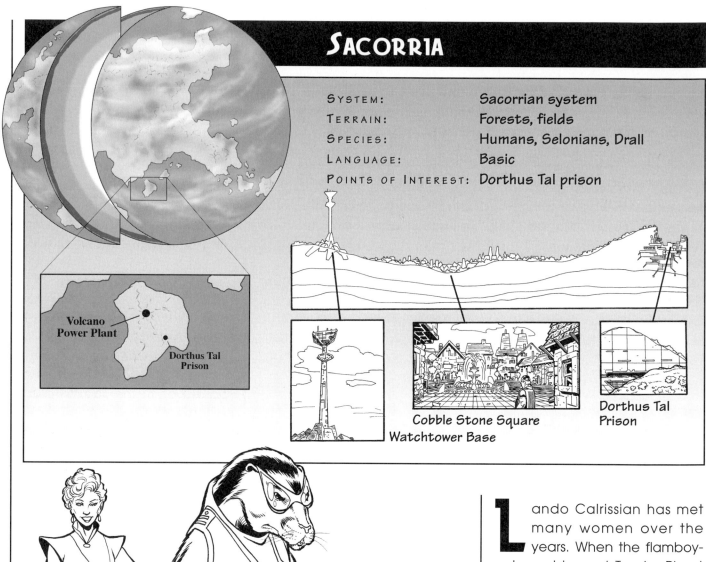

SACORRIA

SYSTEM:	Sacorrian system
TERRAIN:	Forests, fields
SPECIES:	Humans, Selonians, Drall
LANGUAGE:	Basic
POINTS OF INTEREST:	Dorthus Tal prison

Volcano Power Plant

Dorthus Tal Prison

Watchtower Base

Cobble Stone Square

Dorthus Tal Prison

Tendra (left), one of Lando Calrissian's romantic interests, with a Selonian member of the Triad.

Lando Calrissian has met many women over the years. When the flamboyant gambler met Tendra Risant on Sacorria, he thought she might just be the love of his life. Neither of them, however, could foresee the dramatic events unfolding in Sacorria, which would drag them both into a showdown in the Corellian system and shake the foundations of the New Republic.

Sacorria is one of the many "Outlier" systems at the fringes of the Corellian sector that are generally considered backwaters, dwarfed as they are by the powerful and influential Corellian system. The secluded

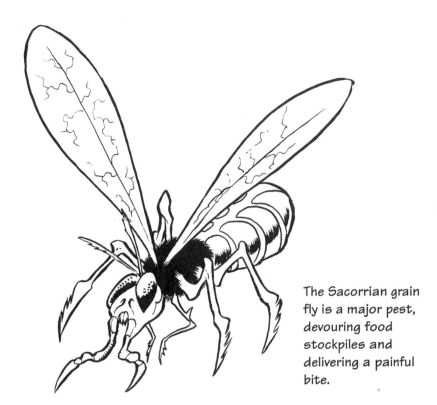

The Sacorrian grain fly is a major pest, devouring food stockpiles and delivering a painful bite.

planet has a single large moon called Sarcophagus, which serves as a vast graveyard for the planet's inhabitants. It is visited only by mourners interring their dead.

The Triad, a shadowy group of three dictators—one human, one Selonian, and one Drall—governs Sacorria. During the Emperor's reign the Triad was merely a mouthpiece for the Diktat of Corellia, but the balance of power shifted greatly after Palpatine's death. As the Diktat gradually lost influence, the Triad secretly consolidated its power.

Agents of the Triad discovered ancient planetary repulsors on the five worlds of the Corellian system and learned how to use Centerpoint Station as a supernova-inducing weapon. Continuing to hide the extent of their authority, the Sacorrian Triad set in motion their plan to become the rulers of an independent Corellian empire.

Fourteen years after the Battle of Endor, during Leia Organa Solo's visit to the Corellian system, Triad-backed rebellions erupted on all five planets. A massive jamming and interdiction field was thrown over the area, and Centerpoint began systematically destroying stars. The New Republic appeared helpless to intervene.

Meanwhile, Lando Calrissian had arrived on Sacorria with Luke Skywalker, looking for a rich woman he could marry for her money. Tendra Risant fit the bill, but once Lando met her, he abandoned his mercenary atti-

tude. Tendra was attractive, friendly, and warm, and she genuinely cared about him. Their budding relationship was cut short, however, when Triad port officials kicked the visitors off Sacorria under a new set of restrictive, xenophobic laws.

Lando left with Luke to investigate the unstable situation in the nearby Corellian system. Tendra, unwilling to lose Lando so easily, left Sacorria in a cut-rate starship and tried to alert him to the Triad war fleet that was slowly assembling in her homeworld's orbit.

Tendra's vital warnings were intercepted by Lando and passed on to the Bakuran cruisers that made up the hastily assembled New Republic armada. As soon as the interdiction field was dropped, the two fleets clashed in a frenzied battle. Despite many deaths, the Triad's navy was smashed and Centerpoint was successfully disabled.

Lando and Tendra at last had time to enjoy each other's company. And as talk turned to the possibility of marriage, they both promised to consider it *very* carefully.

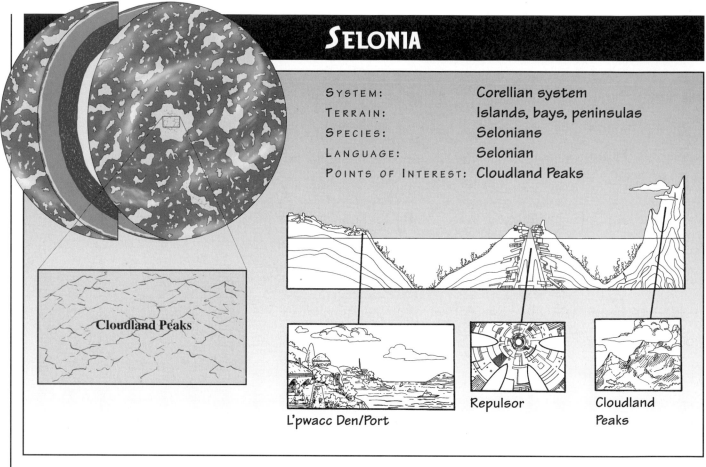

SELONIA

SYSTEM:	Corellian system
TERRAIN:	Islands, bays, peninsulas
SPECIES:	Selonians
LANGUAGE:	Selonian
POINTS OF INTEREST:	Cloudland Peaks

Cloudland Peaks

L'pwacc Den/Port

Repulsor

Cloudland Peaks

Selonians include (from left to right) the sterile female, fertile male, queen female, and adolescent.

As one of the five primary planets in the Corellian system, Selonia sees a great deal of starship traffic pass by on the way to and from the system's massive shipyards. Nevertheless, most visitors and even some native Corellians know very little about the Selonians and their uniquely alien culture.

Selonia has no large land masses or large oceans. The world is covered with a bewildering array of islands, archipelagoes, inlets, and peninsulas separated by narrow seas and shallow waterways. Its most striking geologic feature is the twisting range of volcanic mountains

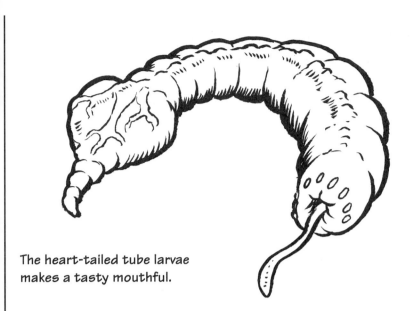

The heart-tailed tube larvae makes a tasty mouthful.

called the Cloudland Peaks.

Sleek and powerful, Selonians are fur-covered carnivores descended from aquatic mammals. They can move just as easily on four legs as on two, and their heavy tails make potent bludgeoning weapons. Despite outward appearances, they have a social structure more common to insectoid races—Selonians are hive animals. Each den includes one queen and a few fertile males, who sire all the members of the den. Fertile Selonians, despite their importance, are treated scornfully as mere "breeding stock."

It is the sterile female workers of the hive who perform all the other functions of Selonian life. Females with the same father are in one "sept" and are genetically identical. Competing dens control regions of territory on Selonia, and the ruling clan is known as the Overden.

Fourteen years after the Battle of Endor chaos erupted in the Corellian system. The Triad of the planet Sacorria, which included members of a long-dishonored Selonian den, masterminded a plan to take over the sector. Han Solo, visiting Corellia, was captured and imprisoned by his cousin Thrackan Sal-Solo, the self-proclaimed Corellian Diktat. Han was forced to battle a powerful Selonian named Dracmus for Thrackan's sadistic amusement, but Dracmus's Selonian friends freed the two captives from jail.

As they boarded the cone-ship that would take them to Selonia, it became clear that Dracmus did not have Han's best interests at heart. Her clan, the Hunchuzuc, wanted to use the famous New Republic hero as a bargaining chip to negotiate with a rival faction back on her homeworld.

Unfortunately, the ruling

Overden had made a deal with the disgraced Selonians of the Sacorrian Triad, and gained control of Selonia's planetary repulsor. A single shot from the ancient weapon destroyed the Bakuran warship *Watchkeeper*. In the face of such power Dracmus submitted, surrendering the Hunchuzuc Den—and Han Solo—to the Overden.

The tables turned when Dracmus learned of the Overden's complicity with the ignominious Selonians of Sacorria. Dishonor and deception are *unforgivable* sins in Selonian society. The leader of the Overden had no choice but to relinquish power in favor of the Hunchuzuc Den, who threw their support behind the New Republic. The crisis in the Corellian system was one step closer to a successful resolution.

SULLUST

SYSTEM: **Sullust system**
TERRAIN: **Underground caves**
SPECIES: **Sullustans**
LANGUAGE: **Sullustan**
POINTS OF INTEREST: **SoroSuub headquarters, Piringiisi**

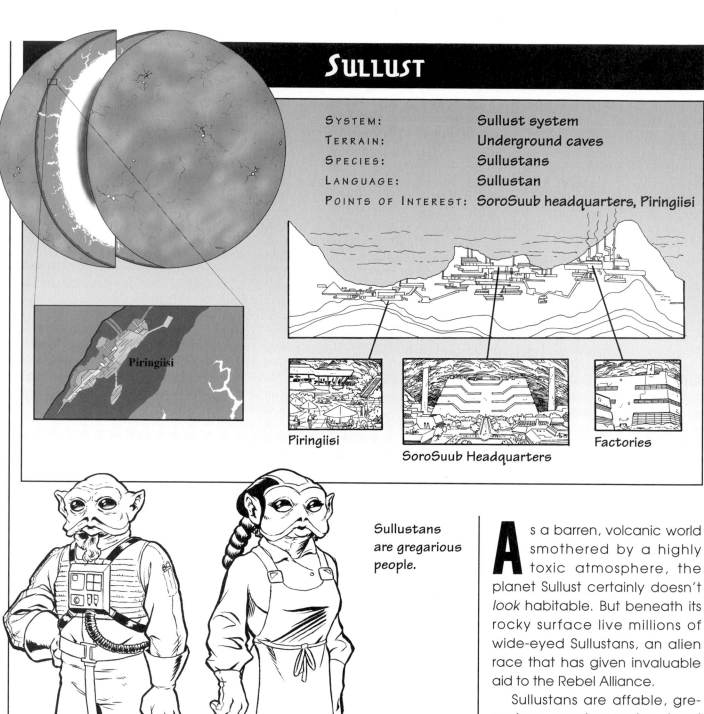

Piringiisi

Piringiisi

SoroSuub Headquarters

Factories

Sullustans are gregarious people.

As a barren, volcanic world smothered by a highly toxic atmosphere, the planet Sullust certainly doesn't *look* habitable. But beneath its rocky surface live millions of wide-eyed Sullustans, an alien race that has given invaluable aid to the Rebel Alliance.

Sullustans are affable, gregarious creatures who stand around 1.5 meters tall and are known for their jowled faces and chattering language. Their subterranean cities are highly advanced and startlingly beautiful—wealthy sightseers from halfway across the galaxy tour Sullust and visit the hot-springs resort of Piringiisi. Dank breeding

Drutash grubs are best served with omaton sauce.

farms produce edible delicacies such as drutash grubs, but most foodstuffs are grown on the agricultural moon of Sulon.

Evolving in a network of dark, mazelike warrens imbued the species with an unfailing sense of direction. Once a Sullustan has traveled a path, the way is *never* forgotten. This innate skill even extends to hyperspace, making Sullustans prized as star navigators and explorers.

SoroSuub, one of the galaxy's largest manufacturing conglomerates, is based on Sullust and employs half the population in its mining, production, and packaging departments. The company makes hundreds of products, from injecto-kit shoes and battle armor to the XP-38 landspeeder. As its economic clout grew, SoroSuub eventually took control of the planetary ruling council, making Sullust one of the few worlds governed by corporate executives.

As an enthusiastic supporter of the Empire, SoroSuub sent its products to fuel the Imperial war machine; its employees were forbidden to voice support for the Rebellion. Many citizens disagreed, but SoroSuub's security officers kept a tight clamp on dissent.

One defiant Sullustan pilot, Nien Nunb, began raiding company shipping convoys and turning the spoils over to the Alliance. Rebel leaders, meanwhile, tried to win the planet and its substantial resources over to their cause. In one incident the starfighter ace Keyan Farlander helped rescue a Sullustan executive from Imperial captivity, a heroic act that helped convince the company to back the Rebels openly several years later.

As a sign of its new support SoroSuub allowed Admiral Ackbar's formidable armada to rendezvous at the planet just before the Battle of Endor. Darth Vader was concerned about this turn of events and made his feelings known to his master. "What of the reports of the Rebel fleet massing near Sullust?"

"It is of no concern," scoffed the Emperor. "Soon the Rebellion will be crushed."

The Rebels were indeed heading into a trap, but their dogged determination was Palpatine's undoing. Nien Nunb, copiloting the *Millennium Falcon* with Lando Calrissian, helped fire the concussion missiles that took down the Death Star and saved the day. Since that triumphant event Nien has become a folk hero among the Sullustans, and his homeworld has become a valued and trusted member of the New Republic.

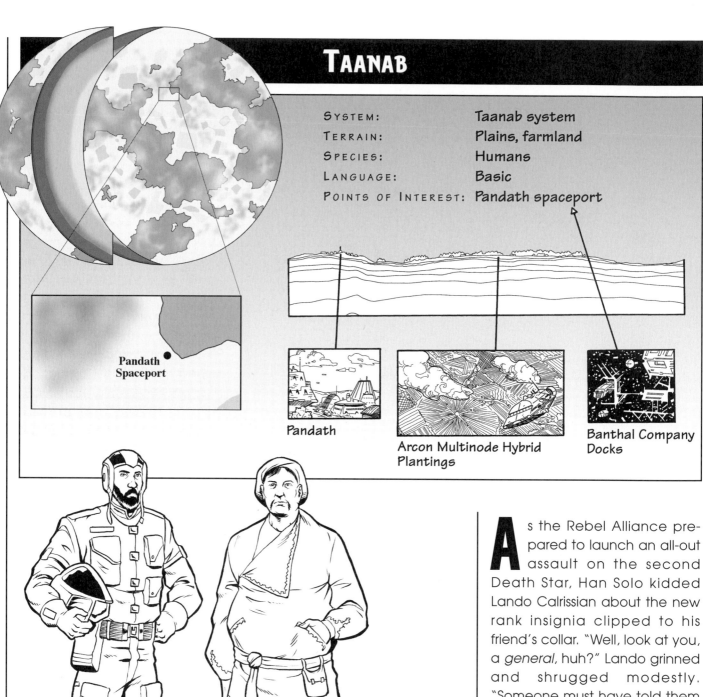

TAANAB

SYSTEM:	Taanab system
TERRAIN:	Plains, farmland
SPECIES:	Humans
LANGUAGE:	Basic
POINTS OF INTEREST:	Pandath spaceport

Pandath Spaceport

Pandath

Arcon Multinode Hybrid Plantings

Banthal Company Docks

A Taanab fleet pilot (left) and wealthy patron (right).

As the Rebel Alliance prepared to launch an all-out assault on the second Death Star, Han Solo kidded Lando Calrissian about the new rank insignia clipped to his friend's collar. "Well, look at you, a *general*, huh?" Lando grinned and shrugged modestly. "Someone must have told them about my little maneuver at the Battle of Taanab."

For once Lando wasn't just boasting. In a fast, furious—and occasionally hilarious—skirmish, the suave con man liberated the peaceful farmers of Taanab from years of persecution at the hands of a local pirate band. Thanks to the piloting skill and

Primary food sources include the Ambrian staga...

tactical genius he exhibited in the one-sided fracas, Calrissian was given command of all Rebel fighter wings during the Battle of Endor.

The celebrated affair began soon after the Alliance's victory at Yavin. Lando, hauling a shipment of freight to Taanab, was killing time in the Pandath cantina when an armada of Norulac pirate ships emerged from hyperspace at the system's fringe.

Taanab's small defensive fleet moved to defend the cargo ships at the Banthal orbital docking array, but they knew it was a useless gesture. The pirates ravaged their planet every year without fail, and the Empire was too preoccupied to protect a small, insignificant farm world.

Lando, intrigued, studied the developing situation on the bar's dented holovid. Seemingly on a whim, he stood up and declared that he could defeat the pirates single-handedly. One wealthy patron, snorting in disbelief, put up the deed to a

...and the roba, both bred and raised on farms.

Clendoran brewery—it was Calrissian's if the cocky captain could pull off his outlandish boast. Amid a chorus of derisive jeers, Lando's freighter lifted off into the clear violet sky.

While the battle-scarred corsairs prepared for their deadly run on the stardock, Lando hid his vessel in the ice ring of Taanab's pale moon. When the raiders were close enough, the gambler raced out into their path—and played his trump card. Stabbing at the hatch release, Lando ejected a full payload of Conner nets smack into the middle of the formation.

The electrified webs of fine mesh unfolded and drifted, hopelessly ensnaring most of the fleet before those ships could take evasive action. As the furious freebooters struggled to unsnarl their ships, Lando gleefully bashed them with heavy ice chunks towed by tractor beam from the moon's frozen ring. Finally, Calrissian rallied the Taanab space force, leading it in a decisive mopping-up operation in which he notched over nineteen kills. The Norulac pirates were utterly annihilated.

Jubilant Taanab officials offered their emancipator a permanent position in their star fleet, but the dashing rogue politely turned them down. Planetary militia officers drew miserable salaries, and he *did* have a brand-new Clendoran brewery to investigate.

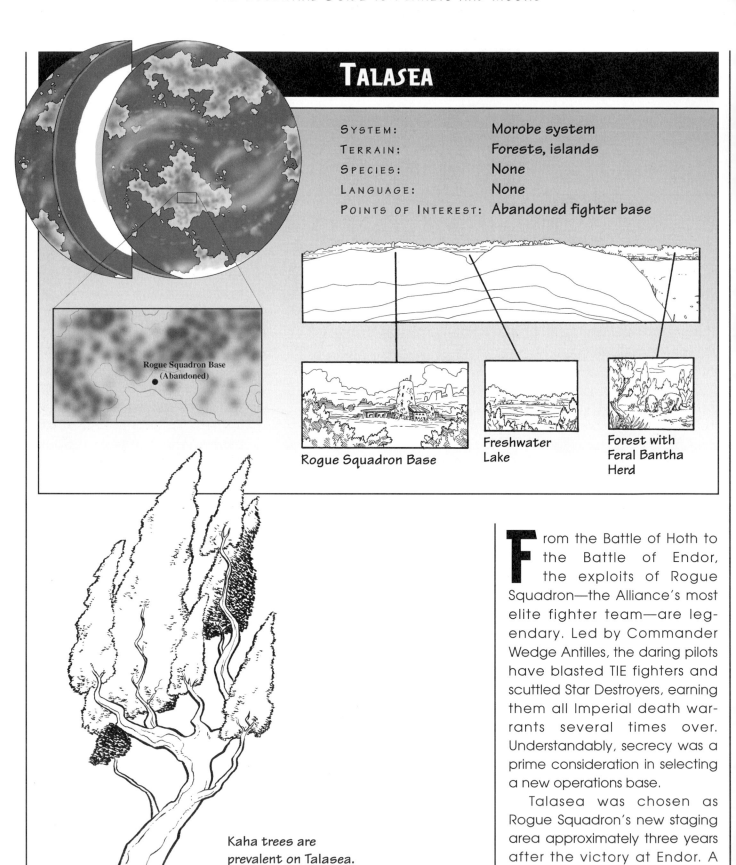

TALASEA

SYSTEM:	Morobe system
TERRAIN:	Forests, islands
SPECIES:	None
LANGUAGE:	None
POINTS OF INTEREST:	Abandoned fighter base

Rogue Squadron Base
(Abandoned)

Rogue Squadron Base

Freshwater Lake

Forest with Feral Bantha Herd

Kaha trees are prevalent on Talasea.

From the Battle of Hoth to the Battle of Endor, the exploits of Rogue Squadron—the Alliance's most elite fighter team—are legendary. Led by Commander Wedge Antilles, the daring pilots have blasted TIE fighters and scuttled Star Destroyers, earning them all Imperial death warrants several times over. Understandably, secrecy was a prime consideration in selecting a new operations base.

Talasea was chosen as Rogue Squadron's new staging area approximately three years after the victory at Endor. A chilly, forested world blanketed by a clinging white mist, the ver-

Feral banthas develop a mean personality and roam at will.

dant planet was uninhabited. It had once housed a small farming colony, but the homesteaders had made the fatal mistake of harboring a desperate Jedi Knight on the run from the Emperor's campaign of genocide. When Darth Vader finally located the fugitive, he murdered every last Talasean for daring to stand in the way of Palpatine's New Order, and their farming herds returned to the wild.

Alliance techs laboriously converted the empty ruins of Talasea's Planetary Governor's palace to a working operations base. Clearing tangles of ivy and evicting nesting animals, work crews converted storage rooms into hangars and sagging cottages into pilots' barracks. Wedge Antilles looked on with pleasure. This remote, overlooked planet would be a perfect spot for launching attacks against the Empire's new leader, Ysanne Isard.

"Iceheart," however, had given the special agent Kirtan Loor the job of ferreting out Rogue Squadron's new rats' nest. Armed with a photographic memory, Loor analyzed sensor data from the Rogues' recent sortie into the Hensara system. Discovering patterns that would have gone unnoticed by lesser men, Loor narrowed the number of candidate worlds down to a handful, then subjected that list to a final criterion—the Rebels' penchant for converting abandoned ruins to their own needs. Only one name remained: Talasea.

A platoon of Imperial stormtroopers made a stealthy landing in the dead of night. Creeping from their darkened transport, the saboteurs affixed explosive charges to the Grand Hall and all the outlying buildings, concentrating on stress points and weakened beams. When the charges were triggered by remote control, those Rebels not killed in the blast would be crushed by collapsing timber.

But the men and women of Rogue Squadron are formidable foes, even outside the cockpits of their X-wing fighters. Corran Horn and Ooryl Qrygg dispatched several invaders with their bare hands and roused the rest of the pilots from their bunks. The Imperials got just what they'd hoped to avoid—a full-scale firefight. Pinned down by blaster bolts, with the element of surprise lost, the outgunned stormtroopers were all captured or killed.

The victory came at great cost. The pilot Lujayne Forge was dead, shot while she slept. Now that Talasea Base was no longer secure, the evacuation began immediately. Rogue Squadron would have to find a new home before taking revenge on Iceheart.

Feral rycrits were once domesticated farm animals.

TALUS AND TRALUS

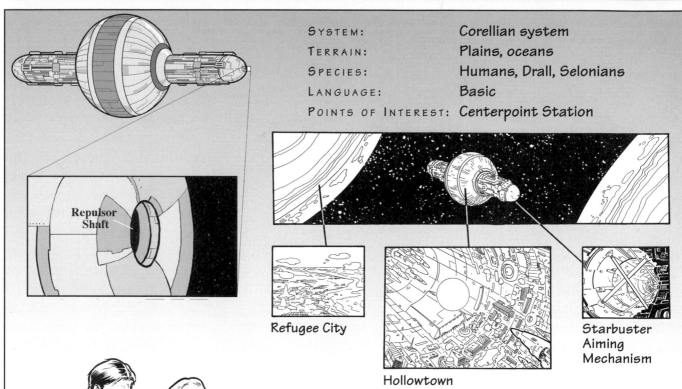

SYSTEM:	Corellian system
TERRAIN:	Plains, oceans
SPECIES:	Humans, Drall, Selonians
LANGUAGE:	Basic
POINTS OF INTEREST:	Centerpoint Station

Repulsor Shaft

Refugee City

Hollowtown

Starbuster Aiming Mechanism

Centerpoint Station survivors migrated to the Double Worlds.

Talus and Tralus are the least populated and least important of the five inhabited Corellian planets. Nevertheless, they hold the key to the entire system's formation, for between them lies Centerpoint Station—an ancient engine capable of moving worlds.

Talus and Tralus, often called the Double Worlds, share much more than similar names. The two planets have the same size, gravity, and terrain types and are governed by the Federation of the Double Worlds, or Fed-Dub. Talus and Tralus also orbit each other as they circle the star Corell. At the barycenter,

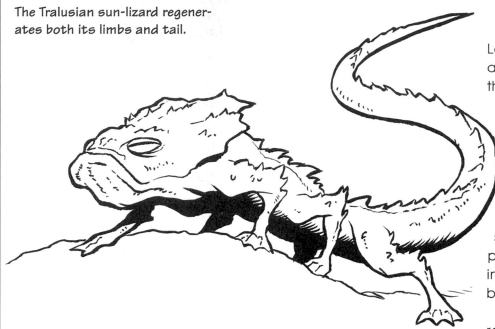

The Tralusian sun-lizard regenerates both its limbs and tail.

or balance point, directly between the two spheres is the gray bulk of Centerpoint Station.

Centerpoint is unimaginably ancient. Over three hundred kilometers long, the space station has existed since the earliest recorded Corellian history. No one knows who built it, and until recent events no one knew *why*. When intersystem space travel first became practical, inhabitants from the Double Worlds settled Centerpoint's hollow interior.

The installation's spacious core, heated and illuminated by an artifical sun called the Glowpoint, was perfect for habitation. Soon homes, lakes, and farms lined the spherical interior, constituting the community of Hollowtown. Artificial gravity was created through centrifugal force as the station slowly spun on its axis.

For millennia Centerpoint remained undisturbed except for the quiet village thriving in its heart. But fourteen years after the destruction of the second Death Star the Sacorrian Triad discovered Centerpoint's true purpose. It had been constructed by a prehistoric and unimaginably powerful alien race to transport all five Corellian planets through hyperspace and into their current orbits. If reactivated, the device could fire a tractor-repulsor burst through hyperspace and cause any star in the galaxy to explode in a supernova.

The Triad implemented its plans. Centerpoint aimed, and the first star was targeted and destroyed. As the deadly repulsor burst built up energy, the Glowpoint flared, burning Hollowtown to a crisp. The devastated survivors fled to Talus and Tralus.

Another star was destroyed before Luke Skywalker and Lando Calrissian finally arrived at Centerpoint to investigate. As the station geared up for a third shot, the heroes found themselves trapped in the blackened ruins of Hollowtown. The Glowpoint released scorching waves of heat in another flare-up. Though they escaped, they could not stop the irreversible firing process—a third star and all its inhabited planets would soon be destroyed.

The key lay in the planetary repulsors buried beneath the surface of each of the Corellian planets. Young Anakin Solo struggled to line up the Drall repulsor for an interference shot at Centerpoint, while the New Republic and Sacorrian Triad fleets clashed in orbit.

The operation was a success, and Centerpoint Station was harmlessly shut down. The immediate crisis was over, but a flock of archaeologists and scientists descended on the Double Worlds. Their investigation into the prehistoric origins of the Corellian system was just beginning.

TATOOINE

SYSTEM:	Tatoo system
TERRAIN:	Deserts
SPECIES:	Humans, Jawas, Sand People
LANGUAGE:	Basic, Bocce, Jawa
POINTS OF INTEREST:	Mos Eisley spaceport, Beggar's Canyon

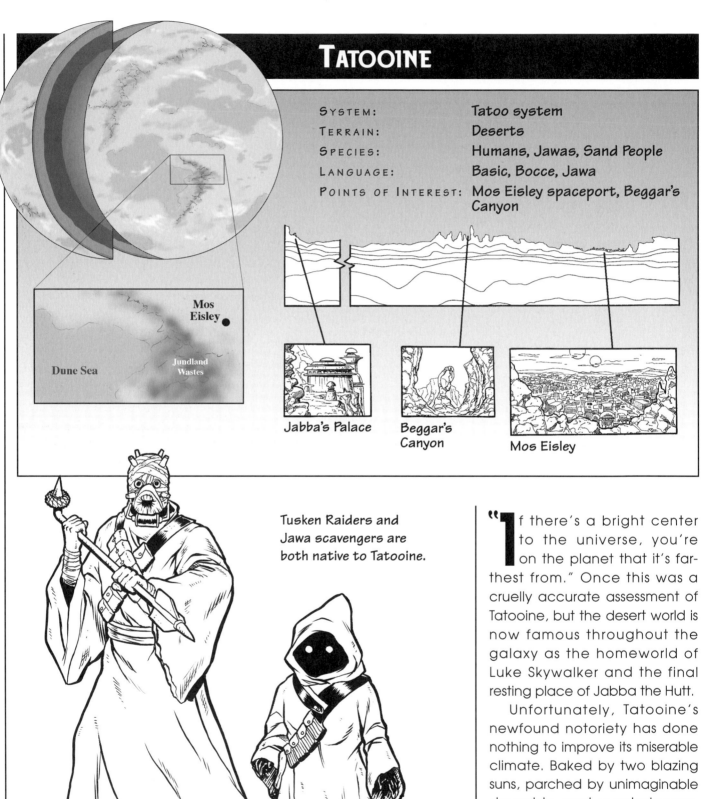

Mos Eisley

Dune Sea

Jundland Wastes

Jabba's Palace

Beggar's Canyon

Mos Eisley

Tusken Raiders and Jawa scavengers are both native to Tatooine.

"If there's a bright center to the universe, you're on the planet that it's farthest from." Once this was a cruelly accurate assessment of Tatooine, but the desert world is now famous throughout the galaxy as the homeworld of Luke Skywalker and the final resting place of Jabba the Hutt.

Unfortunately, Tatooine's newfound notoriety has done nothing to improve its miserable climate. Baked by two blazing suns, parched by unimaginable droughts, and regularly punished with bone-scouring sandstorms, the planet may be an interesting place to visit, but *no one* wants to live there.

Sand People have a special bond with their bantha mount.

Except, of course, for its two indigenous species: Sand People and Jawas. Both races spend their arduous lives swathed in heavy wrappings and dust cloaks, but otherwise they couldn't be more dissimilar. Sand People, or Tusken Raiders, are enigmatic barbarian warriors who live in close-knit tribes with their bantha mounts. The ferocious nomads are perhaps the only beings brave (or foolish) enough to hunt the slavering krayt dragon, which can devour a ronto in three wet bites.

The diminutive Jawas are cowardly yellow-eyed scavengers who roam the vast Dune Sea in colossal sandcrawlers. Abandoned machinery, regardless of condition, is repaired with generous amounts of engine tape and hot spit. The only thing a Jawa loves more than tinkering is haggling with a gullible rancher over the price of a reconditioned—and probably defective—moisture vaporator.

As an infant, Luke Skywalker was taken to the distant desert world by Obi-Wan Kenobi, who placed him with the plainspoken, hardworking farmers Owen and Beru Lars. As the towheaded boy grew into adulthood, his "uncle" Owen sheltered him from the truth about his father. Obi-Wan kept a watchful eye from his hermitage in the Jundland Wastes.

Luke dreamed of far-off adventure while harvesting crops and racing his skyhopper through Beggar's Canyon. Then, one fateful day, his uncle purchased two banged-up droids from Jawas.

In a whirlwind of events Luke witnessed the deaths of his guardians, helped rescue a captive princess, and became a fighter pilot and war hero in the Rebel Alliance. Commander Skywalker had a new life. He had no reason to believe he would ever return to the gritty sands of his youth.

But Jabba the Hutt, a galactic gangster, had an old score to settle with Han Solo. Jabba had the carbonized Corellian delivered to his Tatooine fortress, and Luke and his friends staged a daring rescue above the gaping maw of the Sarlacc. With Jabba dead and his criminal syndicate in ruins, the eerie B'omarr monks crept out in their brain-walkers to claim the Hutt's deserted palace.

Over eight years later Luke

Jawas ride the agreeable ronto when coming to town.

and Han returned to Tatooine to investigate rumors of a new Hutt scheme—the Darksaber project. Cloaked by the Force, the two friends traveled on banthaback with a fierce Tusken tribe.

When they reached Jabba's palace, they found it to be a desiccated sarcophagus. Spiderlike B'omarr armatures were the only things disturbing the heavy dust, but Han found the information they were looking for.

Ferocious krayt dragons live in Tatooine's caves.

TELTI

SYSTEM:	Sistooine system
TERRAIN:	Sand, industrial domes
SPECIES:	Droids, humans
LANGUAGES:	Various droid languages, Basic
POINTS OF INTEREST:	Droid factories

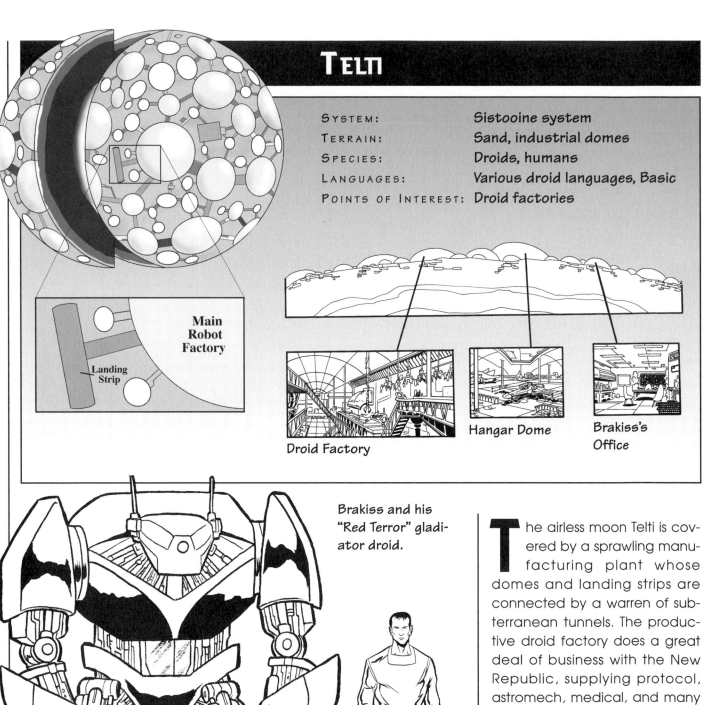

Main Robot Factory

Landing Strip

Droid Factory

Hangar Dome

Brakiss's Office

Brakiss and his "Red Terror" gladiator droid.

The airless moon Telti is covered by a sprawling manufacturing plant whose domes and landing strips are connected by a warren of subterranean tunnels. The productive droid factory does a great deal of business with the New Republic, supplying protocol, astromech, medical, and many other automaton models to the highest levels of the government on Coruscant.

After trying and failing to infiltrate Luke Skywalker's Jedi academy as an Imperial spy, the Force-sensitive human Brakiss found some measure of peace overseeing the day-to-day operations of the Telti assembly plants. But that peace came with a price. The ruthless Almanian Kueller helped subsidize the facility, and in return Brakiss installed an explosive detonator, triggered by remote control, in every droid that rolled off his production lines. Brakiss was the only human on Telti; his assembly procedures were entirely automated, and a squad of five hundred "Red Terror" gladiator droids ensured his privacy.

Thirteen years after the Battle of Endor, following the mysterious bombing of Senate Hall on

C-9PO

Coruscant, Luke Skywalker traveled to Telti to question his former pupil. Landing his X-wing in the hangar dome, Luke was met by the droid C-9PO and led through various assembly areas of the protocol-droid facility. Their eerie tour passed beneath hundreds of dangling, disconnected limbs and metallic appendages while rows of bronze heads and glowing eyes regarded Luke impassively from innumerable shelves.

When Luke reached the main assembly area, Brakiss forced a lightsaber fight but suddenly backed down. He chose instead to warn the Jedi Master away from Kueller, the madman waiting for him on Almania.

Soon afterward C-3PO and R2-D2 persuaded the young mechanic Cole Fardreamer to take them to Telti, since Artoo insisted that that moon was the source of the Senate Hall detonators. The robotic duo investigated the facility while Cole met with Brakiss. The naive mechanic told his host all about the detonators, assuming that one of Brakiss's employees had turned traitor. Unfortunately, the only traitor was Brakiss himself.

Cole was taken to a vast torture chamber operated by EV-9D9.2, a sister model of the sadistic droid once owned by Jabba the Hutt. Meanwhile, Threepio bumbled straight into the Red Terror and R2-D2 was ejected into a junk heap. Many of the droids in this scrap pile, all

EV-9D9.2

barrel-shaped astromech models like Artoo, were still operational. Rallying the discarded droids to his cause, Artoo led his motley army parading down Telti's sterile hallways.

The battered but brave astromechs overpowered the Red Terror (much to Threepio's relief) and confronted Brakiss, who fled from the moon aboard a shuttle. At the last possible instant Artoo disabled a master detonation signal beamed from Almania, preventing all of Brakiss's rigged droids from exploding, and saved countless lives across the galaxy.

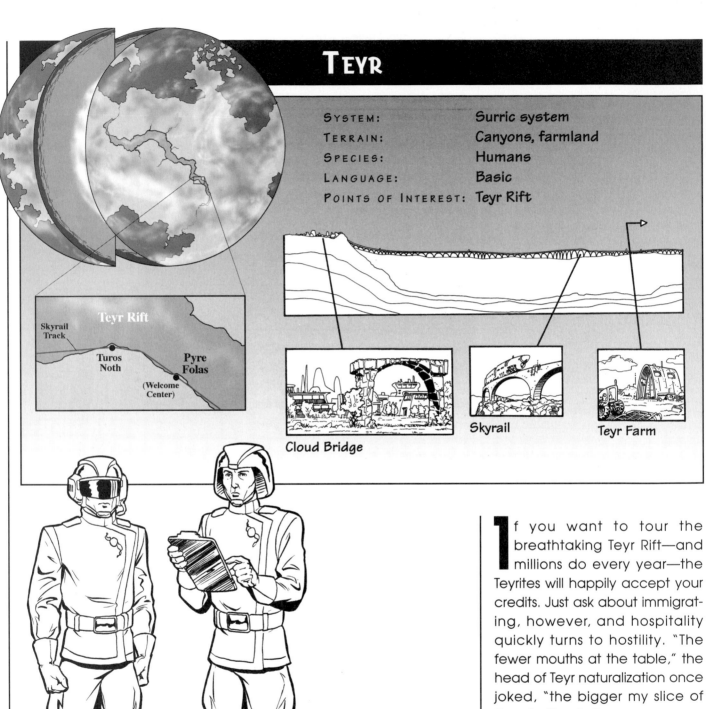

TEYR

SYSTEM:	Surric system
TERRAIN:	Canyons, farmland
SPECIES:	Humans
LANGUAGE:	Basic
POINTS OF INTEREST:	Teyr Rift

Teyr Rift

Skyrail Track

Turos Noth

Pyre Folas

(Welcome Center)

Cloud Bridge

Skyrail

Teyr Farm

Teyrite skyrail operator (left) and port offical (right) help keep tourists on track.

If you want to tour the breathtaking Teyr Rift—and millions do every year—the Teyrites will happily accept your credits. Just ask about immigrating, however, and hospitality quickly turns to hostility. "The fewer mouths at the table," the head of Teyr naturalization once joked, "the bigger my slice of the pikatta pie."

Entry visas are buried beneath a mountain of red tape and a metric ton of bureaucracy, but the payoff is worth it. Teyr Rift is stunning, slashing across more than four thousand kilometers of the planet's face. The canyon's spectacular vistas are unrivaled by anything else in the galaxy.

Thousands of cruise ships, luxury liners, and pleasure yachts arrive each day at the congested orbital docking platforms, and their passengers are shuttled down to the planet below. It's possible to land directly on the surface, at dozens of overcrowded hangars, if you're wealthy (or desperate) enough to pay the three hundred percent premium.

Like preprogrammed droids, every new tourist heads straight for the Rift Skyrail with holocams in hand. This remarkably fast elevated train connects all the canyon stops together and is one of the best places to gasp at the plunging chasms, stratified fissures, and the setting sun's rays as they glint off the golden horns of mesa groats.

Far from the Rift lie other, quieter regions of Teyr, places that aren't dependent on tourism to stay alive. In the heart of the agricultural Greenbelt lies Griann, a sleepy working-class town arrayed in a perfect checkerboard grid. Farther still is Sodonna, a city in decline whose strategic position at the mouth of the Noga River once allowed it to control all merchant traffic on the waterways.

Thirteen years after the Battle of Endor Luke Skywalker went to Teyr, looking for traces of the Fallanassi religious order. His companion Akanah was eager to rejoin her Fallanassi sisters; Luke was desperate to find information on his long-lost mother. Akanah hoped to pick

The mesa groat.

up the trail in the village of Griann.

The Rift Skyrail didn't travel into the unremarkable, bucolic countryside, so Luke rented a small bubbleback speeder and headed west on Flyway 120. Disappointment hit them like a hammer blow when they reached Griann. The home where Akanah's friend had once lived had been obliterated by a cyclone years earlier.

Fortunately, they picked up clues that led them to Sodonna, where the Fallanassi had once owned a group of communal lowhouses. Sneaking past a zealous security droid, Akanah

retrieved a hidden "scribing" message. That missive revealed her Circle sisters' new home: J't'p'tan.

Akanah had business to attend to first—personal business that she couldn't reveal to her traveling companion. They returned to their skiff *Mud Sloth*, and Luke asked her what the message had revealed. "Atzerri," she lied. "We need to go to Atzerri now."

THYFERRA

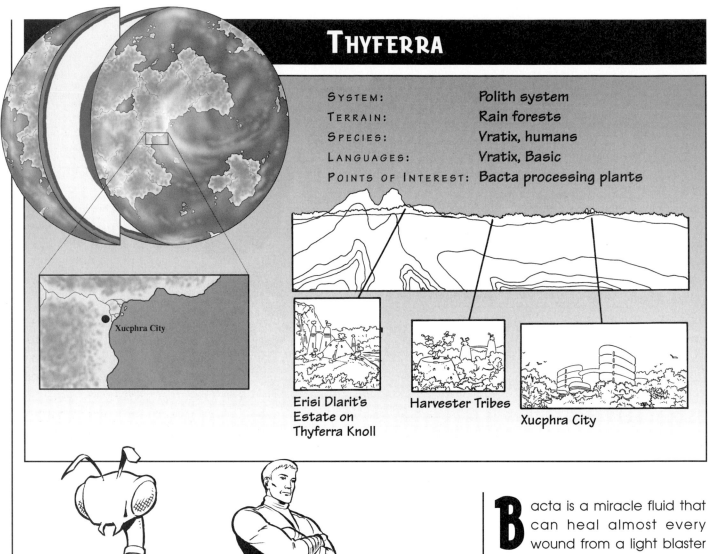

SYSTEM:	Polith system
TERRAIN:	Rain forests
SPECIES:	Vratix, humans
LANGUAGES:	Vratix, Basic
POINTS OF INTEREST:	Bacta processing plants

Xucphra City

Erisi Dlarit's Estate on Thyferra Knoll

Harvester Tribes

Xucphra City

Vratix manufacture bacta while humans manage the economics of Thyferra.

Bacta is a miracle fluid that can heal almost every wound from a light blaster burn to severe medical trauma. And if one needs bacta, there is only one place to get it: Thyferra, home of the Bacta Cartel.

The mantislike Vratix were born in the oppressive humidity of Thyferra's omnipresent rain forests. The hermaphroditic insects inhabited communal towers of mud and saliva and raised small knytix as loyal pets and a tasty food source. Thyferra was dutifully catalogued by Old Republic scouts, then forgotten.

The galaxy quickly took

Knytix make excellent pets, and excellent soup.

notice of this small world when Vratix *verachen*, or "master brewers," created bacta by mixing alazhi plants with the chemical kavam. The new emulsion was a wonder—much more effective at treating wounds than the Pydyrian healing stick—and the Thyferran bacta corporations became very wealthy.

The Vratix's talents, however, were geared toward the mixing of bacta, not the management of galaxywide conglomerates. Ambitious humans began filling the ranks of administrators and executives.

Two of the largest bacta corporations, Xucphra and Zaltin, made a secret deal with the antialien Empire, giving them a shared monopoly over the industry. Ten thousand wealthy, aristocratic humans soon controlled Xucphra and Zaltin, unjustly dominating the Vratix workers. Some Vratix actively opposed their overbearing mas-

ters, forming a terrorist sect known as the Ashern, or "Black Claw."

Xucphra and Zaltin, fierce competitors, collectively maintained a stranglehold on the galaxy's bacta supply by hoarding their staggering profits and routinely engaging in price-fixing. They were often referred to as the "Bacta Cartel" by those fed up with their excessive influence.

Every medclinic needs bacta, and no government could afford to ignore Thyferra. In an effort to gain goodwill, the New Republic recruited two Thyferran humans—one from Xucphra and one from Zaltin—into Rogue Squadron. Within a year the divided planet became a battleground in a conflict known as the Bacta War.

After Ysanne Isard, the Empire's cruel leader, fled from Coruscant, she took her Super Star Destroyer straight to

Thyferra. In a bloodless coup the dictator was appointed head of state by the Xucphra faction. Since "Iceheart" had obtained her new position through legitimate channels, the New Republic government felt it could not move against her. Rogue Squadron, however, lived up to its name—resigning from the military, the X-wing pilots went after Iceheart in an unsanctioned "rogue" operation.

Wedge Antilles and his fighter team harassed Iceheart by raiding her bacta convoys and eliminating her capital ships. Meanwhile, a commando team rallied the maltreated Vratix to their cause. In a final climactic clash—on Thyferra's surface and in the clear skies above—Isard's fleet was smashed and her iron grip on the world was broken. The liberated Vratix vowed to join the New Republic, so the domination of the cartels may soon be a thing of the past.

TYNNA

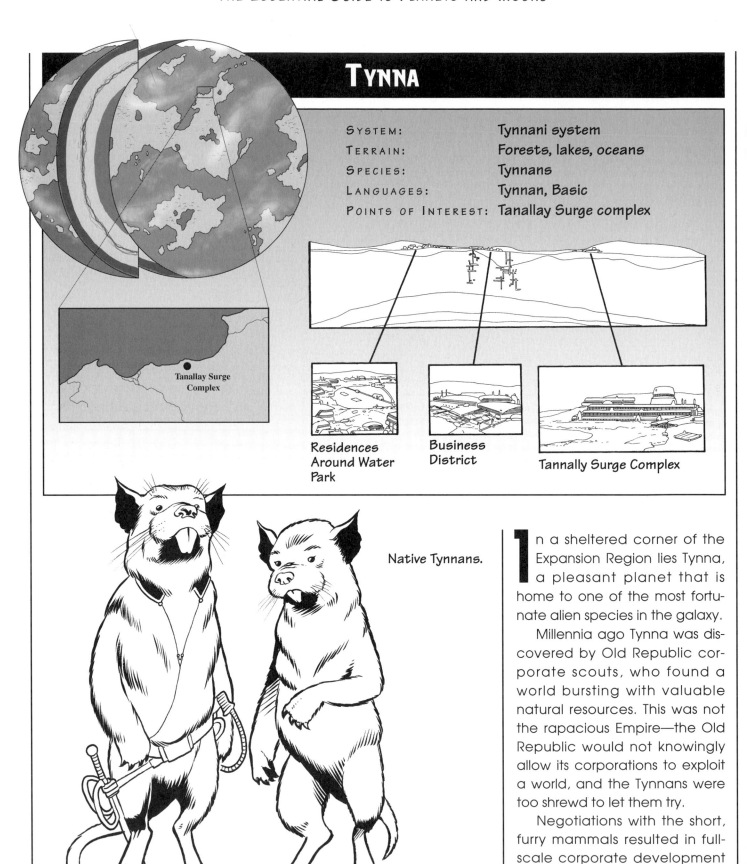

SYSTEM:	Tynnani system
TERRAIN:	Forests, lakes, oceans
SPECIES:	Tynnans
LANGUAGES:	Tynnan, Basic
POINTS OF INTEREST:	Tanallay Surge complex

Tanallay Surge Complex

Residences Around Water Park

Business District

Tannally Surge Complex

Native Tynnans.

In a sheltered corner of the Expansion Region lies Tynna, a pleasant planet that is home to one of the most fortunate alien species in the galaxy.

Millennia ago Tynna was discovered by Old Republic corporate scouts, who found a world bursting with valuable natural resources. This was not the rapacious Empire—the Old Republic would not knowingly allow its corporations to exploit a world, and the Tynnans were too shrewd to let them try.

Negotiations with the short, furry mammals resulted in full-scale corporate development that allowed the planet's natural beauty to remain intact. The

The suuri are a main food source for Tynnans and taste best when capured live.

Tynnans' share of the staggering profits was reinvested in their society. Being for being, they were left with one of the most affluent civilizations in the entire Republic.

Aquatic mammals, Tynnans love swimming in their planet's cold waters and hunting for suuri beneath kelp-covered rocks. They compensate for their poor eyesight with excellent hearing and olfaction as well as quick-witted and highly practical minds.

Tynnan society is entirely state run. All citizens have free access to housing, food, education, and even entertainment. Their wealth allows many to travel the galaxy as tourists, never working a day in their lives, but no one who has ever met a Tynnan would describe them as lazy. The planetary government, ruling from the Tanallay Surge legislative and recreational complex, is selected by lottery. Since *any* citizen can be chosen to serve, the sensible Tynnans always stay informed about important issues.

The galaxy's most famous Tynnan was Odumin, a Corporate Sector Authority (CSA) territorial manager who met his match in two smugglers named Han Solo and Chewbacca. Starting off as a lowly collections agent, Odumin worked his way into CSA management; after he saved the life of the Imperial Grand Inquisitor on board a luxury liner, his success was assured. He soon acquired the services of the notorious gunman Gallandro on retainer.

Odumin uncovered evidence of a widespread slavery ring reaching into the top levels of Authority management. Eager to see if he still possessed the skills for successful fieldwork, he adopted the persona of Spray, a starship skip tracer trying to repossess the *Millennium Falcon* on behalf of several outraged creditors.

Chewbacca, taken in by the ruse, reluctantly agreed to take the bill collector along on their mission to Ammuud. When the *Falcon* crashed in Ammuud's mountains, Odumin kept them alive by catching spiny crustaceans in the icy lakes—an easy task for any native of Tynna but a job deeply appreciated by an arboreal Wookiee.

"Spray" revealed his true identity when the slavers attacked the ship by calling in a *Victory*-class Star Destroyer to apprehend them. Captain Solo, however, proved to be a more bothersome problem. The brash Corellian captured the Tynnan executive, turning him over to the Authority warship in exchange for ten thousand credits and a promise of safe passage out of the territory. Odumin had to give Solo credit for his audacity, but he'd better not try *that* stunt again.

UMGUL

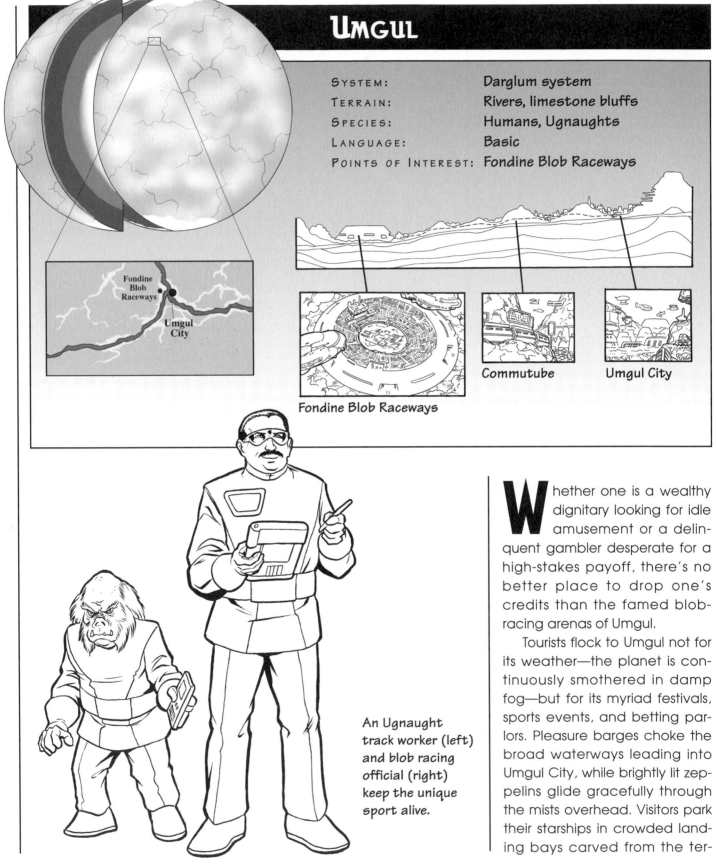

SYSTEM:	Darglum system
TERRAIN:	Rivers, limestone bluffs
SPECIES:	Humans, Ugnaughts
LANGUAGE:	Basic
POINTS OF INTEREST:	Fondine Blob Raceways

Fondine Blob Raceways

Umgul City

Fondine Blob Raceways

Commutube

Umgul City

An Ugnaught track worker (left) and blob racing official (right) keep the unique sport alive.

Whether one is a wealthy dignitary looking for idle amusement or a delinquent gambler desperate for a high-stakes payoff, there's no better place to drop one's credits than the famed blob-racing arenas of Umgul.

Tourists flock to Umgul not for its weather—the planet is continuously smothered in damp fog—but for its myriad festivals, sports events, and betting parlors. Pleasure barges choke the broad waterways leading into Umgul City, while brightly lit zeppelins glide gracefully through the mists overhead. Visitors park their starships in crowded landing bays carved from the ter-

The Umgul racing blob with extended pseudopodia.

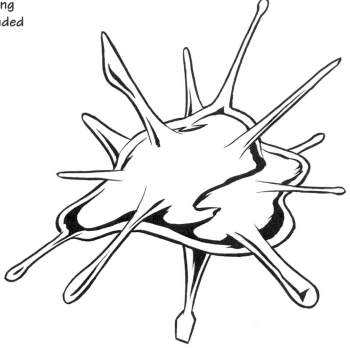

raced limestone cliffs, where they are immediately set upon by a horde of clamoring vendors hawking trinkets, holomaps, and low-interest loans.

Sooner or later, everyone takes the public commutube to the Fondine Blob Raceways, the best of the planet's many thoroughbred tracks. Blob racing is a sport unique to Umgul. The native gelatinous animals possess no central brain. If sliced into pieces, the quivering clumps move independently to fuse back into a complete whole. Small blobs have medicinal and aesthetic uses, but the largest specimens are trained as sprinters from birth.

The Fondine track, which is ringed with powerful fans to blow back the ubiquitous fog, incorporates a constantly changing array of twelve dead-ly obstacles, which each blob must pass to reach the finish line. With millions of credits riding on each race, the roar of the crowd becomes deafening as the syrupy masses ooze through funnels, flow across beds of sharp nails, and squeeze past spinning razor blades.

Before Luke Skywalker opened his Jedi academy, he enlisted Lando Calrissian's help in finding Force-sensitive candidates. Lando located a gambler with a seemingly *supernatural* ability to win at the blob races and traveled to Umgul with R2-D2 and C-3PO in tow.

Disappointingly, Lando's prospect turned out to be a fraud. The young man had been sneaking into the blob corrals at night and implanting micro-motivators beneath the creatures' greasy skin. The devices would later generate a fear reflex, causing the chosen blob to sprint headlong for the finish. Lando apprehended the culprit in a shoot-out at the stables.

The punishment for convicted cheaters on Umgul is death. The poor man's fate seemed sealed until he revealed his secret; his name was Dack, and he was fleeing an unhappy marriage to the smothering Duchess of Dargul, Umgul's sister planet. A million-credit reward had been posted for his safe return.

Deciding they could bend the laws just this once, Lando and the track owner returned Dack to Dargul. A grateful Duchess made Lando a millionaire and ordered the construction of a new subsidiary blobstacle course at the Fondine Raceways—the "Dack Track."

VERGESSO ASTEROIDS

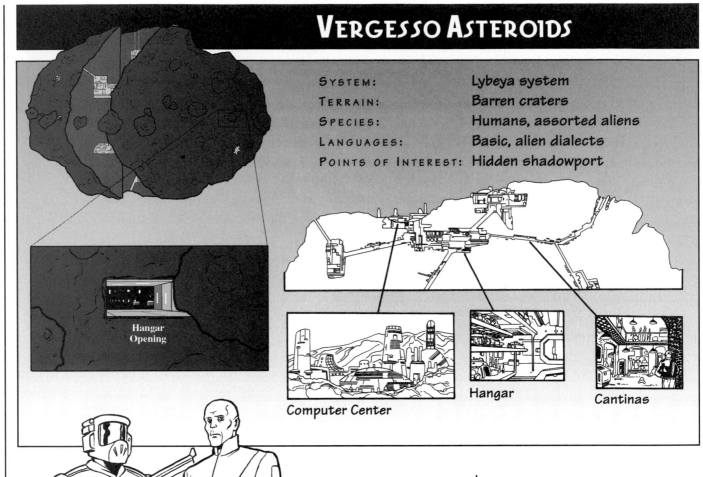

SYSTEM:	Lybeya system
TERRAIN:	Barren craters
SPECIES:	Humans, assorted aliens
LANGUAGES:	Basic, alien dialects
POINTS OF INTEREST:	Hidden shadowport

Hangar Opening

Computer Center

Hangar

Cantinas

Weggit Arpor (right), protected by heavily armed bodyguards, represents the Tenloss syndicate on Vergesso.

The drifting Vergesso Asteroids form five wide bands that orbit the yellow star Lybeya. There are no habitable planets around Lybeya, and its swath of common nickel-iron asteroids holds no mineral wealth. Understandably, legitimate space traffic passes right by this worthless system, providing perfect cover for one of the Outer Rim's largest shadowports.

Built within a huge, moon-sized planetoid in the third asteroid field, Vergesso Base was a haven for smugglers, pirates, criminals, and soldiers of the Rebel Alliance. Owned by Ororo Transportation, a front corporation for the criminal Tenloss syndicate, the facility was a place for the less than lawful to make repairs and conduct business while avoiding the Empire's watchful eye. The Rebel pilots stationed in Vergesso Base were aware of Tenloss's criminal nature but realized that war makes strange allies. Grand Moff Kintaro, the Imperial ruler of Bajic sector, had conveniently found ways to overlook the base whenever the appropriate bribes were offered.

Soon after the Battle of Hoth the Tenloss syndicate attempted to muscle its way to the top of the spice-smuggling pyramid in the Bajic sector. Unfortunately for Tenloss, this put it in direct competition with the galaxy-spanning criminal organization Black Sun. Prince Xizor, the sinister head of Black Sun, sent his human replica droid Guri to assassinate Ororo Transportation's board of directors for their effrontery.

However, this was not thorough enough for Xizor. He revealed the location of Vergesso Base to Darth Vader, claiming that it was a Rebel Alliance stronghold. Xizor knew the Emperor would order it eliminated, and his predictions proved true. Despite Vader's objections that this mission was not worth his time, Palpatine ordered his servant to the Lybeya system to smash the base.

An imposing Imperial battle-

The dianoga infests waste facilities in the market and habitation levels.

fleet led by the Super Star Destroyer *Executor* leapt into the asteroid belt on top of the surprised Rebels and smugglers. Despite nearly hopeless odds, a swarm of defensive fighters boiled out of Vergesso's hangar. While his Star Destroyers engaged the escort frigates and larger ships, Vader climbed into his personal TIE fighter for one-on-one dogfighting against the X-wing pilots.

The Dark Lord of the Sith blasted one fighter after another into glowing dust but was disgusted at how easy it was. He had not faced a worthy adversary since the confrontation with his son at Bespin, and he would not find one here. Annoyed, Vader returned to his command ship to let his underlings finish the mopping up.

Vergesso Base was left in shambles. Thousands of personnel were killed, and hundreds of ships were reduced to scorched, drifting chunks of twisted plasteel. The Rebel Alliance lost dozens of badly needed starfighters, while the Tenloss syndicate learned a valuable lesson—never cross the prince of Black Sun.

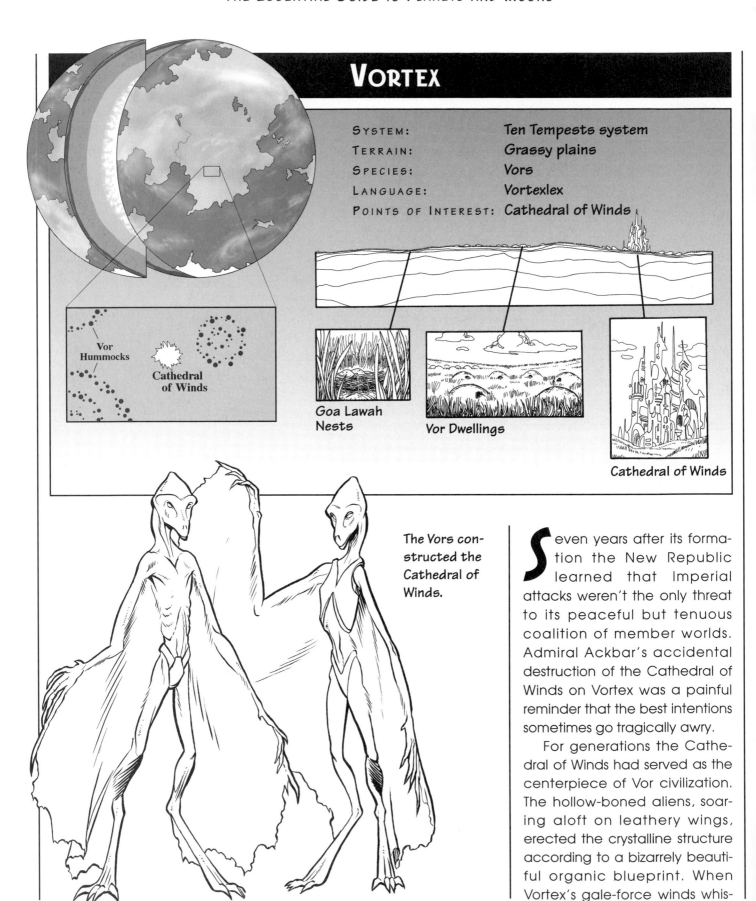

VORTEX

SYSTEM:	Ten Tempests system
TERRAIN:	Grassy plains
SPECIES:	Vors
LANGUAGE:	Vortexlex
POINTS OF INTEREST:	Cathedral of Winds

Vor Hummocks

Cathedral of Winds

Goa Lawah Nests

Vor Dwellings

Cathedral of Winds

The Vors constructed the Cathedral of Winds.

Seven years after its formation the New Republic learned that Imperial attacks weren't the only threat to its peaceful but tenuous coalition of member worlds. Admiral Ackbar's accidental destruction of the Cathedral of Winds on Vortex was a painful reminder that the best intentions sometimes go tragically awry.

For generations the Cathedral of Winds had served as the centerpiece of Vor civilization. The hollow-boned aliens, soaring aloft on leathery wings, erected the crystalline structure according to a bizarrely beautiful organic blueprint. When Vortex's gale-force winds whistled through the glassy spires, the entire edifice acted as a giant pipe organ, resonating with an ethereal alien melody. The Vors, covering portals and vents with their own bodies, directed nature's music according to the songs in their own minds. Since no recording of the annual event was ever permitted, the Concert of Winds' beauty was matched only by its uniqueness.

Ackbar, behind the controls of his malfunctioning B-wing starfighter, plowed into the base of the cathedral like a streaking meteor. Delicate crystal pinnacles toppled and shattered in a cacophony of noise; hundreds of performing Vors were shredded by the razor teeth of broken glass. Though Imperial sabotage would later be revealed as the root cause of the crash, the horrifying incident was an unmitigated disaster for the New Republic.

Ackbar resigned his admiral's commission in disgrace, blaming himself for the 358 Vors killed in the cathedral's collapse. The Republic was made to appear both dangerous and incompetent, an unwelcome perception given its preoccupation with Admiral Daala's recent raids. Mon Mothma immediately dispatched a salvage and repair team to assist the Vors in their cleanup and help restore the government's tarnished image.

Wedge Antilles and the lovely alien scientist Qwi Xux went to Vortex to oversee the recon-

A *goa lawah's* saliva contains toxic bacteria.

struction efforts. It was fortunate, Wedge noted, that the Vors were such an inscrutable, emotionless species. They did not appear to blame Ackbar or anyone else for the catastrophe—they merely wanted to complete a new cathedral as soon as possible. When Qwi picked up a fallen shard and began piping a lilting melody, the lead Vor snatched it away and crushed the transparent flute in his fist. "*No more music,*" he commanded in accented Basic, broken glass digging into his mottled gray palm. "*Not until we are finished here.*"

After months of labor a new, streamlined Cathedral of Winds stood tall beneath the roiling Vortex sky. In a meaningful gesture of reconciliation, many New Republic delegates were invited to attend the cathedral's inaugural performance. Standing amid the circular hummocks of underground Vor dwellings, Ackbar listened contentedly to the gentle strains of a never-to-be-repeated empyrean symphony. The process of healing had begun.

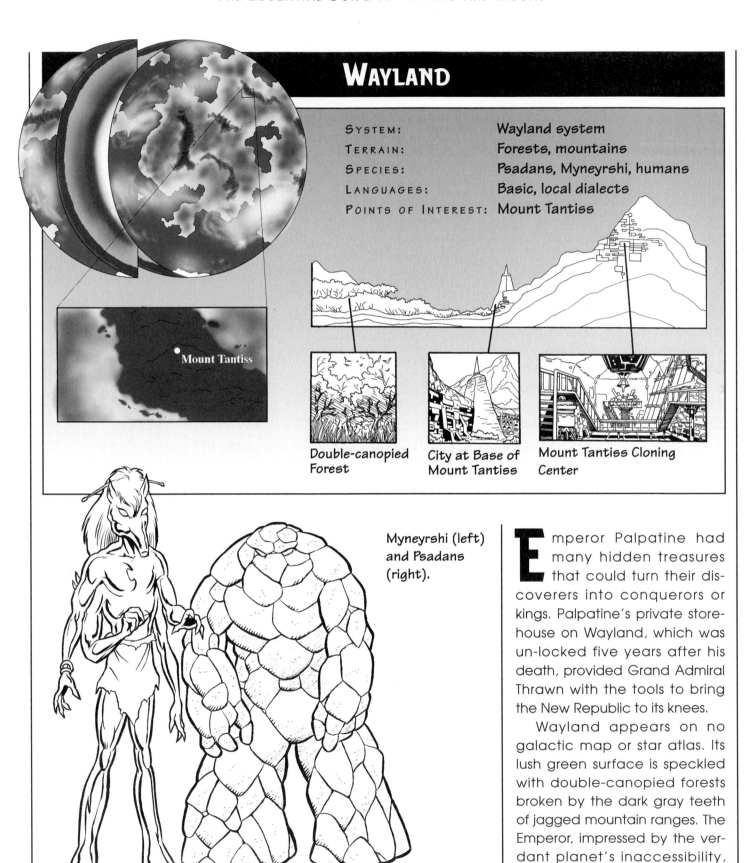

WAYLAND

SYSTEM:	Wayland system
TERRAIN:	Forests, mountains
SPECIES:	Psadans, Myneyrshi, humans
LANGUAGES:	Basic, local dialects
POINTS OF INTEREST:	Mount Tantiss

Mount Tantiss

Double-canopied Forest

City at Base of Mount Tantiss

Mount Tantiss Cloning Center

Myneyrshi (left) and Psadans (right).

Emperor Palpatine had many hidden treasures that could turn their discoverers into conquerors or kings. Palpatine's private storehouse on Wayland, which was un-locked five years after his death, provided Grand Admiral Thrawn with the tools to bring the New Republic to its knees.

Wayland appears on no galactic map or star atlas. Its lush green surface is speckled with double-canopied forests broken by the dark gray teeth of jagged mountain ranges. The Emperor, impressed by the verdant planet's inaccessibility, ordered its development as a repository for his military

Wayland's forests team with wildlife, including clawbirds...

trophies and dark-side artifacts.

His engineers encountered two aboriginal species—Psadans and Myneyrshi—plus a group of humans descended from a long-vanished colony. Dismissing the natives' primitive bows and spears, they began constructing a vast network of chambers deep in the bowels of the most forbidding mountain peak. When completed, the Mount Tantiss complex encompassed extensive treasure vaults, a throne room, and a fully operational cloning facility.

Palpatine refused to attract unwanted attention with a defensive battalion of AT-ATs. Instead, he left behind a single Dark Jedi as guardian. For years Mount Tantiss remained untouched, until Grand Admiral Thrawn learned the location of Wayland during an information raid.

After landing at Mount Tantiss, Thrawn secured the help of a mad Jedi clone, Joruus C'baoth. Though C'baoth claimed to have killed the Emperor's guardian, there is some evidence that C'baoth was the guardian. Regardless, his powers would prove invalu-

able to Thrawn's military campaign. The Grand Admiral also obtained a cloaking device from the vaults and reactivated the monstrous cloning chamber.

With a bottomless source of ready-made soldiers at his disposal, Thrawn threatened to unleash a devastating round of clone wars on the galaxy. The facility *had* to be destroyed if the New Republic was to have any hope of survival.

Fortunately, Mara Jade decided to help the Rebels. Jade, who'd once been the powerful Emperor's Hand, knew many of her master's secrets, including Wayland's coordinates. A strike team of the greatest Alliance heroes landed in the dense forest and covertly made its way to the fortified entrance of Mount Tantiss.

After several days spent hacking through acid root and fighting off clawbirds and vine

...garrals...

...and vine snakes.

snakes, the group infiltrated the mountain through its surface air ducts. While Lando and Chewbacca sabotaged the cloning incubators, Luke and Mara Jade confronted Joruus C'baoth in the Emperor's throne room.

C'baoth's dangerous derangement had become full-blown insanity. When his visitors would not kneel before him as humble servants, he revealed a shocking surprise—"Luuke" Skywalker, a heartless clone warrior grown from the hand Luke had lost on Cloud City. Sabers clashing, Luke battled his duplicate to a standstill, and Mara finished the job with a lethal slash. Master C'baoth met his end soon afterward.

Thanks to Chewie and Lando's handiwork, the cloning chamber and most of the mountain were demolished in a seismic explosion. But the Emperor's storehouse was built to last, and it remains to be seen whether any unpleasant curiosities are still waiting to be discovered beneath the rubble.

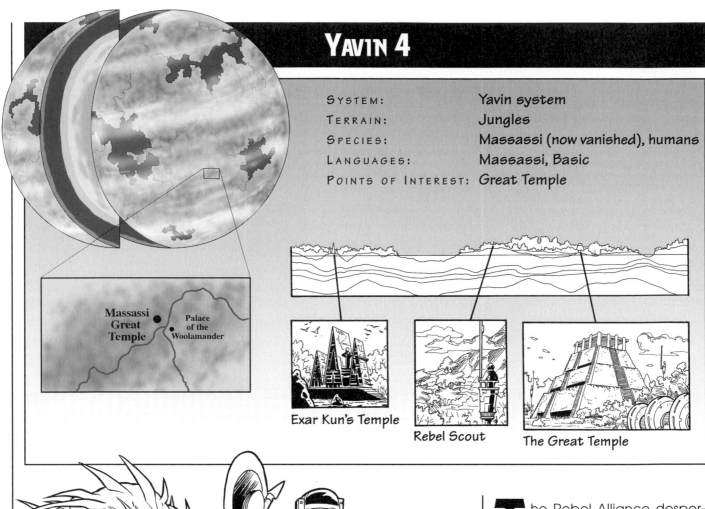

YAVIN 4

SYSTEM: Yavin system
TERRAIN: Jungles
SPECIES: Massassi (now vanished), humans
LANGUAGES: Massassi, Basic
POINTS OF INTEREST: Great Temple

Massassi
Great
Temple

Palace
of the
Woolamander

Exar Kun's Temple

Rebel Scout

The Great Temple

Massassi
warrior (left)
and Rebel
soldier (right).

The Rebel Alliance desperately needed a new base. After fleeing from Dantooine and then skipping across the galaxy one jump ahead of the Imperial fleet, General Dodonna's troops finally selected the remote fourth moon of Yavin. The weary soldiers had no idea that their new home had been a pivotal battleground millennia before and that it would soon change history again.

The lush moon circles the gas giant Yavin. Steamy jungles cover its surface, broken here and there by sluggish rivers and volcanic mountain ranges, all of which explode with life. Whisper

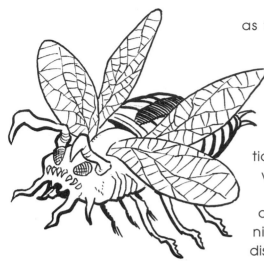

Piranha-beetles emit a death cry before shredding their victims.

birds soar above the brown waters, avoiding spider-anglers on the hunt for small fish and mucous salamanders. Chattering woolamanders swing through the leafy canopy while Yavinian runyips root through the tangled undergrowth. A swarm of piranha-beetles can strip a bristly stintaril to the bone in a handful of seconds.

Nearly five thousand years in the past the Dark Lord Naga Sadow, escaping the fall of the Sith Empire, went to ground on this thriving moon and interred his huge starship. Sadow's warrior bodyguards, the Massassi, remained as guardians of his evil legacy. Over time the Massassi devolved into a primitive and dangerous people.

A thousand years later the fallen Jedi Knight Exar Kun made Yavin 4 his base of operations, constructing new temples as focal points for dark-side energy. In the climactic battle of the Sith War a united Jedi force laid waste to the moon while Kun released his spirit from his body. In the conflagration every last Massassi elder was killed.

The jungles grew back, and it was nearly four millennia before they were again disturbed. The Rebel Alliance decided that the overgrown, abandoned Massassi structures would make excellent hangars and computer centers.

Not long after the establishment of Yavin Base, the Death Star threatened its very existence. The deadly battle station emerged on the far side of Yavin and began a slow orbit of the gas planet. When it cleared this obstruction, one clean shot would blast the moon to rubble.

The Rebels had only one chance. Against all odds, a tiny band of X-wing and Y-wing fighters penetrated its defenses, and Luke Skywalker torpedoed its vulnerable exhaust port. The Battle of Yavin, as it came to be called, was a tremendous victory for the Alliance. The Rebels evacuated the base soon afterward, but Skywalker returned years later to open his Jedi academy, or praxeum. It was far from easy.

During the first year the dormant spirit of Exar Kun reawakened and drove Luke into a state of near death. Later Admiral Daala pummeled the moon with the Super Star Destroyer *Knight Hammer*. Through it all Luke's Jedi trainees bravely used their fledgling powers to defy and defeat evil.

Master Skywalker has recently accepted three new students in his Jedi praxeum: Jacen, Jaina, and Anakin Solo. When these powerful children become full-fledged Knights, the Yavin academy will have left its mark on the next generation.

Mucous salamanders swim formlessly in water, but harden their outer membrane when feeding on land.

YAVIN 8

SYSTEM: Yavin system
TERRAIN: Tundra, mountains
SPECIES: Melodies
LANGUAGE: Melodian
POINTS OF INTEREST: Sistra Mountain

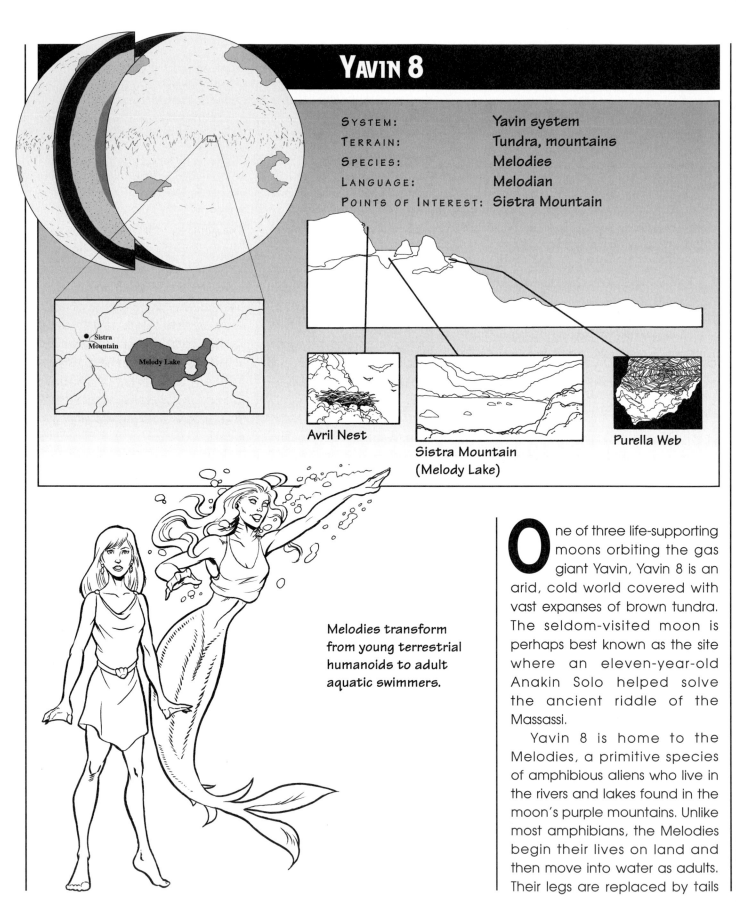

Sistra Mountain
Melody Lake

Avril Nest

Sistra Mountain
(Melody Lake)

Purella Web

Melodies transform from young terrestrial humanoids to adult aquatic swimmers.

One of three life-supporting moons orbiting the gas giant Yavin, Yavin 8 is an arid, cold world covered with vast expanses of brown tundra. The seldom-visited moon is perhaps best known as the site where an eleven-year-old Anakin Solo helped solve the ancient riddle of the Massassi.

Yavin 8 is home to the Melodies, a primitive species of amphibious aliens who live in the rivers and lakes found in the moon's purple mountains. Unlike most amphibians, the Melodies begin their lives on land and then move into water as adults. Their legs are replaced by tails

Large avrils often attack young Melodies.

Reels are a constant threat.

The giant purella spider.

and their lungs by gills during the transformation, which is called the Changing Ceremony.

Since the Melodies are unable to leave their shallow pools during the transformation, they are particularly vulnerable to Yavin 8's large and deadly animals. Snakelike reels can swallow a human in a single bite; huge avril birds can snatch up a bantha in their talons; colossal purella spiders spin webs that can snare a light freighter.

Anakin Solo, the youngest son of Han Solo and Princess Leia Organa, began his training at Luke Skywalker's Jedi academy on Yavin 4 nearly eighteen years after the Battle of Endor. Jedi trainees from all over the galaxy were at the academy, including a young Melody named Lyric who was nearing the end of her nonaquatic stage. Anakin and his friend Tahiri decided to escort Lyric back to Yavin 8 for her Changing Ceremony.

The trip took an unwelcome turn when the moon's carnivores tried to make snacks of the new arrivals. The young Jedi had to battle an avril, a reel, and a pack of toothy raiths, but Lyric successfully made the transition to her adult form.

Anakin also unburied strange symbols carved into the purple rock of Sistra Mountain. When he deciphered the mysterious runes, the boy discovered an amazing secret.

Over four thousand years before, representatives of Yavin 4's Massassi people had gone to their sister moon to seek help for their children, who had been imprisoned in a magical golden sphere by the Dark Jedi Exar Kun. Though the Melodie elders sympathized, they were unable to help. Saddened but still hopeful, the Massassi carved the story of their plight in the rocks of Sistra Mountain, trusting that someone would one day break the curse.

Anakin and Tahiri eventually were able to enter the mystical globe and free the trapped Massassi, thanks to the clues they had gathered from Yavin 8. They also brought back Sannah, another Force-sensitive Melody, for training at the Jedi academy. With the defensive skills Sannah is learning from Luke Skywalker, the Melodies may no longer have to be at the mercy of the moon's predators.

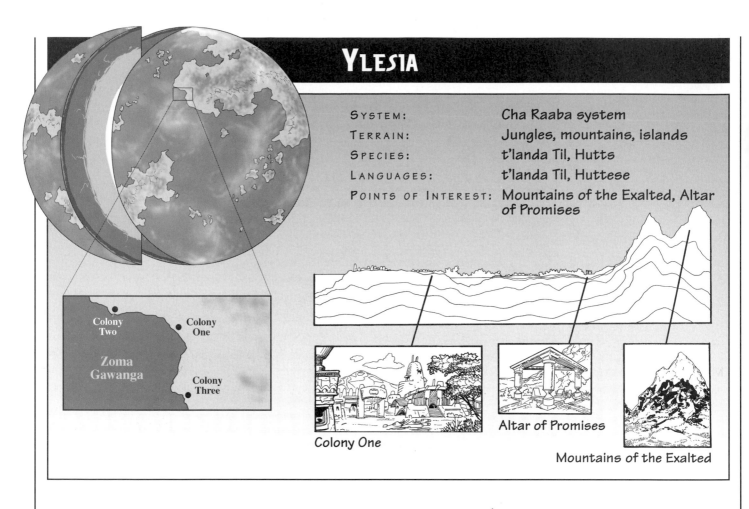

YLESIA

SYSTEM:	Cha Raaba system
TERRAIN:	Jungles, mountains, islands
SPECIES:	t'landa Til, Hutts
LANGUAGES:	t'landa Til, Huttese
POINTS OF INTEREST:	Mountains of the Exalted, Altar of Promises

Colony Two

Colony One

Zoma Gawanga

Colony Three

Colony One

Altar of Promises

Mountains of the Exalted

The t'landa Til and the Hutts rule the slave population on Ylesia.

Religious pilgrims are lured to Ylesia by rumors of a paradise planet where they can experience a sense of fulfillment like nothing they have ever known. Beneath the facade, though, is an ugly web of addiction, slavery, and lies.

The tropical world was established as a major spice-processing center by the criminal kingpin Zavval the Hutt. Realizing that he would need slaves to labor under hellish conditions, the wily Hutt chose not to purchase them. Instead, he came up with a way to *create* slaves.

His lieutenants were of the t'landa Til species and could

Mine workers are often subject to the blood-eating fungus.

therefore emit a natural harmonic that stimulated the pleasure centers in a subject's brain. Lured by the trappings of a pseudo-religion, hundreds of spiritual seekers went to Ylesia to experience this wave of bliss, which was touted as "the Exultation."

The slaves soon became addicted to the sensation, making them weak-minded and easy to control. Living in ascetic colonies, the pilgrims spent their days in backbreaking factory work, refining spice shipped in from Ryloth and Kessel. Every night they scraped parasitic fungus from their calloused hands and crowded into the Altar of Promises, where the t'landa Til "high priests" issued the rapturous Exultation. After a long year of sweat and toil the docile proselytes were shipped off to slave camps and pleasure houses, while their positions were filled by a new batch of converts.

In his late teens Han Solo accepted a job running cargo for Ylesia and got caught up in a great deal of trouble. Piloting a ship through the planet's turbulent atmosphere was hazardous enough, but rival Hutts such as Jabba began attacking the outgoing spice shipments, hoping to steal them without having to pay Zavval. Furthermore, the t'landa Til overseer Teroenza assigned Han a Togorian "bodyguard" named Muuurgh to ensure that the Corellian didn't uncover too much.

Han and the muscular felinoid got along well, for they had one thing in common—both were in love. Muuurgh had come to Ylesia searching for his lost mate, Mrrov, and Han became enamored of a young glitterstim packer named Bria Tharen, who was known to the rest of the colony as Pilgrim 921.

But Bria and Mrrov's days were numbered. Both pilgrims had been on Ylesia nearly a year and would soon be shipped offworld and sold as slaves. Han vowed to rescue them and to become filthy rich in the process.

High Priest Teroenza owned a private display room packed floor to ceiling with some of the rarest and most valuable artifacts in the known galaxy. Han and his companions broke in and stole as many items as they could stuff into their packs. When one of them accidentally tripped an alarm, Zavval and his flunkies burst in with blasters blazing.

Fleeing the firefight, Han hijacked Teroenza's personal ship *Talisman* for their getaway. After rescuing Mrrov from a neighboring colony, the four fugitives rocketed away to safety with treasure in their hands and prices on their heads.

It takes millions of Ylesian white worms to fill a Hutt.

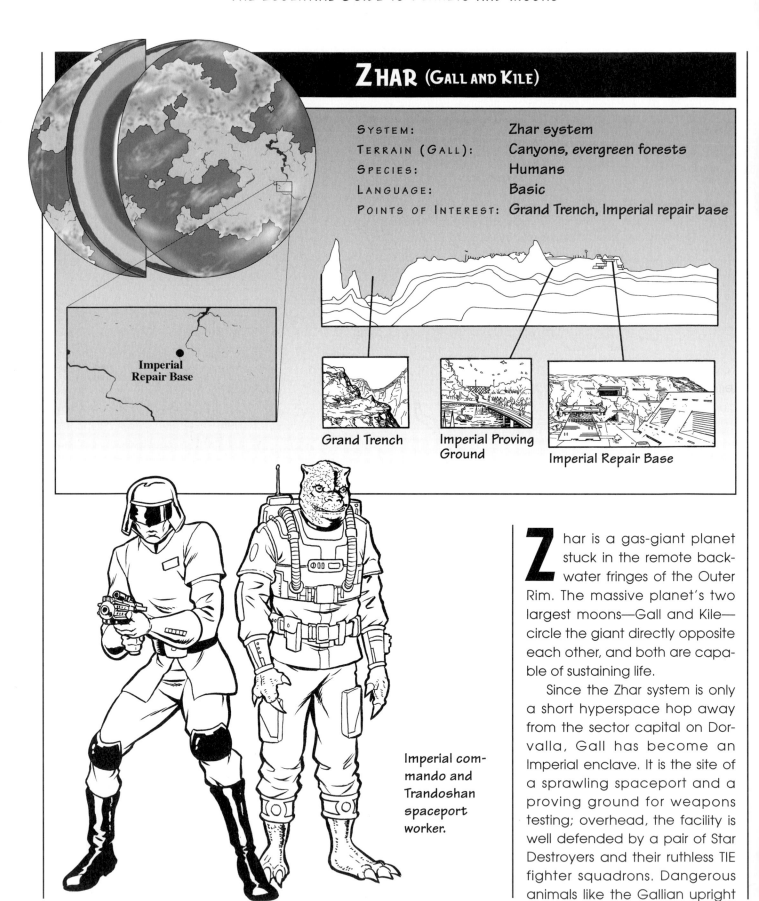

ZHAR (GALL AND KILE)

SYSTEM:	Zhar system
TERRAIN (GALL):	Canyons, evergreen forests
SPECIES:	Humans
LANGUAGE:	Basic
POINTS OF INTEREST:	Grand Trench, Imperial repair base

Imperial Repair Base

Grand Trench

Imperial Proving Ground

Imperial Repair Base

Imperial commando and Trandoshan spaceport worker.

Zhar is a gas-giant planet stuck in the remote backwater fringes of the Outer Rim. The massive planet's two largest moons—Gall and Kile—circle the giant directly opposite each other, and both are capable of sustaining life.

Since the Zhar system is only a short hyperspace hop away from the sector capital on Dorvalla, Gall has become an Imperial enclave. It is the site of a sprawling spaceport and a proving ground for weapons testing; overhead, the facility is well defended by a pair of Star Destroyers and their ruthless TIE fighter squadrons. Dangerous animals like the Gallian upright tripion lurk in the surrounding wilds.

When Han Solo was frozen in carbonite and given to Boba Fett, the bounty hunter immediately brought his human cargo to Tatooine. Unfortunately for Fett, he was ambushed by IG-88 and forced to fly his damaged ship *Slave I* to the Imperial yard on Gall for repairs. The smuggler Dash Rendar located the ship and passed the information on to his former associate Lando Calrissian. An Alliance rescue operation was hurriedly thrown together before Fett could leave the moon.

Wedge Antilles and Rogue Squadron got there first, setting up a temporary operations base on the barren moon of Kile, shielded from Imperial scrutiny by the enormous planet lying between them and Gall. When Lando, Princess Leia, Luke Skywalker, Chewbacca, and the droids arrived, their plan was set in motion. Luke and the pilots of Rogue Squadron drew off most of the Imperial defenses from Gall in a furious space battle, while Dash Rendar led the *Falcon* to the moon's spaceport in his own ship, the *Outrider*.

The two freighters skimmed hair-raisingly close to Gall's evergreen treetops and raced through the red rock canyons of the Grand Trench to escape detection by enemy sensors. As they neared the base, they spied Fett's ship on the landing pad, but Dash abruptly aban-

The Gallian tripion grasps its victims in huge claws while its tail slashes and injects deadly poison.

doned them, pointing out that he'd been hired only to guide, not to fight. The Empire's defensive screen of TIE fighters was simply too much for the rescuers. Amid the chaos of battle, Fett's *Slave I* blasted off into hyperspace. The *Falcon* and its dejected passengers returned to the Kile base.

Meanwhile, Luke was nearly shot down in space by one of his own ships as Wes Janson's X-wing was taken over by a haywire R2 unit. Back on Kile the pilots quickly discovered the culprit—a bribed Alliance crew chief. In a tense blaster face-off

Wedge shot and killed the saboteur.

The heroes could accomplish no more at Zhar. Luke returned to Tatooine to wait for Boba Fett's inevitable return, while Leia and the others went to Rodia to make contact with the criminal organization Black Sun. The hunt for Han Solo would continue elsewhere.

BIBLIOGRAPHY

AC *Ambush at Corellia*, volume one of The Corellian Trilogy, Roger MacBride Allen, Bantam Books, 1995.

AS *Assault at Selonia*, volume two of The Corellian Trilogy, Roger MacBride Allen, Bantam Books, 1995.

BFE *Ewoks: The Battle for Endor*, MGM/UA, 1986.

BTS *Before the Storm*, volume one of The Black Fleet Crisis Trilogy, Michael P. Kube-McDowell, Bantam Books, 1996.

BW *The Bacta War*, volume four of the X-Wing series, Michael A. Stackpole, Bantam Books, 1997.

CCG *Star Wars* customizable card game, Decipher, 1995–1996.

COF *Champions of the Force*, volume three of The Jedi Academy Trilogy, Kevin J. Anderson, Bantam Books, 1994.

COG *Creatures of the Galaxy*, Phil Brucato et al., West End Games, 1994.

COJ *Children of the Jedi*, Barbara Hambly, Bantam Books, 1995.

CPL *The Courtship of Princess Leia*, Dave Wolverton, Bantam Books, 1994.

CS *The Crystal Star*, Vonda McIntyre, Bantam Books, 1995.

CSSB *Han Solo and the Corporate Sector Sourcebook*, Michael Allen Horne, West End Games, 1993.

CSW *Classic Star Wars*, twenty-issue series, Archie Goodwin and Al Williamson, Dark Horse Comics, 1992–1994.

D *Droids*, six-issue series; one-shot, *Rebellion;* and *Season of Revolt* I-8, Dark Horse Comics, 1994–1995.

DA *Dark Apprentice*, volume two of The Jedi Academy Trilogy, Kevin J. Anderson, Bantam Books, 1994.

DE *Dark Empire*, six-issue series, Tom Veitch, Dark Horse Comics, 1991–1992.

DE2 *Dark Empire II*, six-issue series, Tom Veitch, Dark Horse Comics, 1994–1995.

DESB *Dark Empire Sourcebook*, Michael Allen Horne, West End Games, 1993.

DF Dark Forces PC game, LucasArts, 1995.

DFR *Dark Force Rising*, volume two of The Thrawn Trilogy, Timothy Zahn, Bantam Books, 1992.

DFRSB *Dark Force Rising Sourcebook*, Bill Slavicsek, West End Games, 1992.

DLS *Tales of the Jedi: Dark Lords of the Sith*, twelve-issue series, Tom Veitch and Kevin J. Anderson, Dark Horse Comics, 1994–1995.

DS *Darksaber*, Kevin J. Anderson, Bantam Books, 1995.

DSTC *Death Star Technical Companion*, Bill Slavicsek, West End Games, 1991.

DTV *Droids* animated television shows, episodes 1–13, Nelvana, 1985.

EA *The Ewok Adventure (Caravan of Courage)*, MGM/UA, 1984.

EE *Empire's End*, two-issue series, Tom Veitch, Dark Horse Comics, 1995.

ESB *The Empire Strikes Back* film, 20th Century Fox, 1980; novelization, Donald F. Glut, Del Rey Books, 1980.

ESBR *The Empire Strikes Back* National Public Radio dramatizations, Brian Daley, episodes 1–10, 1983; published by Del Rey Books, 1995.

FNU *Tales of the Jedi: The Freedom Nadd Uprising*, two-issue series, Tom Veitch, Dark Horse Comics, 1994–1995.

FP *The Farlander Papers* from the LucasArts PC game X-Wing, reprinted and continued in *X-Wing: The Official Strategy Guide*, Rusel DeMaria, Prima Publishing, 1993.

GAOS *The Golden Age of the Sith*, five-issue series, Kevin J. Anderson,Dark Horse Comics, 1996–1997.

GG2 *Galaxy Guide 2: Yavin and Bespin*, Jonatha Caspian et al., West End Games, 1989.

GG4 *Galaxy Guide 4: Alien Races*, Troy Denning, West End Games, 1989.

GG7 *Galaxy Guide 7: Mos Eisley*, Martin Wixtead, West End Games, 1993.

GG12 *Galaxy Guide 12: Aliens, Enemies, and Allies*, C. Robert Carey et al., West End Games, 1995.

HE *Heir to the Empire*, volume one of The Thrawn Trilogy, Timothy Zahn, Bantam Books, 1991; six-issue comics adaptation, Mike Baron, Dark Horse Comics, 1995–1996.

HESB *Heir to the Empire Sourcebook*, Bill Slavicsek, West End Games, 1992.

HLL *Han Solo and the Lost Legacy*, volume three of the *Han Solo Adventures*, Brian Daley, Del Rey Books, 1979.

HSE *Han Solo at Stars' End*, volume one of the *Han Solo Adventures*, Brian Daley, Del Rey Books, 1979.

HSR *Han Solo's Revenge*, volume two of the *Han Solo Adventures*, Brian Daley, Del Rey Books, 1979.

ISB *Imperial Sourcebook*, Greg Gordon, West End Games, 1989.

ISWU *The Illustrated Star Wars Universe*, Kevin J. Anderson and Ralph McQuarrie, Bantam Books, 1995.

JASB *The Jedi Academy Sourcebook*, Paul Sudlow, West End Games, 1996.

JJK *The Golden Globe* and *Lyric's World*, volumes one and two of the Junior Jedi Knights series, Nancy Richardson, Berkley Books, 1995.

JS *Jedi Search*, volume one of the Jedi Academy trilogy, Kevin J. Anderson,

KT *The Krytos Trap*, volume three of the X-Wing series, Michael A. Stackpole, Bantam Books, 1996.

LC *The Last Command*, volume three of the Thrawn trilogy, Timothy Zahn, Bantam Books, 1993.

LCM *Lando Calrissian and the Mindharp of Sharu*, volume one of the *Lando Calrissian Adventures*, L. Neil Smith, Del Rey Books, 1983.

LCSB *The Last Command Sourcebook*, Eric Trautmann, West End Games, 1994.

MMY *Mission from Mount Yoda*, Paul and Hollace Davids, Bantam Skylark Books, 1992–1993.

MTS *The Movie Trilogy Sourcebook*, Greg Farshtey and Bill Smith, West End Games, 1993.

NR *The New Rebellion*, Kristine Kathryn Rusch, Bantam Books, 1996.

POT *Planet of Twilight*, Barbara Hambly, Bantam Books, 1997.

PS *The Paradise Snare*, volume one of The Han Solo Trilogy, A. C. Crispin, Bantam Books, 1997.

PSG *Platt's Starport Guide*, Peter Schweighofer, West End Games, 1995.

RJ *Return of the Jedi* film, 20th Century Fox, 1983; novelization, James Kahn, Del Rey Books, 1983.

ROC *River of Chaos*, four-issue series, Louise Simonson, Dark Horse Comics, 1995.

RS *Rogue Squadron*, volume one of the X-Wing series, Michael A. Stackpole, Bantam Books, 1996.

RSB *The Rebel Alliance Sourcebook*, Paul Murphy, West End Games, 1990.

SAC *Showdown at Centerpoint*, volume three of The Corellian Trilogy, Roger MacBride Allen, Bantam Books, 1995.

SL *Scoundrel's Luck*, Troy Denning, West End Games,1990.

SME *Splinter of the Mind's Eye*, Alan Dean Foster, Del Rey Books, 1978; four-issue series, Terry Austin, Dark Horse Comics, 1995–1996.

SOL *Shield of Lies*, volume two of The Black Fleet Crisis Trilogy, Michael P. Kube-McDowell, Bantam Books, 1996.

SOTE *Shadows of the Empire*, Steve Perry, Bantam Books, 1996; six-issue series, John Wagner, Dark Horse Comics, 1996; Nintendo 64 video game, LucasArts, 1996.

SOTEALB *Shadows of the Empire* CD liner notes, Varese Sarabande, 1996.

SOTEPG *Shadows of the Empire Planets Guide*, John Beyer et al., West End Games, 1996.

SOTESB *Shadows of the Empire Sourcebook,* Peter Schweighofer, West End Games, 1996.

SW *Star Wars: A New Hope* film, 20th Century Fox, 1977; novelization, George Lucas, Del Rey Books, 1977.

SWAJ *The Official Star Wars Adventure Journal,* issues 1–12, edited by Peter Schweighofer, West End Games, 1994–1997.

SWCG *The Essential Guide to Characters,* Andy Mangels, Del Rey Books, 1995.

SWR *Star Wars* National Public Radio dramatizations, Brian Daley, episodes 1–13, 1981; published by Del Rey Books, 1994.

SWRPG2 *Star Wars: The Roleplaying Game, Second Edition,* Bill Smith, West End Games, 1992.

SWSB *Star Wars Sourcebook,* Bill Slavicsek and Curtis Smith, West End Games, 1987.

SWVG *The Essential Guide to Vehicles and Vessels,* Bill Smith, Del Rey Books, 1996.

SWWS *Star Wars: The Wookiee Storybook,* uncredited, Random House, 1979.

TAB *The Truce at Bakura,* Kathy Tyers, Bantam Books, 1993.

TBH *Tales of the Bounty Hunters,* edited by Kevin J. Anderson, Bantam Books, 1997.

TBSB *The Truce at Bakura Sourcebook,* Kathy Tyers and Eric S. Trautmann, West End Games, 1996.

TJP *Tales from Jabba's Palace,* edited by Kevin J. Anderson, Bantam Books, 1995.

TMEC *Tales from the Mos Eisley Cantina,* edited by Kevin J. Anderson, Bantam Books, 1995.

TOJ *Tales of the Jedi,* five-issue series, Tom Veitch, Dark Horse Comics, 1993–1994.

TOJC *Tales of the Jedi Companion,* George R. Strayton, West End Games, 1996.

TSC *The Stele Chronicles* from the LucasArts PC game TIE Fighter, continued in *TIE Fighter: The Official Strategy Guide,* Rusel DeMaria et al., Prima Publishing, 1994.

TSW *The Sith War,* six-issue series, Kevin J. Anderson, Dark Horse Comics, 1995–1996.

TT *Tyrant's Test,* volume three of the Black Fleet Crisis trilogy, Michael P. Kube-McDowell, Bantam Books, 1997.

WG *Wedge's Gamble,* volume two of the X-Wing series, Michael A. Stackpole, Bantam Books, 1996.

XW *X-Wing: Rogue Squadron,* ongoing series, Dark Horse Comics, 1995–1997.

YJK *Heirs of the Force, Shadow Academy, The Lost Ones, Lightsabers, Darkest Knight,* and *Jedi Under Siege,* volumes one to six of the Young Jedi Knights series,

Kevin J. Anderson and Rebecca Moesta, Berkley Books, 1995–1996.

Abregado-rae	HE, HESB, DFR
Agamar	FP
Alderaan	SW, SWR, ISWU, RJ, JS, SWAJ, BW
Almania	NR
Alzoc III	GG4, TAB, TBSB, TMEC, COJ
Ambria	TOJ, TOJC, TSW, CPL, SWVG
Ammuud	HSR, CSSB
Ando	SW, GG4, COG, DFR, TMEC
Anoth	JS, DA, COF, JASB, DE2
Antar Four	GG4, TAB, ROC, TMEC
Aquaris	CSW
Aridus	CSW
Arkania	TOJ, TOJC, DLS, DESB, DE2, EE
Atzerri	BTS, SOL
Bakura	TAB, TBSB, AS
Balmorra	DE2
Barab I	GG4, SOTE, DFRSB, CPL
Belsavis	COJ
Bespin	ESB, GG2, ISWU, SWVG, TJP, JS, BTS
Bestine	SW, MTS
Bilbringi	LC, LCSB
Bimmisaari	HE, HESB
Bonadan	HSR, CSSB, D
Borleias	RS, WG, KT
Bothawui	HE, HESB, SOTE, SOTESB, SOTEPG
Byss	DE, DESB, DE2, EE
Carida	JS, DA, COF, JASB, TMEC
Carratos	BTS, SOL, TT
Chandrila	KT, RSB, DESB, SWAJ
Corellia	SW, PS, AC, AS, SAC, SWCG
Coruscant	HE, ISWU, SOTE, SOTEALB, DA, AS, CPL, WG, DE, TT, NR
Dagobah	ESB, ISWU, HE, DE
Dantooine	SW, ISWU, DLS, JS, DA, JASB
Da Soocha V	DE, DESB, DE2
Dathomir	CPL, YJK
Dellalt	HLL, GG12
Drall	AC, AS, SAC, HLL
Duro	GG4, MMY, DA, SWVG
Endor	RJ, ISWU, SWSB, EA, BFE, SWCG
Eriadu	DS, DESB, DSTC, COJ
Etti IV	HSE, CSSB, SOTE, SOTESB
Firrerre	CS
Fondor	CSW, HSE, SWAJ
Galantos	BTS, SOL
Gamorr	RJ, SWSB, SWAJ, COJ, ISB, SWCG
Garos IV	SWAJ

Hapes	CPL, YJK
Honoghr	HE, DFR, DFRSB, LC
Hoth	ESB, ESBR, ISWU, CSW, DS
Ithor	SWR, SWSB, COJ, SWAJ, TMEC, DA
J't'p'tan	BTS, SOL, TT
Kalarba	D, SWCG, SWVG
Kashyyyk	HE, YJK, TBH, TT, SWSB, SWWS
Kessel	JS, DA, COF, WG
Khomm	DS, DA
Korriban	DLS, EE, GAOS
Kothlis	HE, SOTE, SOTESB, SOTEPG, TSC
Kuat	PSG, WG, BW, SWAJ
Lwhekk	TAB, TBSB, JS
M'haeli	ROC
Mimban	SME
Mon Calamari	SWSB, DA, DE, JASB
Mrlsst	XW
Munto Codru	CS
Myrkr	HE, HESB, TOJ, DE2, TOJC
Mytus VII	HSE, CSSB
Nal Hutta and Nar Shaddaa	DE, DESB, DE2, D, DF, DS
Nam Chorios	POT
Nim Drovis	POT
Nkllon	HE, HESB, LC, SWVG
N'zoth	BTS, SOL, TT
Onderon	TOJ, FNU, DLS, TSW, TOJC, EE
Ord Mantell	ESB, CSW, SOTE, LCSB, COJ, SL, CCG
Ossus	FNU, DLS, TSW, DE2, EE
Pydyr	NR
Pzob	COJ
Rafa V	LCM
Ralltiir	SWR, SWAJ
Rodia	GG4, SOTE, SOTESB, SOTEPG, TMEC
Roon	DTV, SOTEALB
Ryloth	SWSB, PSG, TJP, KT, XW
Sacorria	AC, AS, SAC
Selonia	AC, AS, SAC
Sullust	ROJ, SWSB, FP, DF, SWCG
Taanab	ROJ, SWAJ
Talasea	RS
Talus and Tralus	AC, AS, SAC
Tatooine	SW, SWR, RJ, ISWU, DS, GG7
Telti	NR
Teyr	SOL
Thyferra	RS, KT, BW, SWAJ, NR
Tynna	HSR, CSSB
Umgul	JS, JASB
Vergesso Asteroids	SOTE, SOTESB, SOTEPG
Vortex	DA, COF, JASB
Wayland	HE, LC, LCSB
Yavin 4	SW, ISWU, GG2, DLS, TSW, COF, DS, YJK
Yavin 8	JJGG, JJLW, GG2
Ylesia	PS
Zhar	SOTE, SOTESB

ABOUT THE AUTHOR

Daniel Wallace is the author of the forthcoming *The Essential Guide to Droids* and coauthor, with Kevin J. Anderson, of *Star Wars: The Essential Chronology*. He inhabits Detroit in the remote Michigan system.

ABOUT THE ARTISTS

Brandon McKinney grew up watching and enjoying the *Star Wars* films. They inspired him to take up drawing, and he got his first professional comic book work at the age of sixteen. He received a degree in Fine Arts at UCLA, where he also studied animation. His short films have run in festivals across the country. Brandon illustrated the "Mighty Chronicles" adaptations of the *Star Wars* trilogy for Chronicle Books, and this book is his second *Star Wars* project. Making his living as a freelance artist, Brandon currently lives with his fiancee and their two cats in Oakland, California. He would like to dedicate his work in this book to his parents, Dan and Kathleen, who took Brandon to see *Star Wars* for the first time and encouraged him to draw; and to Andy Mangels, who steered him in the right direction to be able to illustrate the *Star Wars* universe.

Raised on comic books and cheese in Stevens Point, Wisconsin, **Scott R. Kolins** was forever changed by *Star Wars*. After a few apprenticeships and two years at the Joe Kubert School of Graphic Art and Design, Scott began his artistic career. He has illustrated Spider-Man for Marvel Comics and Green Lantern and Legion of Superheroes for DC Comics. Scott is very proud to have worked on *Star Wars* material and would like to dedicate his work in this book to his brother, Steve. A recent Californian, Scott lives with his fiancee, Kim, in the San Francisco Bay Area.